TAKE A
Chance

Take A Chance – Citrus Pines Book 5

Copyright 2023 © Lila Dawes

The author asserts the moral right to be identified as the owner of this work.

No part of this book may be reproduced or transmitted in any form or by any means, including but not limited to: graphic, electronic, or mechanical, including photocopying, recording, taping, or by any informational storage retrieval system without advanced prior permission in writing from the publisher.

No part of this book, including the cover, has been generated using AI. No part of this publication is to be used to train AI technologies.

This is a work of fiction, and is not based on true events or on real people.

Cover image: Wander Aguiar Photography.
Cover design: Lila Dawes.

Dedication

For my friend and Superwoman, Kate.
Thank you for all your support, fangirling and listening to me ramble about the series, it means more than I can ever express xx

Lila Dawes

Content Info

This book contains themes which some readers may find distressing and start right from the first page, including:

- Domestic violence
- Abandonment
- Abuse
- Anxiety
- Rape
- Violence
- Death
- Details of animal abuse and neglect

Please take care of yourself when reading.

Take A Chance

Contents

Dedication	iii
Content Info	iv
Contents	v
Chapter 1	7
Chapter 2	23
Chapter 3	37
Chapter 4	52
Chapter 5	66
Chapter 6	84
Chapter 7	97
Chapter 8	108
Chapter 9	122
Chapter 10	136
Chapter 11	146
Chapter 12	162
Chapter 13	179
Chapter 14	193
Chapter 15	211
Chapter 16	227
Chapter 17	236
Chapter 18	248
Chapter 19	268

Chapter 20	287
Chapter 21	304
Chapter 22	318
Chapter 23	330
Chapter 24	339
Chapter 25	352
Chapter 26	361
Chapter 27	372
Chapter 28	380
Acknowledgements	396
About the Author	397
Also By Lila Dawes	398

Chapter 1

"*You stupid fucking whore! You thought you could speak to another man without* my *permission? I bet you flirted with him, teased him, didn't you? Begged him for any scrap of attention. Well, I'll give you some fucking attention!*" he grunted as he pinned her down, the delicate bones in her wrist cracking and grinding as he squeezed them together with one meaty, clammy hand. He used the other to unbuckle his pants, his acrid breath wafting in her face. The stench of vodka and Marlboros brought bile creeping up her throat, threatening to spill out. She swallowed it back but only so she could open her mouth to explain.

"*No, I wasn't! I was just being polite, I-*"

She barely had time to register the sharp sting across her cheek from his slap before his fist connected with her stomach. She lost her breath, trying to crunch herself into a ball to cope with the pain but he wouldn't let her. He wanted her to feel every second of it, scraping *against her nerves, like only a man who was completely evil could.*

He gripped her chin roughly, forcing her to face him. "Your lame fucking excuses don't mean shit. I don't know why you bother, who would want to even talk to you?" He laughed in her face, spittle escaping and plastering to her cheeks and she flinched at the contact. "You're so pathetic, it's disgusting. Jesus, even just looking at you makes my skin crawl. I wouldn't touch you but you need to be taught a lesson."

He prised her legs apart. She tried to fight him but she was so weak now from lack of food. She squeezed her eyes closed as the bile crept higher and higher. He spat into his hand and then it disappeared under her torn dress...

"No!" Rebelle cried, so loudly the sound dragged her out of the nightmare. Only it wasn't a nightmare, it was a memory, her most hated one. Tears ran down her cheeks as her breath sawed in and out, her eyes still adjusting to the dark.

Her stomach turned violently, and she managed to pull herself out of the sleeping bag she was tucked into, rolling out onto the concrete floor that hurt her so much to sleep on, and retched in the darkness. The sound of several dogs howling covered up the choking sounds she made as her body tried to expel the phantom food in her belly.

Once she was finished, her small body aching from the effort, she felt around in the dark for the candle and matches she kept close by.

The striking of the match echoed around the storeroom, bouncing off the brick walls and cool concrete floor. She held the match to the wick of the thick, white candle next to her, her hands shaking so much it took a few tries before the room brightened with light. She blew out the match, her breathing still ragged, her eyes still leaking those anguished tears as she sat for a moment trying to pull herself together.

Take A Chance

The howling continued but the sound didn't bother her, she found it comforting. It sounded like home. She took a few deep steadying breaths, the scent of roses wafting from the candle, before getting up and brushing aside the curtain, an old sheet someone discarded at the laundromat. It shielded the storeroom-slash-bedroom from the rest of the animal shelter.

Taking the candle, she went towards the kitchen, which also doubled as an office; she moved slowly, not wanting to risk the flame dying out and having to waste another precious match. She rummaged in the drawers and found a spare cloth and shuffled back, mopping up the little pool of saliva her body felt she didn't need.

On the way back, she turned towards the row of kennels housing the dogs. There were five pens along the wall the storeroom was located on. Five pens in total and all of them full. Not to mention the two cats that lived in the kitchen.

The dog kennels were newly designed with an open top and a half-size barn door style plexiglass entrance. Each one contained a cute wooden dog bed with a very snuggly cushion, food and water bowls and a handful of chew toys to keep them occupied when she wasn't socializing or exercising them.

Rebelle walked past each pen, pausing to soothe the wailing beasts which helped to comfort herself.

The first kennel had Alfie, a Border Collie mix that Rebelle had spotted wandering down the highway with a slight limp one day and promptly pulled over and rescued. The second kennel contained Doug the Pug who had been abandoned at the vet that Rebelle worked closely with. Despite Doug's snorting and the gross problem of his eye popping out of its socket when he got excited, Rebelle had taken to him and insisted he come to the shelter.

Kennel three held Bruiser and Beast, two Chihuahua brothers whose owner had surrendered them to Rebelle when she discovered she had terminal cancer and could no longer look after them.

A white fluffy curiosity of a canine, Sasha, lived in kennel four. She had no discernible breed, was grumpy as hell and liked no one. Rebelle had taken pity on Sasha as Rebelle didn't like anyone either. And kennel five was occupied by Bryan, an elderly Irish Wolfhound who also came from the vet after being seized by the SPCA from some disgusting human who didn't know how to look after animals properly. That was also where the two cats who patroled the kitchen had come from.

Rebelle crooned at them all, convincing each of them that she was fine, except Sasha who didn't care. When she reached Bryan's kennel, he leapt up, hooking his giant paws over the pen door to get to her. His sad face mirrored her own and she held the candle aloft as she buried her face in the coarse fur of his neck to stifle a sob. The rough rasp of his tongue on her neck snapped her out of her misery pretty quickly and he looked repentant as she scolded him.

She shuddered, wiping at her neck. "You know I don't like it when you do that."

She said goodnight to the dogs, not bothering with the cats as she knew they wouldn't be concerned by her trauma. Cats weren't bothered by anything, that was why she loved the heartless little bastards so much.

Rebelle shuffled back to the storeroom and got into her sleeping bag and lay there. She couldn't shake off her nightmare, her memory.

Why is it always in the dead of night that my brain strikes? Sensing weakness and pouncing like it's stalking prey, a lion

Take A Chance

tracking a helpless deer.

Rebelle's mind attacked, flashing back over her life, showing her how it had fractured and how she ended up there and wondering which of her wounds to claw at first.

It all started when her father introduced her to Marcus Black, the new Sheriff of Citrus Pines. Her father had been the deputy and would never progress to anything more; drunks can never hide what they are for too long. Rebelle was sure it was his alcoholism that put her mom in the ground and was the reason her twin sister ran away all those years ago. Evil couldn't hide itself for too long either, but Marcus managed it for years.

He was charming the first time she met him. The next time he came by, he brought her flowers. Her father wasn't home so Rebelle, charmed by the gift and the attention, let him in. When her father came home he didn't seem happy to see his sheriff there waiting but he never said a word; just kept his mouth shut and was more cordial than Rebelle had ever seen him.

Marcus came around a few more times with more gifts, more compliments and more attention. Each time her father came home, she could feel the tension in the room rising, but that good ol' southern hospitality reigned supreme, and Rebelle could never work out what was wrong with her father.

When Rebelle turned eighteen, Marcus proposed. She was unsure about accepting, she didn't really know him that well. But her father's drinking grew even more out of control and Rebelle didn't think she could witness it much longer.

Marcus spun fairytales about taking her away from Citrus Pines, he was proving himself at work and making people take notice. He was going places and taking her with him. He knew how much she cared about animals and promised to help her get started in a career as a veterinarian.

There was nothing in this town for her and Marcus painted such a pretty picture of their future together. He was ten years older, with much more life experience than her so he must know better, right?

She agreed to marry him and when her father came home, they announced the good news.

He was not pleased.

Marcus asked her to wait in her room while he smoothed things over. There was something about his words, the way his mouth lifted into a smirk that turned her stomach combined with the glint of fear that flickered in her father's eye before he blinked it away.

But she left.

She heard muffled voices, rising then dipping to a murmur. They escalated to a fever pitch, and she listened, her heart in her mouth, jolting when a sickening thud caught her ears.

A few moments later, Marcus called her out. She still remembered stepping gingerly into the living room, seeing her father tense and pale with a bleeding lip.

"Dad? Are you okay?"

Rebelle turned to Marcus who just stood there, a smile frozen on his lips. "After a quick moment of reflection, your father has given us his blessing," he said.

She looked towards her father, concerned and confused about what had just happened but after a moment, her father smiled and nodded. "Exciting news!"

"Go and pack a bag, babe. You're moving in with me." Marcus came over to her and kissed her, squeezing her ass possessively. She pulled away, embarrassed at his behavior in front of her father and the suggestion of something physical. They hadn't crossed that line yet,

Take A Chance

Marcus said he would be patient with her, he said he knew she would be worth the wait.

"Let's go!" An edge had crept into Marcus's tone. She jumped and scurried off to her room, packing an overnight bag and grabbing a photo of her mom and dad and another of her with her twin sister. As she headed back to Marcus, she remembered something, and a sudden impulse had her scurrying outside to the dwarf rose bush her sister used to tend to. Rebelle quickly took a small cutting; she couldn't bear to leave it behind to die and lose that connection to her twin.

Marcus was hurrying her out the door so fast she barely had time to say goodbye to her father, but she managed to see him. She just didn't realize it would be the last time. His eyes were bloodshot, likely from the alcohol, but he hadn't moved from his spot.

"Bye, Dad. I'll see you soon?" she called.

He sounded strained when he replied, "Sure thing."

Something felt off but she didn't know what. She prayed on the way to Marcus's house, prayed to Jesus that she had done the right thing.

That night when she left home, she thought her father had mouthed something to her, but with Marcus rushing her out the door, she didn't know what it was. Looking back now she could see it clear as day...*I'm sorry*.

Turns out Sheriff Marcus Black wasn't her knight in shining armor at all and the façade dropped as soon as they were married.

He was an evil, manipulative man. He'd discovered that her father had racked up gambling debts in Palm Valley. Marcus blackmailed her father and ultimately paid them off. But now her father owed Marcus. And Rebelle was his prize.

Marcus Black was a bully, a crook, a thief, a violent

man with a vile temper. His heart and soul were as black as his name, and Rebelle was soon shut off from her family and any remaining friends she had. He abused her, starting right after they said *'I do'*.

Dinner not on the table as soon as he got home? He'd burn her with cigarettes. If she didn't clean properly or talked back? She earned herself a beating. She spoke to another man, any man? Marcus raped her.

And she could never forget the time she brought in an injured bird from the garden and dared to show it some attention when she should have been with Marcus. He killed the bird and starved her as punishment.

The fairytales he'd spun had all been a lie. He didn't want to take her away, to let her spread her wings and fly, let her follow her dreams of veterinary school and helping animals. He wanted her caged, subservient and broken.

And she was.

Until the fateful night she tried to get away.

Marcus had dragged her to an abandoned building he owned on some land on the outskirts of town. It was brick built, the size of a barn with an outhouse that looked more like a crumbling ruin. She asked why they were there and earned a glare for her troubles. He must have been in a good mood because he didn't hit her. When would she learn not to open her mouth?

It was dark, chilly winds had swept through the autumnal night and she shivered. They waited, Marcus chain-smoking his Marlboros until finally some headlights appeared. Two men pulled up in front of them and got out of the vehicle. They were both tall, white with forgettable faces.

"How much?" Marcus said, nodding towards Rebelle. The men scrutinized her, head to toe and she had a prickling awareness tickling her neck.

Take A Chance

One of the men shrugged. "Has she been used?"

"Of course, what do you take me for? She's still pretty tight though, she'll be worth the ride."

Understanding dawned on Rebelle as she realized these men were here to buy her body. Her stomach turned and before she could choke it back, she vomited up the tiny portion of food he'd allowed her to eat.

"Disgusting, look at you. Who would even want you, you make me sick!" Marcus raged, grabbing her by the shoulders and shaking her.

"Let's go, I don't wanna get involved in this," one of the men said and two seconds later they were driving off.

"I knew you would ruin this opportunity for me! You stupid, worthless, piece of sh-"

She spat in his face. That was all she could do, her body screamed at her to do something but with her arms pinned and her body and legs pressed against the car, her choices were limited.

He flinched, shocked, and wiped at his cheek, loosening his hold on her and she took her chance. If she stayed with him any longer, she would die. She could feel Death knocking at her door, it was just a matter of time before she let him in.

So she ran.

In the dark.

Her raggedy shoes didn't protect her feet from the pebbles and rocks that scraped at the sides of her feet as she ran but she kept going, desperation spurring her on.

"Get back here!" he roared, and she could hear him gaining on her.

"No!" A sob slipped out at the thought of him catching her.

Then she heard it, the click of the hammer pulling back on his gun. He was an expert shot and she knew once he pulled that trigger, she was gone.

She didn't look back, just kept running and waited for death to catch her so she could collapse into its warm, sweet embrace.

The gun went off but she didn't fall, didn't feel it anywhere. The silence stopped her, she turned around. The moon peeked out from behind the clouds, lighting up the field, and there he was, rolling in the dirt. She could hear him crying out, a gurgling sound. She tentatively stepped towards him even though her brain was screaming at her to keep going. Her body fighting her flight impulse as her muscles and tendons twitched with urgency to leave.

"Reb-Rebelle," he gasped, the sound watery.

She spotted a rock close by, a large rock that she had dodged but he hadn't been so lucky. He had tripped and shot himself. She watched as blood poured from his chest.

The magnificently lethal Marcus Black had tripped and shot himself.

A hysterical laugh slipped out of her as she watched him choking on his own blood, writhing in the dirt. "Help me...please..." he gurgled, begging her like she had begged him so many times before for some mercy. So, she did exactly what he had done to her every time she begged: absolutely nothing. He reached for her ankle and she stepped back. She sat down close by in the dirt and watched as the light slipped from his eyes. It only took a few minutes and she loved every single one of those blissful seconds...

She prayed for the last time. Not for his soul, that was far beyond saving. She prayed that he was truly gone, that he had been taken into the depths of hell to be tortured for eternity. And with that, she walked back to the car and drove out of town, to the nearest hospital and told them what happened.

His death was ruled an accident: only his fingerprints were on the gun and the trajectory of the bullet matched with her description of what happened. Case closed.

But members of the town were suspicious and soon she heard the whispers.

Widow Black murdered her husband.

She guessed in a way she was responsible for his death; she hadn't tried to help him, and some days that burned at her conscience.

Those days, like today, she let it. She let it drown her.

Rebelle shut her eyes. She couldn't think about it now or she wouldn't pull herself out of the spiral of memories. Tears ran freely down her cheeks.

"Come on now, it's not all bad," she whispered to herself, hiccupping as she mimicked her sister's words to her. When they were children and Rebelle was upset, her twin would always cuddle her and say, *count out what's good*. It was a mantra that had stuck with Rebelle ever since her sister ran away after their mom died. Rebelle hadn't seen her since they were sixteen. Sometimes Rebelle wondered what life would be like if she had stayed. No way would Rebelle have left with Marcus. Maybe her father would still be alive too, instead of having drunk himself to death shortly after she left.

"Count out what's good. You have your health, kinda. The shelter..." she trailed off.

Marcus had debts, big ones and the bank repossessed the house and car, putting Rebelle out on the street. But before she had to leave, she went through all his papers, eventually coming across the bill of sale for the land and abandoned building which he'd had registered in her name. Marcus had been trying to hide the asset from the

IRS, keeping it off the books for some nefarious purpose, and it remained untouchable. For once, he actually did something right. She had somewhere to go, somewhere that was all hers. Even if it was just crumbling concrete with no power.

She worked hard to clear it out and gradually made small improvements to turn it into an animal shelter. It wasn't a great one; she'd had hardly any money so had to do most of the work herself, but it was a shelter nonetheless.

She replanted the small white rose bush she'd liberated from the home before it foreclosed. It was a miracle that she'd somehow managed to keep it going since she left home. Now it flourished outside the shelter as a symbol of hope. It was the start of something good, something that was irretrievably *hers*.

"The animals at the shelter, they're good and you're helping them. Your business is growing," she added.

It was true, the *Take A Chance* shelter was getting busier. People now called her when they found an injured or stray animal. But she needed help, which is why she now advertised for a volunteer. She wasn't a people-person but as much as she hated to admit it, she couldn't do it all. However neither could she afford to pay anyone.

She continued to count out what was good. "Justine and Blake…"

She didn't like people but Blake, the new sheriff of Citrus Pines, had worked his way into her good graces, along with his fiancée, Justine. When Blake first came to town, Rebelle hadn't trusted him one bit. But he'd looked out for her, shown up when she needed him. He believed her about Marcus, had trusted her in turn and worked to rid the department of corrupt officers.

Justine was someone Rebelle had gone to school with

Take A Chance

and was the town psychologist. Although Marcus had died and effectively released Rebelle from her nightmare, she still had lingering anxieties, dreams and flashbacks that she couldn't shake. Rebelle had started having sessions with Justine in order to try to get some help to lead a normal life. She had only had two sessions with Justine so far, needing time in between each one to recalibrate, but she could feel a change happening within herself.

"...and this candle, which you can't afford to keep burning."

Rebelle had little to no money. She didn't eat much and walked everywhere to try and save on gas money for the truck. She preferred to use the small income she received from the vets to look after the animals. She had minimal possessions: her two photographs and a few clothes which she had stolen from the laundromat's lost and found box. She had splurged on the candle, thinking now the nights were drawing in and getting cooler, she should have some lighting.

With a sigh, she blew out the candle and plunged herself into darkness. Alone with her memories she tried to drift off to sleep and as she did, she wondered how the hell she was ever going to survive this life...

*

The next morning, Rebelle got out of bed, rolling up her sleeping bag and tidying it away, stepping behind the curtain that blocked off the storeroom from view.

She dressed in her tattered, borrowed jeans with holes all over and the belt loops torn off. The straps on her tank top had snapped but she managed to tie them together so she could wear it a while longer. The soles on her tennis shoes had torn away and flapped each time she walked but they kept her feet dry which was the main thing. No bra today, she only had one, it was a little on the big side given that it was from someone who was two sizes bigger than her, and she was trying to make it last as long as possible. She wasn't going into town so didn't feel like she needed to wear it. At least she had clean panties, that was a miracle in itself and she already knew it would be top of the list in her *count what's good* session tonight.

Rebelle fed the animals, the dogs howling away for their food while the cats appeared disinterested, but she knew they were hungry really. *Me too buddy, me too.* When had she last eaten? She couldn't remember whether it was breakfast yesterday morning or dinner from two nights ago. She would be fine for another day at least and then she would need to eat.

She was due to start taking some shifts at the local bar, The Rusty Bucket Inn soon and she was looking forward to getting a tiny bit more money coming in so she could eat more and get the dogs some new enrichment toys.

Once they had finished their food, she let the dogs out of the building to run around together, sniff at trees and squirm in the dirt while she cleaned out their kennels. She took a break, feeling lightheaded from lack of food and sleep. She paused for a moment, wiping her hand across her sweaty forehead and then she heard it: gravel flicking up as a car came up the path towards the shelter.

Rebelle's heart pounded in her chest, her pulse throbbed in her ears. She always panicked whenever people came to the shelter. She had recently been the victim of harassment from some of the officers in town who were loyal to her dead husband. They'd come up here, trying to scare her, and boy, had it worked. Blake had saved her and locked them up, and she hadn't had any issues since. But that didn't stop the fear.

The dogs were barking wildly and she stumbled outside, the sun blinding her, and she wrangled the animals inside before they knocked over the visitor. When she finally turned around, she lifted her arm to shield her eyes from the sun, fear pounding through her once again.

It's *him*.

The man she had seen at the bar once. He was tall, hugely built, his white dress shirt pulled tight across his wide chest, his arms corded with muscles and his black pants, held up by suspenders, clung to thighs almost thicker than her hips.

Rebelle hated muscles. All they were was evidence that someone had the strength to hurt you.

His shoes looked like they cost more than the building behind her and don't even get her started on his fancy midlife crisis car, gleaming red in the sunshine. The sun bounced off his hair, strawberry blond and swept to one side, baring his forehead which was creased with faint lines. She could see tattoos crawling up his chest and wrapping around his neck, running down the forearms that were being revealed as he rolled up his shirtsleeves. Expensive-looking sunglasses shielded his eyes but she didn't want to see them.

She wanted him to leave.

Now.

He was a mountain of a man and she had faced men like him before. He terrified her, her fear rooting her to the spot. That fear didn't dissipate even when he pulled off his sunglasses, revealing his bright eyes, one green and one blue. Didn't dissipate when his mouth split wide with a smile, exposing straight, white teeth that practically sparkled in the sun.

In fact, as she took him in her fear only grew, even more so when he opened his mouth and his deep voice, so thick, so *male,* rumbled from him.

"Well, hello there beautiful, fancy seeing you here."

Chapter 2

Will Crawford looked around the small cabin he'd been staying in for the last two weeks, taking in the cramped space filled with wooden furniture that contained numerous chips and cracks. The refrigerator that hummed far too loudly and the leaky bathroom faucet that either ran far too hot or far too cold.

Damn, he was gonna miss this place. It wasn't the Ritz or the Four Seasons or any of the luxury hotels he regularly stayed in, it was far better than that. He was loath to say goodbye but alas, duty called.

"Constantly," he huffed, glaring at his buzzing phone before silencing the damn thing again. He sighed deeply, running his eyes over the place for one final look, trying to commit the cabin to memory. He scrubbed a hand over his chest where it started to ache at the prospect of leaving.

He had come to Citrus Pines for a friend's wedding. He hadn't meant to stay as long as he had, but the second he got to town he couldn't bear the thought of leaving. The townsfolk welcomed him, eager to pull him into their loving fold. He didn't usually have a problem getting people to like him: he was a celebrity, a big one too, like Chris Hemsworth or Kardashian-famous. But this felt warmer, more sincere somehow, like they actually cared about him.

But it wasn't just the people, it was the town itself. The fresh crisp air that carried the scent of lemons on it. The great spruce trees that lined every road and stretched towards the sky like they could reach the sun. The blanket of pine needles that carpeted the ground, cushioning every step. The quaint buildings in town were like something out of a movie and he was immediately attached.

Will had been floundering when he arrived in town, at the end of his tether, not that anyone would know it. It wasn't that he was ungrateful with life, it was just that for the last year or so he had struggled to control the feeling that had crawled into his skin and settled in his veins.

The urge to *escape*.

He didn't know where to, or for how long, and he didn't know why. But he fought to keep it in check, choking it down, pretending everything was fine. Then he'd come to Citrus Pines. To this picturesque safe haven where, away from the Hollywood toxicity, sanity prevailed and he put his foot down, taking a break for the first time in nearly two decades.

Fuck the filming schedule.
Fuck the crew.
Fuck his fellow castmates.

Take A Chance

Fuck the show. The show *he'd* built from the ground up and now everyone else was reaping the rewards. He had *earned* the right to take a break.

When his manager had freaked out, worrying about who would pay everyone's lost wages, Will had instantly wired the money to write the checks. Hell, he could afford it, he was a billionaire.

"It's my show dammit, I'll decide if I want a break," he had growled at his manager, every inch the bad guy the show portrayed him to be. Will was the Mr. Nasty all reality shows needed for entertainment value. He looked the part: tall, built, tattooed head to toe, with a hard stare emanating from his one blue eye and one green eye, as icy as the press reported his heart to be.

When he'd graduated with his MBA, he had barely closed his first business deal when the opportunity for the show came along. *The Viper Pit*, the reality show predating *Shark Tank*, where young entrepreneurs pitched to the four business owners for investment in their start-ups.

Very quickly it was decided what role Will would play. The rude, cruel, aggressive viper. He would intimidate, attack and lash out on camera. Fight with his fellow colleagues, heavily criticize the contestants who were just starting out and trying to make something of themselves, like Will once had been.

When he was approached, he'd been young and naïve and just desperate to make money and get his mom out of the trailer, so he had agreed to play the part and the audience ate it up. People loved it. Women were drawn to him, wanting him to treat them the same way; controlling, aggressive, demanding satisfaction but never giving it.

But his reality-show persona couldn't be further from the real Will Crawford and as time passed, the constant façade wore him down. He would forever be grateful for what the show had given him. So damn grateful to be out of that trailer park and to never again feel the painful ache of true hunger, or be left with another stranger while his mom did what she had to with random men to get money for food. Will had to be grateful and pay his dues, the success of the show depended on his character, so he had to ride it out. Too many people were counting on him.

So, he did it. He gave the producers what they wanted. He gave the fans what they wanted, and he gave women what they wanted. Was sexually dominating, aggressive, and brutal sometimes. And now, he was exhausted. Burnt out. The anxiety of having so much responsibility, so many decisions to make and so many people banking on him had left him completely wrapped up in pleasing everyone. He'd needed a break, a distraction, and someone to take all that responsibility off his shoulders, someone to take control for him. But now his break was over and the idea of returning to the big city left him nauseous.

His phone rang again, distracting him. He glanced down and saw it was the same caller, his *Momager*. The first thing he had done when he made some money was to get his mom out of that trailer and employ her as his manager. Diane Crawford had found her true calling. He taught her everything he knew about business, and she was ruthless in negotiations, completely focused and dedicated to her job. She was a whirlwind; the ultimate female boss and he was so damn proud of what she'd made of herself.

Except sometimes he wished she was the young twenty-year-old, sitting on that dirty trailer floor with him, watching cartoons and eating their daily meal of SpaghettiOs. She was carefree, covered in tomato juice, her red hair wild, chipped nails all different colors from where she'd experimented with her polish, her skin glowing and make-up free.

Nowadays, she looked too put together. Her skin was too tight from her experimentations with Botox. Not a hair out of place and she never missed her bi-weekly manicure at Hollywood's top salon. She always wore immaculate clothing that he hardly dared to touch in case he creased it.

He let the call ring out and the screen darkened. He grabbed his bags, tension tightening his shoulders as he said goodbye to his room, his salvation.

He closed the cabin door and headed down off the porch into the bright sunshine. He closed his eyes, absorbing all the warmth from the sunlight and endorphins flooded him, bringing back his positivity. *You can do this; you can do anything.*

He smiled, face tilted up, letting the rays lovingly caress his fair skin. He could practically feel new freckles sprouting. He got his fair complexion and strawberry blond hair from his mom, although now her hair was showing strands of silver since she had entered her late fifties, her only signs of aging since her dermatologist had erased all the wrinkles and laughter lines that Will missed so much.

He now had his own silver hair showing at his temples. The crinkles at the corner of his eyes had deepened and he could no longer ignore the bags that had taken up residence under his eyes. He was scarily close to his fortieth birthday, and he'd never been more exhausted.

He passed the row of cabins and crossed the porch of The Rusty Bucket Inn. When he opened the door, the scent of stale alcohol hit him, but it wasn't unpleasant, it was comforting. As it was so early, there were only one or two of the old regulars propping up the oak bar.

"The big dog is in the house!" A deep voice boomed, and he looked up to see his best friend, Beau Thompson, behind the bar with his arms wrapped around his stunning red-headed girlfriend, Taylor, the owner of the bar. The sharp ache in Will's chest evaporated and a smile split his face.

Taylor glared at him. "Are you sure your dad isn't Dennis Quaid? Or Heath Ledger? You've got that damn Cheshire cat, panty-dropping grin and I hate it!"

Beau frowned at her. "Hey!"

"I can't help it, sweetheart. I'm only human and he's got those Hollywood good looks that women are helpless to resist," Taylor replied defensively.

"Nearly all women," Will scoffed, looking around the empty bar for the woman with soft doe eyes that were seared into his soul, and who continued to act like he didn't exist.

Rebelle.

He'd seen her a couple of times, a woman so petite he could pick her up with one hand. With wispy dark hair that framed her angular face and gumdrop eyes the color of his favorite whiskey. And don't even get him started on the cute button nose and pink rosebud mouth with the sharp Cupid's bow that visited him in his dreams.

He had seen her a grand total of three times. He'd tried to speak to her each of those three times. He'd been ignored, you guessed it, three times. Her dark eyes always stared straight through him, like he wasn't even there.

"You leaving now?" Beau asked, pulling his focus.

That pang in Will's chest was back and he absently rubbed at the spot and pasted on his trademark smile. "Yep, fun time is over."

Taylor came around the bar and wrapped an arm

Take A Chance

around his waist. "You sure we can't convince you to stay?"

The pang grew sharper. "I'm happy to let you try," he replied, squeezing her to him and shooting Beau a shit-eating grin. His best friend narrowed his eyes, his nostrils flaring before he mouthed *mine*.

Will snickered and released Taylor, not wanting to poke the bear any longer. He'd met Beau nearly ten years ago when he'd hired him as his personal trainer. Beau's passion and dedication inspired Will so much that he offered to partner him if Beau ever decided to open his own gym. Turned out that was exactly what Beau wanted, and a few years later, Beau was the most sought-after personal trainer in Hollywood. Will was so proud of his best friend's success. Even prouder when Beau decided that he wanted nothing to do with the L.A. toxicity anymore and sold up before moving home to Citrus Pines and opening a physical rehab center and gym.

Proud, for sure, but there had been an element of jealousy that Beau had been able to leave it all behind while Will had to keep going. He would never be able to do that, too many people depended on his success for him to be able to jack it all in.

"Seriously man, I'm sad to see you go," Beau said, squeezing his shoulder.

"Me too, trust me. This was the perfect vacation. But that was all it was meant to be. I gotta get back to reality, too many people counting on me." He shrugged before digging in his pants pocket for his key. He pulled it out and reluctantly dropped it into Taylor's waiting palm.

"You okay?" Beau asked.

Will scoffed. "Of course, ready to get back to the action. You know me, can't wait to see what challenge is around the corner, Mr. Happy-Go-Lucky."

"Okay, let me know when you get home. You flying back?"

"Yeah, I'll drop my car off at the airfield."

Beau nodded. "You said goodbye to the others?"

A while ago, Will had been introduced to Beau's other best friend, Dean, who owned the local garage, *Iris Motors*. He had dropped his car in for detailing and he and Dean had quickly formed a friendship. Will was in town these past couple of weeks because Dean was marrying his gorgeous girl, Christy. While here, Will had also met Blake, the new sheriff that Beau and Dean had befriended, and Blake's fiancée Justine. Will and Blake had bonded over their love of animals with Blake sharing the story of how he came to own a domesticated fox.

Will had always loved animals and craved having an animal companion but it just wasn't possible with his lifestyle, it wouldn't be fair to the animal. Will noticed that Blake and Justine seemed close to Rebelle, the woman he couldn't seem to forget, and Blake was incredibly protective of her.

"Yeah, last night when you two disappeared into Taylor's office for an hour." Will raised his pierced brow at them, waiting for them to look sheepish but it never happened. He chuckled and pulled them both into a hug.

"Take care guys, I'll miss you."

"You're gonna visit soon, right?" Taylor's muffled voice sounded thick with emotion.

"Just try and stop me," Will replied, his throat clogged. Beau squeezed his shoulder again tightly, like he could see straight through Will's façade and knew he didn't want to leave.

They broke away and then Will was heading for the door, shooting them a final look over his shoulder before the door swung shut.

Take A Chance

He crossed the quiet parking lot to his red Bugatti. Dumping his bag into the passenger seat, he switched on the engine, and it purred to life, the sound vibrating his legs and Pantera's *Walk* blasted out. Will checked his phone again before beginning his journey and saw he had a message.

Momager: Your plane takes off in an hour, don't miss it. You should get back here in time for new wardrobe fittings and screen test tonight. Then we need to talk about your GQ interview and shoot. Have you been maintaining your weight while you're on this so-called vacation? They want a shirtless shoot...

Will worked his jaw, the loud crack filling the car. The only good thing was the clothes, Will was a fan of a sharp suit and spent most of his time in them. He was not a fan of diets and workouts, which was why he'd had to hire Beau in the first place, to push him to do it.

His brain protested at the thought of being back in L.A. that afternoon, donning his mask of contempt on set and being poked and prodded, hiding his true self. Panic rose up inside him and for a moment he thought he would hurl.

He couldn't face it yet, it was too soon. He just needed more time.

Will: New plan, I'm driving back, see you in three days! Pay whatever the crew are owed, you've got the account deets.

And with that, he silenced his phone and tossed it into the back seat, laughing as he pictured Diane Crawford's face as she read his message. The knot in his chest was still there but had eased slightly; he'd bought himself three more days.

He drove out of the parking lot and headed down Main Street, waving goodbye to some of the locals he spotted on the way. He saw a woman with short dark hair and his heart tripped over itself in his chest but as he drove past her, he saw it wasn't Rebelle.

He continued on down a dirt road, yelling along to Rage Against The Machine, *'Fuck you I won't do what you tell me'*, which had never felt more apt.

He passed the trees and traveled through a more rural area where he spotted a sign, *Take A Chance Animal Shelter - 1 mile ahead.* He hadn't known there was a shelter in town and was tempted to detour for a look but it would only hurt when he gazed into the hopeful eyes of dogs and cats in need of their forever home.

He put the shelter out of his mind until one mile later when he passed the sign for the turning. It took a second for his brain to register it, then he slammed on the brakes and skidded to a stop, clouds of road dust pluming around the car.

He sat there, riddled with indecision before he put the car in reverse and backed up to just before the turn off, leaving the engine running.

It was the same sign as before, a barely there, run down, hardly noticeable sign. How was it supposed to attract attention and potential adopters when it was so small? The shelter really needed to work on their presence and marketing but that wasn't what had caught his attention. It was the fact that this sign had been amended to read: *Take A Chance Animal Shelter. Help wanted/volunteer needed.*

His breathing quickened. It was a sign. It had to be. Well, other than it being a literal sign that is. He'd been looking for an excuse to derail his journey back to his real life and he'd found it. The signiest of all signs.

He spun the steering wheel and turned the car down the dirt track, the sensible part of his brain screaming at

Take A Chance

him to turn back, to go back to L.A., back to his responsibilities and all those people counting on him; he couldn't let them down.

He ignored it all.

There was a reason he had seen this at the best and worst possible time.

He needed this; he could feel it. Call it kismet, fate, dumb fucking luck, whatever, he just knew he was meant to be here. He continued up the road, excitement had him bouncing his knee up and down, looking eagerly through the windshield until a rundown, brick outhouse came into view.

Is this it? It's a mess.

Will killed the engine, wondering if he was even in the right place. He opened the car door and immediately heard the barking. He laughed, full of joy as he saw the mutts come barrelling out of the building towards him before they stopped in their tracks and were herded back inside. Then everything in him became rooted to the spot as he took in the owner.

Her dark brown hair tickled her face with delicate wisps caught in the wind, thick dark brows puckered as she shielded her eyes from the sun. Her rosebud mouth pulled tight, and the sharp jut of her chin lifted defiantly. Gently sunkissed skin enhanced by a white tank top that looked like the straps were tied together on her shoulders. Her jeans were holey and Will spotted a couple of missing belt loops, the tennis shoes that looked like they had once been white but were now a browny gray but it didn't matter. His heart pounded in his chest and he suddenly knew exactly why he'd felt the pull to this place.

He was exactly where he was supposed to be.

He rolled up his shirtsleeves, suddenly sweating but he didn't know if it was from the sun, the hot wave of desire that flooded him at seeing her again or the flames shooting from her eyes.

He pulled off his sunglasses and smiled wide. "Well, hello there beautiful, fancy seeing you here." He was smiling his most charming smile, his *Sexiest Smile 2019* according to *Cosmopolitan*. He knew exactly how it looked, but even his very best smile had zero impact on this woman.

"What do you want?" Her words shot from her, sharp and demanding. The breeze carried her floral scent to him and he inhaled greedily, his mouth watering. The sweet, softly enticing scent completely at odds with the *fuck off* stamped across her puckered forehead.

He took a step towards her, trying to close the huge gap between them but she immediately stepped back, creating more space.

"I'm here about the help wanted sign." He kept his smile wide, cataloging her. Her whiskey eyes darted back and forth from him to the building. She worried at her lip and her knees were bent ever so slightly, like she was prepped to run.

"No thank you," she replied.

He blinked. *What?* "No?"

"That's what I said, no." Her tone was steely.

He can't have heard her right. "But, why not?"

"Lots of reasons."

He plugged his hands on his hips. "Name one."

"You're a man."

He scoffed. "And?"

"I'm looking for a woman."

"That's not what your sign says."

She shrugged. "Then I'll change it."

He chuckled. "You know that's illegal, right?"

"To change my own sign?"

"No, you can't discriminate." He arched a brow at her, enjoying their verbal sparring and wanting to hear more of her rasping voice.

Her frown deepened. "Thanks for the update. Please leave."

Her tone and shuttered expression had him backtracking. He'd fucked this up completely, but he could turn it around, he always did.

He stepped forward again and she stepped back, practically jumping away from him.

"We've got off on the wrong foot." Flashing her a disarming smile he continued. "I'm Will Crawford, pleased to meet you." He held his hand out, but she didn't acknowledge it.

"This conversation is over."

"It's just starting. I've introduced myself, normally you would do the same and say 'Lovely to meet you, come back tomorrow and we'll get to work', and then-"

"Look, Precious. Whatever it is you're selling with your fancy-ass clothes and too expensive midlife crisis car, I ain't buying." Her southern accent thickening delightfully the more she talked.

"Precious?" Will's lip quirked at the nickname. "I'm just trying to sell you my time?"

"Well, I don't want it. Now for the last time, leave," she growled, her cheeks flushed. He took in her fight or flight stance, her hard expression and knew this wasn't going well. He needed to regroup.

He held up his hands in surrender. "Okay, I hear you. I'm going." He paused for a moment, the businessman in him demanding he convince her, but his experience had taught him when he needed to back off or he'd lose altogether. He nodded then shot her another smile, trying to cover the fact that he was memorizing her face.

He sauntered back to his car, his steps light and excitement running through him like he hadn't had in a long time. The thrill of the challenge, the chase. He had a plan, and he would be back in the morning.

He grabbed his phone from the back seat then drove off, calling his *Momager* handsfree.

"Change of plan," he said when she answered.

"Will! What the hell are you doing? Driving from Tennessee to L.A. Are you joking? Are you high?"

"Relax Mom, I'm not doing that," he soothed her ruffled feathers.

"Thank Christ, you gave me a heart attack and I'm too young to die. Okay, so GQ are ready for your 'Fabulous at Forty' shoot on Friday. As I said, it's topless so no solid food after Wednesday and no liquids from Thursday morning. I've booked you a chest wax on Wednesday, hopefully by Friday the swelling and redness will have gone down, you do have such pale skin, Will. Filming starts tomorrow, screentest and wardrobe fitting tonight. They're really wanting to carve out your image this season, still lots of dark prints and cuts to reveal your tattoos, it'll really hammer home the persona and-"

"Mom!"

She sighed. "Yes?"

"Change of plan, I'll be sticking around here for a bit, I'll see you in a couple of weeks."

There was deathly silence then a shriek the likes of which only belonged to fabled Banshees. "What! What the fuck, Will! Are you fucki-"

"Bye Mom, love you!" he called, cutting off her rage before he ended the call. He laughed as he headed back into Citrus Pines to rent out his new favorite cabin for the next few weeks.

Chapter 3

When his car was out of sight, Rebelle gasped out a breath, heaving the air from her lungs. She bent forward at the waist, clutching her trembling knees with shaking hands as she tried not to dry heave.

He'd startled her.

She wasn't expecting to step outside and see him. He, Will, as he'd introduced himself, clearly had no idea how intimidating he was to someone like her. Someone who had been through so much at the hands of a man half Will's size.

She worked to get control of her breathing, but having such an imposing man in close proximity, trying to force his way in, had triggered something. She wiped frantically at her mouth as she felt saliva trying to escape. Panic attacks weren't pretty, but they were frequent. She had been working with Justine to cope with her attacks, but it was taking longer than she had hoped to get a handle on them. Her limbs turned to Jell-O and she collapsed into the dirt.

He could have hit you.
Could have dragged you behind the shelter and-

"Stop!" she gasped out, trying to cease her *'could haves'*. Not every man was abusive, but her brain sure acted like they were. She lay there in the dirt, the sun beaming down on her, covering her in its comforting warmth, bringing life back into her skin. Blood pumped freely through her veins until she came back to herself.

She didn't know how long she had lain there until Bryan, the Irish Wolfhound, came and curled up next to her, resting his head on her outstretched hand. Her palm twitched before she tangled her fingers in his fur, the bristles tickling her skin. She focused on the sensation, using it to calm herself. His dark eyes watched her, his little smudges of eyebrows twitching this way and that.

Her eyes locked on the white rose bush, swaying gently in the breeze and she hauled herself to her feet and went over to it. The moment she stroked her fingers over the soft petals, lost herself in the white swirls of color and inhaled the sweet, floral scent her breathing steadied, a peace flowing through her.

Finally, when she could put off her chores no longer, she headed back into the shelter. Bryan followed her dutifully, staying by her side for the rest of the day as she mucked out the kennels and administered medication to those who needed it. His soulful stare tracked her the entire time, like he was making sure she was okay.

When darkness settled over the shelter as day turned to night, she took Bryan to his kennel and ushered him in.

"Thank you for looking after me today," she cooed at

him when he was reluctant to go in. He waited a beat, but she must have managed to reassure him she was better. He trotted in, circled his bed a few times before collapsing into the cushion with a loud groan and a huff.

She visited each kennel to say goodnight, giving each dog a treat before she did the same to the cats in the kitchen who finally stopped pretending to hate her long enough to yowl for their treats. She gave them scratches and when they shrugged her off, she headed into the storeroom, lighting her candle and inhaling the soft rose scent deeply to calm the nerves which had remained fraught all day.

She tried not to think about Will. Tried to put him out of her mind and not focus on how many times she had looked over her shoulder today, making sure he didn't come back and startle her. Tried to ignore how remarkable his eyes were. They had caught her attention, both bright, the unusual cool colors stark against his pale skin. Her heartbeat increased and her throat tightened.

"No, don't think about it. Count out what's good…" She closed her eyes and blew out the candle, waiting for the good to come but nothing did. Her brain was too exhausted. Her body and soul ached.

"Sometimes the good is that tomorrow is a new day," she mumbled before she fell asleep.

She woke the next morning to silence. Usually, the dogs woke her up howling and growling but this morning they were strangely quiet.

She rubbed the sleep from her eyes before she sat up, her back cracking and she grunted in pain. She rolled up her sleeping bag, moving awkwardly, her spine struggling to straighten after yet another night of lying on cool concrete.

She dressed in the same clothes from the day before

and drew back the sheet that separated her little room from the shelter. Sunlight flooded in from the skylight and she was pleased it was another sunny day, she could already feel it was going to be a good day. Her stomach growled; she hadn't eaten at all yesterday which meant she would need something soon. She went into the kitchen, hunting in the cupboards for anything but they were bare.

Betty, the longhaired black cat twined herself around Rebelle's legs, purring frantically, obviously deciding that she needed to drop the aloof act in favor of getting fed this morning. Rebelle hefted Betty into her arms, struggling slightly with the chonky queen, her arms a little weak from the lack of food. She buried her face in Betty's silky fur, the warmth emanating from her teasing Rebelle's skin. She eventually put the cat down and filled her and her sister, Veronica's food bowls. Betty inhaled it like she hadn't eaten for days let alone last night. Rebelle looked around for Veronica and spotted her sitting on top of an empty bunny cage, enjoying her vantage point.

Rebelle returned to the dogs, grabbing the old cordless phone from its cradle to call the vet to get medicine top ups but she stalled in dialing when she noticed the dog's behavior. Each one of them sat at the front of their kennel, staring through the plexiglass front towards the door of the shelter, alert but not barking.

"What's the matter, guys? You see another mouse?" she asked. None of them replied, obviously. Just acted like she hadn't spoken, their attention fixed. Rebelle headed over to the door, still cradling the cordless phone. "We don't need any more mice here, let's scare it away."

She unlocked the door and leapt outside, smacking straight into the sweaty, hard bare chest of Will Crawford.

"Whoa!" he shouted.

She stumbled back from the impact and his arm shot

out and snaked around her waist, stopping her from falling. She froze at his touch and he dragged her up against him, her palms flattening against his damp, inked chest.

"I got you," he murmured, peering down at her with his eyes, one green, one blue, both cold. The proximity to him set her nerve endings on edge and she pushed herself away.

"What the hell are you doing here?" she demanded. Her feet were screaming at her to leave. Her flight impulse kicked in and she turned and ran back to the shelter, slamming and locking the door behind her. She leaned her forehead against it as she tried desperately to pull air into her lungs. There was silence in the shelter, save for her heavy breathing and she turned around, the dogs all sat there, peering at her through the plexiglass. She shook her head at the furry traitors for not barking and howling.

There was a tap on the door and she leapt back with a yelp, fear spiking her adrenaline.

"Uh, Rebelle?"

"Please leave!" she shouted, panic clawing at her throat.

"Leave? But I've only just started." The rough timbre of his voice came through the door, like there was no barrier between them. It slithered down her spine and she rolled her shoulders in an effort to shake off the unfamiliar sensation.

"What are you even doing here? I don't want your help!" she hissed.

"You said you didn't want it, but you clearly need it. Are you gonna lift all these heavy concrete blocks on your own in this heat?"

It was unseasonably warm for the beginning of

autumn, but she dreaded the cool weather that would inevitably approach, the shelter would be hard to keep warm. She rolled her lips together, hating that he was right and that was why the blocks had sat there so long. She didn't have the energy or strength to do it.

"Besides, I didn't want the dogs hurting their paws on all the brick shards."

That was actually very thoughtful, but she was too far gone to care.

"Well, thanks for what you've done but I'd like you to leave now."

There was no response, but he was still there, she could feel him, and she hated it. "Please just go. Don't make me call the sheriff."

He snorted on the other side of the door. "Really? You'd call Blake on me? Come on out here Rebelle, and just talk to me," he coaxed. But she'd heard that tone from a man before, pretending to just want to talk, just to get her close enough to hurt her. It never ended well for her.

Steely resolve fused her spine and she stepped away, hurrying over to the phone cradle where she had Blake's number saved. She dialed and when he answered, she explained the situation.

"Okay, don't worry, I'll take care of it," Blake said before ending the call. A moment later, Rebelle heard the blare of heavy metal music, then heard Will's voice and hurried back towards the door to listen.

"Y'ello? Blake, my man, how's it going?" His voice faded as he moved away from the building. Rebelle unlocked the door as quietly as possible and peeked outside.

"Nah, I'm helping out at the shelter," Will continued and she watched as his back muscles flexed underneath his decorated skin as he lifted another piece of rock like it weighed nothing. And was he wearing dress pants with suspenders? The suspenders were hanging around his waist, the loops curving around his backside, framing each of the incredibly firm, rounded cheeks. Who did manual labor dressed so formally and where was his shirt? Her eyes were drawn to his chest as the sun glinted off the metal hoop through one of his nipples. Something hot slithered through her and she didn't like it.

"Oh, she did, huh?" Will said, then turned back towards the building. She quickly shut the door and locked it again, listening with bated breath. His footsteps were coming closer. "Okay man. Shit, yeah, I'm leaving now. Thanks, see you soon Blake."

There was silence and Rebelle pushed herself closer to the door, straining her ear to pick up any sound. Another tap on the door had her yelping in surprise.

"Rebelle? I'm leaving now." There was a pause, and she could feel him lingering. "I, uh, I just wanted to help out. I didn't mean to... Look, I'm sorry. I really hope I'll see you around." His voice had previously been booming and confident but now it was soft, quiet and a dash of guilt pricked at her at the hurt lacing his tone.

Her breath released in a *whoosh* when she heard his car start up and the kick of gravel as he drove off. Tears stung her eyes and her adrenaline faded, leaving her weak and dizzy. Caught off guard at the light-headedness, she slumped to the floor. She didn't know how long she stayed like that, but when she came back to herself, her cheeks were still wet with tears, and Betty and Veronica were sat at her feet.

The tears flowed faster as she realized once again just how not okay she was. She didn't want this anymore. Couldn't live like this. Didn't want to be frozen in place by debilitating fear.

She reached for the phone again with shaky fingers and dialed another number.

"Rebelle, you okay?" Justine's concerned voice answered.

Rebelle sniffled. "I, uh, do you think we could schedule one of our chats for later?"

Rebelle could hear the smile in Justine's voice and instantly felt comforted. "Of course, swing by at the usual time. I've got some new fruit teas for us to try!"

*

"So, what do you want to talk about today?" Justine asked as she sat on the couch opposite Rebelle in her office, kicking off her heels and tucking her feet up under her. Her hands absentmindedly stroked her pregnant belly. It might be cheesy to say it but Justine truly glowed with happiness.

Justine's office always gave Rebelle a calm feeling, the natural light from the large windows contrasted with the dark wood furniture and the cream tones of the walls along with large green plants dotted around. The result was a zen atmosphere and Rebelle instantly felt at peace when she came here.

Months ago, after a particularly harrowing nightmare, Rebelle had worked up the courage to come into Justine's office and ask for help. Rebelle had tried to book sessions but Justine had refused to take any money, insisting that they have a weekly catch up over coffee like friends do, and in this time Rebelle could talk about anything she wanted. At first, Rebelle struggled to accept the handout. Her pride and newfound hard-won independence recoiled at the charity. However, she needed help, needed to move

Take A Chance

on and start living her life now she finally had a chance. In the end her desire to shake her fears had overruled her pride and she had accepted the generous offer.

"I want to..." Rebelle trailed off, mashing her lips together, struggling to get the words out.

Justine waited patiently. She looked so elegant in her orange jumpsuit with leopard print heels kicked off, chunky gold earrings adorned her ears and immaculate hair and make-up sent envy crawling through Rebelle. The Latina beauty looked so stunning and 'together' and Rebelle always felt inadequate next to her, next to most women.

She wasn't vain. Marcus had beaten that out of her and constantly told her how disgusting he found her. But she wanted clothes, hell even just bras and panties that weren't second hand or ripped and torn. She wanted to try make-up, she'd only ever worn it as a teenager and when she had tried to as an adult, Marcus would smear it across her face, calling her a whore. She kept her hair short, had learned not to let it grow too long or Marcus could grab hold of it. It had become yet another tool for his abuse.

"Take your time," Justine murmured, sipping the fruit tea she'd made. Rebelle had revealed in their first session that she didn't like coffee, but not why. The stench of it triggered memories of Marcus, looming over her, huffing his stale coffee breath in her face as he assaulted her. With Justine avoiding caffeine during her pregnancy, she had instead bought a box of fruit teas, lots of different flavors and said their goal would be to work through them. This week was raspberry, and it was the most delicious thing Rebelle had ever tasted.

She liked that Justine was patient and always gave her space to pick through her violent, chaotic thoughts and pull her words together in a considered way.

"I want to stop being afraid of men," Rebelle said, immediately taking a sip of her tea to distract herself from the vulnerability her words betrayed. Justine's silence forced Rebelle to make eye contact with her.

"Do you want to tell me the reason that you're afraid of men?" Justine probed quietly. Rebelle drew in a shaky breath and shook her head, no. She had only revealed a few small tidbits in their previous two sessions.

Justine's expression softened. "You know anything you share with me will remain confidential. Just because these are chats and not official sessions doesn't mean I take them any less seriously."

Rebelle's emotions rose as she panicked at having to open doors she wanted to keep bolted shut. She tried to modulate her breathing. She began rubbing her palms over her thighs, pressing deep to create pressure to focus on that feeling, that movement, as a way to self-soothe, like Justine had taught her.

Justine cocked her head. "I'm pleased to see you implementing some of the calming techniques we discussed last time. How are you finding them?"

Jumping at the chance to change the subject, Rebelle replied, "I've got a candle. It's a rose scented one, it reminds me of home." *Of my sister,* she amended in her head.

"That's great. Are you finding the scent soothes you when your anxiety flares up? Or is it the process of lighting the candle that helps distract your mind?"

"I guess both, it doesn't always work though which is why I rub my legs."

"That's fine, it's a sensory technique so scent and touch are great ones to pick. If sensory isn't working for you, we can always work on some breathing techniques if you like?"

Rebelle nodded. "I think that would be good, do we have to do that now, though?"

"No. You could tell me why you're afraid of men instead?"

Rebelle pursed her lips. *Dammit.* Justine was wily and had circled back. Rebelle finished her tea and set the cup down on the coffee table. With nothing in her hands to distract herself, she began picking at the hole in her shorts.

"I know you might not want to talk about it, but talking about it is the first step to overcoming it and I can help you with both," Justine said.

There was another stretch of silence and in that time, Justine refilled their cups with more raspberry tea.

"I think from what I've heard, the previous sheriff wasn't a very nice man. Would that be a fair statement?" Justine asked. Rebelle sucked in another breath and looked Justine in the eye, seeing kindness reflected back at her. "You're safe here, with me, someone who cares about you. I'm your friend, Rebelle, and I want to help."

Stale bitterness rose in Rebelle's throat. Everyone wanted to help now the situation was taken care of but where were they before? She swallowed that bitterness down like she did each time, trying not to focus on the way she felt the town had failed her. She knew Justine cared, she wouldn't give her valuable time away for free if she didn't.

"He hurt me," Rebelle replied, softly.

"How did he hurt you?"

She picked at a ragged nail bed. "With words, sliced me open with each cruel insult or curse. With his fists, his belt, his cigarettes, sometimes anything he could get his hands on."

Justine's warm skin paled slightly as Rebelle spoke. This is what she'd been afraid of, the pity that the truth brings. But Rebelle had started, had opened the dam and now she couldn't stop.

"He cut off all my communication with friends and family. If I spoke to strangers, he accused me of flirting and raped me as punishment. He would shut me in the bedroom all day, locking the door and not letting me out to eat or drink or go to the bathroom. Sometimes he'd leave me in there for twenty hours or more, I couldn't always hold it. When he would let me out and see I hadn't been able to hold it, he'd punish me, tell me I was disgusting. So I guess yeah, you could say he wasn't a nice man." Sickness churned Rebelle's stomach at rehashing some of the worst moments.

Justine swallowed loudly. "Rebelle, I'm so sorry. Can I give you a hug, please?"

Justine's words tugged at her chest and Rebelle looked up to see tears filling her eyes. She appreciated that Justine had asked but she still had issues being touched.

"I appreciate that but I'm not great with touch yet."

"I understand and I want to respect your boundaries. I also want to wrap you in my arms and take you away from here."

Rebelle chuckled softly at the image that represented. She saw Justine cradle her swollen stomach and Rebelle knew she would be an amazing mom.

"*Dios mio*, I'm glad that *pendejo* is dead!" Justine spat before slapping a hand over her mouth, her horrified gaze lifting to Rebelle's.

"It's fine, I am too."

Justine shook her head. "Thank you for sharing that with me, it must have been incredibly painful, but I feel like now we can work on helping you."

Rebelle worried at her lip. "And you won't tell anyone?"

"Not Blake, not Christy or your new boss Taylor."

"Not that Will guy?" Rebelle didn't know why she said that.

Justine's dark brow furrowed. "Will? No, of course not. This stays between us."

Rebelle's cheeks grew warm under Justine's scrutiny. She didn't know why she cared about Will, maybe she still felt guilty after calling Blake on him.

"So, is there a reason as to why you want to work on your fears *now*?" Justine asked.

Because I don't ever again want to be afraid of a man like I was yesterday. "Now I'm working at the bar, I'll be around men a lot. And if I got a, uh, male volunteer at the shelter it would be nice to not be afraid of them."

Justine eyed her again. "When Blake came by for lunch today, he mentioned Will turning up at the shelter. Is that what you're thinking, that it would be him?"

Dammit! How did she know everything? Rebelle gave a noncommittal shrug.

"The bar will be a great place to start, as you'll have Taylor's full support if you ever feel uncomfortable. Also the new guy, Ben, is a sweetheart and you'll have Kayleigh there too so you won't be on your own too much. It'll be a good way to ease yourself into interacting with men again. And if you find yourself struggling then take a break, give yourself some space and use the techniques we've worked on."

Rebelle nodded, this sounded doable. There were places she could escape if she felt overwhelmed and vulnerable.

"Breathing techniques will be useful to you. Interacting with men isn't necessarily something you can control but your breathing is. Using techniques to gain your control back will truly help you. They're simple, if you find yourself struggling with a situation then take a step back, imagine you're blowing up a balloon or blowing out a candle. Take a breath in and release it in a slow exhale," Justine added.

They practiced a couple of times and then it was time for Rebelle to leave.

"Raspberry is the nicest so far," Rebelle mumbled, looking for something to talk to Justine about that wasn't therapy.

"Oh yeah? I'm glad you liked it, it was nice and sweet but I bet now I have a red tongue?" Justine stuck her tongue out which was indeed striped candy red. Rebelle nodded then stuck hers out and Justine smiled wide.

"Next time let's try blackcurrant?"

"Deal," Rebelle replied. She swayed slightly on her feet.

"Are you okay?" Justine asked, her eagle eyes missing nothing.

"Yeah, just a bit of headrush, must have stood up too quick," Rebelle lied, and she knew Justine knew she was lying.

"When did you last eat?"

"This morning," Rebelle lied again.

"Wanna have dinner with us tonight? I know Blake would love that."

"Thank you but I need to get back to the shelter."

"At this time of night? Aren't you going home?"

Fear pulsed inside Rebelle at her slip up. "Late night feeding then I'll go home."

Justine looked like she wanted to argue but she didn't say anything, and they both headed to the door of the office, Justine preparing to lock up.

"Next week, you can tell me all about your first shift at The Bucket but if you need me before then, just call."

"I will, thank you for this evening. I really appreciate what you're doing for me."

"It's what friends do." Justine shrugged. "I'll just say, we know Will. He's one of the good ones but I know that doesn't mean much right now. I don't know of any reason that you need to be afraid of him. Hell, if he ever did anything wrong the whole world would know about it in seconds anyway!"

Rebelle frowned, not knowing what Justine meant by that.

"But even so, you can count on us that if something happened, we would help you. Blake would be there in a heartbeat. We're here for you," she added.

Emotion clogged Rebelle's throat and she nodded in lieu of responding. They went their separate ways, Rebelle watching as Blake met Justine outside her office to drive home together, the joy in their faces as they looked at one another couldn't be denied.

Rebelle began the long walk back to the shelter, mulling over Justine's words and wondering if maybe she had been too hasty in calling Blake on Will earlier.

Chapter 4

"Adjust your plan. Pivot, use your creative thinking." By now, Will was used to rejection and it wasn't the first time he'd had to alter a strategy. He hadn't failed, he just needed a minute to reconsider his options. He got back in his car and drove away from the shelter.

He couldn't believe Rebelle had called Blake on him. Why was she so resistant to his help? Blake had warned him away from her before, but Will had just thought Blake was being an overprotective big brother figure and looking out for her. He had told Will that Rebelle was anxious around strangers and was likely scared Will would hurt her. On reflection Will could see that he was intimidating and had often used that to his advantage in the business world. Being tall, built and covered in tattoos didn't exactly scream, *"I'm completely harmless!"*, neither did his reputation as a Viper. He couldn't blame anyone for not wanting to get caught up in hungry paparazzi and journalists scavenging for a story.

He needed to befriend Rebelle, show her he wasn't a creep and work his way into her good graces. And he could volunteer at the shelter, do something worthwhile for once. Then maybe she would see he was actually a pretty good guy and he could take her out.

Her whiskey eyes were all he was seeing in his dreams lately and he'd love to see them glow with warmth when she looked at him. He really wanted her to look at him with desire and delight but at this stage, he'd settle for warmth.

He parked up at The Bucket and headed straight inside. Although it was early in the morning there were already a couple of locals warming the worn barstools. Taylor and Beau were chatting to each other, their faces so full of love it was kinda sickening.

"Oh my Lord!" Taylor gasped as she saw him, her hand shooting out to grab Beau as she fell into a very dramatic swoon. "Warn a girl before you walk around looking like that!"

Will glanced down seeing that he'd forgotten to put his shirt back on after working at the shelter this morning, a sheen of sweat still coating his chest. The temperature was in the low eighties and he was happy with the unseasonable warmth, anything to stave off the cool temperatures that pre-empted Christmas. He didn't want a reminder of the approaching holiday season.

"You know I'm the reason he looks that good, right?" Beau grumbled, folding his arms over his wide chest and pouting. Taylor patted his arm in consolation.

Will laughed. "Speaking of, why are you never at work?"

"Heading there now, asshole. You gonna come and see what real work looks like?" Beau goaded.

Will laughed. "Yeah, sure. My morning just freed up and I've got a lot of energy to expend. I'll grab my gym gear and I'll meet you there."

Beau's Bodies was located on the edge of town. Beau had built the gym from the ground up to help the local residents. Will loved the place, not just because he was proud of his best friend and former business partner but because there were so many different types of people coming here, looking for his help. Teenagers, yoga moms, older men and women using the pool and sauna for rehabilitation. No one was dicking around trying to impress anyone. No duck pouting photoshoots. No dude bros making women feel uncomfortable. It was just…nice.

Beau tossed some boxing gloves at him when he entered, and Will's smile widened.

"My favorite, how did you guess?" Will didn't know how people could jump on a treadmill for an hour, he got bored with that in seconds. Boxing was his jam. Physical, aggressive, hard work. He strapped his hands in and followed Beau over to the large punching bag.

"We'll do a quick warmup before we go onto the bag," Beau said, then proceeded to reel off combos for Will to try. Left hook, right uppercut, jab, jab, squat down, uppercut. They repeated these a few times, Will getting into the zone with the rhythmic slap of gloves on pads, leather on leather, before they progressed to the bag.

An hour later, dripping with sweat, Beau called time out. He grabbed two drinks from the mini fridge at the back of the gym. Will wiped his face and chest on a towel before taking one of the bottles from Beau.

"Uh-uh, this will make me gassy and bloated. I need

still, not sparkling," Will said.

Beau rolled his eyes and muttered something that sounded like *precious* under his breath but switched the bottles over. They sipped their drinks in silence, catching their breath before Will's enthusiasm for the gym couldn't be contained.

"This place is amazing, I'm so proud of you, man!"

"Thanks, that means a lot coming from you. I'm on the lookout for another physical therapist if you know any looking for a new, exciting location?"

Will mulled it over. His stepbrother's fiancée, Ava used to do that, but Will had a feeling she had quit. Will didn't spend a lot of time with his new stepfather and brother, he wasn't a massive fan, but he liked Ava who seemed sweet.

"I'm not sure, let me think on it and see if I know anyone," he replied.

"Cool. So what's the plan, what are you doing here?"

Will didn't really know how to answer that. "I'm just extending my vacation, that's all."

"Well, I'm glad. You never make time for yourself but how's the show taken it?"

"As long as everybody's getting paid, I think they take it quite well," Will joked, but Beau wouldn't be distracted.

"Anything you're trying to run away from?"

My entire career and life? "Nope, just wanted a longer break."

Beau frowned at him, he could always call Will on his shit, but this time he didn't. "I like having you here, I'm not trying to chase you away. I'd love it if you stayed, but I just want to make sure you're good. You can always talk to me, you know."

Will's phone rang and he looked at the caller ID. "Shit, I gotta take this. Thanks for the session. Drinks tomorrow night?"

"Sure thing."

With a wave, Will was running out of the gym and getting into his car. "And how's my favorite reporter today?" he asked when he answered the call.

"Wondering what the hell you're doing!" Adrienne snapped.

When Will first started out, he was vilified in the press. He had an attitude and didn't want to deal with the paps and there were some incidents. He had a chip on his shoulder he had to shake, and it took him a while to learn that if you worked with the sharks rather than against them, they let you know when something big was about to come out and let you get ahead of it.

Adrienne had come to him years ago, desperate and hungry to prove herself in a world full of men. She had uncovered the trailer park childhood that he'd worked so hard to bury, not for himself but for his mother. He could imagine exactly what the sharks would do when they found out that the number one female manager in the biz used to give blowjobs to put food on the table.

But Adrienne had also grown up in a trailer park and was sympathetic, she wanted to warn him it was going to be printed. So Will did the one thing he knew how: he made a deal. If Adri squashed it, then he'd give her every exclusive about him and his family as it came up. He guessed she was calling because he'd been slacking.

"I had to find out from that pig Gary at TMZ that you missed filming? TMZ Will, TM fucking Z and fucking Gary. That was humiliating as shit!" she shouted.

"I'm sorry Adri, honestly it slipped my mind," he replied smoothly, trying to soothe her ruffled feathers.

"Where are you and why did you miss filming? Are you leaving the show? Finally had enough of playing the villain?"

If only.

"Nah, I came to Citrus Pines for a wedding a few weeks ago and just extended my vacay to spend time with friends. You know how it is."

She harrumphed, not satisfied with that.

"I promise I'll tell you when I'm coming back. In the meantime, maybe follow my stepdaddy around, he's always doing something shady." Will chuckled to himself.

"Which friends were getting married, anyone I know?"

He realized her killer instinct for a story was perking up. "No, just friends in town, not celebrities."

"Okay, fine but I'll be in touch."

He ended the call, frustration starting to build but he shoved it down. He was in a better situation in life than a majority of people. So he strapped on his big boy positivity pants and started up the car, heading back to the cabin to shower.

*

The next night, Will walked into the bar only to find it completely packed. Beau waved at him from a booth he'd managed to secure.

"What's going on tonight?" His voice raised over the crowd.

"Taylor's got some Elvis tribute act on tonight, apparently the guy has drawn a crowd," Beau replied.

"I'll say."

"Have a seat, I'll grab us a couple of beers. I've got connections here," Beau joked, sliding out of the booth.

"No, gassy, bloaty, remember?"

Beau rolled his eyes again and Will popped him on the shoulder, then out of the corner of his eye he caught a glimpse of familiar short, dark hair. He craned his neck and saw Rebelle, standing behind the bar, looking a little harried as she served customers. Taylor was helping her out and kept darting her encouraging smiles. Rebelle dropped a bottle and it smashed, her terrified eyes swung to Taylor and her brows dipped in. Taylor immediately rushed over and soothed her.

"Actually, I'll get the drinks, you stay here," Will said. Beau looked over his shoulder and spotted the object of Will's attention.

He shook his head. "Don't let Blake catch you, I don't wanna plan your funeral."

"Relax man, I'm just ordering some drinks at the bar. Anyway, I'm going to see *your* woman, we both know she prefers me." Will shot Beau a wink before heading to the bar.

A few people tried to get his attention, no doubt wanting a selfie or an autograph or to tell him about their great business venture, but he ignored them. He only had eyes for one person.

He used his height and build to his advantage, pushing through the crowd and waiting until she was ready to serve him. She turned those gumdrop eyes on him which widened impossibly when she realized who was towering over her.

He arched a brow, stooping down to her height. "Shall we talk about the fact that you called the sheriff on me?"

*

Rebelle's throat dried at his words and she braced herself. She expected him to be angry but as she looked into his enchanting eyes, they sparkled playfully and she could hear the teasing lilt to his deep voice.

"Hey man, I'm a big fan! Can I get a picture for the

Take A Chance

wife? She'll get such a kick out of it!" Some guy slung his arm around Will's shoulder and Rebelle watched as his expression shuttered. The muscles in his jaw worked before he replied with a clipped, "Sure thing."

Rebelle backed away, she could see the change in him, and it brought her memories and fear to the surface. Her hands began to shake and she waved to Taylor. "I just need a minute."

Taylor smiled. "Of course, just take a breather, sweetheart. You're doing amazing tonight!"

Rebelle smiled weakly at the redhead's praise.

"Hey you big sexy lug, what can I get you?" Taylor said, and Rebelle turned back to see her leaning across the bar to hug Will.

Rebelle escaped to the bathroom, trying to calm her thoughts and nerves, using the controlled breathing technique Justine had taught her, resting her forehead against the cool ceramic wall tiles. Rebelle liked the idea of this technique, being in control, of taking charge when for so long she had to put up with what someone else wanted, having her choices taken away from her and feeling insignificant. Going along with what Marcus wanted and never having what *she* wanted. As she focused on the control, her breathing slowly settled and the tremor in her hands ceased.

She heard Taylor announce the Elvis tribute act which happened to be Ben, the other newbie working at the bar. Rebelle had met him tonight and he seemed sweet, but time would tell. People rarely showed their true colors up front.

She headed back out to the bar, pushing her way through the crowd, keeping her eyes down. Thankfully when she came back, all the patrons were gathered by the stage watching Ben's performance, so she had some more breathing space.

She tidied up the empty glasses left behind and wiped down the bar, listening to the music and trying to enjoy normal life. Her eyes swept over the crowd. If she hadn't married Marcus, would she have made friends and been here with them tonight, letting her hair down? Would she be out there dancing with Taylor and Beau and…her eyes met Will's and she fumbled the bottles she was holding. *Why is he watching me?* He blinked and his eyes flicked back to the stage and she released the breath she'd been holding.

Rebelle didn't know too much about modern music, she couldn't say who was at the top of the charts or trendy to listen to, did charts even exist now? But Ben had a great voice and his guitar skills were excellent.

Taylor rejoined her at the bar. "How's it going?" she yelled over the music. Rebelle thought it was nice that Taylor kept checking on her and making sure she was okay, but she felt bad at the number of glasses she'd broken.

"Okay I think. Sorry again about those glasses. Make sure you take them from my paycheck."

Taylor shook her head. "Why the hell would I do that? Shit happens, sweetheart and I'm certainly not going to take money off you for being human and having a clumsy moment."

Rebelle tried to protest but Taylor shouted her down which she was secretly grateful for, she needed every cent she could get her hands on.

"For what it's worth, I think you're doing great." Taylor squeezed her arm briefly, so quickly she wouldn't have noticed the way Rebelle tensed up and took a slight step back.

Ben's performance ended and everyone flocked to the

bar for a refill, including the tall, intimidating man with ocean eyes who wouldn't stop staring at her. *God, why are you comparing his eyes to the ocean?* Luckily Taylor filled his order and Rebelle's eyes were glued to his retreating back as he headed towards his booth with Beau.

As the evening wore on, her eyes refused to leave the booth he was in for barely more than a few minutes. She studied him, looking for any signs, any hint of the anger she'd seen earlier when that guy interrupted them. She noticed she wasn't the only person watching him. People flocked to his booth all night to talk to him, some randomly took pictures with him - what was that about? How did he know so many people in town when he'd only just shown up? And surely if he *was* a bad guy then people would stay away from him? She'd seen people behave the same way with her sheriff husband but when they approached him there was always an undercurrent of fear in their expressions. That wasn't the case when they looked at Will. There was nothing but friendliness and eagerness. Awe even.

Taylor liked him and so did Beau. Maybe she had been too hasty in calling Blake? Maybe she should let him help out at the shelter, heaven knows she needed those damn muscles of his. What she could do with that strength down at the shelter.

The evening came to an end with only one or two hardcore regulars still around. Rebelle had been watching Will discreetly over the top of a cocktail menu, observing his easy banter with Beau. Beau was also good friends with Blake and Justine, two of the only people that Rebelle truly trusted. She replayed Justine's words from the other night. If they trusted Will then maybe Rebelle could too.

The guys stood up and Taylor went over to them,

reaching her arms up and linking them around Beau's neck, kissing him tenderly and Rebelle's pulse thudded at the intimacy between them. Rebelle had never experienced that kind of connection with someone.

Then Will dropped a kiss on Taylor's cheek, fist bumped Beau and headed towards the bar. Rebelle squeaked and dropped the menu, scurrying to look busy and like she hadn't been watching him.

He deposited their empty glasses on the bar top and lingered, her eyes darted to his and immediately bounced away. She focused intently on drying the glass in her hand, her body turned away from him but still able to watch him from the corner of her eye.

He tapped the bar top. "Goodnight, beautiful."

He was nearly at the door before she found her voice but with the place practically empty, her soft words carried.

"I'm sorry I called Blake on you."

Will halted in front of the door. Taylor and Beau's attention slid to Rebelle before looking back to Will. He shifted on his feet and turned towards her, his expression unreadable. Rebelle's skin heated, something hot spreading through her and her throat dried.

"I-I do need some help at the shelter."

Her stare dipped from his ocean eyes towards his lips, noticing his mouth tick up on one side. He walked back toward the bar, a slow lithe prowl and she held her breath.

"I'd say so, yeah," he murmured, his voice low.

"If you think you'd maybe have some time to spare then maybe," her voice faltered, *damn dry throat*. "Then maybe you could swing by and maybe help out."

His mouth spread into a full smile, and something tugged deep inside her. He rubbed the side of his neck and her eyes drifted to the tattoo there, a dark skull with dollar signs for eyes and she shivered at the sight.

"I can't afford to pay you," she rushed out.

He scoffed. "I don't need money, beautiful."

Indignation fired her up. "Don't call me that."

He cocked his head to the side. "Why not?"

"If you want to come to the shelter, you can't call me that. It's unprofessional. You'll call me Rebelle." *Shit, where did that authority come from?*

His eyes darkened, his voice thick when he replied, "Yes, ma'am."

There was a pause where they just stared at each other and something approaching hysteria crawled up her throat under the intensity of his gaze.

"So, do you want to or not?"

"Want to what?"

"Volunteer!" she snapped.

His grin spread again, and she realized he was toying with her. *God he's infuriatingly smiley.* "I guess I have some free time."

"Then I'll see you tomorrow."

He nodded. "What time do you usually get there? You were there pretty early the other day."

Shit. No way could he find out she was *living* there.

"Get there by eight," she said, giving herself an extra hour to make sure she was up and ready and had tidied away her sleeping bag and hidden the evidence in the storeroom properly.

"I'll see you at seven fifty-five," he said, and she frowned. "Sleep well, Rebelle." The way he said her name riled her, slowly rolling the syllables over his tongue like he was enjoying their flavor. He smiled at her one more time before he left, waving to Taylor and Beau who stood there looking dumbfounded.

When the door to the bar closed behind him, tension released from her shoulders and she pushed out a slow breath, like she was blowing out her candle, just like Justine taught her.

"You can take off now, sweetheart. I got it from here," Taylor said, coming up next to her.

Rebelle just nodded and handed Taylor the glass she was drying and Taylor smiled at her.

"If you ever wanna talk about boys, I'm totally down." The redhead waggled her eyebrows.

"Talk about boys?"

"Yeah, gossip with the girls. Christy and Justine too, I know they'd love to spend more time with you."

"Thanks, but I'm not a *talk about boys* kinda girl," Rebelle mumbled.

"Doesn't just have to be about boys. Just think about it, we're here if you need us." Taylor shrugged and ushered Rebelle out from behind the bar. "You need Beau to take you home?"

Rebelle shook her head. "I'm fine, thanks. So can I come back?"

Taylor laughed. "Of course, I'll give you a couple of shifts a week, just tell me when you can work and we'll sort out the schedule."

Rebelle left the bar and began the long walk back to the shelter, wishing she hadn't left the truck at home to save on gas.

She'd done it. She'd made it through her first shift.

She'd been around people, men in particular, and she'd only had to use her breathing techniques a couple of times. She should feel great but her brain was preoccupied with the fact that Will was going to be at the shelter in the morning.

Just the two of them.

Take A Chance

Maybe she could just put him to work and stay away from him. Or go to the vets and leave him to look after the animals.

Either way, she would try to put as much distance between them as possible.

Chapter 5

Will would be lying if he said he'd gotten any sleep last night. Lying on his back, hands tucked behind his head and blankets tangled around his waist, he stared up at the ceiling in the dark, picturing the constellations that sparkled beyond, and thinking about Rebelle.

He couldn't get a read on her. She was stubborn, serious and incredibly guarded and all he wanted was to take a sledgehammer to her walls and explore what she was truly like.

He didn't buy that this was who she was. There was more to her, he could feel it. And what his mind fixated on the most was the warning he'd seen in her whiskey eyes and the pound of his pulse when she *commanded* that he call her Rebelle. He knew he liked it when someone else took charge, taking the pressure off of him for once but he hadn't realized just how much he liked it until *she* took control.

A lot, his dick piped up, but Will ignored it.

She intrigued him in a way no woman had before. She didn't seem anything like the type of women that he was usually around and it was a breath of fresh air. She had awoken something inside of him and he wanted to get to know her, to get her to drop her guard so he could see who she really was.

Is there any point when you're not sticking around? his brain interjected.

"Jesus, I'm not going to marry her. I'm just taking a longer vacation than I planned and looking to make a new friend."

You don't want to be her friend...

Will scoffed, feeling ridiculous for having an argument with his own thoughts. He tried to switch them off and stop thinking about Rebelle and start thinking about the shelter. He was excited to get there in the morning. He hadn't felt this energized about a project in a while; probably not since he and Beau worked together on Beau's first gym; and how long ago had that been?

He couldn't wait to meet all the animals properly, clear away some of that rubble and help turn the place around. If he did a good job, would Rebelle be pleased? Would she smile? He was desperate to see her smile.

When the sun finally rose he decided to stop trying to sleep and got up, showered and put on his dress pants, suspenders and shirt. He wasn't exactly dressed for manual labor but he hadn't brought a lot of clothing options with him and besides, he was comfortable and looked good, so win-win.

He set off early, swinging by Ruby's Diner on Main Street to grab two coffees figuring he would make a good impression and maybe get a smile from Rebelle. Because who didn't love coffee?

"Well, if it isn't my favorite billionaire," came the gruff voice of the owner, Ruby. Will chuckled, taking in her wide, pink-lipsticked smile and purple hair curled to perfection. She was wearing a leopard print jumpsuit and if she was a day under eighty, he would be shocked.

"You're here early, have you come to finally take me away from this place?"

"One day, Rubes, one day," he winked, bending to kiss her cheek. They had become good friends since he'd come to town. He had used the diner as a work base for the last couple of weeks and enjoyed her banter.

She tsked. "Promises, promises."

"In the meantime, can I get two coffees to go?"

"Sure thing, sugar lips. Where you off to so early?"

"I'm volunteering at the shelter," he replied, taking a seat at the Formica counter.

Ruby paused and turned to stare at him, one overly penciled eyebrow raised. "The Take A Chance shelter that Rebelle Black runs?"

"That's the one."

She turned back to grab the coffee pot and fill two take-out cups. "Be careful, you know what they say about her, don't you?"

He sat up straighter, intrigued and desperate for any information about Rebelle. "No, what?"

She turned back and placed the two cups on the counter and when her hands fumbled trying to put the lids on, he took the lids from her and did it himself. She patted his shoulder in thanks and managed a mischievous squeeze of his bicep.

"They say she murdered her husband…"

He fumbled the lids, surely he hadn't heard that right.

Take A Chance

"Come again?"

"Not that I believe it, mind you, but *something* happened up there that night. Just be careful, I'm not sure I could cope if I lost you."

He laughed. "I'm sure you'd be straight onto the next strapping young man who stumbled into town like the maneater you are."

"True, you are a little old for me. What are you, forty?"

"Hey, watch it, Grandma. I'm still thirty-nine."

She winked at him. "Exactly, too old for me."

He shook his head, chuckling, thinking about what she'd said about Rebelle. It sounded too ridiculous to be true, no way could she have killed someone. If she had, surely she would be behind bars? Maybe he needed to speak to Blake, clearly the sheriff knew something if he had warned Will away the other day.

"Just the coffees?"

"Gimme a couple of those donuts too, I need to make a good impression."

Ruby snorted. "I'll say."

She rang up the amount on the register and he paid, giving her a fifty-dollar tip before kissing her cheek again and leaving.

He got back into his car and drove out to the shelter, mulling over Ruby's words. He didn't believe small town gossip and, call him naïve, but he didn't think Rebelle would harm a fly.

He glanced at the time as he turned down the dirt road towards the shelter and saw it had just turned eight. He was right on time.

When he pulled up and got out of the car, he spotted her leaning against the building, an unreadable expression on her beautiful face and a large gray Irish Wolfhound slumped at her feet. He put on his trademark smile, his heart kicking in his chest at the sight of her and grabbed the coffees and bag of donuts.

"Good morning, isn't it a glorious day?" he called, slamming the car door with his hip. The hound got to his feet and trudged over to Will.

"You're late," Rebelle said, her tone flat.

"I'm right on time," he replied.

"It's after eight, you said seven fifty-five."

He chuckled. "But I got coffee and donuts, that's worth the five minutes surely?"

"I don't like coffee and I'm not hungry."

"Then there's more for me," he replied happily. He wouldn't be deterred by her standoffish behavior. He knew she would be a challenge, but he believed she was worth it, rumored murderer or not.

"Glad to see what kind of work ethic you have," she grunted.

He hid his smile, she clearly had no idea who he was and he had to admit it was refreshing. He damn well wasn't afraid of hard work. "Then by all means, put me to work, beauti-Rebelle."

Her hard stare didn't waver, and he didn't back down, thrilled at the eye contact. "How long will you be here today?" she asked.

"As long as you need me."

"You have nowhere else to be?"

"Nope," he said, his lips popped on the *p*.

"Fine, let's start with cleaning out the kennels then, follow me. You can eat your donuts while I tell you what to do but don't drop any crumbs, we have an issue with mice."

Before he could respond she swiveled on her heel and stalked off, leaving him and the hound trailing after her.

He crammed in one donut before they made it inside to the kennels and when she turned and spotted his bulging cheeks, she frowned but didn't comment.

She took him through how to shut the dogs into their outside pen so he could have full access to the inside to clean, change bedding and replace toys. He noticed that when she did turn to look at him her eyes drifted to his mouth and then flitted away again.

"You sure you don't want a donut?" he interrupted, holding one out to her.

"I told you, I'm not hungry," she replied curtly. Then there was a low growl and she clapped her hand over her stomach.

"I think someone's lying," he teased. Instead of coaxing a smile from her, she pivoted on her heel again and went into the kitchen opposite the kennels and came back with a bucket of water and a mop.

Her arms trembled slightly at the weight of the bucket and he rushed to meet her and relieve her but she glared at him before dropping it down, water sloshing over the edge.

"You don't have a hose?" he asked, thinking that would be easier than filling a bucket and dragging it out each time. Had she been doing this all by herself? It was a lot of work.

She didn't meet his stare. "No."

"How come?"

"They cost money."

"If the shelter needs money, then I can-"

"I'll be outside if you need me," she interrupted and then scurried off.

He frowned after her, not sure how to reach her. He was charming as hell but so far, she wasn't interested in niceties. *Maybe you'll win her over with hard work,* his ever-optimistic brain chimed in.

He drank his coffee and felt something touch his leg. He glanced down and found a long-haired black cat winding itself around him. Its gold eyes shining in the light from the window.

"Hello, you. Aren't you a beauty?" he cooed, bending down to pet the cat who let him stroke once and then bit him. "You play hard to get, huh? Just like someone else I know," he mumbled as the cat scurried off.

Will cleaned down the kennels, enjoying the physical work, the fruits of his labor, but soon he was pulling down his suspenders and unbuttoning his shirt. He flapped the tails, trying to get some air onto his body and considered tossing the bucket of water over himself just to cool off. He continued on and thought he could feel eyes watching him but each time he turned around, there was no one there.

After another hour he whipped his shirt off, unable to take it anymore. When he finally finished with the kennels, he went to find Rebelle. He found her outside, hauling bricks like he had done a few days before. She struggled with a particularly large one and as he saw her tiny legs buckle, he raced over to catch it before she dropped it on her toe.

"Thanks," she mumbled, not meeting his stare.

"You really shouldn't be doing this stuff on your own. Why didn't you ask me to help?"

"I can do it," she replied.

"Just because you can, doesn't mean you should."

She finally looked at him and her eyes swept over his bare chest, lingering here and there and he wondered if she was taking in the various tattoos he had inked across his skin.

She swallowed. "Can you put your shirt back on?"

"It's nearly a hundred degrees in there and there's no air conditioning," he replied, taking in the damp circle at the neck of her t-shirt. Was that the same one she was wearing at the bar last night? It had the same hole in the shoulder.

"I would feel more comfortable if you had your shirt on," she insisted.

He was about to rebuff her but there was something about her tone that gave him pause. He tugged his shirt back on, noticing the guarded expression on her face and wanting to ease the tension he could see bunching her shoulders.

He helped her move the rest of the rocks and then they took a break, both panting and drenched in sweat. He was mesmerized by the way her skin glowed and the dark hair slicked to the back of her neck. He wanted to push it to one side and run his tongue over her skin, savoring the salty taste.

He shook his head, dislodging the fantasy before his pants started getting tight.

They spent the afternoon working side by side, although any time he got too close, she stepped away. She tried to be discreet, but he noticed it. He attempted to engage her in conversation, but she gave clipped, one-word responses.

"You can leave now, we're done for the day," she said softly.

Thank God, he was exhausted. Lack of sleep and the heat had made today much harder than he anticipated but he'd loved every minute of it. Loved getting to know the animals, helping them and seeing the fruits of his labor.

He smiled. "Great, do you want a lift home?"

"No, I'm fine thank you," she said, avoiding his gaze again.

"It's no trouble."

"I've got some things to do and then I'll go. But uh, thanks for today," she added reluctantly.

He puffed up with pride from her appreciative words. "Sure thing, same time tomorrow?"

She met his stare, her dark eyes narrowed slightly, then he watched as they dipped to his mouth like she had done earlier.

"If you would like to come back, then that would be fine."

He smiled again, eager for another chance to spend more time with her. "Great, see you in the morning."

He waited for her to turn her back and leave but she didn't, she was waiting him out. "If you don't like coffee, what can I bring you in the morning?"

She pursed her lips. "Nothing. I don't want anything from you," she said, the unfriendly back in her tone. He had pushed her too far again and he wasn't even sure how. He was slowly learning her boundaries though. He'd get around them, he'd lower her defenses and she would let him in, he had time.

"Goodbye, Rebelle."

That night, he slept like the dead and when he got up in the morning, muscles that he didn't even know he had ached. He had done a hard day's work yesterday and his body was screaming in pain but his soul felt rejuvenated. He hadn't thought about the mess his life seemed to be or the responsibility weighing heavy on his shoulders. How he was almost ready to throw his entire career away. Or what was waiting for him when he got home and he hadn't felt that knot constrict his chest recently.

He was *happy*.

Will stopped by Ruby's Diner, grabbed a coffee for him and a hot cocoa for Rebelle, figuring maybe she liked

Take A Chance

that instead. He was determined to find out what she liked. He grabbed a couple more donuts and drove over to the shelter.

Rebelle was waiting for him again, her pale skin shining in the sunlight but this time he noticed dark circles under her eyes.

"Hot cocoa fan?" he asked as he made his way over to her, holding a cup out to her.

"No. I told you not to get me anything," she grumbled.

"You said you didn't *want* anything from me," he replied, and her plump lips pursed at his words.

Rebelle might not want something from him but he was starting to want many things from her and it was looking more and more likely he wasn't going to get any of them. He was used to getting what he wanted, and call him a brat, but it only made him try harder.

She turned away and headed inside the shelter and he trailed after her. He looked in each of the kennels and stroked the heads of the dogs waiting for him, their tails wagging, tongues lolling out of their mouths. Except for the Irish Wolfhound who was already out of his kennel and trotting after Rebelle.

"Looks like someone has a crush on you," Will commented.

Rebelle looked down at the hound who gazed up at her lovingly and Will thought he saw a flicker of a smile. She stroked over the dog's head and cupped his jowl. "Hurt recognizes hurt," Rebelle murmured and then jolted, like she realized she said it out loud.

Questions flooded Will's mind and he wanted to pull her into his arms and rid her of the misery that cloaked her expression. Although he didn't know her that well, he already knew she wouldn't want any of that.

"You can clean the kennels again today. Betty and Veronica are feeling particularly grumpy so maybe stay out of their way," she said.

"Betty and Veronica?" His lips quirked up at the names.

"The cats, they're sisters."

"Did you name them?"

"No, they came like that from their owner."

He cocked his head, assessing her. "Do you name any of them?"

"Let me know once you've finished the kennels," she said by way of an answer and he felt the dismissal like a kick to the gut. But he wouldn't be discouraged, he was resilient, he had to be in his life. He watched her walk away, the soles of her shoes flapping where they had come unstuck, and he couldn't fight the frown that pinched his brows.

*

Rebelle walked away from him, feeling the slide of his cool eyes across her back, prickling her skin. She had spent half of yesterday caught between begging him to leave and feeling grateful he'd stayed. She hadn't gotten so much done in one day the entire time she'd had the shelter and it had been so satisfying.

But she could feel his presence constantly. Every rumble of his rough voice felt like it was touching exposed nerves, tickling them for the sheer hell of it and leaving her an uncomfortable mess. His can-do attitude and constant smile irked her whilst she also found comfort in having company. She was a cluster of opposing feelings.

As a teenager she'd loved having friends and being

around others. But a jealous and controlling husband brought a life of isolation, and her social skills weren't what they used to be. *Post-Marcus* Rebelle wasn't quite used to *people* yet. Especially men who were as intimidating as Will was.

Rebelle still found the sight of Will's bare chest, his muscled and inked skin, his piercings unnerving as well as intriguing. She couldn't seem to stop her eyes from their journey across his skin, taking in the designs and she found herself wanting to ask about them. Did they have a meaning, or did he just get them for the sheer hell of it? There were so many colorful patterns and intricate designs, and she couldn't seem to stop staring at the collection of roses across his chest.

She shook her head and turned her attention to her rose that had flourished in the soil. She sniffed the white flowers, inhaling their soft scent. She stroked the silky petals and for a moment, felt closer to her absent sibling before turning her attention back to the land around her. Time to indulge her little fantasy.

She lifted her arms, creating a frame with her fingers and she spun slowly, picturing each section of land and what she hoped to do with it. In one space, the cattery she envisioned, then in another, a place with huge hutches and a run for rabbits and guinea pigs. In another the small paddock she already had but fenced off so horses and donkeys could graze there.

She wanted to take in all the wayward animals and rehome them. For a while, she had planned on opening up to the public, intending to advertise in town inviting people to *adopt, don't shop* and *take a chance on a new friend*. But she was too busy to entertain members of the public as well, at least that's what she told herself. Maybe now with Will helping out she would be able to do it.

She was starting to see what she could achieve with him being here and suddenly felt a wave of gratitude towards him. That feeling lingered and when he found her later, needing something to do, she agreed to let him come with her to the vet to collect an animal and more medicine. Will was so pleased that she agreed, he bounced around like a big kid.

They drove the entire way in silence, and it might have been comfortable for Will but Rebelle was increasingly uncomfortable in the tight, confined space. The rattle of the engine filled the cab of the truck, making it impossible to talk which Rebelle was grateful for but as she glanced around all she could see were the faults of her beat up old truck. His car, which she assumed was a rental, was so fancy she was scared to even look at it. It probably cost more than Rebelle could even imagine.

Will appeared perfectly relaxed through the journey, his big body folded up, his long legs spread wide and she was thankful for the space between them so that he wouldn't have his large thigh pressed up against hers. He was close enough that his scent drifted into her nostrils, salt and sandalwood and annoying. His palm rested on one broad thigh, fingers tapping happily to an imaginary beat and her eyes kept dropping down to look at the pale skin dusted with freckles and fingers free from tattoos. He was in dress pants again and a shirt that she noticed was the same shade of blue as his left eye.

She bit her cheek, she needed to stop noticing details about him.

Relief swept through her when the vet's office came into view. She pulled up outside the door and hopped out of the truck too quickly and dizziness swamped her. She was only a few days away from getting her paycheck from the bar so food was limited. She'd had a protein bar last

Take A Chance

night and eaten it so slowly, savoring every mouthful and went to bed feeling somewhat satisfied.

Will was hot on her heels as she went inside and greeted Darlene at reception whose eyes nearly bugged out of her head when she spotted Will.

"Oh my God, it's you, isn't it?" Darlene said.

"Probably, yeah," Will replied, and unleashed that wide smile of his that Rebelle sometimes found herself staring at.

"Rebelle, thanks for coming," Dr. Jae-Seung Park called, distracting her from Will's interaction. She turned and faced him, his small smile greeting her as usual. He couldn't be more than thirty and had a shock of black hair, his dark eyes were always friendly, and he was trying to grow a beard, the stubble dotted along his jawline was a little patchy.

"What have you got for me today?" Rebelle asked, noticing how Dr. Park's eyes lingered on Will who was standing too close to Rebelle. She sidestepped to put space between them.

"I've got a tabby cat who's been through a rough time. Follow me," he said and Rebelle trailed after him into a consultation room.

Dr. Park went to get the tabby and Rebelle glanced around the room; the rubber top of the table streaked with claw marks from unhappy visitors. The room had that clinical disinfectant smell, and the walls were painted white but had a cloth wall hanging of a tiger with Hangul script, vintage Korean street posters lined another wall as well a stunning travel print of Seoul.

He reappeared lugging a cat box behind him and Rebelle could already hear the unhappy grumble emanating from the box.

"I think he's been hit by a car. He's not chipped so no

idea who he belongs to, but no one has come forward to claim him and I haven't got room to keep him here. He's lost the tip of his ear and has a sore paw which I've bandaged so my gift to you comes with medication, but you're used to that now. Unless your apprentice here is going to take over for you?" Dr. Park's lips lifted in a smile as he nodded towards Will.

Rebelle's frown slipped into place as she glanced at Will who had an *aw shucks* expression on his face. She couldn't understand why everyone seemed so fascinated by the man.

"Thanks, I'll bring him back next week for a check-up," she said, taking the grumbling bundle from the doctor and pivoting on her heel, bumping right into Will. She mumbled her apology, but he wasn't moving so she looked up at him, her eyes lingering on his lips.

"Give me the cat, he looks heavy," Will said.

"I can carry him," she hissed.

Will leaned forward and she had no room to step back so his breath brushed her ear in an all too pleasant way. "You look like you can barely stand right now. Give me the cat, Rebelle."

How did he know she was struggling? She hated that it was so obvious. She pushed past him and out the door, humiliated that Dr. Park witnessed the exchange.

She was in the truck and starting the engine before Will jogged out from the office and she had half a mind to leave him there, her earlier gratitude towards him gone.

On the way back to the shelter, he seemed perfectly content to sit in silence again, tapping his damn fingers on his knee like he hadn't a care in the world.

"Why does everyone know you?" She raised her voice over the sound of the engine. She kept her eyes on the road but felt his flit to her.

"You really don't know who I am?"

She shook her head.

He laughed gently. "I'm kinda famous."

She snorted. "Kinda famous? For what?"

"A lot of things," he replied, and she felt his stare leave her. He didn't elaborate and she didn't press him either. They made it back to the shelter and he was taking the growling cat box from her before she could bat an eyelid. She raced ahead of him, unlocking the shelter and he sauntered right past her.

"Do you even know what to do with that cat right now?" she snapped, hating how he acted like he owned the place.

His cool eyes swept to hers. "Well, I was gonna grab a crate and blanket from the storeroom and set him up in the kitchen. Figured I'd keep him in there, cover the top with a blanket so it's sheltered, and he feels safe until he's acclimated."

Rebelle clamped her lips shut, pausing. That was exactly what she would have done. He was learning quickly which was *not at all* impressive. She realized he was headed for the storeroom and her heart leapt into her throat. She darted after him, grabbing his bicep.

"Wait! There aren't any blankets in there!"

"Oh, where are they then?" He turned and looked down to where her hand was gripping him. Her eyes dropped to her hand latched around his arm, her fingers nowhere near meeting around the hard flesh that was heating underneath her palm. She snatched her hand away, warmth suffusing her cheeks and her heart pounding. She *never* touched people.

"Uh, just grab one from the clean pile in the kitchen," she said.

"Do we have a washer here?"

We. He said we.

"No, I use the laundromat in town," she replied.

He considered her. "You drag these blankets and towels into town every time they need washing, like every two, three days?"

"Yes, it's not a big deal."

"Why don't you have a washer here? Or use the one at your place at least and save the journey?"

Why is he always asking questions that I don't want to answer? "Once you've got our new resident set up, you can leave. I don't need any more help today."

He cocked his head to the side and regarded her gently. "Rebelle, don't be like that."

"See you tomorrow, Will." She spun on her heel and made herself scarce.

Once he left, she snuck into Bryan's kennel and snuggled down with him, she had missed him today. She dug her fingers into his wiry fur and held on tight, thinking about how she had raised her voice at Will, had *touched* him. She had surprised herself at both actions, the fact that it had felt natural, and she hadn't noticed she'd done it. That she felt *comfortable* enough to do that.

He had only come here twice and somehow he already had her defenses slipping. She didn't like it, didn't like that he also clearly had kept it from her that he was some kind of celebrity. She didn't like dishonesty or secrets and she certainly didn't like being in the dark. She needed to know who he was.

She kissed Bryan on his snout and grabbed the keys to the truck. She drove to Palm Valley and parked outside the library. Once inside, she headed straight for the row of computers they had.

Once when Marcus had left his laptop out she had searched the internet to look for any trace of her sister.

So, she sat down, opened up Google and typed in Will...*shit what was his last name again?* Luckily Google filled in the rest for her and she clicked on *Will Crawford* and thousands of pages came up. His incredible net worth - her cheeks flamed as she remembered saying she couldn't afford to pay him. He was right, he didn't need money. He never needed to work again. He was set for life, for thousands of lives.

Rebelle gasped at the sheer volume of articles and information on him and scrolled endlessly.

Bad Boy of Business.
Hot Head.
Temper Tantrums.
Assault.
Violent Rages.

Sickness churned her gut as more articles highlighting his behavior came up. Fights, aggression. All the things that terrified her. She clicked a link to a YouTube video of him on his show. He raged at one of the contestants, got in their face, yelling before knocking over the stand their presentation was on, flipping the table where the other judges sat before storming out.

Rebelle's breath was heaving out of her as she saw more and more videos of his anger popping up. Her hands began to shake with knowledge that she'd let this man fool her. She'd let his good-natured façade and sunny smile trick her into thinking he was someone worth letting into her shelter.

Dear God, what if he turned his violent temper on her? Or the animals?

She'd been so gullible, so foolish.

Not anymore.

Chapter 6

Whistling an old Metallica tune, Will pushed open the door to Ruby's Diner, excitement coursing through his veins as he thought about getting to the shelter and looking after the animals, and seeing Rebelle.

He was starting to break down her walls, he could feel it. She was letting him in, showing him more tasks at the shelter and she even let him accompany her to the vet.

Confined in her truck, he'd let the silence between them settle, not needing to break it, just enjoying the time together. The warmth emanating from her body kept his temperature up. Her scent, that delicious soft floral made his mouth water. He'd longed to reach for her, bury his face in her neck and inhale her sweet scent, taste her rosebud lips but he'd kept his hands to himself.

He hadn't been this excited about anything for so long. All for picking up dogshit and spending time with a beautiful prickly female? Call him crazy but he finally felt alive.

"What're you so happy about, Mr. Billionaire?" Ruby's gruff voice broke into his thoughts.

"Just another beautiful day, and I get to see you, of course." He shot her his award-winning smile and she smirked at him before waving him off.

"Coffee?"

"Extra strong, and a couple of those delicious donuts please, Ruby."

As Ruby turned away to prep his coffee, Will spotted Justine at a booth, eyeing him warily as she shoveled pancakes into her mouth.

"It's the baby," she mumbled around a mouthful.

He laughed and made his way over to her. "I ain't judging."

She swallowed and shook her head. "I'm just so hungry all the time. Blake made me toast, eggs and bacon this morning and yet I'm sneaking off here desperate to get my hands on pancakes."

"If you want pancakes, then eat them. Don't deny yourself, otherwise no one is happy. Also, I'm sure Blake would love to make you pancakes, he thinks the sun shines out of your-"

She arched a brow at him.

"-smile?" he finished lamely.

"Nice save," she smirked, pouring more syrup over her pancakes. "What are you doing here?"

"Just grabbing a coffee before heading to the shelter."

She side-eyed him while munching on another forkful of pancakes. "How's that going?"

He took his coffee from Ruby and dropped a kiss on her cheek, leaving her another fifty-dollar tip.

"It's going great. I love spending time with the

animals, doing something to help them and I've got a few ideas on how to help the shelter with marketing to get some more money coming in."

"And what about the owner of the shelter? You treating her right?"

Will actually felt his cheeks redden under her intense mama bear stare. "I'm trying, she won't let me. Any tips for handling Rebelle would be much appreciated." He put his hands together, begging.

She scrutinized him for a moment before she sighed. "Blake will kill me for helping you with her. I can kiss extra pancakes goodbye but try raspberry tea."

He pumped his fist. "Yes! Thank you, girl, you will not regret helping me." He bent and kissed her cheek.

"Don't give me a reason to regret it. My future husband and baby daddy is a very powerful man."

He swiped a wedge of pancake. "Don't I know it."

"Did you just take a pregnant woman's food?"

"Yup!"

She shook her head at him, smiling and he waved goodbye, heading back to the counter to sweet talk Ruby into making him a raspberry tea, which she thankfully had.

He sang along to the Iron Maiden track blasting from the car's sound system as he drove out towards the shelter, cradling the raspberry tea like his life depended on it. It was his lifeline to Rebelle.

When he arrived, he noticed the door to the shelter wasn't open like it usually was and she wasn't waiting for him.

Concern furrowed his brow which had developed even more freckles from his time in the sun. He stuffed the donut bag under his arm, grabbed the tea and his coffee and headed towards the door, turning the handle but it didn't budge. He tried again and nothing.

He knocked. "Rebelle? You there?"

There was silence but he could have sworn he caught her scent and the hitch of her breathing through the door.

He knocked again. "Rebelle? Can you let me in? I've got something I think you're going to like," he teased, trying to reel her in with intrigue but it didn't work.

Will pressed his ear to the door and heard movement. "I know you're in there. Rebelle, what's going on?"

"I don't need your help anymore, Will. You can leave," came her voice. The sadness in her tone had him worried.

"What do you mean? There's loads to do. Is everything okay? Are you okay?"

"I'm..." she trailed off and he held his breath waiting for her to say more. "Just please go, Will."

"Belle, just tell me what's going on. You can trust me."

He heard her adorable snort through the door. "Can I?"

"Can you open the door? At least let's talk in riddles face to face," he tried to joke.

There was more silence then a firm, "I Googled you."

His stomach lurched. This is why he hadn't wanted to play the celebrity card with her, hadn't wanted her getting some preconceived notion of him when he only wanted to be himself with her.

"Rebelle, I can explain-"

"You've been lying to me, misrepresenting yourself. You're not who I thought you were. The man I saw on those clips, he was..." The quiver in her voice nearly broke him. "I don't know him, and I don't want to. I don't want anything to do with him. Please leave, I don't want you around me or my shelter."

"You're not even going to let me explain?"

"Don't make me call Blake again."

She would do it, he knew she would, and that was the last thing he wanted. Hurt that they had reverted back to this tried to prick at him but he refused to feel discouraged. He just needed to try another angle.

"You know, I Googled you too." More silence. "And you know something, I knew that wasn't you. Not for a second did I believe you were some black widow, husband-murdering evil woman. But did you stop to think that maybe what you saw isn't me either?"

"It's different, I actually saw your behavior."

"On TV, for entertainment. That's...that's not the real me, Rebelle, it's just a part I play. I'd like to show you the real me, if you'll let me?"

He heard shuffling behind the door, then a softly muttered, "I should have known better."

When it became clear the door wasn't going to open he bent down and left the donuts and raspberry tea on the doorstep. "I'm gonna go, give you time to think on it. There's some breakfast and a raspberry tea out here for you which a reliable source tells me you're going to enjoy. I'll come back in a few days."

"Please don't." The wobble in her tone hit him like a punch to the gut.

"I'm here if you ever need me," he tried again, desperate to reach her, to not lose what they had started to build. Which really was nothing in the grand scheme of things but it had felt like the beginning of *something*.

*

Will meandered through the rest of the week, struggling to turn his frown upside down, which was unlike him, but he was dejected after his encounter with Rebelle. Or rather, her door.

Take A Chance

He also missed the dogs and Betty and Veronica. And he wanted to know how the new cat, Oscar, was getting on. Was he ruling the place or were Betty and Veronica keeping him in line? Was Bryan still following Rebelle around all day making moon eyes at her? Had any new animals come into the shelter?

It sucked big balls that he didn't know the answers to any of those things and he was missing Rebelle. Her warm whiskey eyes that he could drown in. Her stern voice admonishing him, making him put a shirt on when she clearly found his shirtless torso interesting, even if she tried not to stare.

Tonight, he was at the bar, like he was every night, praying she was working. He hadn't seen her for five days and he was getting withdrawal symptoms. She avoided him like he avoided his mom's calls.

The knot in his chest was back. His anxiety soared at the mere thought of all those people counting on him, waiting for him to come back to work. Charities needing his attention. And he was hiding out in Citrus Pines because he couldn't bear the thought of dealing with them all. Guilt burned in his throat, he tried to swallow it down, tried to shrug it off but the knot stretched tighter, stealing his breath.

Then she entered his atmosphere, distracting him, his whole body humming and on alert just in her presence. He was playing pool with Beau when she came in. His eyes flew to her, taking in her slight frame, the dark circles ringing her eyes and the stiff way she held herself. Their eyes connected and she stilled, only moving when the door banged closed behind her, startling her. The noise broke their connection and she rushed toward the bar. He heard her rushed apologies to Taylor as Taylor gently shushed her.

"Hey, bozo! It's your turn," Beau said, waving his hand in front of Will's face.

Will blinked, tearing his attention away from Rebelle and focusing on making his shot. He sank his last two balls before the black, shooting Beau a smug smile.

Beau pouted. "Best two outta three?"

"You're on. Rack 'em up while I get us a couple more drinks."

Beau followed his gaze to Rebelle then shook his head. "Man, you've got a death wish, don't you?"

Will's eyes flicked to Beau and he bristled. "What's that supposed to mean?"

"It means, no matter how much Blake warns you away, you're determined to keep trying with Rebelle, aren't you?"

His shoulders relaxed, realizing that Beau wasn't referring to Rebelle's past and whatever happened that night with her husband.

Will had meant it when he'd told Rebelle he Googled her. He hadn't found much except a couple of poorly written local news articles that gave very few facts and a whole lot of hearsay. In his opinion Rebelle could have sued for defamation and made a tidy sum to help out with her shelter. But based on what little he knew about her, he figured she stayed away from the news. The only thing that Will took away from the detail he'd found was that she was married to a fucking asshole who left her with nothing.

"I'm glad Blake's protective of her, she needs someone looking out for her."

"Uh huh. And you want it to be you from now on?"

Will inspected his cuticles. "Maybe."

Beau whistled. "Damn, Will. You really care about her? I've never seen you this interested in a woman before."

Will shrugged him off and headed to the bar, his eyes never leaving Rebelle as she bustled about fetching drinks. Although she didn't once meet his stare, she avoided him consistently like she knew he was there.

Eventually, when he was seconds away from having a bitch fit and demanding she look at him, Taylor appeared and served him. He slunk back to the pool table with his tail between his legs.

He played another round of pool, beating Beau again despite his attention being focused on the beauty behind the bar who refused to look his way all evening. Finally, he decided enough was enough and he went back to his cabin.

While he lay in bed, mulling over how to reach her, an idea struck him. Sometimes people needed something tangible, they needed to see the detail, the evidence to make an informed decision. Just like when he made a big business deal, he needed to see it laid out in black and white. The numbers, the facts, to tell him whether it was the right investment or not.

Will messaged Blake asking if he could swing by the station in the morning, then placed a call to his favorite reporter, asking for her to email him every article, good and bad that had been written about him. He contacted his clients and other people he'd worked with asking for a reference. He woke up his accountant and got access to his financial records. Pulled his contract with *The Viper Pit*. And in the morning, he was up bright and early, that pep back in his step because he had a plan.

Will went to Palm Valley, stopping by the general store to buy a manila folder and went to the library and printed off all the emails he'd received and compiled everything.

It was all there, in black and white.

All his evidence.

His life laid out, every moment illuminated and exposed. He jumped in his Bugatti, his midlife crisis car as she'd called it, the thick folder on his passenger seat and drove back to Citrus Pines.

He spotted her standing by the rose bush, inspecting the blooms and petals. He'd caught her staring at it numerous times now. She was wearing a pair of faded black jeans with the ankles rolled up and a bit of rope as a belt. Her tank top was more gray-looking than white and covered with rips, exposing slashes of pale, smooth skin. He swallowed thickly as he got out of his car.

The dogs were barking and covered the sound of his approach. He waved his arms trying to get her attention, not wanting to scare her.

She startled when she saw him, her stare darting back towards the shelter. "I told you not to come back," she snapped.

Even though she was annoyed, he liked seeing the fire behind her eyes. "I know and I will leave, I just wanted to give you this." He waved the folder at her.

Her eyes narrowed. "What is it?"

"Reasons to trust me. A shit load of them."

A thick dark brow raised skeptically and she didn't move to take it.

"This is kinda heavy…" he teased, still holding the folder out to her.

He thought her lip quirked up and his pulse pounded. "I'm sure you can manage it," she replied but still didn't make a move to take it. He saw the wariness was back in her eyes, and decided not to push her.

"I'll leave it here and go. I really hope you look at it, Rebelle. I'll come back tomorrow and if you decide you don't want me here then that's fine, I'll take your word

Take A Chance

and I'll leave you alone."

She didn't say anything as he placed the folder on the ground and backed away, turning and heading towards his car.

Before he drove off he called out to her, "Sometimes you need to take a chance. Sometimes it pays off."

*

Rebelle watched as his fancy car drove off, kicking up a plume of dust which floated after him. She looked down at the ground, the breeze had lifted open the folder that was full of documents. Curiosity got the better of her and she picked it up, taking it into the shelter and placing it on the table, staring at it.

Bryan nudged her with his wet nose before licking her and she hissed in surprise. "You know I don't like it when you do that," she scowled at him, rubbing the wet patch on her arm before bending and giving him a hug.

Ever since she demanded Will leave the shelter the other day, she had been restless, not knowing what she needed to feel right again. When she'd seen him at the bar last night, her stomach had twisted itself into knots, feeling guilty again and wondering if she regretted her decision to fire her volunteer. She scoffed to herself at the thought of a billionaire volunteering at her shelter.

Rebelle lifted the front of the folder, peeking at the page inside which, having a quick glance over it, held Will's financial records. She flushed and slammed the folder closed, feeling like she was invading his privacy.

She cleared her throat and continued with her chores. When she finished cleaning everyone and administering medicine, she found herself wandering around, at a loss with what to do next. She went into the kitchen and found some scrap paper, jotting down some ideas and designing little posters to put up around the town.

She distracted herself all day from thinking about the contents of that folder until night fell and she lit her candle, the scent of roses calming her as unrolled her sleeping bag across the cold, unforgiving concrete floor.

Then she finally gave in. She grabbed the folder, pulled her sleeping bag around her and opened it up.

It was all there.

The complete history of William Joseph Crawford.

Rebelle discovered his dad left when he was a kid, that he had grown up in a trailer park. That he worked his way up through business school and how he became the fearsome man he was today. She looked at his financial records, flushing at just how much money was in the bank, but also how much money he was giving away. To support colleagues and small businesses, to support foundations and help charities.

She read through his contract for *The Viper Pit* and saw the clauses he'd highlighted that outlined the behavior expected of him on set and during filming. There was even a report card from his high school teacher which went into detail about what a bright young man Will was and how he cared for others.

Testimonies from friends and fellow entrepreneurs, news articles showing the bad and good that had been reported on Will.

Rebelle devoured the information. Reading each document with precision, until wax was dripping onto her sleeping bag and her eyes drooped, fatigue overtaking her. She read for hours, until the early morning rays appeared and she blew out the candle, finally drifting into a peaceful sleep knowing the complete history of Will.

And she realized as she slipped into slumber that she

Take A Chance

had once again made a mistake sending this man away.

When she awoke later it was just in time to hear a car door slam outside. Her heart pounded in her chest, her pulse thudding in her ears as panic rose up inside her. She frantically tidied away the papers, shoving the sleeping bag to one side just as she heard a knock on the door.

"Rebelle?" his voice echoed through the door.

"Shit," she hissed, leaping out of bed, her back cracking from the sudden movement. She rubbed sleep from her eyes and slapped her cheeks hoping to get some color in them so that she didn't look like she'd just got out of bed.

She threw on her top from yesterday and slid into the same old worn denim that scraped across her skin, tightening the rope belt. She ducked out from behind the curtain and said a quick good morning to the dogs, the cats glaring from the doorway of the kitchen, completely unimpressed that breakfast was so late.

Rebelle paused at the door, taking a deep breath, her head swimming slightly. She had picked up her paycheck from the bar but hadn't had time to buy food yet. Her stomach rumbled sharply, nausea rose in her throat, and she swallowed it down.

She unlocked the door, a brief tremor of fear moved through her as she opened it and her eyes connected with his cold stare, focusing on his green eye. The tremor moved through her but didn't develop further which was a relief.

From all her reading, Rebelle felt like she knew him better than any other person in her life and although she was still wary of his behavior, she was willing to give him the benefit of the doubt, a courtesy she had never extended to anyone else.

"Morning." His deep voice washed over her, his

mouth quirked up at the corner before it widened to its full potential, his white teeth gleaming at her.

"Morning," she replied, her voice a rough morning rasp.

His cool stare warmed the longer she looked at it. "Did you read the folder?"

She nodded once.

"And?" He rocked forward on his feet, feet that were encased in extravagant dress shoes. Now she knew his clothing allowance was $100,000 a month she understood where his nice clothes came from and why he wore them all the time.

She paused, experience cautioning her, but her gut said to stay strong. Then she stepped to the side and opened the door wide enough for his hulking frame to enter.

He tried to hide his surprise but failed. He wandered in, sauntering past her and the scent of salt and sandalwood drifted over her. She turned, the movement sending her lightheaded. She waited for it to pass but it didn't. Instead, the swimming sensation increased, black dots winking over her vision.

"Rebelle?" he called but his voice sounded like he was under water.

She reached out for something to steady herself as her vision blurred more. A rushing sound filled her head and then she was falling, already bracing for the impact of hitting the hard floor but she never did.

She was floating.

She was weightless.

Chapter 7

"Rebelle?" Will watched her closely, saw all color leave her skin. Her eyes rolled back and he was dropping the raspberry tea and donuts, reaching for her before she hit the ground.

She was like silk in his arms, ethereal. She weighed nothing. The concrete blocks he'd been shifting last week were heavier than her. Her skin slid against his as her arms dropped, her head lolled to the side and he sank to his knees.

"Rebelle? Can you hear me?" He tried to ignore the edge of hysteria that crept into his tone. He placed his hand against her forehead, immediately struck by the stark contrast of her pale skin underneath his tattooed hand. Her forehead was clammy, her lips thin and the deep red that they usually appeared was muted. He shook her gently and she moaned.

"Shit," he muttered. "I need to get you to a hospital."

She moaned again and shook her head. "No." Her eyes fluttered open and locked with his.

"What's going on? I'm worried."

She tried to sit up and pushed his arms off her. "I don't like being touched," she groaned but immediately her arms flopped to her side like she ran out of energy.

"You might not like it, but you need it. You can't move on your own and I wasn't about to let you hit the concrete."

A low growl emanated from her, and he realized it was her stomach and his own clenched in response. "When was the last time you ate?"

"Who knows?" she replied, her tongue loose in her current state.

"Shit, Belle. Come here." He glanced behind him and snagged the bag of donuts that was currently sitting in a puddle of red raspberry tea. He pulled out a glazed donut and held it out to her. She tried to lift her arm and mewled when the limb didn't want to cooperate. He fought his instinct to draw her tighter to him, wanting to protect her, figure her out. There was so much he didn't know, didn't understand about her.

She began shivering and he glanced around, not seeing anything to cover her with. He lifted her into his arms and went towards the storeroom in search for clean blankets.

She lifted her head. "No!" she cried when she saw where he was going.

"Yes, you need a blanket."

"No, don't go in there!" she shouted, her voice breaking, and she struggled in his arms, her small ineffectual hands fighting against him.

He pulled back the raggedy curtain shielding the storeroom and stopped dead.

Dread slithered down his spine as he took in the candle, the sleeping bag, the tiny pile of ruined clothes and the manila folder containing his life story. Overwhelmed by the lump in his throat and the tears that threatened to sting his eyes he couldn't move. So many of the things he didn't understand about her just slid into place.

He swallowed around the lump and her shuddering breath jolted him back into action. He bent down, snagging the sleeping bag and moved back into the shelter, wrapping it around her and heading back to the donuts. A high-pitched whine had him looking over to where the dogs were all standing at the front of their kennels, watching them through the plexiglass. The whine emanated from Bryan who was pacing, clearly concerned for Rebelle. *That makes two of us, buddy.*

Will sat on the floor, Rebelle perched in his lap as he held a donut to her lips.

She didn't take a bite, just stared up at him with doe eyes, trying to read his expression but he shuttered it.

"You saw it, didn't you?" she whispered. The fear in her eyes sliced into his gut.

"We'll talk about it later. Eat," he replied, holding the donut to her lips again.

There was a pause, her nostrils flared and he knew her pride and independence was taking a blow. But then she nibbled the edge of the donut, sliding her tongue across her lips and it was like she went into a frenzy. She moaned and bit into the donut, taking one mouthful, then another and another. He'd never seen a donut eaten so quickly that he struggled to get the next one to her in time.

"Feeling better?" he asked, brushing a lock of hair from her face.

She flinched and leaned away, trying to extricate herself from him and this time he let her. She swayed slightly when she got to her feet and he lifted to his knees in front of her.

Rebelle stared down at him, defiance in her expression. Her moment of weakness was over but he stayed there, at her mercy, waiting for whatever she threw at him. He knew her pride was torn and she could lash out at him from embarrassment.

She drew in a shaky breath and he watched with amazement at how she put herself back together. Her expression froze, the blank mask fell back into place but his whole perspective had shifted in the last few moments.

"So, let's get to work. Lots to do today." She sounded like a drill sergeant.

He glanced back towards the storeroom. "You live here?"

She spun away and picked up the dropped cups, refusing to answer him and acknowledge the truth. He knew she wanted to act like nothing happened, but he couldn't. He had seen too much and he was not the sort of man who would pretend he hadn't seen anything. He had never been accused of inaction in his life and he wouldn't be now.

"I've gotta go. I'll be back later," he said.

With a final look at her rigid shoulders, he fled.

*

Rebelle got on with her tasks, trying to ignore the incident from this morning. Ignoring the pit in her stomach that was, for once, not from hunger. Her humiliation burned her cheeks and had her attacking her tasks, throwing herself into them with every fiber of her being. Anything to distract her from the look on Will's face when he found out just one of her many secrets. And how he had run out of here like all the dogs were snapping at his heels.

He wanted to be here so badly and she'd finally accepted that and let him in and then he was gone like a shot.

She let the dogs out to play together, Bruiser and Beast wrestled over a toy while Sasha ran circles around them, trying to herd everyone together. Doug the Pug was enjoying Sasha's energy and tried to match it which was when Rebelle intervened. She didn't want to have to pop his eye back in again, just the thought turned her stomach.

While they enjoyed themselves in the cool sunshine, Rebelle cleaned out Betty, Veronica and Oscar's litter boxes and gave them clean blankets to lay on in their crates and a cardboard box she'd been saving. Oscar immediately came over to investigate. Rebelle liked his swagger and the way he stomped around the place, wafting his tail in Betty and Veronica's faces, like he didn't have half an ear missing or a limp. Oscar forced them to take notice, just like Will had refused to back down from her.

"Stop thinking about him. He doesn't want to help out anymore, that's fine. We got by just fine before him and we'll get by just fine after him," she told the cats. Her eyes welled but she took a deep breath, focusing on the exercises that Justine had given her, refusing to let the events of the day tangle with her emotions.

It was early evening when she heard the noise. A low

rumble that got louder and louder, followed by shouting. Multiple men shouting and panic gripped her at their raised voices. She grabbed the cordless phone and ran toward the door and looked out.

"Oh my God!" she cried, taking in the enormous truck that was backing onto her land. A truck that contained a trailer home. Will's car was parked out front and he was heading towards her, a no-nonsense expression on his face in place of where his bright smile usually was.

"Where do you want it?" he demanded.

"Wha-?" She looked around, scared from all the loud noises, people and confusion.

"Where do you want it to go? I saw you that time when you were mapping out the landscape of this place. In the design in your mind, where would your home go?"

A lump filled her throat at the idea that he had witnessed her mapping out her dream. That she never at any point in this dream shelter planned for a space for herself.

"I hadn't thought…"

His face softened a fraction before his persona slipped into place. Only now, she understood it. From watching the YouTube videos, she realized he was in business mode.

"What about over there? You're close to the shelter so you can roll right out of bed and go to work. Close to the animals but there's room for development and hell if you change your mind, we'll just move it again."

Her wounded pride resurfaced. She worked hard for what she had, it might be close to nothing but it was hers and he swooped in and tried to save her at the last minute? No.

"Why are you doing this? I didn't ask for any of this, I don't want it." Her heart pounded in her chest as she glanced around at her space changing. "Take it away, leave. I'm fine on my own and I don't need you to rescue me!" she shouted and slapped a hand over her mouth. She hadn't shouted at anyone in a very long time and the last time she did, there were painful consequences.

She paused, waiting for Will to lash out the way that Marcus had.

Instead, Will threw back his head and laughed, the deep boom of it rattled her chest and flared her anxiety. "Right there is fine, guys," he called to the men. She heard the whir of machinery and the clunk as it dropped onto the ground.

"It's not funny. You think you can just turn up here and make changes to *my* property because you're some bigshot with money?"

"I know what you're doing," he replied, a soft smile on his face that lit the fire inside her even more.

She stuck her hands on her hips. "What am I doing?"

He grabbed her hand and slapped the keys to the trailer home into the palm and she tore herself away from him.

"I won't use it."

"I figured you'd say that, all that damn pride you've got must be exhausting to carry around. So, I had a backup." He smiled again, and it did funny things to her stomach. No, it must have been all the sugar from those donuts.

Will turned and stalked into the shelter, unbothered that she trailed after him spluttering protests. She didn't know whether to follow him or to make sure the men weren't doing anything to her land. Will appeared a moment later with her sleeping bag, candle, the torn down curtain that had hid her secret, the stack of ratty clothing and the manila folder.

"I'm confiscating this, you can have it back when you're settled in your new home," he said.

Her mind was swimming again from all the change. She didn't like change and didn't like the forcefulness Will was exhibiting.

"Why are you doing this?" she asked, her voice low as tears threatened. Humiliation at all the men witnessing her and Will's exchange and knowing she couldn't look after herself.

He fixed her with a piercing stare. "Because you won't do it for yourself. You won't help yourself or let anyone else help you. I'm leaving you no choice."

"I'll never owe anyone a thing!" she hissed.

"Sometimes we need people to help us and not owe them anything. That's me speaking from experience. It's not mine, you won't owe me anything. The title is in your name. Welcome to your new home, Rebelle." And with that he walked away from her, carrying her minimal belongings.

A knot of anxiety caught in her chest. "Wait! The candle, I need that, please!"

He turned back and he must have seen something in her expression because he relented. He held out the candle and she snatched it from him. "Surely you agree I need clothes?" she muttered, hugging the candle close and breathing in its calming scent, letting the memories of her sister soothe her nerves.

He ran his eyes over her, barely concealing the lust. His cold stare heating as it inched over her flesh and the look had her recoiling.

She snatched her clothes from him and stalked back into the shelter, needing comfort.

Too much change, too many people. Decisions she couldn't control, and it was all too much. She climbed into Bryan's pen and sat down, her back against the plexiglass. He came over and with a groan, collapsed into her lap. She tried to ground herself, her emotions a maelstrom that slowly calmed as she focused on the sensation of stroking his wiry fur.

As the sun began to set, the noises outside died down to nothing and it was just her and Bryan and her breathing techniques. There was a shuffle behind her and Will cleared his throat.

"They're done, it's all ready for you. The fridge is stocked, the bed is made. It's all yours, Rebelle. There's a washing machine coming tomorrow, I'm sorry I couldn't get it today, but I think I used all my persuasive powers getting the trailer home here."

Her words tangled in her throat, torn between wanting to cry and scream and seeming ungrateful for what life and Will had dropped at her feet. But he was ruining all her plans to save herself.

"I'll see you tomorrow," he said and then the door closed.

She stayed on the ground with Bryan for hours until her curiosity finally won out. She got off the floor and took Bryan with her as she went outside into the night.

The trailer glowed in the dark, warm lighting coming from the windows and lanterns adorned the white decking that surrounded the front. It was all cream with sky blue shutters hugging the windows.

It was cute.

She still held the keys, and she raised a shaky hand to unlock the door. Part of her didn't want to go inside, she wanted to ignore the home. Pretend it wasn't there but her petulance faded the longer she looked at the adorable blue shutters and the glowing lanterns.

She stepped inside. The low ceilings made the home

cozy and snug. The cream-colored walls continued throughout the home and a chrome kitchenette was all set up with the necessities. She noticed a full stock of raspberry tea and her stomach did a little flip as she realized it was unlikely the home came with those: Will had picked them out for her.

She trailed her hand along the countertops, the cool chrome effect making her shiver. Opposite the kitchenette was a little living area with a TV, coffee table and plush corner sofa that her aching back begged her to sink into.

She continued to explore, following the hallway through to a bedroom in the back. Sage green walls calmed her mind the moment she entered and plush white carpeting snuggled her feet. The light wood furniture and bed with its thick comforter welcomed her and she sighed before turning away to find the small bathroom that had a shower, toilet and sink. Toiletries adorned the slim unit next to the sink and there was shampoo and conditioner in the shower stall. She longed to get under the warm water and her chest expanded with an excited breath.

She wanted to hate it, but she couldn't.

It was perfect.

She couldn't have picked a better place herself. She went back to the bedroom and placed her tattered clothes in the top drawer of the wooden dresser and put the rose candle on the end table next to the bed. Bryan jumped onto the bed and circled a few times before flopping down with a deep rumble and immediately went to sleep. She guessed he was happy enough here too.

She went back into the bathroom, stripped off her clothes and turned on the shower. Stepping underneath the warm water, she sighed and let the stress of the day trickle off her skin along with the water. She popped open the cap of the shampoo and immediately the scent of Will surrounded her. She brought the shampoo to her nose and inhaled deeply, sea salt and sandalwood, and goosebumps rose along her skin.

When she finished her shower she went into the kitchen and opened the fridge, her stomach rumbling sharply when she took in all the food stocked inside. She gorged herself on meat, cheese and fruits and when she went to bed, trying to squeeze under the soft comforter around Bryan, her belly full, her body clean, she felt better than she had in a long time.

The scent of Will surrounded her and at first, it irked her, then after a while she found the rich, earthy aroma comforting, and she drifted into a deep sleep.

Chapter 8

He shouldn't have left her last night.
He should have stayed.
He shouldn't have been so harsh.
He should have made sure she was okay.
He shouldn't have taken her meager belongings.
He should have insisted he move in so he could look after her.
But he couldn't. He didn't think he would be able to go inside the trailer, too many memories of his childhood made his stomach clench if he thought about them hard enough. Like it clenched when he realized she had been *living* at the shelter. Probably hadn't been eating properly. Had definitely taken her clothes from the lost and found that was likely at the laundromat she said she'd been going to.

Take A Chance

Will had all the money for ten lifetimes over and here was this hardworking, dedicated woman who was barely scraping by because some asshole didn't provide for her adequately and then died.

The struggles he imagined she must've been through recently blew his mind. No wonder she was standoffish. No wonder she wasn't a lady to be charmed by his award-winning smile. No wonder she refused help and was so independent. She'd had to fight for every single thing she had. Nothing had been handed to her.

In a way it reminded him of his mother and how she had done what she needed to in order to survive. Rebelle had done the same and it broke his heart.

As soon as he'd finalized the deal on the home, now officially the most satisfying deal of his life, he knew she would fight him every step of the way. But he was right in what he'd said, even if he shouldn't have said it quite the way he did. If she couldn't, *wouldn't*, help herself then he would help her whether she liked it or not. And she definitely hadn't. She really wouldn't like what else he wanted to discuss with her but he decided to wait until she was settled before he suggested anything so huge to her.

Will wanted to confront Blake and Justine about Rebelle's situation, frustrated that no one else had realized and sought to help her sooner. But then he remembered how much he fought to hide his past, not just for him but for his mom. Maybe no one knew about Rebelle's situation, and she hid it for a reason. He wouldn't break her confidence, wouldn't reveal her secrets.

As he approached the shelter, Black Sabbath blasting out from his car's state of the art sound system, he was *nervous*. He didn't know what kind of reception he was going to get from Rebelle. Had she stayed in the shelter or had she stayed in the home?

He slowed as he approached and spotted her outside the shelter, bent over a cardboard box. She pulled back the flaps and covered her mouth with one delicately boned hand.

He slammed on the brakes and was out of the car and by her side in seconds. "Belle? What is it?"

She looked up at him, her brows knitted then pointed down at the box and his gaze dropped to where a calico cat reclined on a soft blanket. A very fat calico.

His blood boiled, anger rushing through him, his fists balling at his sides. "What sort of fucking person dumps a cat in a box?" he shouted.

Rebelle jerked next to him at the sudden increase in volume. She darted around him and grabbed the box with the now hissing calico and headed towards the shelter, shrinking away from him. He'd noticed before she didn't like yelling. He huffed, annoyed with himself for his uncharacteristic outburst.

"Sorry, I didn't mean to yell. I was just shocked," he said, trailing after her.

"I'm shocked too but I'm not yelling," she muttered. She placed the box in the kitchen and dug in one of the cabinets for some cat treats and offered them to the calico who greedily accepted them. "This is what I wanted."

He shifted behind her and watched as the tension crept back into her shoulders. "What do you mean?"

"Someone has taken care of her, see? She's in good condition. She was loved and now for some reason, someone isn't able to care for her and brought her to the one place that could look after her," Rebelle said, meeting his eyes.

"Some idiot-"

Take A Chance

"Some *person* who for whatever reason, financial, medical, whatever, has left her with us. I want people to feel like they can turn to us for help."

"Us?" He smiled.

She shook her head. "Me. The shelter."

She had a point. This result was much better than a potential alternative that he didn't even want to think about. While he ruminated on this, Rebelle stroked the calico whose purr vibrated off the cardboard box walls. When Rebelle reached the cat's incredibly large stomach the calico patted her hand in warning, but Will noticed her claws remained retracted.

"She's also about to have kittens," Rebelle sighed.

"She is? We've got a baby mama in the house?" Will could barely keep the excitement out of his voice. He freaking loved kittens.

"I need to get her to the vet to get her checked out, but I haven't fed and cleaned the animals yet." Her eyes swung up to Will's. This was a big moment, he could tell. She wasn't asking him for help, he didn't think she would be able to do that, but she was signaling for it.

"I can do it, assuming I'm allowed to volunteer again?"

Her brows knitted and her rosebud mouth puckered in her telltale frown. "You're still here, aren't you?"

He fought back the smirk at her graciousness, damn he loved their verbal sparring. "I am, I got this. You take Parfait to the vets."

Her button nose wrinkled adorably. "Parfait?"

"Yes, Parfait. Just look at that face, it's perfect." He folded his arms over his chest defiantly, he named the cat and he wasn't afraid to own it.

"It's not a good idea to name them," she murmured, stroking Parfait's rounded belly, this time without any warning from the cat. He was amazed at how quickly the little calico had been won over by Rebelle's touch.

Before he could get her to elaborate, she added, "I haven't left anyone here alone before. I'm trusting you."

His chest swelled with pride at the fact that he had earned enough of her trust that she would leave him here, even if only for a short time.

"I won't let you down," he said.

She opened her mouth but then closed it and left without another word, carrying the box that held a purring Parfait.

He sped through the cleaning, eager to impress Rebelle, and had some time to play with the dogs afterwards. When he came back inside the building, he found himself drawn to the storage room. He glared around the dank concrete space, eyeing it with disgust at what she'd had to do before he realized it no longer contained any of her belongings: she had stayed in the trailer. Relief, followed swiftly by joy flowed through him.

He set to work clearing out the space and tidying it. Restacking all the towels and bowls, he found a couple more dog toys and put them on the side to wash before handing them over to new recipients.

Betty and Veronica came and investigated the space with him, weaving around him and sniffing everything, sneezing when they put their noses in the dust and cobwebs tangled around their whiskers.

When he was finished, he grabbed the toys from the table but stopped when his eye caught the invoices sitting on top. Will flicked through them, seeing how much she was paying for pet food and delivery. His eyebrows winged up at all the additional charges the company was billing her for and he got out his phone, ignoring the missed calls from his mom, and immediately started looking for a new supplier.

Take A Chance

He made a note of some companies and called them up, discussed costs over the phone, negotiated his way to a better bulk order price with free delivery included.

He waited for the adrenaline high he usually got from closing a successful business deal, but it never came. Instead, he was excited for Rebelle to come back so he could tell her how he'd managed to switch the suppliers and save the shelter more money.

Will was waiting for her as her old truck pulled up outside the shelter and she got out, the cardboard box in her arms.

"I think you're going to be very happy when you hear what I have to say," he called as she came towards him. Her eyes were wary as she headed past him, giving him a wide berth like she was afraid to accidentally touch him. He caught a whiff of her scent as she sped by him and smiled when he realized she had used his shampoo.

She surveyed each of the dog pens, making sure they were okay before she inspected the cats. She was checking nothing had gone wrong while she was out and that he'd done what she asked.

"I'm not even going to comment on how much you're checking up on what I did, I'm just glad you're back because-"

"What have you done to the storeroom?" Her tone was frigid.

"I tidied it, considering it can now be used for actual storage."

She spun to face him, her eyes sharp. "But I didn't ask you to do that."

He paused. "True, you didn't. But I just thought it would help."

She pursed her lips but didn't say anything, just grabbed a blanket. "I need to set up Parfait, the vet said she's due over the next couple of weeks."

"Wow, really? I'm going to get to see the kittens being born?"

"Unlikely, she'll probably have them when it's quiet and she's alone. Or at nighttime, when you definitely won't be here."

A muscle ticked under his eye at the comment. "Where are you going to put her?"

"I'll put her in the crate."

"What crate?"

"The one in the storage room."

"There isn't a crate in the, now newly tidied, storage room."

She spun to him. "What?"

He held up his hands. "No crate. It went to Oscar."

She cursed and popped her hands on her narrow hips. He could see her brain working at what to do next.

"I don't have anywhere." Her tone was laced with defeat and her shoulders slumped on a big sigh. He stepped towards her, wanting to put his arm around her but remembering she said she didn't like being touched, he held off.

"It's going to be fine, Rebelle. I'll go and buy-"

"No! I don't need you to swoop in and save the day, William!" she snapped and fuck if her full naming him didn't have his throat running dry and a slither of awareness shooting down his spine. Had he ever liked being called William before? He didn't think any woman had ever called him by his full name before, not even his mom. But he liked it when *this* woman did.

He shook off the arousal that began unfurling inside him. "Okay, if you don't want me to buy anything then let's put her in the trailer. That way she's comfortable and it's quiet. She can nest."

Rebelle's eyes narrowed on him before her mouth relaxed. "Yeah, okay. That's actually a good idea." Her expression suggested she was struggling to admit that, and he bit back a smile.

"Come on, let's take Parfait home."

Rebelle rolled her eyes at his exuberance and he took the box holding Parfait from her and headed out towards the home. The closer he got, the more his excitement waned as he realized he didn't think he could actually go inside the home, too many bad memories from his childhood overwhelmed him. When they walked up the steps to the little deck by the front door he stepped back and offered Parfait to Rebelle.

"I thought you were excited to get her settled?" Rebelle glanced at him quizzically, her dark eyes catching on his mouth before shifting to meet his stare.

"I think you've got it from here. Three's a crowd." He gestured to the box and Rebelle took it from him, their fingers gently brushing. She shook her head at him and went inside. He hovered before heading back to the shelter, annoyed at himself.

Back inside, he noticed Bryan at the front of his kennel, his head hanging over the door, a hangdog expression on his face.

Will stroked his head. "You missing her?" He'd seen the way the hound watched her and followed her around. He stepped back when Rebelle came back into the shelter.

"Didn't you have something you wanted to tell me?" she asked Will.

Before he could reply, a man appeared in the doorway. "I've got a delivery?" he asked.

Rebelle yelped in surprise, taken aback by another person being at the shelter.

"Yes, bring it in and let's see where you can hook it up," Will replied.

"Wait, what?" Rebelle looked after the man who left the building.

"I told you I bought a washing machine, so you didn't have to lug everything down to the laundromat anymore."

Her eyes widened. "I thought you were kidding!"

He laughed. "Why would I joke about that?"

"Why would you buy a washing machine? Jesus Christ, I didn't ask you for any of this! This is my shelter and I decide what happens here, not you. If I need you to do something I'll tell you and then you go and do it, you got that?" Her voice raised slightly, and defiance flashed in her eyes. His breath snagged in his throat at her demand.

Fuck.

He liked it when she got like this, stern and controlling, demanding and telling him what to do and putting him in his place. The only problem was his place felt like it was at her feet and he fought the urge to sink to his knees before her. He could just picture her, standing over him, instructing him on what to do and he shivered at the image.

He brought himself out of the haze of thoughts that he would *definitely* pick over when he was alone later. "I hear you, I do. But you need this, the animals need this."

She looked away from him, frustration radiating from her, her hands balled into fists and then she huffed and stormed off. He didn't like railroading her, didn't want to do this but again, she needed it.

Will went through his messages as the washing machine was installed. The knot in his chest tightened and his guilt grew by the second that he wasn't back on set, that he was holding up production, but he couldn't leave now. There was so much to do here, he was needed *here*, not on set.

The washing machine was on a test cycle when Rebelle reappeared with Bryan at her side.

"How's Parfait?"

"Fine, thank you. And…thank you for the washing machine," she said, practically through gritted teeth and he flashed her a smile.

"You're welcome, Belle."

Her iconic frown slid into place but she didn't question the nickname. It had slipped out a few times now and he liked it. Belle, *beauty*. She certainly was. There was a glow to her skin that he hadn't seen until today, rosy like the haze of the morning sun.

"Did you say you wanted to tell me something?" she asked.

He hesitated, knowing how hard it had been for her to accept the changes he'd made today so he rolled his lips inwards and shook his head.

"No?"

"Well, it was just that I had rearranged the storeroom," he lied. He would tell her about the dog food another day.

*

"He just won't stop sticking his stupid nose in where it doesn't belong!" Rebelle huffed as she paced up and down Justine's office. "He bought me a trailer, who even does that?"

"He did? Damn, he's a keeper," Justine said.

Rebelle frowned at her and Justine made the *zipping my mouth* motion.

"I'm not keeping anyone. Anyway, he's just come in and decided I needed a washing machine and my storage room tidying and he's everywhere all the time with his smile and can-do attitude and big ideas and I don't like it."

"So kick him out, tell him to take a hike," Justine shrugged.

She chewed on her nail. "I tried that once and it didn't take."

"What happened?"

"He...never mind."

"Rebelle," Justine warned. "You know you need to work on opening up..."

Rebelle sighed. Her emotions were taut and ready to snap. So much change in a short time, so much out of her control. She was only just getting used to being around Will now but that didn't mean it was easy. Combined with the trailer home, which she hated to admit she loved and the washing machine. Ugh, she knew she was being ridiculous but her whole life felt like it was turned upside down. It may not have been perfect but what she had before was *hers*. She had earned it all, no one else, just her.

"I Googled him and I freaked out when I saw what he was like on his show. I had no clue he was a freaking billionaire which just made it all worse."

Justine's eyes bugged. "You didn't know? I thought you knew!"

Rebelle shook her head.

"Well, most women would be very happy to discover they had a billionaire wanting to spend all his time with them," Justine snorted.

"Well, not me. And he doesn't want to spend time with me, he's spending it with the animals. I panicked when I saw how aggressive he was. It was so like Marcus that I just... couldn't. So I kicked him out."

"Understandable."

"Then he pulled together a file of his entire life and gave it to me. Just opened himself up to a complete stranger, like it was *nothing*!"

"He did? Oh my God that's so..." Justine trailed off at Rebelle's glare.

"Anyway, then I fainted and he cared for me, bought me a trailer and here we are."

Justine sat forward in her seat. "Wait, why did you faint? Are you okay? Why did he buy you a home? Where is your home?"

There was a heavy pause, the atmosphere became oppressive. Rebelle could feel Justine eyeballing her hard. She pivoted on her heel, her foot sliding out from the sandal as another strap split. Cursing, she met Justine's stare. She expected censure, scolding but not the tears welling in her new friends' eyes.

"Where have you been living, Rebelle?" she whispered.

Rebelle pushed out her breath, her eyes closing as she gave up. She surrendered her secret.

"I've been living at the shelter, in one of the storerooms."

There was a choked sound and she had the urge to hug Justine and tell her it was okay. Which was bizarre because Rebelle never touched people and she sure as shit didn't comfort anyone. Especially not when that comforting bitterness crept up in her throat and threatened to spill out and blame everyone else for what happened to her.

"Marcus had debts. He died, and the house went with him. Everything went with him, and I had nothing except the shelter, due to some legal loophole. It was all I had so that's where I stayed," she shrugged, not knowing what else to say.

"So, you've been sleeping there? Eating there?

Showering?" Justine's words were hardly more than a whisper.

Rebelle flinched. "I think it's better if I don't answer these questions, it'll just make us both feel worse."

Justine nodded vigorously. "Rebelle, I'm so sorry I didn't do more. That none of us did more."

Something cracked in Rebelle's chest and spilled out, warm and soothing. "Don't. Don't do that, that's not what I want. And look, I'm getting free therapy so really, I'm doing okay," she joked weakly.

Justine pushed out a shaky breath. "Thank you for sharing that with me."

"You're welcome. Thanks for putting us back on track," Rebelle replied, feeling her lip quirk up on one side.

Justine gaped at her. "I'm sorry. Is that a smile?"

Rebelle fought against the muscles trying to widen the grin on her face. "I don't know what you mean."

Justine snorted, "It is! It's a smile. Do it again, do it again!"

"That's not how smiles work."

"It is when you're around people who make you smile." Justine's words landed heavily. Rebelle didn't know the last time she had been around people who made her smile, except for this moment. And maybe when she told Will that Parfait was pregnant, that made him so happy, excited like a little kid.

"What're you thinking about right now?" Justine interrupted.

Rebelle jolted, shaking the thought away. "Huh? Nothing, why?"

"Because you smiled again."

Rebelle scoffed. "Lies."

Justine got up from the couch, her belly looking much

Take A Chance

rounder even though it had only been two weeks since Rebelle had last seen her. She came over to Rebelle, standing slightly too close and Rebelle fought her instinct to take a slight step back.

"Are we at a hugging stage yet?" The eagerness in Justine's face took a sledgehammer to Rebelle's walls. She still didn't like being touched; she wasn't sure if that would ever go away. But she was starting to recognize that not everyone who touched her did it to hurt her.

She sighed. "Quickly."

A small squeal slipped from Justine as she pulled Rebelle into her arms and half a second later she was free again.

But in that half a second she could feel the love pouring off Justine, washing over her and she didn't hate it.

Chapter 9

Rebelle had her raspberry tea on the deck of her home that morning as the sun rose, creating a diamond carpet as it twinkled off the dew drops in the grass. Her feet were tucked up under her, snuggled into the white and blue striped cushion accompanying the rattan chair. Bryan was curled up at her feet and let out a world-weary sigh as he turned over.

She closed her eyes and tipped her head back, letting the morning sun's rays wash over her. The breeze tickled her cheeks and she inhaled deeply, the scent of pine and grass in the air.

And sandalwood.

Her eyes snapped open and there he was. The man who had bulldozed his way into her shelter and continued to push his way through, whether she wanted him to or not. Will stood at a slight distance from the home, not near it but not away either which was strange, he didn't usually keep his distance from her.

He cleared his throat. "I see someone has been sneaking out of his kennel," he said with a pointed stare at her guard dog.

"Problem with that?"

He shook his head, smiling and her eyes zeroed in on his mouth like they seemed to do recently. She frowned and extricated her limbs from the hungry cushion trying to swallow her whole. Bryan heaved himself to his feet with great effort, his thin tail gently waving back and forth as he looked up at her.

"Where do you want me?" Will said, his voice low, and something hot slithered through Rebelle. She looked at him, his cool eyes twinkling with amusement and maybe even a challenge.

"Start where you normally do, the dogs," she replied, turning away, not wanting to keep staring at him or she would notice how the sun highlighted the gold and auburn tones in his mussed hair or the fine lines that crinkled around his eyes whenever he smiled.

She washed up her mug, pottering around her little kitchenette and loving that the home was beginning to feel more and more like...home.

She stopped by Parfait's box to give the little lady some attention. The pregnant beast waddled to her feet and went to inspect her food bowl. Rebelle had tried to get Parfait to leave the cardboard box but the feline liked it and Rebelle didn't want to force her, so she put a clean blanket inside and set out some food and water.

Rebelle watched her, checking for any signs she wasn't okay. Her stomach bulged and Rebelle was sure that she could see movement in there. Then Parfait wandered back to bed and dropped down onto her side in a half squirm, peeking up at Rebelle from under her arm and purring violently. It was moments like this that brought Rebelle peace. Connection with another living thing that was so pure, so beautiful and so lacking in any motivation. She tickled Parfait some more before she and Bryan headed over to the shelter.

She worked side by side with Will in silence. Every now and then she felt his eyes on her and her own found their way over to him too. Taking in his dress pants and white button up shirt, the sleeves rolled up and his suspenders off his shoulders and looped around his hips again. His shirt taut against his back and she could almost see the design of his tattoos through the thin material. She was staring intently, trying to work out the patterns and shapes when she heard a vehicle pull up outside.

Suspicion instantly pricked at her, she wasn't expecting anyone. She went outside and saw a truck, the driver unloading pallets of dog food, but it wasn't her normal supplier.

"No, I think there's been a mistake," she called to him.

The driver, a grizzled guy in his fifties with dirty overalls, looked at the clipboard.

"Take A Chance shelter?"

Rebelle frowned. "Yes."

"Then there ain't no mistake, sweetheart," he replied.

She prickled, hating the condescending nickname.

Will appeared at her side. "Ah, there was something I didn't get around to telling you," he said with a sheepish smile.

Her blood cooled. "What did you do?"

His grin faltered momentarily but then he reinforced it. "I switched our supplier, ta-da!" He did a flourish towards the grumpy driver who had finished unloading the pallets and came over to them.

"Are you Will?" he grunted.

"Yes."

"Sign here," he shoved the clipboard at Will who signed and then the driver tore off an invoice and tipped his imaginary hat. "Y'all have a nice day," he said with a distinct lack of enthusiasm.

Rebelle could feel her anger ratcheting up again as one more thing had been taken out of her hands, in her own damn shelter.

Will began inspecting the pallets, oblivious to her swelling temper.

"I switched the pet food supplier and we're going to save a chunk of money from our next delivery, isn't that great?"

"You did that without speaking to me?" she growled and that got his attention. He looked over at her and his sunny smile tipped her over the edge. The anger and frustration over the last few days of him barging into her life and deciding it needed fixing spilled over. "Why do you think that was something acceptable for you to do? It's not up to you where the dog food comes from!"

He was taken aback by her anger. "But they're charging you a fortune, it was the most expensive one across the market."

"I don't care."

"You don't care? But the money it's costing could go so much further. Based on some of the things you want to do here, you need to cut costs and that's a big expense that can be easily reduced."

"It *can* be, but I don't *want* to. These animals have been through hell and back and the least they could do is have a nice damn dinner and you had no right to interfere with that!" she shouted, then sucked in a breath when she realized how much she had raised her voice.

The habitual fear that was instilled in her reared its head, terrified of the consequences of her anger and raising her voice to a man. Fear that increased tenfold when Will raised his arm to run his hand through his hair and she flinched, leaping back. Immediately she realized what she'd done and judging from the expression on his face he'd seen it too. Rebelle blanked her features, willing the tension hovering in the air to disperse.

"I would never hurt you. We're just arguing, it's how passionate people get their point across," he said, his words calm, his voice moderated.

There was a pause before she absorbed his words, focusing on one thing. "You think I'm passionate?"

"Of course you are, you're these dogs' momma. I know you'd do anything possible to make their lives better." There was a pause before he added, "Including spending far too much money on their food when you weren't spending any on your own."

Before she could rebut him, he continued. "It's something I've been wanting to speak to you about actually. I want to partner with you on the shelter. Be your financial investor or a director, whatever you want. I know you have plans and I want to help you achieve them."

She scoffed. "You're unbelievable, you know that?"

They had spent a lot of time together but for the first time she saw his sunny expression fall. Not when she barked orders at him or was rude to him, but now.

"For wanting to help?"

Her throat closed up, tears threatened to spill from her eyes and the thought of crying in front of him had her fighting them back. "Stop trying to save me, save this place. We don't need you. We were doing fine, just fine without you."

"You were doing the best you could," he replied gently, and she stumbled back at the pity in his words. "I don't want to take anything away from you, I just want to help move it forward. For the animals, for you. Please just say you'll think about it?"

"I don't want your money."

His expression softened. "Belle, you need *someone's* money, it might as well be mine."

She needed to go, get away from the big man with big money and a big heart who threatened all her plans to do this all on her own. To prove to the world that she could do it, that she was fine without anyone, she didn't need anyone. She would do it on her own or she would die trying. After Marcus she made a promise to herself; she would never rely on anyone else, especially not a man, ever.

She didn't want much from this life, had learned not to try and shoot for the stars a long time ago. She had simple, achievable dreams and yet they seemed like they were forever out of reach.

She was a failure.

She left the shelter and headed towards her home, the home *he* had bought for her, and a sob tangled in her throat. She made it inside and into her room, closing the door. Her breath heaved as sobs tried to escape and she wrestled them back, but fighting was pointless, it hadn't gotten her anywhere and she let them out. Gave them free reign and collapsed onto the floor, burying her face in her hands.

When her sobs finally subsided, the faint purring from beside her drew her attention. Parfait sat peering at her with inquisitive eyes. A whining from the other side of the door, followed by a heavy scratching had Rebelle scooching forward and opening it to let Bryan in, and between the two of them they smothered her in love.

She sat there for hours, mulling things over, picking apart her dreams and trying to reimagine them, but it was tough. The reason she was so protective of *Take A Chance* was because after Marcus had taken so many choices and experiences away from her, maintaining control of the shelter and everything that happened here had been the only way to get her life back and start the healing journey.

The shelter was her passion, and she knew she needed to put the animals first over her feelings and her need to claw out her independence. Look what happened with Parfait yesterday, how many more times would an animal in need turn up and she was already out of space?

She needed to expand, to start adoptions, and Will's support could kickstart all her plans for the shelter. The ones that had her standing outside each day and mapping out where everything would go. But still she rebelled against the idea of accepting help, she couldn't shake it.

The sun set and she couldn't believe she'd spent all day hiding away in her room. She went back to the shelter, relaxing slightly when she saw Will's car had gone but also feeling a twinge of guilt that she'd abandoned the shelter to him all day. It was her shift that evening at The Rusty Bucket Inn so she had a shower, put on her least torn clothes and made her way over.

It was a busy evening, lots of noise and bustle and close contact with people. Ben was working with her this evening as well as Taylor and she was surprised how gentle and helpful Ben was with her. Rebelle was trying to work on the things Justine had advised would help her. She made herself have regular interactions with strangers and acquaintances to work on building relationships, but it still intimidated her to approach people.

Take A Chance

"Well done on your Elvis performance the other week, it was great," she said, shyly.

Ben smiled. "Why thank you, it was great to perform again. I'm so grateful to Taylor for supporting me."

His words produced a lightbulb moment in Rebelle's brain. *Taylor, of course!* When it was time to close down the bar she lingered behind.

"You can take off now, sweetheart," Taylor said, spotting Rebelle still behind the bar. When Taylor called her sweetheart she kinda didn't mind, she knew it was a term of affection and it made her feel warm inside to know Taylor was friendly enough with her to do that.

"I wanted to speak to you, if that's okay?"

Taylor looked up from cashing up the register. "Oh yeah? What about?"

Rebelle played with the bottom of her shirt, tugging at a slight tear. "I was wondering how you got started at the bar?"

"Well, it's a long story, if you've got time?" The redhead had a gleam in her eye. Rebelle nodded and then Taylor beamed at her, grabbed two beers from the fridge under the bar and popped the tops off, gesturing to one of the booths.

Rebelle seated herself in the booth, Taylor slid across from her and placed a beer in front of Rebelle before taking a swig from her own. Rebelle tentatively picked up the bottle and Taylor clinked the necks together before launching into her story. She told Rebelle about looking after her sick father and needing somewhere to escape to. Stumbling across the bar and begging the owner for a job, working part time and earning her position as manager through grit and determination.

"When Bob said he wanted to sell, I thought I was shit out of luck." Taylor shook her head. "I had plans for this place, big plans that I didn't want to give up. Then I realized if I wanted it, I had to fight for it. I turned to Dean to borrow the deposit for the bar and took out a loan to cover the rest. It took years before I made enough to pay him back and then I had to work my ass off to make enough to buy the other half from Bob. Which I did, just a couple of months ago." Taylor grinned.

Rebelle shook her head. "That's amazing, congratulations."

"Yep, I'm a ten-year overnight success. And I'm hella grateful for the help, it got me to where I needed to be. Now I own it all, all on my own."

"So you don't regret asking for help and sacrificing what you wanted to get it?"

Taylor focussed her stare on Rebelle, but for once, she didn't look away but met the fierce redhead straight on.

"Never. I worked too hard for so long on my own and when I finally had help, it stopped being quite so hard. No one can get through life without help from others, it's not physically possible. But if that's something you struggle with then you need to pick your battles. I'm sensing you're asking about this for a reason?"

Rebelle nodded and swallowed around the lump in her throat. "Yes. I wanted to build the shelter from the ground up but it's taken longer than I thought. Funds are…tight. And now I'm doubting whether I can do it myself after all. There's this, benefactor, who's offered to help me out, but I can't get past the thought of not doing it all on my own."

"Does this benefactor happen to be taller than a giant with strawberry blond hair, tattooed head to toe with much more money than sense?"

Rebelle nearly laughed at Taylor's description of Will. "Maybe."

"Sweetheart, if he's offering it, *take it*. At the end of the day, you have to compromise sometimes on your dreams in order to achieve them. I get why you want to do it yourself, trust me. But if you want it to happen at all, you need him. In ten years' time are you going to look back and think, *damn, I hate that I had help achieving all of this* or are you going to look back and think *wow, look at everything I achieved?*"

Taylor was right. Would Rebelle care in ten years' time? Would there even be a shelter in ten years' time at the rate she was going on her own?

"There are much worse people that could be offering to help you, Will's one of the good ones. He's my man's bestie which means he's good people. If he's putting his hand in his very deep pockets, then let him," Taylor added with a shrug.

Rebelle chewed on her lip, thinking over Taylor's words and they finished their beers in silence. When Rebelle realized the time, she got up. "Thank you for the chat, I appreciate your advice."

"I appreciate you asking me. I really enjoyed this, we should do it more often." The redhead beamed at her.

Rebelle nodded, she had also enjoyed the chat. Getting perspective from another strong independent woman and not feeling judged had been really special.

They said goodbye and as Rebelle walked back to the shelter, she mulled the situation over. Her talk with Taylor had definitely shifted her perception of things. Despite the ache in her chest, and the apprehension about accepting help, there was a fizzle of excitement too at the thought of the changes she could make and actually achieving her dreams.

For once, she had hope.

Only she had stipulations. She needed to be in charge,

that was the only way she would do it.

*

"I have conditions."

Rebelle's voice distracted Will from cleaning Bruiser and Beast's pen. He stood upright, dropping the brush he was using to scrub off God knows what from the floor. He turned to face her and met her usual wary expression. He wished like hell she wouldn't be so on edge around him. It hurt that she wasn't relaxed in his presence when all he could think about each night as he fell into a deep sleep was the fact that he couldn't wait to see her again the next day.

Every morning he woke, his blood alive in his veins, his heart a rhythmic thump that screamed at him to get to the shelter, to get to Rebelle. Even if she spent all day looking at him with her signature frown in place. Hell, at least she's looking.

Except he'd seen her flinch yesterday when he raised his arm during their discussion. Like it was her instinctive reaction and that brought up more questions. She was such an enigma, and although he had uncovered some of her secrets, he wanted to know them all. He wanted her soul bared to him.

He wanted nothing more than to be a good thing in her world and recently he was thinking he had stepped over an invisible line and pushed them too far the other way. But if she had conditions, then maybe things weren't so bad after all. It meant she was open to the idea, and nothing made him happier.

"Oh yeah?" he said, wiping the back of his hand across his brow.

She spread her arms wide. "I don't know how any of

this works. You have me over a barrel there. But I want what's best for the animals and that means accepting your kind offer that I wasn't too gracious about. I'm sorry for that, I...well I wanted to do it on my own."

He didn't say anything, just watched her wringing her hands together and looking about. He took a step forward, wanting to ease her discomfort but not knowing how. Realizing instead that him trying to do anything with her made her discomfort worse.

She hit him with her whiskey eyes, so full of emotion it stole the breath from his lungs. "I don't know how to do this, but I *need* to. I need your help because it turns out, I can't do it all on my own. However, I will remain completely in charge of the shelter. All decisions need to be run by me and what I say is final. If that's something you don't think you can handle, then I guess we're done with this conversation. But I really hope not." Her voice lifted at the end in anticipation.

Will didn't have a problem with her needing control, if anything he liked it more than he should. "I think I can agree to that, but I have conditions of my own."

She nodded, a sharp jerky movement and began tugging at the bottom of her shirt.

"I know a lot about business so although you might have final say on decisions, you have to hear me out when I propose something. Without interrupting," he added when he saw her open her mouth. "I will dictate how much money gets spent so if costs need cutting then it'll happen and if we need to spend more then, you will be on board with that too."

"You can't change the dog food."

"I won't change the food *if* you take a salary," he countered.

Her frown dropped into place, her forehead

puckering, her dark brows sliding together. Her mouth opened, floundering, ready to rebuff him.

He folded his arms over his chest. "It's non-negotiable. You're not the only one who has hard limits."

She huffed. "Fine," she muttered through gritted teeth.

His triumphant smile took over his face and he stuck his hand out, his triumph only dipping for a moment when he thought about the flash of fear in her eyes yesterday.

He began to withdraw his hand, knowing that she wouldn't want to touch him, but Rebelle surprised him. She tentatively slid her soft palm into his, his large hand engulfing hers and he wrapped his fingers around her, eager to feel her skin rub against his. They shook once and she was withdrawing her hand before he had time to register the stark, perfect contrast of her delicate skin surrounded by his tattooed hand.

She shuffled her feet and tucked her hands in her back pockets. "Now what?"

He laughed, the sound echoing off the shelter walls and her eyes shot to his mouth before flicking away again.

"Give me today to make some notes and get ideas down to take you through. I need to duck out for a while later on if that's cool. Shall we have a work meeting at Ruby's later, say seven o'clock?"

He figured he was pushing his luck and he could already see the *no* forming before she opened her mouth but he wanted her all to himself.

"Being off site will be good for both of us. Consider it a team meeting."

She nodded slowly, then swiveled and disappeared. His enthusiasm grew as he got to work planning in his mind. So many times he reached for his phone to contact

Take A Chance

his mom to organize something or get someone's number but then he remembered, he didn't want any outside help. He wanted this to be his private project with Rebelle. Didn't want anyone knowing what he was doing and bursting the little bubble of happiness that he'd found for himself.

He left in the afternoon, pausing briefly in front of his car to turn and face the shelter. He stood there with his hands on his hips, taking in his surroundings and he was struck by a phrase he'd heard a thousand times before: *today is the first day of the rest of your life*. Something about that resonated with him today, like this journey he was about to go on with the shelter and Rebelle was something more. Something *significant*. Like he was starting out as an intern at a huge conglomerate, which was a ridiculous notion because Will already had an incredibly successful career...*that isn't satisfying you at all*, his brain added.

He got in his car and headed out of Citrus Pines to the next town over in order to get some supplies and as the sun set, he headed back to Ruby's Diner, eager to see Rebelle.

Chapter 10

Rebelle hovered outside Ruby's Diner, peeking in the window to see if Will had arrived yet.

You're an independent woman, remember? You can go inside and sit down on your own.

She smoothed a hand down her dress, a dress that Taylor had sneakily snuck into her bag one day at the laundromat months ago so that she had something to wear to Christy and Dean's wedding. It wasn't fancy, it was a plain navy cotton dress, but it was Rebelle's favorite garment, and she didn't want to think about why she'd felt the urge to put it on to meet Will.

She pushed open the door and entered. A quick glance around the diner had Rebelle relaxing. There were a few people inside but no one that she knew. She hurried to a cracked, red vinyl booth.

Take A Chance

"Well look at you, pretty lady." Ruby whistled low as Rebelle passed.

Rebelle ducked her head in embarrassment and picked up the pace, sliding into the booth and burying her face in the menu. She didn't like drawing attention to herself. She never wanted to stand out, always wanting to blend in like a wallflower. There but missable, that way she would be left alone. A shadow appeared next to her and it was apparent that today was not that day.

"How you doing, sweetie?" Ruby's croaky voice drifted over her. Although it sounded like she smoked thirty cigarettes a day, it had a pleasing effect on Rebelle's sense.

"Fine, thank you," Rebelle replied quickly and faced her menu again.

"Every day he comes in here, you know, that fine-ass billionaire, looking for something nice to bring to you each morning," Ruby said, her tone curious.

Rebelle swallowed thickly, "I...I didn't ask him to."

"No sweetie, I know that. I'll bet you didn't want him to bring you anything, did you?"

Rebelle shook her head forcefully.

"But that's how big his heart is, that he was so desperate to find something to please you. That's very interesting, don't you think?" Ruby cocked her brow and one side of her red lipsticked mouth quirked up.

Before Rebelle could reply, Will's booming voice echoed around the diner. "There's my two favorite girls!" He approached them, still in the same formal attire he was in this morning, his smile wide and Rebelle's eyes immediately flicked away from his lips.

"There's my man, I missed you," Ruby sighed and leaned into him when he was close enough.

Will shocked Rebelle by dropping a kiss on Ruby's

cheek and she was surprised to see the old woman blushing furiously.

"It's only been a few hours, but I just couldn't stay away," he replied, and Ruby giggled, pushing him away in that *aw shucks* way. Did Will manage to charm everyone he met? For some reason it annoyed Rebelle to see that he was the same with everyone, his easy charm, his friendly smiles and booming voice and laughter. None of it was for show. And she wasn't special, this was just who he was.

"Sorry I'm a few minutes late, I'm usually very punctual," he said sheepishly when Ruby finally left them alone.

Rebelle couldn't help herself. "Not in my experience."

But her tone wouldn't deter his stupid smile. "It was like four minutes late, same as today and it gave you time to catch up with Ruby. Now then, what're you thinking of having?"

She placed her menu down, ignoring her rumbling stomach. "Oh, nothing for me, thanks."

His eyes flicked to her over the top of his menu. She always latched onto his green eye first, finding the shade so startling that she looked to the other one to escape the intensity, only to find herself drowning in the deep ocean blue color.

"Did you eat today?"

She prickled at his question, unable to shift away from the burning intensity of his gaze. "Yes."

His smile turned playful. "Liar. What did you eat?"

She arched a brow. "You want me to list my food?"

"I want you to list your food," he chuckled.

"An apple and…erm…" she floundered.

"Exactly. So, what are you eating tonight?"

"I'm not having you pay for dinner," she hissed.

"I won't be. This is a working dinner, we'll expense it. It's a write-off," he shrugged.

Ruby came over with a little notepad and pencil. "What'll it be, kids?"

Will looked pointedly at Rebelle and she sighed and gave in. "Just a water and the tomato soup with a grilled cheese sandwich, please?"

Will hummed. "Sounds good, make it two please, Ruby. And a side of fries, blueberry waffles, hash browns and a chocolate milkshake."

Rebelle stared at him in disbelief. He just grinned, patted his stomach and she could see the muscled ridges through his shirt. "I'm a growing boy."

"So, how long have you lived in Citrus Pines?" he asked when Ruby left to place their order.

She frowned. "Isn't this a work dinner?"

He cocked his head. "Exactly, I'm getting to know my boss."

"I'm not your boss," she replied.

"But you're going to tell me what to do," he said, his eyes twinkling, and she squirmed at how deep his voice went.

"My whole life," she replied, her frustration growing.

"Did you meet your husband here?"

She bristled; she refused to think about that vile man. "So, how does this all work now, then?"

He blinked but didn't reply, just waited her out. She knew he wanted an answer, but she wasn't going to give one.

"Either we talk about work, or I leave. So start talking," she said quietly, her tone leaving no room for discussion.

His nostrils flared and his expression shuttered. She thought for a moment he was angry and her pulse kicked but when he opened his eyes, there was an unmistakable heat to them. Heat that made her feel all itchy.

"I didn't want to make you uncomfortable. I thought chatting beforehand would ease you into our new relationship." He paused before the word *relationship* and her mouth ran dry at the implication of the word. She needed to pull herself together, but she was all out of sorts. She was out, socializing, well, working but in a social atmosphere. This was so unlike her, and her nerves were struggling with it. She closed her eyes, feeling her panic beginning to rise and she decided to count out what's good. *The shelter, Parfait's health, Justine expecting a baby, the home...*

When she finished, her eyes opened as her food was placed in front of her. She could feel the intensity of Will's stare on her and refused to meet his gaze. The delicious scent of tomato soup wafted up from the steaming bowl and her stomach growled appreciatively. There was something so comforting about grilled cheese and tomato soup, and she eagerly dived in.

They ate in silence, and she observed Will's table manners. He ate a bit of each meal, like he didn't know where to start and was worried it would be taken away from him before he got to each plate.

Her cheeks heated when his lips pursed around the fork. She cataloged the details of him, the way he dabbed gently at his mouth with his napkin. He ran his finger around the rim of his glass slowly, his long-tapered fingers with short nails. Marcus had never trimmed his nails and they were filthy and scratched at her. She shuddered slightly at the memory and turned her attention back to Will. She admired that he took care of himself.

When they finished, he pulled out a file that she hadn't

noticed and slid it across the table to her. She tentatively took it and opened it, gasping. It contained a business plan, ambitions for five, seven and ten years of the shelter. The paperwork to start registering as a non-profit organization. She flicked through it, not understanding what some of it even was but it looked important. She saw contracts drawn up for suppliers, a new bank account that had a sum of money in it that made her eyes water.

"Will…" she shook her head, flicking through the rest in amazement. "How did you do this in a few hours?"

He shrugged like it was nothing. "I've got some experience in this kind of thing."

She snorted at his nonchalance, flicking through and finding the invoice for a domain name www.takeachanceshelter.org and it all looked so official, tears began to well in her eyes.

"You think that's good, wait until you see this," he said and slid a piece of paper across the table to her. She looked at it and frowned at all the zeros.

"What's this?" she asked, taking a sip of water.

"Your salary."

She choked on an ice cube, clapping her hand to her chest. "Absolutely not," she growled.

Instead of being intimidated, he seemed to enjoy her anger, laughing. "Why not? Remember it's non-negotiable."

"I'll take a quarter of that."

"Three quarters," he countered.

"Half," she snapped back and too late she saw the triumph in his eyes.

"Perfect, just what I was hoping you would say. You need to get better at negotiating, but we can work on that."

His smugness irked her. "Says the man who just

negotiated a non-negotiable."

He barked out another laugh, the deep sound startling her and when she saw the joy on his chiseled face, she nearly smiled in return. *Nearly*.

For the next hour they talked plans. He had someone coming to take pictures for the website and their social media.

"You can control all the social posts if you wish, or we can find someone who wants experience in media management and give them a trial run."

"How would I manage that?" she asked, quizzically.

"With this," he said, pushing a small box across the table to her. She opened it up and gasped when she pulled out a brand new cellphone.

"No, one hundred percent no. I can't afford this!"

"You can on your new salary. But it's been paid for, you'll only have to pay for minutes."

She eyed the device warily. She'd had an old school Nokia when she was a teenager but when it broke she was with Marcus and he wouldn't let her get another one. This looked so sleek and *expensive* she was worried about breaking it.

"I can't accept this."

"Look, you wanted to be in control. This way you control social media, the website once it's built and you can approve invoices on there. I even took the liberty of plugging in my number, your lowly volunteer," he teased.

He took the device from her gently and switched it on. When the screen lit up, he turned it to face her. "If you want to contact me just open up this book thing here, tap my name and hit call or message or Facetime. Whatever you need, I'm here."

She looked at the phone in wonder, his name on the screen. She tapped his profile and a picture of Will

Take A Chance

flooded the screen. His smile wide, his eyes bright and she struggled not to stare at the image. Forgetting she wasn't alone, she ran her finger over the screen.

He cleared his throat, jolting her out of her daydream. "Moving on, we need to look for strategic partners, get some corporate sponsorships. Also contractors who can work with you on the development of the shelter. We need funding and lots of it which is where I come in. I have contacts, rich people who want to spend their money on good causes. They just need wooing first," his mouth quirked up.

She shook her head. "I don't know about that. I'm bad company."

"Oh yeah, says who?"

"Me."

"Well, I'll be the judge of that. Luckily for you, I have someone to organize these kinds of things. Rich people love an event, so we'll host a charity ball."

Rebelle didn't really understand how people dressing up raised funds but if it meant people with money gave the shelter money then she was down for that. They continued talking until it was time to leave. Will paid the check despite Rebelle's protests and they left together, Ruby giving Rebelle a saucy wink as she did.

When they stepped out into the cool air, she watched as Will tipped his head back and looked at the sky. Her eyes slid down the column of his throat, lingering on the dip below his Adam's apple.

"Damn," he said softly.

"What is it?"

He shook his head. "Nothing. Come on, my car is this way," he said, stepping to the side and gesturing for her to take the lead.

"It's okay, it's a nice evening, I'll walk."

"It'll be at least thirty minutes, no. Come with me," he insisted.

"I do it all the time, it's fine."

"If you won't come with me then I'll walk you."

Her eyes widened. "Oh, no. I can see myself home."

"Don't be silly, come on Rebelle. You can tell me more about the shelter on the way," he said. He had that determined look in his eye which was probably how he got all those billions in the first place, and she knew it was pointless arguing.

She trudged ahead and they fell into polite conversation. The further from the town they got, the darker the night grew and every now and then Will paused and tipped his head back. After he did it the third time she realized what he was doing.

"You like stars?" she asked, intrigued.

He made a humming sound in the back of his throat and she felt it vibrate through her bones. "There's too much light pollution here to see the stars well but further out, I can see some."

They continued on in silence, him pausing regularly and humming in assent every now and then and she didn't comment. It probably took them twice as long to make it back, but she didn't mind.

"Wow," he gasped.

"What?" she yelped, worried.

"Look at them all," he said, awe in his tone and peering up at the sky. She tipped her head back, feeling slightly dizzy. The sky twinkled brightly with all the stars that had come out to greet them.

"Yeah, there's not much light out here so you can always see the stars. Sometimes you can see shooting stars too."

"Do you ever make a wish?"

"Not anymore."

He grunted in response then brought a hand up to rub his jaw. "Do you think I could bring my telescope up here sometime?" He had such a cautious look on his face, and she relished his vulnerability, finally someone other than her was revealing secrets.

She arched a brow. "You have your telescope with you here?"

"It's in my car, I take it everywhere."

She fought a smile but failed miserably and looked at her feet, trying to hide it.

"Double wow," he whistled low, and she looked up to find him smiling down at her. "An elusive smile. You should do that more often."

She shook her head, this was feeling all too comfortable. "Yes, you can bring your telescope here. I can't say no to the man who's single-handedly funding the shelter and bought my home."

"I didn't think you would, but I didn't want to push my luck," he joked.

"Goodnight, William."

His eyes flared. "Night Rebelle, see you in the morning."

Chapter 11

The next two weeks flew by in a flurry of activity. The photographer turned up to take pictures of the shelter and animals for the website and to start their social media off with some content before handing over the reins to Rebelle.

She had shown Will her basic drawings of where she wanted the shelter to develop and instead of mocking her scribbles, he stared at them intently before complimenting her. She tried to shrug off the warmth that filled her at his praise. He took the pen from her, their fingers brushing, and she jerked back slightly at the electricity that jumped between them. She made a point of ignoring the wicked smirk he was shooting her.

He added to her drawings, expanding certain areas based on the growth projection he'd calculated they would have over the next few years. She couldn't ignore the way her heart clenched when he drew a line straight through the storeroom and grunted, "We're knocking that down, I don't ever want to see it again." He added a walkway between the kennels and the new cattery in its place.

"It's no good planning for just the next few months, or we'll just have to build all over again. You need to plan for the next five years at least until we expand into other States."

She blinked. "Other States?"

He peered down at her, and she tried to ignore the warmth that she'd seen enter his eyes every time he looked at her. "Yeah. Expanding into other States, out from Tennessee. Although at first, we could open up a few more shelters maybe in Palm Valley or Nashville."

Rebelle's throat constricted at the magnitude of what this was turning into, her lungs straining for oxygen. She had always wanted to grow the shelter, but felt like it was all happening too fast. He must have seen the fear in her eyes and his hand slipped to her lower back, stroking small circles of comfort.

"Hey, Belle. Deep breaths. We don't need to talk about this now if you don't want?"

Her breathing deepened but not from fear. He was touching her and she...didn't hate it. Which scared her more.

She pulled away, pacing with her hands on her hips, trying to get her thoughts under control. "I knew that would happen, I guess, it's just a bit sudden is all."

"It is a lot to process. We can just focus on this one for now. I'm getting way ahead of us."

She met his stare, her eyes slipping to his lips and her throat dried. She shook her head and met his stare again.

His eyes probing her in a way that unsettled her and heated her skin.

She cleared her throat, adding more space between them. "Yeah, I think that's for the best."

They finished mapping out areas of the shelter and he left to call some contractors. The shelter grew quiet without him. It annoyed her that normally she would have no problem being on her own here, now she *noticed* when he wasn't around and she didn't like it.

She was used to doing this all on her own. She didn't want to start relying on him. Except she kind of needed to. He knew who to contact, what paperwork they needed, what approvals to get. She was relying on him and she hated it. She could feel a sense of helplessness building up so she tried to focus on the positives.

"Count out what's good," she whispered. "The animals are happy. The animals are healthy and loved. You're getting stronger by the day. Your life is *beginning*."

The last one was a helpful reminder of how far she'd come in the last few weeks. *Even if it is all down to him.* She growled at the errant thought and turned away to grab the worm medicine.

Rebelle headed back to the trailer to check on Parfait who was still incredibly pregnant. By Rebelle's count she should have given birth about three days ago and still was bulging at the sides. She considered calling Dr. Park but decided to wait another day or two. Parfait didn't seem to be in distress, maybe she had just made such a nice home for her kittens that they were reluctant to leave.

When Rebelle went back to the shelter, she found Will talking to Betty, Veronica and Oscar as they wound around his legs, howling for the food he was putting onto dishes for them.

Rebelle leaned against the wall, watching him and

enjoying listening to his easy chatter. He certainly was a talker, the complete opposite to her less than chatty disposition. The man hadn't met a word he didn't like, and she felt a smile creeping onto her face. Just as he sensed her, turning around, she fixed her mouth.

"Oh, I didn't realize you were there." He flushed, his freckles standing out. Her eyes ran over his face eagerly, imagining the constellations she could make from his freckles. She had never thought about stars before until their chat a couple of weeks ago.

"Why do you like stars?" she asked before she could stop herself.

He placed the food down for the cats and they immediately abandoned him for the meat.

He straightened up, rubbing the back of his neck and appearing awkward for the first time and she wondered if she touched a nerve. She was about to change the subject when he began.

"When we lived in the trailer park, my mom would…" he paused. "Entertain men for money. It was a small home we lived in and although I know she tried her hardest I would sometimes hear them. There was a ladder attached to the back of the home and one night I climbed it to escape the noise and that's when I noticed the stars. I took a pillow up one night and lay there, mapping them all out. I found a book at the library and taught myself which ones were which. I found it soothing and something about the night sky being so vast, so much bigger than myself, just helped me ignore what was happening and focus on the future. It made me want something more from life. To get away from there so my mom would never have to do that again. So we would never go hungry again or without heat again."

Rebelle didn't know what she was expecting but it

wasn't this. She didn't know what to say.

"I can't believe I just told you that," he said, his brows pinched in confusion.

"Thank you for sharing that with me." The words rasped from her dry throat. She knew how hard it was to share with people and an inexplicable wave of pleasure spread through her that he shared something so private with her.

"Let's talk about something else," he said brightly.

She looked to Betty and Veronica who had already licked their dishes clean and were washing and gazing up at Will lovingly. "You seem to have an affinity with felines. Did you have cats growing up?"

He shook his head. "We couldn't afford them. I envied the friends who had pets. I've always loved animals. Even animals that people traditionally don't like, snakes and spiders. Dogs might be loyal but they like everybody. Cats are pickier, more discerning. If you get a cat's approval, then you know you've done something right." He shrugged and gave her a lop-sided version of his smile and her heart pounded in her chest, a warm pulsing from between her legs startled her and she twitched on the spot. *That was weird.*

"They remind me of you," he said, distracting her from wondering what her traitorous body was doing.

"Excuse me?" she choked out, pointedly looking down at Betty who was mid ass-lick.

Will barked out a laugh that echoed off the walls, startling Rebelle but also had her fighting not to join in. "No, I mean you're picky about who you let in. You're discerning too and I'm very grateful that you let it be me."

She pursed her lips. "You didn't give me a choice."

"Exactly."

Take A Chance

The air grew heavy between them as the small space in the kitchen seemed to shrink. His eyes were locked with hers, refusing to let her look away. They hypnotized her and she found herself taking a step towards him.

What are you doing?

She snapped out of whatever spell he cast on her by opening up to her. She had eagerly accepted his vulnerability, enjoying knowing what hid beneath his surface. But she didn't know what she had been about to do and that frightened her.

"I think you can take off now," she said harshly, taking out her confusion on him.

Will gave no reaction to the harshness of her words, just smiled at her in that frustrating way and said goodbye.

*

He watched her move behind the bar. Her confidence had grown and she no longer looked terrified of every sound and movement someone made. Although tonight there was something different about her. She seemed distracted.

She had avoided him all day and he didn't know why. He enjoyed their chat in the kitchen yesterday, even if it was him baring his soul and all the yucky parts of his childhood that he tried to hide from everyone. He felt safe sharing with her.

"Yo, you there buddy?" Dean asked, distracting him.

Will glanced back at his friend. "Sorry man. How's married life?"

If Will had to describe the kind of smile Dean gave him, he would call it dreamy. "It's great. Just perfect. We're enjoying it being the two of us, for now."

Will arched a brow. "For now?"

Dean shrugged. "We know we want kids but we're gonna wait a little bit. You want kids?"

Will was approaching forty, he knew if he wanted kids, he needed to start planning now but he didn't have that urge. Call him crazy but he preferred the thought of having lots of animals to children. He'd never been around them as a child himself, never had a sibling to look after or cousins. His stepbrother was a fully grown asshole and although Will would have some step-nieces or nephews in future, when he thought about having his own children, he felt nothing.

"Nah, I don't think that's in the cards for me. I've never pictured a life with kids so I'm good."

"Fair enough. What about settling down, you've been single what, your whole life?"

Will slid his gaze to Rebelle. There was only one woman who intrigued him right now and although she was warming up to him, he didn't think she would ever be interested in anything romantic with him. His jaw ticked in annoyance and the ticking increased when he watched some guy reach across the bar and paw at Rebelle. Will was on his feet in seconds and over there, forcing himself between them.

"You okay, Rebelle?" he asked, glaring down at the idiot who thought he was good enough to touch her.

"It's fine, Will. Please," Rebelle hissed.

He turned to her, knowing she hated displays of aggression and immediately schooled his features into something resembling his normal expression.

The other guy tripped over himself trying to get away from Will.

"I need to hear you're okay, beautiful."

"I'm fine," she said but she didn't seem like it. Hadn't

Take A Chance

seemed like herself all night.

He fought the urge to cup her jaw. "Tell me what's wrong?"

She nibbled her lip and looked away.

"Rebelle? Come on, you can tell me what's wrong."

"I'm worried about Parfait."

"How come?"

She twined her fingers, squeezing tightly. "I think she was going into labor when I left. I know it can take hours and probably nothing is happening and cats have been doing this for centuries and mostly in the wild where no one will watch over them and-"

"Hey, breathe," Will commanded, placing his hands on her shoulders. "What do you need?"

She wrung her hands again and it pained him to see her so worried. "I left and I should have stayed. Do you-" She snapped her lips shut but she'd been about to ask him for something. He knew she found it so hard to ask for help so he just waited her out until she could form the words.

"Do you think you could swing by and check on her?" She held her breath like she was waiting for him to refuse.

Understanding dawned on him. "She's in the trailer."

Rebelle nodded and indecision flitted through him. He looked away, nibbling his bottom lip as he thought about the fact that he would have to enter her home. A home like one he had lived in before and he knew the memories would come back full force. But Rebelle needed him, for the first time was asking him for help and he couldn't, *wouldn't* let her down. Besides Parfait's health was far more important.

"Sure thing. Keys?"

Her face flooded with relief. "Oh, thank you, Will. I know it's tough for you with the home and everything and I just-"

He shook his head, hating that she knew how hard it would be, his weakness. "It's not tough. Not once you asked me. I told you I'm here for you. Knowing Parfait might need me is all the motivation I need."

She regarded him, he kept his expression soft as he regarded her in return, drinking in the look on her face. "Still, I'm grateful." She handed him her keys and he gave her a little wave. "You got your phone?"

She flushed. "Ah, I may have left it at the home."

He shot her a knowing look. "Why am I not surprised? I'll stay with her until you get back. Have a good shift and don't stress." He winked at her before heading back to his friend.

"Sorry Dean, something's come up and I gotta head out to the shelter."

"Everything okay, you need anything?" Dean asked.

Will loved that his friend wasn't annoyed at him for skipping out on their catch up and immediately offered help, that was Dean's way. If someone needed something he was there, no matter what.

"Do you think you could give Rebelle a ride back when her shift is done? I think she left her truck at home." *Probably to save on gas money*, he thought and gritted his teeth in annoyance that she was only just starting to make enough money to not have to worry about those things. He wished he'd pulled his head out of his ass and made his offer to support her sooner.

"Of course, you got it," Dean nodded, clapping Will on the shoulder.

"Thanks, I owe you one. See you later," Will said and with a final look at Rebelle, he left the bar.

He drove out towards the shelter, his gut twisting with unease as he worried about his past and if Parfait was okay. Rebelle was right, cats had been doing this for centuries without human interference, but something could go wrong and he couldn't bear the thought of not intervening if tragedy struck.

He parked up and headed to the home, pausing at the entrance, his hand on the door handle. He couldn't seem to open it. He took a few deep breaths, closed his eyes and was bombarded by memories. His mom sitting on the floor with him, watching cartoons and eating another store-bought mac and cheese TV dinner split between them. For the third day in a row it had been the only meal they'd eaten. The sadness in her eyes as she told him that *me and Mr. Marshall are just going to go to hang out in my room for a little bit, turn the TV up, bud.* The look on the man's face still haunted Will. Grief from what his mother had to do, guilt at the way he was ignoring her now all swamped him.

"Goddammit!" he shouted, frustrated with himself and his inability to go inside the tiny home.

A whining from the other side of the door penetrated his unwanted trip down memory lane. Bryan was inside and Will loved that Rebelle was keeping the hound in her home, like she couldn't let him go.

The thought of Rebelle, that she *needed* him, had garnered her courage and asked for his help settled his nerves. If she could do that, then he could do this. For Rebelle. For Parfait. For himself.

He unlocked the door with a shaking hand and pushed it open. The scent of roses teased his nostrils as he went inside. Lust clenched low in his belly at the smell, reminding him of Rebelle and how much he wanted her.

He flicked on the lights and there was Bryan, looking worryingly towards the bedroom.

"It's okay buddy, it's going to be fine," Will said,

unsure whether he was trying to convince the dog or himself.

He went into the bedroom and found Parfait in her box, laying on her side and panting. He knew he was imagining it, but he was sure she looked relieved when she spotted him.

"Hello girl, how are you?" he cooed as he sat down next to her and gently stroked her head. She gave a soft whine as her stomach clenched sharply and her panting increased.

Will had done some research weeks ago when she first arrived. He knew she could do this on her own, but it was tough to see her so uncomfortable. She kept sitting up and peering between her legs like she knew something was going on. After thirty minutes the first kitten appeared.

"That's it," he praised. Instinctively Parfait knew what to do and began washing the tiny kitten. Will's heart was in his throat as the kitten didn't move and he didn't know whether to intervene or not and then suddenly the kitten's sharp little squeaks filled the room.

"Jesus," Will sighed, leaning back against the wall and breathing a sigh of relief. This was traumatic, a rollercoaster of emotions, and he felt like he'd aged ten years just in that moment. He wished Rebelle was here to keep him calm.

The kitten nuzzled in Parfait's fur, looking for its first feed and Parfait began purring and padding her paws in the air whilst looking at Will, like she was reaching for him.

He lay down next to her, propping himself up on one arm and spoke to her gently whilst her body prepped for the next kitten.

Over the course of the evening another three appeared

and Will's heart was in his mouth for each one. When it was all over, Parfait peered up at him, four kittens sprawled on her belly, quietly mewling and she blinked up at Will. He felt his throat close up, tears stung his eyes at getting to witness this beautiful moment and he was only sad that Rebelle hadn't been here to witness it with him.

It truly felt like a blessing, something he never would have witnessed if he had been back in L.A. He wondered how on earth he was ever going to leave this place when the time came.

*

Rebelle's shift dragged. Although she knew Will would look after Parfait, not knowing was driving her insane. The bar stayed busy with Christy turning up at one point and joining a lonely Dean. She watched the couple discreetly, seeing Christy perched on his lap. No one else even entered their atmosphere, they only had eyes for each other, and Rebelle felt a strange ache in her chest as she watched them.

Christy and Rebelle had been close when they were teenagers, bonding over their mothers' deaths. When Christy left town, Rebelle had been devastated to lose the one person she was close to and wanted to stay in touch with, but Marcus already had his talons in her at that point.

When it was finally time to close the bar, she rushed through cleaning up, eager to get home to Will and check on Parfait.

Dean came up behind her. "Will said you might need a lift home?"

She knew Dean from school but she didn't know him personally and it made her nervous to think of him driving her back.

"Oh, uh you don't need to do that," she replied, wiping down the bar.

"It's no trouble, you're on the way to our place." Dean shot her an easy smile. Like he was trying to show just how non-threatening he was. At least if Christy would be with them, she would feel more at ease. Christy bounced over, wrapping an arm around Dean's waist and leaning on his shoulder.

Rebelle nodded. "Okay, if you don't mind, that would be nice."

They headed out to his vehicle, and she realized he had a truck like hers and asked him about it.

"She's a beauty alright, she's kept going for fifteen years now. Got a good engine and never let me down," Dean said, patting the hood affectionately. "Especially when I had to follow this one across town in a race against time as she was on her way to leaving Citrus Pines for good." Dean added, jerking his thumb at Christy as he helped her into the truck.

Rebelle didn't know a lot about their story, she knew Christy hadn't been his biggest fan at school, but she guessed that must have changed over time.

"He just wouldn't let me go and I couldn't be more grateful," Christy sighed, shifting over to allow room for Rebelle.

Rebelle hopped into the cab and squeezed in beside Christy. "I had no idea you thought of leaving again?"

Dean started the engine and the truck roared to life, the sound reminding Rebelle of her own and comforting her. Like a security blanket.

"Yeah, it was tough after my dad died. Then I thought this guy didn't want me so I hightailed it out of town, but he didn't give up on me. He came after me and practically

Take A Chance

begged me to come back." She smiled mischievously at Rebelle.

Dean snorted. "Oh, now that's not how it happened at all! Lies, all lies. See this is what really happened..."

Justine had previously told her about how she and Blake had gotten together, and Rebelle enjoyed hearing the stories of other couples, hearing what trials and tribulations they overcame. Dean began telling her their couple story with Christy interrupting every now and then to set the record straight. Rebelle liked listening to their easy back and forth, seeing how in sync they were and in no time at all, Dean was pulling up outside the shelter and she was a little bummed that the ride was over so soon.

"Thanks for the ride, I really appreciate it," she said, hopping out.

"Any time," Dean replied.

"We should do this again, but somewhere that's not a truck and with drinks," Christy said, grinning.

Rebelle hesitated for a moment before nodding. "Sure."

They waved goodbye and then she was heading inside, eager to see Will and Parfait. She went straight into her bedroom and found Will sitting with his back propped against the bed, his eyes closed. Parfait rested on a blanket on his lap with four adorable, wiggling bundles.

Rebelle gasped and this prompted one of Will's eyes to pop open.

"She did it!"

He wiped at his mouth and sat up. "She did. She did so good as well. When I got here she was panting and crying out. Then afterwards she wouldn't settle, just kept trying to get in my lap so I put the blanket over me, and we all had a group nap."

Rebelle knelt beside him, stroking Parfait who rolled

onto her side in a purring frenzy, dislodging her feeding kittens. "You did so good, mama," she cooed. She looked up to find Will watching her; she hadn't realized how close they were. It must be because she came home to find him snuggling a cat mom and her newborns but there was a flutter in her stomach and she suddenly found him very attractive.

She cleared her throat, breaking eye contact. "It's a great honor that she chose you. It means she feels comfortable with you and trusts you." *Like I do.*

"I didn't really do anything. Just talked to her, tried to give a motivational speech that's got me through some tough times," he joked, smiling at her.

"You did good too," Rebelle teased, and he stared at her before she wiped the smile off her face.

Will eased the blanket back into the box, careful not to dislodge any kittens. Parfait immediately tried to find her way back to Will, even picking up one of her newborns and bringing it to him. Rebelle was stunned. Usually cats were very protective of their newborns but the fact that she was bringing them to Will was truly astounding. The birth must have really bonded them, and Rebelle was devastated she'd missed it.

"What do I do?" he asked, concern pinching his brow.

"I don't know. Maybe just put it back and we'll leave so she can have some peace."

Rebelle placed Parfait back in her box and Will put the kitten on her side and eventually it latched on to feed and Parfait stayed down, just peering up at them padding her paws and blinking.

They left her to it, the home suddenly feeling very small with Will's broad shoulders taking up all the space.

"Thanks so much, I really appreciate you doing this. I know it must have been hard coming in here what with your memories and everything," she said.

He shrugged. "Yeah, there are memories, but it was a long time ago and you have to move on eventually. You can't be scared of something forever, it's just not feasible. It helps that now I have a really beautiful memory of being here. And like I said, I would do anything you asked me to."

There was so much weight to his words that Rebelle struggled to breathe for a moment. His eyes held hers and her skin pebbled under his perusal. Arousal fluttered to life inside her and for a moment she wondered what it would be like to act on it.

She jolted, shocked at the thought. "Anyway, I won't keep you. Thanks again."

He smirked at her, like he knew exactly where her thoughts had travelled but thankfully didn't mention it and headed for the door.

When he left, he took all the air out of the home with him and once again she was struck by how a place could feel so empty without him.

Chapter 12

It was a packed Friday night at the bar which Rebelle really should have expected, but it still took her by surprise. Luckily, she had Ben and Taylor helping out.

"I can jump behind if you need me to?" Kayleigh called from her seat at the bar, putting down her notepad and pen. Ben leaned across the bar and dropped a kiss on her cheek.

"No way, bad girl. You quit, remember?" he shouted over the noise.

Rebelle had only worked with Kayleigh briefly before she quit, but Rebelle had enjoyed her company. She didn't understand why Ben called her bad girl though, she was incredibly sweet. She also hadn't realized that Kayleigh and Ben were a couple. Her eyes flicked between the two of them and she spotted the tender look on Ben's face before he went back to serving customers. Rebelle wanted to ask them how they'd gotten together, eager for more stories of couples falling in love but she didn't want to be nosy.

For some reason, Rebelle was so curious about everyone's love lives, what a healthy relationship looked like and understanding the mechanics of how they broke that boundary and became something more.

"Hi Rebelle!" Justine called as she appeared through the crowd. Blake was clearing the way to the bar, glaring at everyone until they moved to let his pregnant fiancée through.

"How are you doing?" Blake asked, his intense stare running over Rebelle like he was checking for any injuries.

"Good, Taylor is taking good care of me," she replied.

"What about Will?" Blake grumbled before Justine elbowed him in the stomach.

"Ignore Sheriff Broody, how are things?" Justine asked, her eyebrows raising in meaning. "Anything or any*one* been making you smile recently?"

The eagerness in Justine's face had Rebelle fighting a smile. She didn't know how Justine did it, but she managed to always soothe Rebelle's prickly nature and get her to drop her walls. She shook her head and refused to answer, turning away to fetch Blake a whiskey.

"And what would the pregnant lady like?" she asked when she returned.

"Just some apple juice please," Justine pouted. Rebelle turned away to fill the glass and when she turned back, Will had entered the bar and was heading their way.

Even though she had only seen him a few hours earlier, when they made eye contact, she felt herself relax. That feeling in itself had her pausing and questioning what it meant. It unnerved her so much that she moved down to the other end of the bar, leaving Taylor to serve him so she could pull herself together.

She avoided him all evening but kept him in her periphery. Unease trickled through her as she became aware of a constant need to look over at him. What was going on with her? She noticed how many people approached him, and annoyance plagued her that people continually wanted something from him. Why couldn't they leave him alone? And why did it make her angry to see the volume of women draping themselves over him? She watched as he gently removed some woman's unwanted arm from around his waist.

As the evening wore on the crowds died down enough that Taylor retreated to her office and Rebelle realized she could no longer avoid Will. She was restacking glasses, watching as he sauntered lazily over to her, his whiskey in one hand, the other in the pocket of his slacks.

"Hey," he said, taking a swig from his glass, a drop of amber liquid lingering on his lip. His tongue darted out to swipe it up and her gaze zeroed in on it. Her cheeks flushed and her eyes immediately swerved away, darting here and there and not able to focus on anything so long as she avoided his crimson lips. Why couldn't she stop staring at them?

Moments later her eyes landed right back on them. She noticed her curious eyes drifting to his mouth more and more and she couldn't work out why she was so fascinated. Was it because his lips looked so plump and pillowy soft? Was it because they were stretched so wide she could only imagine how it felt to have them encompass hers? A sharp jolt from between her legs signalled that that was exactly the reason she was so fixated on them.

Horror crawled through her.

Take A Chance

Oh my God...I like him. Like...like him.

No. No, she couldn't like him, she didn't like *anyone*. Just because she had a sexual thought about him didn't mean anything. Although she hadn't had sexual thoughts for a long time, not since she was a teenager.

"-corporate partnerships...Belle? Are you listening?" His voice penetrated her fog. Her hands trembled and she met his stare, his head tilted and those damn lips quirked up on one side.

"Justine," she blurted out. "I need Justine!"

Rebelle hurried around from the bar and over to where Justine and Blake were sitting.

"I need you," she said to Justine. "I'm so sorry, I know you're trying to have a nice evening but I-"

"Say no more, let's go," Justine said with a smile and got up, heading towards Taylor's office. Rebelle trailed after her, trying to do her breathing exercises until they were safely ensconced inside.

"Taylor, can you give us a minute?" Justine asked.

Taylor looked around. "But it's my office?"

"I know honey, but we just need a minute," Justine replied. Their bickering wasn't helping, and Rebelle was seconds away from blurting out the feelings bubbling up inside her.

"I always get asked to leave my own office," Taylor grumbled, and Rebelle couldn't take it anymore.

"Stop please! Lord, Taylor, stay, I don't care!" Rebelle exclaimed.

Both women turned to stare at her in surprise. Taylor got up and came over to stand next to Justine.

"What's wrong Rebelle?" she asked, her green eyes pools of confusion.

"I..." she trailed off.

"Just give her a moment," Justine said. Rebelle began

pacing and tugging at the bottom of her shirt, trying to sift through her cluttered thoughts.

"He's…" she began and again cut herself off. She paced some more until Justine broke the silence.

"Is it Will?"

Rebelle stopped pacing and faced them, nodding.

"What did the bastard do?" Taylor growled and Justine elbowed her.

"He hasn't done anything, right?" Justine asked Rebelle, her eyebrow raised like she knew *exactly* what the problem was.

Rebelle scrubbed a hand over her face. "I can't stop staring at his mouth," she squeaked out.

Taylor whooped loudly. "I was so freaking hoping for this!"

Justine nudged her again and scolded her. "Will you stop?"

"Why is this such a biggie? Just go out there and lay one on him, stake your claim. Then all those fame groupies will leave him alone," Taylor said.

At the thought Rebelle started hyperventilating and Justine pulled out a chair and pushed Rebelle down onto it. "Head between your knees, deep breaths." After a moment, Rebelle's breathing eased and she sat back; gulping in huge lungfuls of air.

"This is why I wanted you to leave," Justine growled at Taylor.

Taylor's face lost its glee. "I'm sorry, I didn't realize-"

Taylor didn't get to finish as the door burst open and Christy walked inside. "There you are, I've been looking for you all over! What are we doing in here?" Christy looked around, her blue eyes landing on Rebelle. "Rebelle, are you okay, what's going on?"

"I think we need to clear the room. Both of you, out!"

Take A Chance

Justine said, clapping her hands together.

"I'm not going anywhere until I know Rebelle is alright," Christy replied. Rebelle glanced around at the three women in front of her, all determined to make sure she was okay and a warm feeling unfurled inside her.

"It's fine," Rebelle told Justine. "Actually, this is kinda nice," she whispered, scared to admit it in case they didn't feel the same.

"Well, duh! We've been trying to get you to hang out with us for years. It's about time it happened, just maybe not quite like this," Taylor said.

"If you feel like you want to talk about it, then tell us what's going on?" Justine spoke softly.

"I don't know what's going on, that's the problem. My brain is doing stupid things and I freaked out."

"What's your brain doing?" Christy asked.

Rebelle paused before answering, looking down at her hands tangled in her lap. "I can't stop staring at Will's mouth and I realized just now…I think I want to," she swallowed hard, "kiss him."

There was silence and Rebelle eventually looked at each woman in turn and found them either grinning or trying to smother a grin.

"It's about damn time," Taylor replied.

"That boy has been mooning over you since my wedding," Christy added.

Rebelles eyes felt like they were about to bug out of her head like Doug the Pug's did. "What!"

"You didn't realize?"

"No! Why would I know that?" Rebelle gasped out.

"You're not that clued up on men, are you?"

"Taylor!" Justine scolded, coming to Rebelle's defence because she knew the history, which neither of these women did.

"No, I'm not. My dead husband was an abusive, manipulative asshole so I'm not great at reading normal signals," Rebelle said quietly. She eyed them all, watching the pity taking over their faces. "And you can get rid of those pitying looks right now, I don't need it. I am fine. Just not when it comes to Will's smile apparently," she muttered.

"It is award-winning," Christy conceded.

Taylor snorted. "Just ask him."

"Do you think you're ready for something like that? To explore a sexual relationship?" Justine asked, gently.

"I don't know, how would I know?"

"Well, are you horny? Are you masturbating?"

Rebelle spluttered. "You can't ask me that!"

Christy snorted. "I think she just did."

"Look, we're all adults here. We've all done *it*. And not only that, but we're also girlfriends, right?" Taylor said, looking to Rebelle who nodded, reluctantly. "And that's who you tell all your secrets to. So out with it, are you?"

Rebelle shook her head. "No, I never really have before."

Justine shrugged. "Maybe give that a try?"

"It won't be hard to get over the line with that one, ha!" Christy guffawed. "Just imagine, all those muscles, picking you up and throwing you around, holding you down and making you his," she sighed dreamily.

Rebelle tried to picture it but immediately squeezed her eyes shut, not liking the image. "I don't think I could ever relax enough to let a man take control like that again and lead the way."

"So then why don't you take control? You lead the way. You could own exactly what happens, when and how," Justine said.

Rebelle mulled it over and the idea appealed to her. To

have him at *her* mercy was much more alluring than the other way around.

"I think she likes that," Taylor whispered.

Rebelle felt her cheeks heating again and she turned away from them.

"Can you give us a minute?" Justine asked. The other two nodded and left the office, Taylor pausing. "We need to hang out together more," she added before closing the door.

"I'm sorry if that was a lot," Justine said.

Rebelle nodded. "It was, but not necessarily in a bad way."

"I'll give you a few minutes but obviously if you need anything then please know, we're all here for you, but I'm also here in a professional capacity as well as a friend."

Rebelle smiled softly. "I know, thank you."

"Look at that, girl. Another smile!" Justine squealed and Rebelle shook her head, trying to stop a laugh from slipping out.

Justine left the office and after a few moments, Rebelle collected herself then she left too.

She headed back into the bar, trying to avoid looking at Will but he made it hard by seeking her out. "Is everything okay? You kinda ran away earlier?"

She nodded sharply. "Fine, everything's fine."

"You want me to give you a ride home?" he offered.

Home. Not the shelter, it was now home.

She opened her mouth to decline but honestly, her feet were hurting, and the walk back would be hell on them. "Sure."

He blinked in surprise. "Great, I'll be outside, just come out when you're ready."

When she closed up with Taylor, Beau was outside waiting for the redhead. Taylor winked at her and then they left. Rebelle headed over to Will who was leaning against his car, head tilted back and staring at the stars. The column of his throat exposing creamy skin to the moonlight. She wanted to trace it with her tongue. She gasped at the thought, turning the sound into words to disguise it.

"How much have you had to drink?" she asked.

He levelled a look at her. "I've had one drink, Officer Belle," he teased.

She pursed her lips, he'd used that damn nickname again.

"Your chariot awaits," he said, unlocking the car and holding the passenger door open for her. She slipped around him, trying not to touch him and felt the cool leather of the seat kiss the backs of her bare thighs. He started the car and loud rock music blared from the complicated looking stereo; he turned it down, apologizing.

They drove back to the shelter in silence, Rebelle shooting him curious glances on the way, wondering what it would be like to kiss him, to touch him, until she was a mess inside. When they pulled up outside her home, he got out and ran around the car to open the door for her. He offered her his hand and she was ready to dismiss it but instead, she took it, skimming her palm against his and he made that humming noise again.

They stood outside the door, and she didn't know where it came from but there was an air of expectation surrounding them. Heavy and urgent and she didn't know what to do with it, only that wasn't ready to say goodbye to him yet.

"Do you want to come in and see Parfait?" she mumbled.

He smiled, pulling his bottom lip between his teeth

and rubbing one hand along his jaw. "Yeah, I'd like that."

She opened the door, turning on the lights and walked into her bedroom with him trailing behind her.

"Hello, gorgeous," he fussed, and Rebelle's insides clenched uncomfortably. Parfait stumbled to her feet, trampling her kittens in her eagerness to get to Will. She rubbed around his thick calves and as he bent down to stroke her, she leapt up to meet him. Rebelle fought an eyeroll at how he managed to charm practically every female he encountered. *You included…*

The longer she stared at him, the less she could deny her attraction to him. With the wise words of her new friends firing around in her head and her body eager and needy she decided that, while she still had her courage, she was going to make a move.

*

"She looks like she's doing so good. Is Belle taking good care of you? Of course she is," he cooed at Parfait, tickling her whiskers and she treated him to a sharp grate of her tooth down his hand as she rubbed around him, marking him.

After a few more strokes, he got to his feet and was surprised to find Rebelle standing incredibly close. He looked down into her wide doe eyes, so dark he could drown in them. She worried her lip and he was desperate to suck it between his and see if she tasted like raspberries from all those teas she drank.

Her shoulders didn't seem quite so hunched in anymore and her cheeks were slightly rounder now she was eating properly. Her skin glowed with health and vitality, and she looked at least five years younger now the dark circles were gone from under her eyes.

She was exquisite and every nerve in him ached to touch her.

She looked away, breaking the spell and seemed to realize they were in her bedroom. Twin spots of pink appeared on her cheeks, and he wondered what had made her blush.

"Let's go back out there," she gestured towards the living room.

He backed out, not wanting to make her feel uncomfortable. He expected to leave now he'd seen Parfait, but Rebelle surprised him again.

"Doyouwantadrink?" she rushed out.

He fought a smile at her nervous energy. What was going on with her? She had always been something of an enigma to him and he was struggling to gauge her behavior right now. But he certainly wasn't going to pass up the chance to spend more time with her.

"Sure. How about one of those raspberry teas you like so much?"

She nodded and busied herself in the kitchenette while he got comfy on the sofa, stretching his long legs the best he could with her coffee table blocking his ability to manspread.

He watched her move, cataloging the small things she did. He knew he was a goner for her, but he found it fascinating watching her complete mundane everyday tasks, like making a drink. She came over with the steaming mug and he adjusted himself in his pants, not wanting her to see the effect she was having on him.

"Thanks," he said. She took a seat in the armchair opposite him, folded her hands in her lap and hit him with her curious stare.

"So, you like heavy metal music?"

He narrowed his eyes at her. Don't get him wrong, he

was enjoying this, but it wasn't like her to make small talk, she was notoriously monosyllabic when dealing with him.

"Yeah, I do."

She nodded then there was silence for a few moments. He reached forward for his mug, the steam caressing his face as he brought it to his lips, eager for a taste. The warm, sweet flavor exploded on his tongue, and he just knew she would taste exactly like this.

"Seems such a contrast to your bubbly personality, how did you get into it?"

He choked on the tea and set it down, clearing his throat.

"Are you trying to get to know me better?" he teased and watched as pink fused her cheeks and she looked away.

"Sorry, I'm new to all this," she said, stiffly.

He cocked his head to the side and studied her, something about her was different. "New to what?"

She squeezed her eyes shut and shook her head. "I apologize."

"Don't do that. I was just teasing you. Like friends do," he said, softly.

"Friends," she repeated.

"Yeah, we're friends, aren't we? As well as colleagues?"

Her eyes slid to his mouth like he'd seen so many times recently and he could have sworn her stare darkened. Her gaze didn't waver and flicker away like it normally did, if anything she doubled down on the staring.

A heat developed between them that hadn't existed before until now. He sure as shit would have noticed it if there was. He didn't know what was driving the change but his heart pounded in his ears as awareness crawled through him.

"You're staring at my mouth, Belle," he murmured. She didn't move and he swiped his tongue along his bottom lip. "Why are you staring at my mouth?" his voice was all gravel now at the heat in her stare, the intensity on her face that he watched morph into arousal. *Fuck*.

"Unbutton your shirt. Start at the collar and work your way down, slowly," she commanded and his cock responded instantly.

"What?" he choked out. He was stunned at the words that just came out of her mouth. He had to be imagining it. Her expression shuttered immediately and he instantly regretted his word vomit.

"I'm sorry. I thought…I don't know. Oh God, I'm so sorry." She looked tortured and embarrassed.

Was she making a move and he'd been too blindsided to appreciate it? "Are you…is this happening?" he said, gesturing between them.

Her hands gripped her knees, knuckles blanching. "I take it you're interested…sexually?"

Will's eyes practically bugged out of his head.

"Forget I said anything," she rushed out when he didn't say anything.

"No, no, no! I'm *very* interested." Will had never been accused of being a stupid man and he wasn't about to start being one now. He slowly began unbuttoning his shirt, his hands fumbling with excitement at the way she was watching him. Was he dreaming? If so, he never wanted to wake up.

There was a long pause where she just stared at him, not that he was complaining but it seemed like she didn't know what to do next. She had commanded him, he knew she liked having control around the shelter but fuck, would she like it in the bedroom too? Heaven knows he was desperate to give it up, could they be more perfect together? But now she radiated a shyness that hadn't been there a few moments ago. Maybe she wanted to take control but wasn't sure how, maybe he just needed to coax it out of her.

His voice heavy, he asked. "Now what?"

Her tongue swiped across her lip. "Pull it to the side."

His pulse pounded at her words, her tone. He opened up his shirt, baring his chest and stomach to her. He nodded to her and smirked, telling her it was okay. Her eyes roved over him salaciously and he loved it.

"What do you want me to do next?" he asked.

"Tr...trail your hand down your chest. Tug the ring through your nipple." Her voice grew more confident and with each command that spilled from her lips, he grew harder. He stroked his hand down his skin, leaving a trail of goosebumps and diverted to his nipple, looping his finger through the ring and giving it a tug, his eyelids fluttering closed at the sensation.

"Did you like that?" her voice a low purr.

His gaze shot to her, amazed. How did she know? How did she know exactly what he wanted?

"Answer me," she demanded.

"Yes," he choked out. "What next? Tell me what to do, Belle."

"You want me to give you orders?"

The look in her eye was provocative, the dark brown depths swirled seductively, and he could barely restrain his, "Yes!"

"Keep going, rub your hand over your crotch. I can see you're enjoying this already," she said pointedly, her stare dropping lower to where his arousal was trying to bust out of his pants. He nodded, eager to obey her. He rubbed his hand over his crotch, the bulge throbbing underneath the material.

"That's right, now squeeze it."

He fisted himself and his whole body tightened with anticipation, his eyes rolling back in his head.

"Does that feel good?"

"Yes," he hissed.

"Do it again."

He did as she said, and a grunt slipped from his lips. A harsh sound and he didn't want to scare her but if anything, she seemed to like it more. Sitting there with her hands folded primly in her lap, looking casual but he could see the passion in her eyes. She was enjoying it too and the knowledge resonated in his chest.

"Unzip your pants."

His pulse pounded with each new order. He lowered the zip and lifted his hips, pulling them down to mid-thigh until he was free. Her lips pursed as she took him in and his eyes were greedily drinking in every detail of her expression, the way her eyes widened and her grip tightened in her lap.

"What are you thinking, Belle?" he begged, needing to know what was going on in that pretty little head of hers.

"You're a big boy, aren't you, William?" she murmured, her voice deepening. Then she rolled her lips inwards like she hadn't meant to say that.

"Holy shit," he huffed at her words, squeezing himself harder, not being able to control his reactions.

Her head tilted to one side. "Do you like it when I talk to you like that?"

"Yes," he gritted out.

She nibbled her lip. "Do…do you want me to talk you through this?"

"God, yes." Breathing became a struggle as his fantasy took over. He had always been the one in charge, knowing it wasn't really what he wanted although he still managed to get off. But this was different, like she had picked through the corners of his mind to uncover his most desperate, unattainable fantasy and placed it in his lap.

He liked her taking charge, relinquishing control to her and being at her mercy. His hips rolled, pushing his cock up through his fist and he moaned, looking at her, waiting desperately for the next words from her lips.

"I think if we keep going like this, you're not going to last very long, are you?"

He shook his head. Didn't even try to deny it.

"So keep going. Pump your hand, thrust up into it."

He did, eagerly. The couch creaking under his hips, his breathing labored and echoing around the room but he didn't care, didn't try to get it under control. He didn't want to change a second of this moment, too scared it would wreck the magic she was weaving. Scared she would stop.

She leaned forward, resting her clenched hands on her knees. "That's so good, William. Just like that."

He needed her touch, her warm skin, her intimacy. "Can I touch you?" he begged.

"No."

A shudder moved through him. Apparently he was equally turned on by her denying him as her taking control.

"Keep going," she said, her eyes afire. "Don't stop."

His hand moved faster, squeezing tighter, needing to get there. He wanted to please her, to give her what she wanted. Sweat slicked his skin, making his path slicker, faster and so much better.

"I'm gonna come," he warned.

"I want to see it, William," she murmured.

"Get it all over yourself."

"Oh, my God," Will groaned at her words, loving every moment. He felt it seconds later, his release creeping closer, just in reach. His spine tingled, his toes curled and he watched as streams of white covered the inked designs on his stomach. He continued wringing each drop and when he finally finished, the shuddering breath he hadn't realized he was holding released in a *whoosh*. His arms were weak, he shifted his legs and they were like jelly.

He was wrung dry and never more satisfied.

Chapter 13

Rebelle's pulse raced, her fingers clenched around her knees so tight her knuckles had whitened and her breath came as heavy as his. Her eyes devoured him, relaxed against the couch, his arms spread wide, head thrown back. Sweat beaded his temple. His body lax. His glistening skin shifting in a slow wave, navel dipping then chest expanding with each ragged breath he drew in.

She was in awe of him. A gradual, sleepy smile spread across his lips and her grip tightened on her knees. The sharp pounding in her core and her skittering pulse increased when her gaze latched onto the arousal coating his stomach.

Rebelle leapt to her feet and ran for the bathroom, locking herself in and sinking to the floor. She wrapped her arms around her knees and her breathing grew deeper as she tried to calm herself.

What the hell had she just done? She didn't even recognize the person who spoke those words, who had the thoughts she had, and had commanded him to do those things. She had degraded him, demeaned him and made him do private things to himself all for her attention. And what was worse, what horrified her the most: she *liked* it.

She wanted more.

She raised a hand, her trembling out of control as she brushed her hair back from her face.

There was a knock at the door and her stomach dipped.

"Uh, Rebelle?" his voice wavered. She had *never* heard his voice waver in all the weeks they had spent together. Not when he argued with suppliers on the phone, not when he discovered what horrible things humans could do to animals, not at any of her sniping comments and there had been *plenty*. Nothing had affected him and dulled his attitude. It was now; in the wake of what she made him do that his voice betrayed him.

Guilt twisted her stomach and she nearly retched. What the hell had she done? She swallowed past the spikes in her throat. "I'm sorry, Will. You can just go, it's fine."

"But Belle, I want to talk ab-"

"I said it's fine, we'll talk in the morning!"

There was silence from the other side of the door and then a moment later she heard the banging of the front door in the frame and squeezed her eyes shut. Her anxiety flared, her breathing still struggled. She needed her candle.

She fled the bathroom and ran into her bedroom, grabbing for the candle and squeezing it to her chest, breathing in its scent. She waited but it didn't calm her. She ran through the techniques Justine had shown her and settled on one.

"S-STOPP," she scolded herself. "Stop. Pause a moment. Take a deep breath." She inhaled deeply, the rose scent starting to take the edge off her anxiety. "Observe. What are you reacting to and what are the sensations in your body. Pull Back and Perspective. What is the bigger picture?"

She faced herself in the mirror on the dressing table, examining her wild eyes. She took a deep breath and considered what she was reacting to: her sexual encounter with Will. The first sexual encounter she'd had with *anyone* in a very long time. She had done it, had taken control of the moment and what frightened her, what had set her off, was how much she had enjoyed doing it. And doing it to Will specifically. This big strong man who was larger than life had been so vulnerable with her, so open and her body still tingled and ached for him even now.

She tried to pull back, take the helicopter view, just as Justine had taught her, and gain some perspective. Except that perspective worried her. She had just crossed a major line with Will considering the professional relationship they had now.

A low rumbling broke into her thoughts and she glanced down to find Parfait watching her with enquiring bright eyes as her kittens mewled around her. There seemed to be some judgement in the feline's gaze but Rebelle knew she was imagining it.

She got into bed, hoping to push this evening's events to the back of her brain. Ignoring the need her body was trying to get her to alleviate, she tried to fall asleep, but sleep would not come. Her mind whirred away with old memories of Marcus and new ones of Will.

When the sun rose in the morning, she gave up trying to sleep and got ready for a day at the shelter. She left the bedroom and as soon as she entered the living room and spotted the two mugs of raspberry tea, images from last night consumed her. Will's groans and sighs of pleasure, the way he worked himself. She grabbed the mugs and spun away, washing the cups out in the sink and leaving them to drain on the side.

She gave Parfait some pats, hoping the cat would forgive her for her actions against Will and she left for the shelter. She visited each pen, greeting the dogs and giving them a stroke before she reached Bryan's kennel. The hound was lying in his bed and refused to come over to her.

She sighed when she realized she had been distracted when Will dropped her off and hadn't collected Bryan to bring him into the trailer for the night.

"I'm sorry, Bryan. It was a hectic evening, I didn't mean to forget you," she crooned. His eyebrows worked overtime as he flicked his puppy dog stare over her before he gave in, hefting himself to his feet and coming over. She ruffled his coarse fur and opened his kennel, letting him out, knowing he would stay by her side.

The sound of footsteps had her stomach clenching and she swiveled slowly and watched Will come in through the door, the sun haloing him from behind. His crisp white shirt looking freshly pressed, his black suspenders holding his black slacks in place.

"Morning," he said, giving her that megawatt smile and his eyes crinkled at the corners. The familiar smell of sandalwood wafted towards her, and it was like Pavlov's scent. She practically started salivating.

She noticed the takeout cups in his hands and waited for the overpowering scent of coffee to hit her and make her nauseous but it didn't. He held out one to her and she glanced down, seeing the raspberry tea. After everything she'd done, he was still so good to her. She had to make this right.

She pulled herself to her full height, which wasn't much but it felt like a power pose and she drew strength from it.

"I would like to apologize, for, uh, last night," she stuttered, tugging at the end of her shirt. "I crossed a line between us and it shouldn-"

He cocked his head. "No."

She blinked. "No?"

"I don't accept."

Her mouth flapped as she floundered for words. "But-"

His grin widened. "I loved it."

Her thoughts stopped whirring and became strangely quiet as she absorbed what he said. They regarded each other; his eyes never waning from hers.

"But I force-"

"Oh hell no you didn't. Like I said, I *loved* it. It was consensual, there wasn't a single part about what we did that I didn't love. Except the end that is, when you ran way and hid from me instead of discussing it like adults." His mouth drew into a straight line before he continued. "It was perfect. How could you think I didn't like it? Did you not see how quick on the trigger I was?"

Her brow furrowed. "Quick on the what? Did you say trigger?"

"Yeah, you know..." He mimicked an explosion with his hands and the flush started at her toes and worked its way right up to her neck and cheeks.

She cleared her throat as something hot bloomed inside her. "Oh, well, that's good to know, I guess."

"It was amazing, illuminating, like you," he said, softly. Her insides twisted at his words. He enjoyed what they did. He *wanted* it like that. Her knees turned weak after she realized they had both enjoyed last night.

"When can we do it again?" His voice deepened and her mouth ran dry at the way his eyes darkened with heat. He was a stunning man, so contradictory. Tall and far too strong, his body covered in tattoos. He was bright and happy but could be hard and stubborn, determined to get what he needed. Yet he was soft on the inside and wanted to relinquish all control to her.

She was suddenly eager to explore with him, to throw off the shackles and experiment with pleasure but she couldn't. It was a slippery slope. She didn't want to get attached, to rely on him or any man again. She had experimented with her desires, and it had been amazing but that was all it could be. The shelter was what mattered to her, above everything else and she couldn't let a dalliance with a gorgeous billionaire get in the way of that.

"We can't. Will, it was a mistake, we work together. The shelter is my priority, and I won't let anything get in the way of that." She paused, worried what his response would be, and his smile briefly lost some of its wattage but then returned full force.

"I completely agree, the shelter is the priority, and I don't plan on doing anything to change that," he said calmly.

She narrowed her eyes. He was taking this much better than she thought he would. Maybe after all the pretty words from his pretty lips, he wasn't that interested in her after all.

"Great, then I guess we can just go back to normal," she said, placing her hands on her hips. Bryan came up behind her and nudged her.

"Sure," he replied, rocking forward on the balls of his feet. She didn't like his cheerful exterior, he was plotting something, she could feel it. He eyed her as he ran his tongue over his bottom lip and her eyes were glued to it.

"It's feeling a bit warm today, don't you think?" he asked nonchalantly. His hand skimming up his body and loosening the top button of his shirt.

"Not at all, it's actually very cool considering it's fall," she replied, her eyes shifting away from the hollow at the base of his throat that was now exposed. She realized what he was doing. He was not the type of man to give up at the first hurdle, but she wouldn't be moved.

He began lifting the giant bags of dog food from the newest delivery and moving them from one side of the room to the storage area. Lifting two at a time, the muscles of his forearms flexing, the material of his shirt straining to contain his biceps. When he caught her staring, he shot her a wink.

She bit her cheek. "I know what you're doing."

He faced her, a mischievous smile on his lips. "Oh yeah? What's that then?"

"You're trying to turn me on. You think it's sexy that you have muscles? That you can pick up and put down heavy objects?"

"You think my muscles are sexy?" A teasing note had entered his voice.

She ignored his statement. "You're not impressing me."

The corners of his mouth quirked, annoying her. "I'm not trying to."

"I'm not finding you attractive."

He prowled over to her, caging her against the table so she couldn't move. He bent down, hovering next to her ear. "Methinks thou doth protest too much."

She looked him dead in the eyes, trying to ignore the delight banked in them. "Methinks thou art deluded," she said, shoving him away and ducking her head, trying to hide her reaction to him. She spun on her heel and headed into the kitchen, his deep chuckle following her.

She fed the cats and rearranged the medicine cabinet for the animals before she cleaned the kitchen top to bottom.

"You didn't forget, did you?" Will said from behind her, making her jump.

"Forget what?"

"It's the charity ball this weekend. Have you got a dress?" he asked.

She stilled. "Why would I need a dress? I'm not going."

He scoffed. "You're the owner, you can't not go."

"Okay, let me rephrase, I don't want to go," she shrugged.

His hands clamped down on his hips. "Why don't you want to go?"

"Because that's just not my scene. I'm not one of them and I never will be."

He arched a light brown brow. "Them?"

"Yes, rich assholes with more money than sense!"

His hand slid across his jaw, scratching the stubble there. "Hmm, like me, you mean?"

She blinked at the hurt in his eyes before he quickly masked it. She swallowed. "No. You're not like that."

"Don't you trust me to pick the right kind of people to invest in the shelter? You think you'd have some more faith in me by now, it's been weeks." He turned to leave and she moved in front of him, blocking his path.

"Will, wait-"

"You're not the only one who cares about the shelter,

you know? What do I need to do to get you to trust me?" He brushed past her as he exited the room.

She stood in the kitchen, her mind and heart warring with each other. Rebelle didn't fit in at events like that and what would she even wear? She didn't own any of her own clothes. Everything was second hand and torn because she couldn't afford any.

*Not anymore...*her brain piped up. Now she was getting a regular paycheck, she was able to buy her groceries and pay the bills and she could afford clothes too. Except she didn't know where to go or what to buy. There was someone who could help her though.

She took out the phone that contained only three numbers: Will, Dr. Park and Justine. She opened a new chat with Justine.

Rebelle: Hey, it's Rebelle. I just wondered if you could recommend somewhere to get a nice dress? Like a dress someone would wear to a ball?

The reply was instantaneous.

Justine: I can do better; I can show you. When do you want to go?

Rebelle paused. She had wanted to do this on her own, hadn't been asking for Justine to accompany her but the thought of trying to find a dress so fancy left her feeling overwhelmed. Maybe going on her own wouldn't be the best thing.

Rebelle: Is tomorrow too soon?

Justine: Not at all. We can get lunch too. You need just a dress or anything else?

Rebelle's fingers fumbled as she typed, still not used to messaging.

Rebelle: A formal dress, maybe shoes? A bag? Jewelry? I don't know.

Justine: Okay, we'll need reinforcements.

"Reinforcements, what does that mean?" Rebelle asked Bryan who was curled up at her feet and just stared at her lovingly. A moment later she received a notification that she has been added to something called *Rebelle's Angels* and there was an image of what looked like a movie poster with the *Charlie* crossed out and *Rebelle* placed over the top.

Christy: We're in!

Taylor: Love a shopping day, let's go to Palm Valley #roadtrip!

Realization of what, or who, the reinforcements were settled in.

Justine: Love a girls' day out but don't get distracted, this is for Rebelle. We need to get a dress for the ball.

Taylor: Perfect, I need one too.

Rebelle: You're coming to the ball?

Taylor: Hells yes!

Christy: We all are, we're VIPs darlin'.

Another wave of guilt washed over Rebelle. Of course, Will would invite good people, he was a decent man with strong morals and big beating heart in his chest. It was one of the reasons she had agreed to let him work on the shelter with her. She should have known better.

As though her thoughts conjured him, he appeared in the doorway. "I'm gonna take off. I've got a meeting with a contractor about expanding the back for a doggie play area and building a cattery. I'll let you know if they sound like the ones for the job, it'll be a big commission for them if they impress me given how much work we want to do here." He didn't lift his eyes from his phone.

"Okay, great." She expected him to say more but he just turned on his heel and left. The shelter grew cold and empty with his absence, but she shrugged it off. Instead, she thought about the cattery she wanted building and started sketching out ideas for the interior.

She tried to concentrate but her mind kept flashing back to the look of hurt that crossed his face earlier. The dip in his normally smooth brow, the hint of sadness in his ocean eyes that he tried to hide, the flat line of his mouth that usually held its trademark award-winning smile. She tried to brush it off but couldn't and later that evening when she was curled up on the sofa with Bryan at her feet, she messaged him.

She was annoyed at being the one to give in and message him. He'd said he would update her so why was she having to chase him? She angrily jabbed at the phone screen.

Rebelle: So? How did it go?

She saw him come online, the gray ticks turned blue and then he was typing.

Will: Are you actually messaging me first?

She scowled at his message, could practically see his smug grin, and grumbled to herself as she replied.

Rebelle: I instantly regretted it.

Will: Did you just make a funny?

Forgetting herself, a smile slipped free and she snorted before rearranging her scowl.

Rebelle: For the first and last time.

Will: It's late, get some sleep. I'll tell you about it tomorrow.

Rebelle: About that…I was thinking of taking one of those days off you mentioned.

She nibbled her lip as he began typing, waiting for his response. She would get up even earlier in the morning to sort the animals if she needed to, if he couldn't manage it.

Then an image of a random man just blinking appeared.

Will: I don't think I read that right.

Will: You?
Will: Take a day off?

She smiled again, she could hear the sarcasm. She didn't reply, instead she brushed her teeth. She decided to keep Bryan in the home tonight, she didn't want to take him back to the shelter. She settled him on the couch and kissed Parfait goodnight and got into bed. Her phone started vibrating and she looked down.

Will video call.

She panicked. How did she answer this? Did she even want to? She tapped the screen but nothing happened and then it disappeared.

Will: You have to swipe up. Ready?

She barely had time to read the message before he was calling again. She slid her finger over the screen and then his face appeared.

"Why do you want a day off?" he asked, without preamble. She took him in, his wide mouth pinched in displeasure, but his eyes were sparkling as usual, so she wasn't worried he was actually mad and as usual his green eye snagged her attention. Her tongue grew twenty times heavier as he ran a hand through the scruff on his chin and jaw and the rasp echoed down the line.

"Uh, errands?"

His nostrils flared. "You sure about that?"

"Yes."

"Who are these supposed errands with?"

"Justine," she replied and that seemed to placate him. Just then Parfait jumped onto the bed and began purring around the phone.

"Your girlfriend is missing you," Rebelle grumbled, turning the phone to Parfait.

"Of course she is," he replied smugly.

"Can I go to sleep now?" Rebelle could hear how pissy

she sounded.

"You're in bed too?" he asked, his voice dipping the way it had yesterday when she was talking him through his-

"Yep!" she cut off her thoughts, heat suffusing her cheeks. He pulled the phone back and she could see his bare shoulders and chest.

"I'm in my bed. You're in your bed. Kinda feels like one of us is in the wrong bed..." he trailed off, his eyelids dipped suggestively, and she felt it all the way to her toes.

"Sounds like we're in exactly the right beds to me. Good night, William," she said, tersely.

He grunted and raked a hand across his chest and she saw it travel to the ring through his nipple and he tugged gently.

"If you're looking to keep this strictly professional then don't call me William in that tone. It gets me all riled up." His voice dropped a few octaves and suddenly the blankets were too much for her, she kicked them off.

"That's enough of that," she mumbled, not making eye contact through the phone in case he moved his hands anywhere else.

He smirked. "Sweet dreams, Belle." There was so much insinuation in his tone that she pursed her lips to fight back a moan. His laugh echoed around her room until she ended the call. Parfait, disappointed that her hero didn't materialize, went back to her kittens.

Rebelle lay there in the dark but sleep was gone from her. She shifted her legs restlessly as images of Will flooded her mind and her breathing grew labored. Her hand trailed down her damp skin and her eyes fluttered closed as she pictured him how he'd been last night, his face basked in pleasure, his eyes begging her.

A deep pulsing between her legs had a hand fisting the

sheets as the other slid from her stomach to the seam of her panties. She hovered there, playing with the material, in two minds. She hadn't done this for a very long time.

Eventually her hand dipped beneath the edge and found her wet center. She circled around her clit, her breath releasing in a deep sigh as more images of Will invaded her mind. She worked faster, her hips lifting to meet her hand, her body moving in sync.

She could feel it building, far too quickly and the image of him watching himself orgasm threw her violently over the edge. She cried out as her climax slammed through her, her body seizing then releasing for an endless time.

She lay there, trying to catch her breath but it evaded her and soon her breath grew more labored as she tried to restrain the emotions flooding her. She fought to control her lungs, taking deep breaths and trying to beat back the emotion rising in her throat and choking her. She couldn't swallow it down and she burst into tears. She sobbed, loud and messy, not able to control herself. Bryan must have heard her as he came stumbling into the room and heaved himself onto the bed. Rebelle grabbed him and buried her face in his wiry fur.

Her eyes finally drifted closed when she exhausted herself and a final thought floated through her mind just before sleep claimed her. *I wish Will was here...*

Chapter 14

A loud banging woke her and she bolted upright in bed, her heart thudding in her chest and dislodging Bryan in the process.

"Rebelle!" a voice shouted. *Was that Justine?*

"Oh God," Rebelle groaned, relaxing slightly. Realizing she had overslept on shopping day, she stumbled out of bed. "I'll be just a minute!" she called through the front door.

She ran around the home, getting ready, pausing as she looked in the drawer at her sparse clothing and grabbed them all in her arms. She carried them through the kitchen and dumped them all in the metal trash can. The clang of the lid closing rang through the home, filling her with a deep sense of satisfaction. After today, she would never have to wear someone else's discarded clothes again.

She regarded the canine who traipsed behind her. "Come on you, back to the shelter." Bryan grumbled and reluctantly followed her out. She opened the door and found Christy, Justine and Taylor all standing there with big grins on their faces.

"It's shopping day!" Taylor cheered and they revealed the party poppers they'd brought with them. After a loud bang that didn't startle Rebelle as much as she expected, confetti rained over her, the ribbons of it gliding down her face and settling in her hair.

She sighed but was secretly pleased at their enthusiasm to spend time with her. "You're morning people, aren't you?"

"We sure are, darlin'!" Christy crowed.

"Let's get this show on the road, we've got some damage to do." Taylor turned towards the car parked outside.

"He picked a good one," Justine said quietly as the others moved on.

Rebelle glanced back at the trailer. "Yeah, he did."

Justine's lips twitched. "I meant you." She headed after the others, jumping into the driver's side, her big belly just about squeezing behind the wheel. Rebelle paused, mulling over Justine's words before shaking them off and shutting Bryan back in the shelter.

When she came back to the car, Christy and Taylor were grinning at her from the back seats. Rebelle settled herself inside then jumped at the sound of a cork popping.

"To new traditions!" Christy exclaimed, handing her a plastic champagne flute. They clacked their flutes together, including Justine. "It's non-alcoholic," Justine explained.

Rebelle shook her head. "You guys are so extra."

"Thank you," Taylor said earnestly, pressing a hand to her chest and a chuckle slipped from Rebelle.

"There she is!" Justine cheered and they were on their way, all bickering like sisters and a pang hit Rebelle's chest at the thought of her missing twin. She wondered where she was, what she was doing now and if she ever thought of Rebelle and coming home.

"So..." Christy began, raising her eyebrows suggestively. "Did you do *it*?"

"It?" Rebelle downed the rest of her faux champagne.

"You know...*it*," Taylor winked. Rebelle's cheeks flushed and she slapped a hand over her mouth, smothering a hiccup.

Taylor hooted. "That's a yes!"

Justine held up a hand. "Wait! On your own or with Will?"

"Oh, erm..." Rebelle's cheeks darkened further.

Christy squealed. "Definitely both!"

Four eyes bored into her head from behind and she could feel Justine darting glances at her periodically. Rebelle threw her hands in the air. "Yes! Are you happy now?"

"Hell yes!"

"I'd be happier if you shared details."

"Did you take control?" Justine asked, the more sensible of the questions that were peppered at her.

Rebelle played with her champagne flute. "I did."

"And? How did that feel?"

The two in the back were finally quiet, just listening and it felt like she was in a therapy session with Justine. "Really good. Too good. But we've agreed it won't happen again."

Taylor snorted. "Been there, sweetheart."

"Same," Christy added. "And it's never *just once*."

Rebelle faced them. "Oh no, it has to be. He's partnering with me on the shelter and that comes first."

"I bet it wasn't the only thing to come first," Taylor muttered behind her flute and Christy snorted her drink. "Stop it! That went up my nose!"

Justine's inquisitive eyes flicked back to Rebelle. "Did you *both* agree it was just once?"

Rebelle squirmed in her seat thinking about it. "Um, I'm not sure."

"Did you just tell him it was only once?"

"Maybe."

"So if he didn't agree and he didn't disagree...he would do it again, right?"

"I don't know."

"I think you should pursue it," Justine said.

"I second that."

"I third it!"

Justine shushed Taylor and Christy before turning to Rebelle again. "You've changed so much in such a short time and I think it's helped you grow and given you confidence. You seem less closed off, more open to people and you barely reacted to the party poppers. Maybe you're ready to explore a new relationship?"

"But the shelter is my priority. I can't-"

"We know it's important to you. It's important to Will too. He won't let anything happen to it, or you. No matter what happens between you," Taylor added. Rebelle chewed on her lip, mulling their words over for the rest of the journey.

When they arrived at the mall, Rebelle checked her phone and saw a message.

Will: Have fun with your errands *smiley face*.

She wanted to reply but didn't know what to say

except;

Rebelle: Thanks. Can you check on Parfait while I'm gone?

He replied with a thumbs up and then she was whisked away by the girls. They grabbed pastries for breakfast then hit the stores. Rebelle couldn't believe the clothes she saw, snagging multiple jeans and t-shirts, a skirt and some sweaters now the weather was cooler.

The others kept finding clothes that would 'make her eyes pop' or 'her ass stand out' and 'her breasts look great' along with a number of other things that all ended up with making Will drool apparently. They completely ignored her protests that she didn't want him to drool over her, their relationship was purely professional.

Then Rebelle picked up a few pairs of tennis shoes and boots for the dirtier parts of shelter life along with some adorable ballet flats before she stumbled into the lingerie department.

The sea of colors and fabrics fascinated her and she couldn't stop herself from trailing her fingers over them, like a kid in a candy store. She knew she needed basic underwear but after wearing second hand ones for so long she just couldn't do it. She craved luxury. She bought satin, lace and silk in various colors and styles and loved every second of it.

Next, they went into a store so fancy if Rebelle had been on her own, she would have been too intimidated to enter. But today, she had back up.

Justine found a gorgeous orange wrap dress that fit around her belly and made her look like a Goddess. Christy went for a classic black cocktail dress and Taylor snagged a pink satin floor length gown.

"What color are you wanting Rebelle?" Christy asked.

Taylor looked up from her phone, her gleaming eyes

fixing on Rebelle. "Something tells me that red would be the best color for you to wear to the ball." Red was such a bold, daring color that Rebelle halted. She wanted to blend into the background, to disappear and draw no attention.

The women dug through the racks of dresses until Christy gasped and pulled out a long, rose red backless dress with a full satin skirt. Justine squealed and Taylor clapped. "It's perfect!"

"No, it's too..." Rebelle trailed off.

"Are you kidding? This is damn perfection!"

"No, it's too much, I can't..."

The women closed around her and Taylor squeezed her hand. "Sweetheart, sometimes too much is just right."

"You're allowed to be too much, there's nothing wrong with that."

They bundled her, protesting all the way, into the changing room, they drew the curtain and silence embraced Rebelle and the dress. She swiveled. Ignoring her reflection in the mirror, she eyed the dress with undisguised curiosity. What would it feel like to wear something this beautiful? Her fingers twisted into the fabric, snaking it around her hand as anticipation grew.

She hastily undressed and removed the bra that was two sizes too big and stared at herself in the mirror. She assessed her body. The small breasts that seemed unimpressive. The ribs that didn't protrude quite as much as they used to. The hips that didn't flare out as far as on other women and her short legs which had grown muscular from hard work. She spotted the marks, the scars, and the bone on her elbow that would always stick out more where it wasn't fixed properly. It hurt to look at herself and see the map of abuse.

"Is it on?" came an eager voice, snapping her out of

her perusal. She removed the dress from the hanger and stepped into it, pulling it up and slipping her arms through the straps that skimmed down the sides of her waist, leaving her back bare. She smoothed the material and looked up at her reflection. She clapped a hand over her mouth and tears filled her eyes. She barely recognized herself. She was beautiful, delicate and feminine.

She let out a small sob and the curtain was pulled back and her three new friends rushed her, pulling her into a hug. She didn't fight the contact, in fact, she welcomed it. They gently shushed her, stroking her arms and comforting her until she took a deep, shuddering breath and pulled away, wiping her puffy eyes. She never had been a pretty crier.

"You look spectacular," Christy said.

"This color and style looks amazing on you. You're like a princess, Rebelle!"

"Will is going to lose his shit," Taylor tsked, a sly smirk on her face.

"No doubt," Justine agreed.

They had her twirl for them and she marveled as the skirt flared out. They discussed the type of shoes that would be best and then they left the fitting room and she was alone once more.

She didn't want to take the dress off, eager for the next time she could wear it again. Eventually she removed it and this time when she saw herself, she didn't critique her body, she didn't pay attention to the scars or bones. She had always felt weak with Marcus, annoyed at her body for failing her, for not being strong enough to fight back or recovering quick enough after abuse but now she saw it for what it was. Hers. It told a story of her life; her growth. The body that worked hard to keep her moving, keep her strong and kept her living, *surviving*.

Once she was dressed again, she made her way to the register, passing a table full of accessories that included suspenders. She looked over the different designs before spotting a pair with constellations on them. She couldn't resist the purchase and growled, "Not a word," at the tittering trio with their raised eyebrows.

They stopped for lunch before heading back for shoes and purses and more clothes before they finally headed home, chatting excitedly about their purchases.

She caught Justine staring at her. "What?"

"Nothing. I was just thinking that sometimes retail therapy can be as effective as normal therapy."

Rebelle didn't respond, just considered her words. She did feel like something had shifted inside her today. Spending time with the women, getting her own clothes, spending money she had earned and flexing her independence felt *good*.

She watched the sun set on the drive back, listening to Christy and Taylor ribbing each other and smiling here and there at the insults that were clearly full of love.

"Do you think we can get ready together next week?" Rebelle asked tentatively when Justine pulled up outside the shelter.

"Oh my God, yes!"

"It'll be like we're going to prom!"

"We can do hair and make-up, it'll be so fun!"

"Thank you for today," Rebelle said to them and then got out with all her purchases before she got teary-eyed again. They agreed to head to Justine's before the ball to get ready and Justine agreed to look after her dress as she could steam it.

Waving goodbye, Rebelle headed home, stopping when she noticed Will on the deck of the trailer, peering through a telescope.

*

"Mom, I know!" Will's exasperated sigh bounced off the walls of the shelter. Her screeched response was so loud that he pulled his phone away from his ear and a couple of the dogs began howling.

"This is unacceptable! What am I supposed to tell GQ? And Time Magazine, Will. Time freaking Magazine!"

He pinched the bridge of his nose. "Tell them whatever you like, just make them go away."

"You can't hide forever," she said, her voice softer and part of him wanted to give in and give her what she wanted but he knew better.

"Stop trying to guilt me."

"What are you even doing there? What is so damn important that you've put your entire career and life, and the lives of so many others, on hold? People are running in circles trying to clean up and mitigate the impact of your absence and what the hell are you even doing it for?"

Will didn't want to tell her because he wanted to protect what he was doing here, it was private, just for him. But his mom knew how much he loved animals and he hoped she would be pleased he found something he was passionate about.

His enthusiasm spilled out. "It's an animal shelter. I'm working with the owner to help it grow and it's turned into a passion project."

His mother made an excited noise. "This is perfect for your brand, I'm so proud of you! What great publicity this will be. I'll start calling around our talk show host friends to book a slot for you to talk about it and oh! GQ are going to just lap this up!"

She continued on in her excitement as Will's heart plummeted to his feet. Part of him was surprised that she was so cold blooded in her way of thinking and part of him wasn't surprised at all.

He missed the woman who sat on the floor with him playing Uno, eating SpaghettiOs from the can and watching cartoons. The woman who was too young for a child but managed anyway. The woman whose imagination turned the couch cushions into a fort and the floor to lava and created their own island to live on. The woman who had him giggling hysterically at the way she told stories, all her facial expressions, accents and voices she used. The woman who inspired him with her positive attitude and optimistic outlook on life despite the trainwreck theirs was.

"What happened to you?"

There was deathly silence on the other end of the phone but Will plowed on. "I miss her, you know. My friend, when it was just the two of us. Sometimes I don't even recognize you anymore."

A dismissive sniff. "I don't know what you're talking about."

"Yes you do! Where's the woman who stole Christmas lights from the front yards of the rich neighborhoods just so we would have some inside Lucille? You remember Lucille, don't you?" he asked, referencing the trailer home which he now looked back on with fondness. Maybe spending so much time around Rebelle's and seeing how she appreciated it had changed his opinion.

She sighed. "Will, you've clearly had a long day and-"

He ended the call, he didn't need his mother trying to gaslight him. He tried to put on his positivity pants but struggled and paced the shelter, frustrated and needing something to vent his frustration. He wanted Belle. Her presence calmed him and he was at ease around her.

Will felt a lot of things around her and their encounter the other night played on repeat in his memory. An encounter unlike any he'd ever experienced before. She'd driven him wild, found his untapped fantasies and made him see stars, so many and so clear that he could have almost picked out each constellation if he hadn't been so wrung dry.

Except while she'd watched him with a pleasure and intensity he would never forget, he hadn't been able to touch her. And now she was insisting they keep things strictly professional, and he didn't know where to go from here.

Damn her practicality and the fact that she had a level-headedness that he struggled to display around her. He just wanted to prove to her all the ways it would be so much better if it wasn't just one time.

His phone beeped and he looked down, praying it was another message from Rebelle but it was from Taylor.

Taylor: What color is your suit jacket for the ball?

Will: Navy blue, why?

Taylor: Just want to make sure you and Beau aren't twinning.

He stuffed his phone back into his pocket, not sure why it mattered if he and Beau were twinning. Grown men could wear the same color if they wanted.

Now he was thinking about the ball and Rebelle's refusal to come. Was he disappointed he wouldn't get her in a social setting? Yes. But he was also disappointed from a work point of view too. No one was more knowledgeable or passionate about the shelter than she was, and he wanted her to use that passion to inspire others to be involved. Sure, he could get his fat cat friends to part with their easily earned cash, but she was the ultimate ambassador for the shelter.

He tried to shrug off her words. Did she really think he was just another rich asshole with more money than sense? He didn't want her to think like that about him. He wanted to mean more to her than an bottomless bank account. He wanted to do something more with his money. Something meaningful. Did she think he was just flashing his cash and not caring about the shelter? Or her?

A soft press against his leg distracted him and he looked down to find Oscar, the stray cat from the vets, peering up at him.

Will bent down and scooped Oscar into his arms and buried his face in Oscars soft fur. Will had been spending time with the old bruiser, trying to socialize him and get him used to company. Like most stray cats there had been an affectionate beast inside Oscar trying to break out which was now freed. Oscar's deep rumbling purr soothed Will's raw nerves until he was calm again.

"Thanks buddy, I needed that feline therapy," Will said, putting Oscar down and the cat immediately ran over to Betty and began rubbing around her, his tail wafting under her nose. She didn't seem impressed. Why were the women of this shelter so damn hard to impress?

Will finished cleaning, the routine of it soothing him, then spent the afternoon on the phone to the new contractor arranging dates and any permits needed to develop the land.

All of a sudden it was evening, like Will just blinked and darkness had come. He shut up the shelter and drove back to his room at The Rusty Bucket Inn and showered. He stopped by the diner for dinner and a chat with Ruby before he went back to the cabin.

He paced, restless. He didn't want to go to the bar, he

couldn't handle the fans tonight, he just wanted peace. He wanted Rebelle.

"Fuck it," he grunted and headed for his Bugatti. Ten minutes later he was outside her home but the lights were off. *Where was she? Was she on a date?* Jealousy flared before he could stop it and he took deep breaths to calm himself before he got back behind the wheel.

He tilted his head back, looking at the sky for comfort. The stars and moon so blindingly bright that suddenly he knew exactly what he wanted. He opened the trunk and pulled out his telescope, assembled it on the deck of the home and lost himself in the stars.

He checked off the usual constellations, looking for something *more* and was so lost in his quest that he didn't notice Rebelle until her scent caught him.

"Hi," she said, softly. Not quite smiling but not *not* smiling either. Just seeing her brought him a happiness that was unrivalled. He ran his eyes over her, spotting the bags weighing her down and smiled when he realized she'd been shopping. He was glad she'd had a day with a friend and focused on herself for once, spent some of her money. She deserved to be spoiled, she deserved everything.

"Hey you," he replied, his voice deepening with lust. She glowed under the moonlight, an aura of happiness emanating from her. The tension that she carried in her shoulders had evaporated and the caution had fled from her eyes. "Nice day?"

Her eyes darted to the telescope. "Yes, thank you. How was everyone?"

He shrugged. "Just fine. Oscar's the big man of the kitchen now. I think he's got a thing for Betty but she's playing hard to get." He hoped the double meaning in his words would be clear. She either missed it or chose to ignore it, he suspected the latter.

"Doing some stargazing?"

"Yep, it helps to calm me when I'm feeling stressed."

She cocked her head. "It does? How so?"

He rubbed his thumb across his lip, considering. "I don't know really. It gives me something to focus on and distract myself. Something about it being bigger, vaster than anything here puts it all into perspective, I guess."

She nodded, looking about them, then pinned him with her dark stare. "What're you stressed about?"

He made a dismissive noise and waved his hand. "Nothing for you to worry about. Just business," he lied.

She pursed her lips ready to call him on his shit, he could tell. He needed to distract her and pointed at the telescope. "Want to see?"

Rebelle's expression changed and she nodded eagerly, dropping her bags and stepping closer to him. He moved back to give her access but there wasn't much room and soon she was stepping in front of him; the heat from her warming him in the cool autumn air. He bent down to her ear, her hair blowing across his face in the breeze, a silky strand lingering on his lip, teasing him.

"Just look through here." He tapped the eyepiece, and she leaned forward, her hand coming up to rest on the optical tube.

"Can you find the brightest star?" he whispered and watched as goosebumps spread across the length of her exposed neck and he fought every impulse to trace them with his tongue and press his lips to her neck. He tried to remind his libido that she didn't want to pursue any entanglements because of *reasons* but his body didn't get the message.

"The northern star? I think so," she interrupted his growing thoughts.

Take A Chance

"Actually that's not the brightest, it's Sirius. Also called the Dog Star, very fitting for us, don't you think?"

"I see it," she breathed. "It's stunning." *Tell me about it.*

"Which one is your favorite?" she asked, keeping her eye to the telescope.

"Cassiopeia," he replied instantly.

"Show me."

He loved the command in her voice. He moved the telescope so it faced north and took up place in front of her, trying to find it.

"She's hard to spot so far south but sometimes if you're lucky or you know what you're looking for you can see her." He stepped back. "Here."

Rebelle leaned to the eye piece again. "I can't see anything."

Will couldn't resist cupping her jaw and tilting her head up a fraction, trailing his fingers away softly and he watched the shiver move through her and bit back a moan. She was so sensitive to touch, so reactive. He didn't want to stop touching her so placed one palm on her narrow shoulder.

"This is the best time to see her, late fall. She kinda looks like a squished W. The star in the middle shines brighter than the sun and is much bigger. She's the queen of energy but is destined to explode one day. She shines bright but it'll be fleeting."

"She's beautiful."

"She is."

"Tell me more?"

He smiled to himself, loving her thirst for knowledge and finding someone who found stars as fascinating as him. "That one, Rho Cassiopeia, is also destined to explode as a Supernova which is essentially the biggest explosion that humans see. It's when a star has reached the end of its life, and it goes out in a burst of light. It's ten thousand light-years away which makes it one of the most distant stars."

Rebelle gasped softly. "I can't believe we're able to see it!"

"And Rho Cas is in the process of doing that. It recently expelled twenty times more material than is contained in our combined solar system."

"She's powerful." Awe dripped from Rebelle's tone.

"She is, but temperamental. Just like you," he whispered. Rebelle pulled away and looked up at him with wide eyes, so bright they reflected the stars right back at him.

"Will…" she warned.

He stepped closer, bringing them flush to each other, her soft body fitting to his and he fought a moan.

"Rebelle…"

"We can't," she said, firmly. It was that tone of voice that drove him wild. Before he could touch her, she moved back, breaking the spell. "Thank you for my astrology lesson."

He smiled. "Astronomy."

"And for today, I got you something." She rummaged in her bags.

His smile widened. "You got me something?"

"It's nothing really. I don't know why I thought you would like them. I mean, what do you buy a billionaire, right? And it's not like you would wear them, you probably have much more refined taste and-"

"I'll love them," he interrupted her rambling.

"It's okay if you don't like them. I can take them back or see if someone else would have them." She shook her head then held out a black box to him. He opened it and when he saw the gift, his stomach clenched sharply. It was a pair of black, silk suspenders decorated with constellations. He trailed his fingers over them, touched beyond belief at the thoughtfulness of her gift. He'd had plenty of gifts in his lifetime, expensive gifts, meaningless gifts, but he'd never had one more thoughtful than this.

"Hopefully these are okay. I mean I don't know much about suspenders but-"

He closed the box and pulled her into his arms, enveloping her tiny frame and she stiffened.

"What are you doing?" came her muffled voice.

"Hugging you," he growled, his fierceness for her overwhelming him.

"You're hugging me?"

He huffed a laugh at her statement. "Why yes, I am and honestly, you're taking it like a champ." They hugged in silence until she finally relaxed against him, giving in and that was precisely the moment he let go.

"I love them. They're the best gift I've ever had."

She ducked her head. "You're just saying that."

He gripped her chin and tilted her whiskey eyes to his. "No, Belle. I'm really not."

Her eyes dipped to his lips, like he'd seen before and he was willing her with every fiber of his being to kiss him.

"Great, good. I'm glad." She looked about her awkwardly. "Well, I'm gonna go to bed. I'll see you in the morning?"

"Of course," he replied. Fighting his disappointment, he watched as she moved about, clumsily reaching for her bags, enjoying that for once it was Rebelle who was flustered instead of him.

She looked back over her shoulder. "Well, goodnight."

"Night."

She fumbled unlocking the door to the home. "Night

then."

He fought a smirk. "Goodnight, Belle."

"Night," she said again and then shut the door. He stayed on the deck for a while, watching the stars and listening to the comforting sounds of her moving about inside the home and he felt calmer than he had in years.

Chapter 15

"I'm gonna head off." Will poked his head around the door and Rebelle's stomach did that weird fluttering thing it had been doing since the night he compared her to his favorite constellation. No one had ever compared her to anything before let alone something as beautiful and bright as the stars.

"Great, thanks for sorting out the meds," she replied, trying to keep the squeak out of her voice.

He snorted. "Next time, you're taking Oscar's temperature. He sat down on the thermometer and it disappeared."

She rolled her lips inwards to fight a smile.

"I had to go in and get it, Rebelle." He shuddered and his skin paled at the memory, his freckles coming into focus. "Anyway, the contractor has finished setting up and he'll start working on Monday. Are you excited to see your cattery dreams come to life?"

She nodded eagerly. "I can't wait to see it. Is it weird that I'm nervous?"

"Not at all." He cocked his head at her, watching her with aqua eyes and she busied herself tidying paperwork and avoiding his penetrating stare. "Are you sure I can't convince you to come tonight?" he asked softly.

She stalled. She could hear the underlying hope and question in his tone, *please come tonight?* She hadn't told him yet, she wanted it to be a surprise. That and she genuinely wasn't sure if she could actually make it through the doors to The Rusty Bucket Inn without hyperventilating. Justine had been messaging her all week checking in, sending breathing techniques and soothing mantras like she knew exactly how stressed Rebelle was about the crowd and noise that awaited her.

"I'm sure. I know you're going to do great though. You're a successful businessman; if you can't squeeze money out of these people by telling them about sad kittens and puppies then no one can."

He shrugged. "I know, but I wanted you by my side. Partners in crime." His stare lingered on her mouth. Heat sizzled in her veins at reminders of their encounter.

She cleared her throat. "*Business* partners in crime," she reiterated. Although she had to admit the line kept blurring. Some days when she was telling him what to do, she could swear he was enjoying it too much and then she enjoyed him enjoying it and now it was getting messy.

His expression shuttered. "Of course," he replied.

She turned away from the expression on his face before it bothered her too much and carried on filing invoices. "I'll see you in the morning then."

She couldn't face his disappointment, or she would

blurt out the truth: that she would see him in just a few short hours. "Have a good night. Can't wait to hear about it tomorrow."

Then he was gone.

She checked the time and her stomach clenched with anxiety when she realized there was only a couple of hours until the event. Her brain rejected the idea of socializing and crowds but she just needed to do one thing at a time to make it manageable. And the first thing was closing up the shelter and going home.

She checked Parfait had enough food and her kittens were all fine. At three weeks old they were moving around and squawking now. Parfait had taken such good care of them and by the time they were ready to be separated from their mom, the new cattery would be up and running.

Her throat thickened at the thought of saying goodbye to them. "This is why we don't name you, because we get attached," she grumbled as Parfait butted her head around Rebelle's hand.

"Right, the first step was coming home. Second step, shower. You can do this."

She lathered up, remembering to shave as multiple body parts would be on display this evening. The thought caused the sharp clenching in her stomach again and she tried to distract herself with some breathing techniques and ended up choking on water.

"Third step, clothes." She headed to her drawers and tugged them open and as she glanced down feeling a supreme sense of satisfaction at seeing her own clothes bundled inside. She dressed, not adding a bra as instructed by Justine so that by the time her dress was on, any strap marks would have disappeared.

"Fourth step, leave and go to Justine's." She

swallowed a few times, her throat drier than the Sahara. She grabbed her purse and keys, kissed Parfait goodbye and gave herself a pep talk during the drive to Justine's.

When she arrived; chaos greeted her. Taylor was walking around half-dressed. Christy had one eye made up and her hair in curlers. Justine was fully made up but sat in pajamas eating pizza.

"She's here!" Justine called around a mouthful of meat feast.

Taylor and Christy squealed, and Rebelle was sucked into the chaos. Pizza was shoved in her face, music was blaring and champagne was in front of her. She watched in awe as the women did their hair and make-up, amazed and envious of the ease with which they did it. The whole atmosphere was joyful, girly and feminine and Rebelle lapped it up, feeling like she was part of something, like she belonged somewhere. *Finally*.

"How do you want your hair?" Christy asked, clacking the heated tongs.

"Curl it, Rebelle. It'll look so cute!" Taylor piped up.

"Yes! It'll show off your jawline and earrings too," Justine added.

Rebelle tugged on her earlobe. "I don't have pierced ears." Each woman stopped what they were doing and slowly turned to her. The music dropped at that moment and there was a significant silence.

Taylor turned to the others with a glint in her eye that filled Rebelle with apprehension. "I'll do it, I did my own."

Christy's eyes also filled with that same glint. "À la *Grease*!"

Unease skittered through Rebelle. "What's a grease?"

Christy snorted in disbelief. "How have you not seen *Grease*?"

Rebelle's anxiety and stress bubbled over, causing her to word-vomit something she would have rather kept to herself. "Because my husband locked me in the house all day, every day, and never let me watch anything that wasn't sport or violence…"

Tension filled the room after her revelation, and she panicked that she'd made things so awkward. She was having a nice time and now she'd ruined it because she hadn't learned not to blurt out inappropriate things in polite company when she was stressed. She wondered if she should start grabbing her things.

"Fucking bastard!" Taylor spat, surprising Rebelle with her vehemence.

"If I could, I'd kill him all over again," Christy growled.

Was this what it felt like to have someone on your side? Someone who had your back? A family? Rebelle couldn't help it, she burst into tears.

"Oh, we're sorry!" The women swarmed her, group hugging her, and she didn't fight it, she welcomed it. Welcomed their friendship, their loyalty and love and they earned hers in return.

Justine clapped her hands, drawing their attention. "No crying, Cinderella needs to get ready for the ball. Christy, get her make-up ready. I'll do her hair and Taylor if she lets you near her ears then make it quick and painless. We're running out of time!"

Taylor turned towards her, a brow arched. Rebelle tugged her bare lobe and then looked at the gorgeous earrings each woman wore, and she wanted something beautiful and shiny too.

"You won't regret it," Taylor said, and Rebelle nodded.

Turns out she regretted it for about five seconds when

it stung then burned and then she was distracted by the sparkling gems that nestled into her ear lobe. She touched them, carefully so as not to anger her throbbing ear, awed at the decadence of the jewels.

The women got to work, curling her hair into bouncy waves that skimmed her jaw. Her eyes were smokey, her cheeks contoured and her lips slicked with a stunning red tone and a gloss at her cupids bow which drew her eye every time she looked at her reflection. Then she was in her red gown and strapping on the gold shoes, facing her friends who all looked stunning.

"We need a selfie! We look too good not to document it," Christy said.

Normally Rebelle hated having her picture taken but she wanted one of them, of this moment. They posed and Rebelle smiled wide, the flash blinding her briefly.

Justine drove them to the bar and Rebelle lost herself in the excited chatter, trying to forget the nerves churning in her stomach. She knew now that if she hadn't gone to Justine's to get ready, she never would have made it, her nerves wouldn't have allowed her. The nerves that hounded her now telling her she couldn't cope with the crowd, the loud, sudden noise of the bar, getting tongue-tied when talking to potential investors. But all of that paled in comparison to the nerves she felt at the thought of seeing Will.

They arrived and hurried her towards the bar but before they could drag her inside, she paused. "You go in. I just need a minute."

Christy squeezed her hand. Taylor kissed her cheek, murmuring, "You look fine as fuck. He's a fool if he doesn't trip over his tongue trying to get to you."

Justine lingered behind. "If you need me for anything then just come and get me. I'll give you a minute, but

Take A Chance

you've got this, honey. Trust me and yourself." Then she was gone in a flash of orange, disappearing into the bar.

Rebelle drew in deep breaths, working them through her tightening throat. Her knees were like Jell-o and her hands shook. She caught her reflection in the window and was startled at her appearance. Her brain immediately reacted and told her that she didn't look like herself.

"Or do you look exactly like who you're supposed to be?" she murmured, smoothing her hands down her dress. "Final step, walk inside that bar."

She took a deep breath, closed her eyes and released slowly. Thinking of her sister, counting out what's good, thinking about her candle, the rose bush, Bryan, Parfait, the shelter, Will, all the things that gave her joy. Until she had the strength to push open the door and waltz inside.

The noise enveloped her, but she was used to that now she'd done a few shifts at the bar. The warmth from the room welcomed her as she glanced around the spectacularly made-up bar. She barely recognized it. Fairy lights hung from the ceiling, reflecting against the wooden floor. The tables were pushed back, creating a large space in the middle where most people congregated. Large balloon stands dotted around the room with pearlescent balloons and more lights. There was a slideshow playing on a projector featuring images of the shelter and animals, a couple of her which she was dismayed to see.

She took in the guests, all dressed up in their finest outfits. She couldn't even conceive how expensive some of them were. Everyone looked like they bathed in money. She began to feel intimidated until she remembered why she was here.

And then she saw him.

Tall and fair, his strawberry blond hair combed back off his forehead. His eyes shining bright, his freckles standing out across his sharp cheekbones and hard intimidating jawline. He wore a navy velvet suit jacket with a black bowtie and black tailored pants but her pulse pounded when she spotted the constellation suspenders she had given him peeking out from under the jacket. His tattoos spilled out the collar of his shirt, giving him that edge that she now realized she was drawn to. He looked powerful, strong and daunting. As a man, he was overwhelming, but she knew underneath that exterior was a good, soft soul with a giant heart.

"Breathe," she murmured to herself. Smoothing her expression, she headed towards him.

*

Will's fake laugh was killing him. If he had to do it one more time he thought his jaw would explode into a bunch of crying laughing emojis.

He didn't like fake people, in fact he strongly disliked them, but he would fake it with the best of them if it meant getting money for Rebelle and the shelter. He'd ask about the Hamiltons' kids. He'd agree to summer in Barcelona with the painfully dull Rosbergs and he'd invest in the Richardsons' daughters start-up that sounded like it was destined for failure. He'd do whatever it took for Rebelle, for the animals and he'd do it all with a big, fat fake smile on his face and have another hearty laugh ready for someone's bullshit joke.

He sighed with mirth, tugging at the bowtie that was currently trying to choke him out, then smoothed a hand over the deep blue velvet jacket which was his personal favorite. "Good one, Phillip; where do you come up with these?"

The elderly Phillip tapped a thick finger against his

bulbous nose. "If I told you I'd have to kill you!"

Will guffawed, his head thrown back until Phillip believed he truly found him hilarious. The only way this would have been bearable was if Rebelle had been with him, then they could have kept each other going. He was determined not to miss her but was failing miserably.

He wiped a non-existent tear from his eye before firming his gaze. "Now that we're getting on so well, Phillip, let me tell you about the opportunity you have before you to really change the world," Will began.

Phillip was the richest man in the room, even more so than Will. The only reason he was here tonight was to try to collect Will's friendship. Phillip had Celebrity Worship Syndrome and Will was in his sights. He may be the richest and obsessed with celebrity, but he would also be the toughest nut to crack tonight and that didn't stop Will from having his shot.

He got ready to launch into his spiel but a delicate hand and a softly spoken, "William?" stopped him.

He looked down, his words halting in his throat and a tangled cough escaped. His breath abandoned him and he ran his hungry gaze over Rebelle. His shock at seeing her was quickly replaced by arousal and a need to drop to his knees before this goddess who had graced them all with her presence.

Her dark hair curled gently, framing her face and he'd give anything to touch the glossy ribbons. Her make-up highlighted her features without being overpowering and her eyes were so sensual he was getting warm just looking at them. Her beautiful red dress fit to her frame but billowed at the skirt making her look like a princess. He ran his eyes back over her, not able to take her all in in one go. He was stunned, blinded by her. She glowed and not just from the dazzling earrings that reflected the light off each facet. It was like she glowed from within, and his heart seized in his chest.

He wasn't the only one who noticed her. Multiple heads turned in her direction. Right about now he should be having some overprotective, macho thoughts about how she was *his* but oh no, the shoe was completely on the other foot. He was all hers. Hers for the taking. He would do anything this woman asked him. He was a mess for her, a simp, a stan, whatever you wanted to call it, that was him. She had him in the palm of her hand. Not that she even wanted him there.

"I think you've stunned him," Phillip guffawed, breaking the spell that had Will so ensnared in. He covered the small hand she'd placed on his arm with his own, his skin practically vibrating at her touch.

"You look…" he floundered. "There aren't words…"

"Try and find some!" Phillip joked and Will fought every instinct to tell Phillip to *fuck off*. His eyes swiveled to Phillip and his mouth opened, unsure what would come out, especially when he saw the appreciative looks that Phillip was giving Rebelle.

"She looks-"

"Incandescent," Will interrupted.

Rebelle's cheeks flushed prettily and she looked like a demure wallflower. But he knew the sharpness of her tongue and he wasn't fooled one bit. He pulled himself together, remembering it was the shelter that was important tonight.

"Phillip, I would like to introduce you to the owner of the amazing organization we're here for tonight, Rebelle Black."

Phillip puffed up his chest, his pride engaged and held out his hand to Rebelle. Will watched as Rebelle glanced down at it and saw her wage an internal war before she eventually slid her palm into Phillip's.

"Delighted to meet you, thank you so much for coming tonight," Rebelle said, politely.

Will couldn't tear his eyes from her as she and Phillip sank into conversation and she charmed the rich old fool, doing a better job than Will ever could of talking up the shelter. That was exactly why he had wanted her here tonight.

He couldn't believe she had turned up. No way could she have gotten this dress together last minute. He looked around and spotted Justine and Taylor huddled together, watching them closely and realization set in. He smiled and lifted his champagne glass in their direction. Taylor spun away like she'd been caught doing something she shouldn't have, but Justine smiled back and snuggled into Blake, whose scowl immediately softened at her touch. Will noticed Justine soothed Blake's sharp edges and glanced down at Rebelle and wondered if he did the same for her.

Phillip wanted to steal her away to introduce her to some of his friends and Will tightened his hold on her. Her eyes slid to his before she dipped her head, signaling she was fine, and he released her.

He watched her make her way around the room, each time she glanced over her shoulder and caught his eye, he would give her an encouraging smile and that seemed to relax her. His eyes trailed down her bare back, the elegant slope and the mouthwatering dips at the base of her spine that had him thinking some very *uncharitable* thoughts.

Blake appeared next to him. "Crawford."

"Blakey," he crooned, loving to get under the gruff deputy sheriff's skin. Blake swung his frown towards Will. "I thought we were friends but you don't look too friendly right now," he joked.

"I know. I apologize for that," Blake replied, clenching his jaw.

Will clicked his tongue. "Wow. I wasn't expecting that." He and Blake had been firm friends until Will set his sights on Rebelle, since then Blake had been slightly less friendly.

The deputy sheriff sighed. "It's come to my attention that I've been hard on you and overprotective of Rebelle."

"Did it come to your attention when your fiancée told you to back off?"

Blake's response was a clipped "Yes."

Will laughed. "It's cool, man. I know why you did it and I would have been the same."

Blake sipped his drink. "Justine tells me Rebelle's doing real good and I've noticed she's…thriving. I'm going to say that's down to you."

Will shrugged, not really knowing what to say to that but profoundly happy at the thought of having a positive impact on Rebelle's life.

"Don't fuck it up. I will murder you, slowly, and I'll get away with it too. I'll bury any evidence and all traces that I ever met you," Blake said, darkly.

Will gulped. "You still need my help with your campaign for sheriff?"

"Yep."

"Then you got it, sheriff." Will grinned at him and was shocked when Blake grinned back, his teeth white beneath his beard, and slapped him on the back before heading back to Justine.

Will finished his break from wooing the guests and jumped back to it, following Rebelle around and they tag-teamed a bunch of potential new investors, partners to the core.

She amazed him at the confidence she displayed talking about the shelter and the animals, her ambitions. He was falling for the charm the way everyone else was, ready and excited to go on this journey with her.

Once they had gotten around everyone, Will took to the stage, making a heartfelt speech about the shelter and what it meant to him. He was about to finish and declare the rest of the evening for dancing and drinking but he decided that the person everyone wanted to hear from should speak.

"Now for some final remarks before you can all enjoy yourself and we'll stop asking for money. Please welcome to the stage the owner of the Take A Chance animal shelter, who's been there from the very beginning, Rebelle Black!" The alarm in her eyes wasn't surprising but the willingness with which she approached the stage was. He handed her the mic and went to step down but she tugged on his hand and he saw her whiskey eyes fill with worry. He squeezed her fingers knowing she wanted him to stay but she needed to do this on her own.

"Erm, hi," she began shyly, shuffling her feet and looking at the ground before her shoulders lowered and her stare fixed on Will again.

"We, and the shelter, appreciate the time you've taken out of your very busy lives to be here and support Take A Chance." There was a pause while she found her words. "Will's not exaggerating, he's had a tremendous impact on the shelter, he's managed to charm all the animals, they'll be lost without him when he leaves," she began quietly. Her words hit him in the chest and that knot appeared again. He'd been trying to avoid thinking about when he would leave and go back to his life.

"I wouldn't be here, in this room, without Will." The look in her eyes when they flicked to him and lingered was full of gratitude and he could barely stand the weight of it. "And the animals wouldn't be here without any of you. So please support where you can, nothing is too small and if you can't afford it, donate your time. It costs nothing and means everything. Oh and, adopt, don't shop." She ended with a firm nod, her features schooled in the kind of expression that made him weak for her.

Applause and cheers echoed around before the lights dimmed and music filled the room. Shadows fell around him, and he watched as she stepped down from the stage and was immediately enveloped by the future trustees. Just as he'd suspected, they loved her. He observed her find her voice and speak, every now and then she threw him a concerned look, but she continued on. He felt so proud of her.

After a while, couples filled the makeshift dancefloor, and an opportunity reared its head. And after all, Will never ignored an opportunity.

He sidled over to her and waited until she finished with the gentleman in front of her before leaning down and brushing a dark curl to one side with his nose.

"You look like you're a good dancer," he murmured, his lips stroking the shell of her ear. He pulled back, watching her eyelashes flutter closed for a split second before her eyes burst open and locked on him suspiciously.

"Do I?"

He nodded, grinning down at her. "Yeah. You definitely look like you're wanting to dance."

Her arms crossed over her chest. "I don't think I am."

"Come on," he took her hand. "Put your sassy eyebrow down and dance with me."

"I don't have a sassy eyebrow!"

"Belle? Shut up and dance with me, please."

She paused and his *please* had her relenting just as he knew it would. He drew her over to the floor and she placed her hand on his shoulder. He slid his arm around her waist, his palm flattening on her bare back and he swallowed a moan at her warm satin skin. She sucked in a breath and he waited, wanting to see if she would pull away but she surprised him by settling against his chest. He rested his chin on the soft billow of her hair and closed his eyes, swaying them slowly and reveling in holding her tiny form in his arms.

After a moment he heard her sigh. "I'm not sure how you convinced me to do this."

He smiled, eyes still closed. "It's because I said *please*. You like it when I ask you nicely, don't you?" he dropped his voice suggestively. "When I beg you."

As he expected she didn't respond. He was definitely learning how to read her. She wasn't as complicated as he'd initially thought. Or maybe he just understood her better now. He dipped his head, resting his cheek to hers and inhaled deeply, satisfaction filling him at having her in his arms.

"Did you just sniff me?" she rasped, clearly as affected by their closeness as he was and trying to distract herself from the reality of it.

"You can't blame me, you smell amazing."

"Is that some dig about me not wearing perfume? Because until recently it wasn't exactly at the top of my grocery list. And I'm not trying to impress anyone so-"

He cut off her insecure, grumpy ramblings. "No, I wasn't. I think you genuinely smell amazing, like roses and wildflowers."

She cleared her throat. "Oh…"

He shook his head, smiling at her lack of response. They swayed slowly until the song faded away and when the next one started he expected them to part ways, but neither of them made a move to leave. At least two more songs went by, Will lost in the thought of all the places in the world he had traveled and all the places he could be, yet he wouldn't be anywhere but right here with her.

He felt someone appear next to them, then heard the icy tone that was so familiar.

"Will, darling, aren't you going to say hello to your mother?"

Chapter 16

Rebelle couldn't focus on anything except the sensation of Will's rough palm grazing her spine. The feeling was sending delicious tingles through her but instead of fear, she felt at ease. She melted into him, astonished at her lack of concern at their closeness, the contact between them and putting herself in a position of vulnerability. Will could easily hurt her. She knew this. But she knew *him*.

You thought you knew Marcus too...the dark thought slithered through her mind like the snake in the garden of Eden. It gave her pause before she reminded herself she had been young and naïve when she first met Marcus, she hadn't yet learned what she knew now. Will had shown more kindness to her, and the animals, than Marcus ever had. Being around all these people tonight gave her a new perspective on Will. She'd discovered what a powerhouse he was in the business world. Sure, she knew what was in his bank account, but now, seeing how respected and sought after he was, the partnerships he had created, she struggled to understand what on earth he was still doing here in Citrus Pines.

"Will, darling, aren't you going to say hello to your mother?"

Rebelle drew back at the interruption and turned, meeting blue eyes as icy as the voice had been. She took in the white blonde curls with not a hair out of place, the perfectly arched brow and smooth features. There was so much behind those blue eyes, so much history that belied the smooth features. A classic red dress with a white fur wrap sitting around her shoulders. She was a formidable woman and Rebelle could feel herself shrinking to two inches tall next to such an elegant, put together lady.

"Mom, what are you doing here?" Will's jaw clenched tight and his whole posture became rigid.

"Can't a mother visit her only son's charity event? I'm curious what you've been doing all these weeks," his mother replied, her cool stare flicking to Rebelle, giving her a dismissive once over, her mouth slipping into a tight smile. "Or should I say, *who* you're doing?"

"Stop. Right now," Will growled, his hands balling into giant fists. The air grew heavy with all the things unsaid between them and now Rebelle needed to leave, her anxiety rocketing by the second.

"It's fine, Will. I'm a big girl." She leveled a stare at his mom. "I'll leave you to speak, clearly someone has something to say."

She turned, heading towards the bar to get some water and seek out her friends. God she couldn't believe she had *friends*.

Take A Chance

"Excuse me, hi, is it Rebelle?"

Rebelle turned and saw a young woman with flowing chestnut waves and deep hazel eyes standing there. An eager smile graced her lips, and her hand cupped her rounded stomach. A man hovered slightly behind her, tall, dark-eyed, suited and booted and glued to his phone.

"I'm Ava and this is Kyle," she said, gesturing to the man who lifted his head long enough to give Rebelle a bored smile before returning to the device. Rebelle decided she didn't care for Kyle.

"Kyle is Will's stepbrother and I'm Kyle's fiancée."

She held out her hand and Rebelle shook it gently. "Pleased to meet you," Rebelle replied, peering over Ava's shoulder to see Will and his mom locked in a heated debate.

"I hope you'll forgive us for crashing your event, but I was eager to hear about the work you've been doing?" Rebelle instantly warmed to Ava's eagerness. She recognized part of her old self in Ava: she was a people-pleaser.

"What would you like to know?"

"Only everything!"

Rebelle smiled at her exuberance and launched into the spiel she had worked on this evening, explaining the background of the shelter and her plans for it moving forward.

"Sold!" Ava exclaimed.

Rebelle cocked her head to the side in confusion. "Sold?"

"I'll write a check or transfer some money. I've been looking for an investment for my trust fund and this sounds perfect. I want to do something good with my money, something meaningful."

"Babe, don't be stupid. Save your money, you won't

get your investment back, be smart about this. Better yet, let me invest it for you, I'll find you something that will actually return," Kyle piped up, sealing the spot Rebelle had been prepping for him in the *Asshole Hall of Fame*.

Ava's cheeks pinkened and her smile turned a little shaky and Rebelle hated seeing her discomfort and embarrassment at the hands of an arrogant man.

"It *is* a worthy cause," Rebelle growled at Kyle, staring him down. She could see the disdain in his eyes as she stood up to him.

Ava looked between them. "Uh, well maybe I could set up a monthly donation then? I'm a physical therapist so I am earning money too, I'm not just a trust fund baby," Ava assured her. Rebelle could see she didn't want to be tarred with the rich woman brush and wanted to do more, and her like for Ava grew.

"I'm sure you're a lot of things and I'd be very grateful for your support. There's plenty of time to think about how you'd like to do it. Maybe have a drink and mull it over and we can talk again, just the two of us," Rebelle said. Ava's megawatt smile dimmed slightly but she nodded emphatically before Kyle dragged her away. Kyle met Rebelle's stare as he walked past and the look in his eyes had Rebelle feeling icky.

Alone again, Rebelle glanced around, stuck at an event she hadn't wanted to come to, surrounded by people she wouldn't choose to spend her time with, except those she was already connected to.

Everyone was sticking their two cents in on how to run the shelter and she felt like she was drowning. She needed to put her foot down, to exercise control over all these strangers telling her how to run her shelter. It had been an overwhelming evening but suddenly she needed space to breathe and take back control. She headed into

Taylor's office for some peace, away from prying eyes.

She paced the room, practising some breathing exercises and sorting through her emotions and frazzled nerves but none of her techniques were taking the edge off.

She needed something more.

The door opened and Will entered, closing it and leaning against it, his head tilted back, eyes closed.

He sighed. "I'm sorry about that, I hope it didn't ruin your night."

The long column of his throat worked in a swallow and Rebelle felt her own throat drying. She had a feeling she knew what she needed to take the edge off.

"Let's go home," she said.

He looked at her. "You want me to take you home? Now?"

"Do they need us?"

"I guess not." He shrugged, tucking his thumbs into his suspenders. Suspenders she had bought him, and he had liked enough to wear. The reality of him wearing something she gave him for some inexplicable reason made her feel slightly savage.

"Then let's go."

Her chaotic thoughts quieted on the drive back. They pulled up outside the home and he followed her to the door. She unlocked it and went inside.

"Well, goodnight," Will said, then turned to leave.

Rebelle held the door open. "William, get in here."

His mismatched eyes widened before he swiped a hand over his mouth, concealing his grin.

"Yes, ma'am," he said, holding eye contact and anticipation sizzled in her veins at his acquiescence.

She spun on her heel and marched towards her bedroom and picked up the bed that held Parfait and her kittens and rehomed them in the living room. This time when she headed towards her bedroom, Will followed.

Rebelle stood at her dresser, lighting the rose candle that lit up the room in an enticing glow before she faced Will, her gaze running over him head to toe, taking in the way he pulled at the cufflinks of his shirt, the way his suspenders molded his shirt to his chest and abs that she had discreetly admired and secretly hungered for. The way his cold eyes burned so bright as they devoured her and his thick bottom lip pulled between his teeth.

She inhaled deeply, slowly. "Take off your clothes."

*

His pulse thudded at her words. His dick, which had been at half-mast as he'd watch her all night went to full.

He didn't pause. Didn't falter. Didn't question her when she had that firm glint in her eyes. He knew now it meant only good things for him.

His eager fingers worked at his bowtie, fumbling with his excitement until he whipped it off. He dropped his suit jacket, not bothering if it got crumpled and ruined, he couldn't wait for her to ruin *him*.

He shrugged out of the constellation suspenders she gifted him that he treasured more than any other item in his bulging, exclusive designer wardrobe. Pulling his shirt from the waist of his pants, he unbuttoned it and threw it to the floor. He paused, waiting for her reaction.

"*All* your clothes."

He fought a smirk. His dick twitched at the bored tone of her voice that belied so much. He unzipped his pants, removed his shoes and socks and hooked his thumb into the waistband of his boxers and tugged them down. He stood before her, completely naked and aroused.

Rebelle's eyes ran over him, burning every inch of his skin with her intensity. Taking in his tattoos, his muscles before they landed firmly on his heavy erection.

"What do you like?" she asked, caution entering her eyes and he wanted to chase it away. He didn't want her cautious with him *ever*.

"Anything you do. Nothing is off limits, you can do anything you want to me, and I'll love it, I swear," he rasped, trying to keep the desperation from his voice. Anticipation traveled along his skin, raising the hairs on his arm all the way up to the back of his neck.

She circled him like a lioness playing with her prey but he wasn't scared, he was excited and he fought a shiver that tried to roll through him.

Her fingers coasted over his shoulders and down his back, pressing into the dips at the base of his spine before coming around the front of him. She stared into his eyes and he sank into the whiskey depths, drowning in them. She pushed him and he fell backwards onto the bed and she tumbled on top of him. Fingers dancing over his chest, pressing into his pecs. She thumbed his nipples, drawing ragged breaths from him before tugging at the ring and he hummed low in his throat.

Rebelle explored his body, stroking over him, every sensation driving his need higher. She lifted his arm, stroking his sensitive armpit and tugging gently at the hair before working her way down, assuaging her curiosity with slow hands.

She continued her exploration, both hands trailing down the V of his hips, skimming over his throbbing dick that screamed for more attention and lifted his sac, testing the weight of him before going back and wrapping a hand around his shaft. She pumped him with an interest that had his chest heaving, breaths panting until she squeezed tightly and his breath disappeared altogether.

Sweat broke out on his brow and before he could piece his thoughts back together, she was shoving him, rolling him onto his stomach.

She tugged on his toes, pressed her fingers into the balls of his feet, pushed her palms into the muscles of his calves and ran her fingers through the hair on his thighs.

What she was doing wasn't innately sexual but he was harder than he'd ever been before and ready to blow over her inspection of his body. His spine tingled at her scrutiny, waiting to see if she found him worthy.

His hips pumped, working himself against the rough sheets and he began to see stars, his breaths getting deeper but she gripped his calves, squeezing in warning and he stopped at her denial.

She tickled the backs of his knees, ghosted her fingers up his thighs and the higher she went, the tenser he grew. He was panting like he'd ran a marathon when he hadn't done anything more than lay here and enjoy her touch and lay in anticipation of what she would do next, his body begging, *dying* for whatever she would give.

She massaged his thighs and pushed them apart before her hands rested on the cheeks of his ass. His breath held, praying she would give him what he was too scared to ask for. He'd given her free rein of his body and wanted her to take from him.

She traced a finger down the seam of his cheeks, his eyes squeezing closed and his groan breaking free from his lips. He was entirely at her mercy, her control and it threw him to the point of no return. The kind of intimacy, the kind of sex he'd wanted for so long.

He thrust again, his hips swinging out of urgency for relief, desperate for friction and she squeezed his backside. He grunted in satisfaction, fisting the sheets.

"Patience," she whispered. Then she ran the tip of her fingers down the split of his cheeks again before slipping between them and pressing against the tight ring of muscles and inside him. She twisted her finger, curling it and he was gone.

He cried out as he came, hard, jetting over her sheets, his entire body shaking endlessly at the intensity as pure pleasure glided through his veins. He struggled to get his breathing under control, his pulse hammering. He rested his damp head against his forearms, stunned as his body gradually relaxed.

She'd shattered him. Her scrutiny and curiosity had teased and taunted him, driven him past his peak and he'd never been more satisfied. Each encounter with her had been unlike anything he'd ever experienced and he felt safe at her mercy.

Far away he heard the rustle of her dress, felt her slight weight settle over him as she lay on his back and her head rested on his shoulder as she gently stroked his biceps and tears filled his eyes.

Will wasn't sure where the emotion came from, whether it was happiness or gratitude or affection. They didn't fall, just rested on his lower eyelids. He felt sleep pulling him under and he slowly drifted off, coming awake sometime later as she whispered:

"I'm ready for you to touch me now."

Chapter 17

Rebelle held her breath, waiting for his response. Was he asleep? His steady breathing suggested so but there was a change in the pattern when she'd spoken. Was everything okay? Had she gone too far with him?

She had revelled in her exploration of his body. Enjoyed discovering what halted his breath or made his pulse pound and had him rub himself for relief. She had never been allowed free rein like she had tonight. Had never wanted to until she'd met Will. Something had consumed her, a need to brand him with her touch and make him hers.

She had owned his flesh and sensations. She had owned his pleasure and spiked her own in the process. The trust he placed in her was a turn on like no other and she was finally ready to let him touch her, desperate for it even. She was ready to give him a part of herself, a part she hadn't truly, willingly given anyone before.

He stirred beneath her and she realized she was still splayed out on top of him. She rolled off and he turned to face her, his eyes at half-mast.

"You're ready?" he rasped.

She nodded and reached for him, pausing before she touched him, unsure. "I don't know what to do now."

"I can take it from here, beautiful," he murmured and moved towards her, pulling himself up so he towered over her.

She didn't find it intimidating, she found it exciting. He ran his hand through her hair, her curls snaking around his fingers and not letting him go. He cupped her jaw, his big palm encompassing her and she tilted her head, placing a kiss to the heel of his hand.

He pulled himself closer, nuzzling her cheek with his nose and her eyes slipped closed as his stubble scraped her skin. There was a pause that was long enough to have her eyes opening. He was just a breath away, waiting, with a desperation in his eyes as he looked at her mouth.

"Kiss me," he begged, just how she liked. He was showing her what to do but she was in charge. The butterflies in her stomach flapped wildly at the thought of kissing the mouth that she hadn't stopped thinking about for weeks. The butterflies tried to escape as she slowly closed the distance and pressed her lips against his.

He grunted at the contact and met her pressure, then increased his, pushing back, wrapping his arm around her waist and pulling her into his naked lap. He tilted his head so his wide lips would encompass hers. They were soft, pliant and she could definitely see how his mouth was award-winning. She held herself back, not sure how to feel about the sensations riding her. Heat pulsed at her core, so hot and sharp she could feel it building with intensity.

He pulled away, resting his forehead to hers and cupping her cheeks. "You gonna let me in?"

He could feel her hesitancy and instead of taking what he wanted, like others had, he was asking her. Putting the power back with her.

Empowered, she dove back in, pressing their lips together and this time she ran her tongue across the seam of his plump lips and he opened on a moan as her tongue invaded his mouth, seeking out his. They met and danced together, a rush of pleasure trickled down her spine, goosebumps bursting to life as his flavor exploded in her mouth.

It was a kiss that lit up her world, chasing away every shadow, like the rising sun chasing away the lingering darkness from the night sky. She was bared, vulnerable and there was nowhere to hide, she could only embrace it and give in. His thumbs stroked across the apple of her cheeks, spreading moisture and Rebelle realized she was crying. He pulled back, resting his forehead to hers, his lips swollen from her mouth.

"We'll stop. If it's too much, we can stop," he panted, and his concern and care shattered any lingering doubts that this was the man she wanted.

She dragged him back to her mouth, swallowing his concerns and chasing them away with her lips and tongue. He tugged her even closer and her hands rested against his pecs and kneaded the muscles there. Strength. Such strength that would have previously terrified her, now fascinated her. Maybe it was because he chose to display his strength in different ways than she had witnessed from Marcus.

Will kissed her cheeks and jaw, trailed down her neck,

leaving warm wet seals of desire as he went. She tangled her hands in his hair and held him to her throat. A ragged moan flew from her lips when he sucked hard.

"Make me feel good," she whispered.

He paused, then continued placing reverent, gentle kisses down her neck, to her collar bone and shoulder. He hooked his fingers into the strap of her dress and pulled it to the side, kissing every inch of skin he unveiled until her dress pooled at her waist. She held her breath, waiting to see his reaction to her small, unremarkable chest. He glanced up, his eyes locked onto hers and the desire and need shining from them astonished her. He placed his palm over her chest, resting on the skin over her heart.

"You're so beautiful and this is my favorite part of you," he murmured, and she wondered if he could feel the organ beating its way out of her chest, desperate to get to him. He dipped his head, pressing a kiss to the skin and her head tilted back. His lips traveled down the valley between her breasts, leaving a trail of tingles before he veered off.

"Although these have to be the prettiest things I've ever seen," his gravelly tone sent shivers racing through her. He captured one nipple, taking it into the warm, wet cavern of his mouth, sucking gently and a gasp slipped from her. His tongue flicked back and forth, wringing delicious sensations from her.

"More!" she demanded, holding his head closer. He moved to her other nipple, sucking it while rolling the damp one between his thumb and finger. Her hips shifted of their own accord, seeking him and she felt his hardness through the soft material of her dress. A deep rumble emanated from his throat when she came into contact with him and her nipple popped free from his mouth as he wrapped his arms around her and ground against her, slanting his mouth over hers, devouring her.

"More William. I need more," she whined. His hand tunneled under her skirts, finding her panties and rubbing his knuckle over the damp front as she bit back a curse.

"Is that what you needed, Belle?" he said against her lips, his pressure increasing to a point where she could only grunt in response.

"I can make it feel so good. Will you let me?" he asked.

She nodded and his hand shifted the material to the side and he slid a finger inside her. Her head tipped back on a moan and she tightened around him. He sighed, nibbling her exposed throat. "Goddamn, you're perfect." He added a second finger and she felt a slight burn that soon faded as he pumped them slowly before stroking his thumb over the heart of her.

"Harder," she huffed out and he immediately increased the pressure until she was almost mindless. She needed to touch him, delving between them and trailing her fingers down his chest before wrapping one hand around his hard cock and squeezing. She smiled at his shuddered breath and proceeded to work him until he was as mindless as she.

Then he was moving, shifting them towards the edge of the bed and she wrapped her legs around him as he stood up.

"What are you doing?" she mumbled inbetween kisses.

"Condom in pants," came his muffled reply. At least he was thinking sensibly, maybe he wasn't as mindless with pleasure as she was. Then he was sitting them back on the bed and tugging her underwear off.

She sighed. "I was wrong. It is attractive that you can pick up and put down heavy objects."

He laughed quietly, a throaty huff against her skin.

"You're not heavy, you're perfect." She heard a packet rip, then there was movement beneath her.

She was too eager for what came next and grew restless. He fixed her with a look, lids lowered. "Take over, I know you want to."

The fact that he *wanted* her to made it all the sweeter. She rose up on her knees, her nipples rubbing against his chest and his sharp intake of breath tickled her skin. She gripped his length. "You like it when I take control?" she whispered, their lips a breath apart. His tongue flicked out and swiped across her lower lip. "You want me to ride you while you lie back and take it like a good boy?" She sank down onto him slowly.

"Oh shit," he huffed, squeezing her hips tight. It took a few tries. He stretched her, that sweet burn making her pause until she was ready. She clenched around him, enjoying the feeling of him filling her, this strong man relinquishing power to her.

His breath stuttered out and she rocked her hips. She kept the pace slow, enjoying every sensation being dragged out, memorizing each detail of his face, twisted in exquisite agony and the fact that it was *her* who had put that look on his face.

He tried to increase the pace but she held firm. "I want you to feel every second of this. Every single sensation," she said, loving the strength she felt at being with him. His head dipped back, his eyes squeezed shut, his mouth open in ecstasy and her gaze devoured him.

Something changed.

Her chest cracked.

Her nerve endings flexed, hyperaware.

He brought his hand to her again, his fingers swirling fast, slick circles over her clit and her breathing increased, her hips moved faster and his head came forward, eyes clashing with hers. Emotion overwhelmed her and she tried to look away but he wouldn't let her.

"No, Belle. Right here, stay right here," he grunted, his eyes refusing to let her go.

It took her by surprise, a sudden explosion that rocked her entire body, seizing and she screamed as she was flung over the edge. Will cried out, burying his face in her neck, his teeth nipping at her skin as he shuddered with her, both of them quivering together.

The crack in her chest widened and split open and tears flooded her cheeks, worse than when she'd climaxed on her own. Her sobs wouldn't be contained and broke free.

"Rebelle?" Will's concern made it worse. He cupped her cheeks, brushing her hair back from her face and swiping his thumbs over her tears. She brushed his arms aside and clung to him, wrapping her arms and legs around him, scrabbling to get closer, she couldn't get close enough to him. Her fist gripped his hair as she sobbed into his neck.

"Don't let me go!" she gasped through her tears. She tried to climb him to get better purchase and he didn't fight her, just held on.

"Belle, I'm worried."

Like someone pulled the plug that held all her thoughts and feelings inside, it all spilled from her. The abuse, the violence, the cold, dark words, the rape, Marcus's cruel ways and eventual death and how she did nothing to help him. She told Will everything.

The whole time she didn't move, couldn't look at Will's face for fear of what she would see. He stroked her back throughout it all but didn't say anything.

By the time she had it all out, exhaustion was taking over and she didn't fight it, she would deal with the consequences of all this tomorrow. As she drifted to sleep, she wiped her face, thinking it was strange that her cheeks were damp when she no longer was crying.

*

Will swiped at his eyes, the tears finally slowing. He was shocked, horrified and enraged at what she had just revealed to him. His stomach turned at the awful things she had told him. At what she had suffered at the hands of the man who was supposed to love and protect her. At the hands of someone who resembled the devil.

Will was glad Sheriff Black was dead, only he thought that Marcus hadn't suffered nearly enough to satisfy Will.

He took a shuddering breath, trying not to jolt her too much. He still stroked her back, soothing her as she slept. Now he was soothing himself except it wasn't working.

His rage burned bright, his skin vibrating with it and the need to act. He needed to get this out, he could feel it bubbling up inside and soon he would erupt. He needed Beau.

Will slowly laid her down, not wanting to wake her and alert her to the level of instability he was feeling. After everything she'd been through, he didn't want to scare her.

He shifted her, gently rolling her to the side but was reluctant to let her go. She stirred, snuffling softly in her sleep and he pressed a kiss to her shoulder, then her cheek and pressed his forehead to her hot skin, his eyes squeezed closed, wondering how the hell someone could hurt this woman.

He eventually left her, heading into the bathroom to dispose of the condom and then out to his car to grab the spare gym clothes he kept in there. He dressed then let

Parfait into the bedroom as she paced outside the door, like she needed to check on Rebelle.

"Look after her, I'll be back soon," he whispered to the fussing calico.

He glanced at Rebelle again before he slipped out of the trailer and began jogging. He didn't trust himself to drive with the way his mind was whirring away. He jogged to the gym and up the porch that ran around the house attached to the side of the gym.

He banged on the door, feeling a momentary release at the aggression. He continued pounding until the light came on and the door was flung open, Beau glaring out with Taylor peeking over his shoulder. Beau's glare softened when he saw Will. "Everything good, man?"

Will couldn't shake his agitated state. "I need to train."

Disbelief crossed Beau's face. "Now?"

An emphatic shake of his head was all Will could muster. He caught Taylor's eye over Beau's shoulder and her face betrayed her. She knew. She knew exactly what was wrong.

"Beau, go. He needs you," she said, squeezing Beau's bicep. Beau looked between them then nodded. "Head around and I'll grab the gloves."

Beau let them into the gym and they strapped on their gloves in silence before they turned towards the punching bag.

"You wanna talk about it or just punch the shit out of stuff?"

"Punch the shit out of stuff," Will grunted.

"Guess that answers that. Right, let's go, don't fucking slack off because I'm not gonna go easy on you. Combo one on the bag!" Beau shouted, knowing exactly how to handle Will right now and Will couldn't express his gratitude except to hit each combo as hard as he fucking could. He proceeded to pound all his rage and frustration into the bag, completing combo after combo until sweat poured from him and his knuckles and wrists ached from the impact.

"Again!" Beau barked when they were done and proceeded to rattle through the next combo. With each hit to the bag Will remembered a different snippet of Rebelle's story. How Marcus had used her as an ash tray, marring her delicate skin. How he'd starved her. How he'd taken away everything she loved. How he'd used her body.

"Again!" Will shouted this time, adrenaline not slowing yet. When they finished on the bag, Beau grabbed the pads and strapped them to his hands.

Will hesitated. He didn't want to hurt his friend.

"Come on!" Beau bellowed and Will decided his friend could handle it after all and then rattled off another combo. "Jab, jab, uppercut, hook, left kick, right kick, duck!"

He attacked. Beau took each impact and pushed right back, and they continued their dance.

"Fuck, shit, shit, fuck!" Will screamed with frustration, throwing his rage into each punch until he was exhausted, depleted but the rage burned bright.

He sagged against Beau, there was a pause and then his friends' arm circled his back and patted it.

"Let it out, Will," Beau murmured and it was the permission Will needed. His tears burned hot, choking him.

"I know...know everything th-that he did to her," he stammered. Beau didn't reply just continued being his rock. "Everything."

It was a while before he quieted, the rage was gone and a helpless feeling took its place. "You'll do free self-defense classes, right? We can set it up and I'll fund it, whatever you need." Will pulled back, not bothering to dry his tears.

"Already do, my man. Right after what happened with Tay," Beau replied, a dark look crossing his face at the memory.

That useless feeling prodded at Will again. "God, of course you do."

"Look, you can't change what happened to her. Just be there for her, it's all you can do. You'll feel ineffectual but it's the only thing she needs you to do right now. She'll tell you if she needs something more."

Will knew Beau had some experience, he trusted his friend, trusted his words. He cleared his throat, using the hem of his shirt to wipe his face. "Thanks, for this," Will gestured around them. "And for being there, I appreciate it."

Beau shrugged. "No sweat, it's what friends are for."

They packed up the gear and closed the gym, the sun starting to rise, a deep chill in the air and Will realized it was mid-December and Christmas was on the way. He didn't have the familiar sense of dread over the holiday season as he usually did.

Beau paused on the front porch. "You need a ride back?"

"Nah it's fine. Give Taylor my love and apologies for the intrusion."

"Apology won't be enough, she'll want her pound of flesh for interrupting our snuggle time."

Will snorted. "I'll sleep with one eye open."

"Drinks this week?"

"Sounds good, see you then." He waited until Beau went inside before he headed back to the shelter. He checked on Rebelle who was still sound asleep and his heart panged as he took in the delicate features that belied the hardass personality she had. No wonder she had been so closed off, and so cautious of him.

Parfait was curled up next to her and gave Will a slow blink when she saw him. He ducked out and showered, rinsing the sweat off. The hot water burned his skin and the steam filled his lungs as he worked out the aches in his arm. He slid back into Rebelle's bed, pulling her into his arms. "I've got it from here, girl," he told a purring Parfait, and she blinked again before heading back to her kittens.

Will stroked Rebelle's silky hair, breathed in her sweet rose scent and a feeling of calm settled in him as he tumbled into sleep.

Chapter 18

When Will awoke later, he was alone in bed. The chill in the air had him drawing the comforter around him. He looked around, not seeing any hint of Rebelle. He had been looking forward to seeing if she enjoyed morning cuddles. Something told him she would like them, just resist it every step of the way.

His eagerness to find her and check she was okay after last night had him vaulting out of bed, tugging on his dress pants and shirt from yesterday. He pulled his shoes on and headed out to the shelter. He was halfway over when he spotted her by the rose bush. She seemed so captivated by the pure white flowers and he stopped to watch the way she gingerly touched the petals before she pruned them, flinching when she cut like she didn't want to hurt it.

"Morning beautiful!" he called.

Her wary eyes flicked to him then away again and she spun on her heel and headed back inside.

Will chuckled to himself, of course she would be difficult over the *morning after,* it was Rebelle. His brows dipped as he remembered everything she had told him the night before and he realized with chagrin that this morning would be tough for her.

He went after her, his long legs no match for her slight steps. He slipped an arm around her shoulder and turned her to face him. A pretty flush had spread through her cheeks and she nibbled her lip, looking at her sneakers which he noticed looked new, not the old tattered ones she had. Her purple knit sweater hugged her slight frame and just made him want to hug her more. He was pleased she was using the money she was earning to get herself the things she needed. He had been worried she would be too stubborn to spend it.

"Are you avoiding me?"

"Yes," she replied.

He laughed at her trademark honesty. "Why?"

"Because I'm trying to sort out my feelings. I don't have a lot of experience with this, and it doesn't help when you're everywhere I turn, looking so..."

He smirked. "So, what?"

She huffed at his teasing and he laughed again. "I understand. But just so you know, I don't have any experience with *this* either." He sighed, dropping his forehead to hers.

"With sex?"

He rolled his eyes playfully. "Is that all you think about, Belle?" She tried to shove him off but he pulled her back. "No, with this," he gestured between them. "With *more.*"

"Oh…" was all she said.

"But, I will say that last night was my number one of all time."

She shook her head. "Will, I-"

He interrupted her denials. "You rocked my world, Rebelle."

She snorted and shoved him away again.

"I'm serious." His grip circled her wrist and pulled her to him, her palms coming up against his chest and he turned her hand over placing a kiss to the center of her palm. Then another to the scar on her wrist that he now knew was a cigarette burn, working his way up until he was at her neck, inhaling her wildly seductive scent and flicking his tongue over her hammering pulse.

"Will," she sighed, leaning against him, her hands trailing down his back and resting on his ass possessively. A tremor of anticipation moved through him, he liked when she owned him.

His nose brushed over her cheek, his lips moved against her ear. "Round two?"

Her phone rang loudly, and he groaned. "I'm regretting getting you that."

Rebelle answered and moved away so Will went by each of the kennels, petting the dogs who had been watching them curiously. Then he went to inspect the work going on in the new cattery.

Rebelle appeared at his side. "That was the vet. They've got a dog who needs looking after for a while. It was quite cryptic so I'm not sure what we're dealing with."

"Want me to come with?"

She shook her head. "I'll go. I could do with some air."

He didn't push her, couldn't imagine the maelstrom of

emotions she would be dealing with. He followed her back into the main area and watched as she surveyed the full kennels.

"Need more space," she muttered, her frown in place.

He broached the subject he knew she was avoiding. "We need to start adoptions. The website should be done. I'll get a local photographer to come down and take some pictures of them all and get things moving." Her lips pulled into a mulish line, just like they did every time he mentioned adoptions. "You can't keep them all, Belle. They need homes," he said softly, stroking her arm.

"I know!" she snapped, pulling away.

"Then what's the issue?"

"No one is good enough for them," she growled.

His expression softened, he loved her love for them and how fiercely she cared. "What if I promise you an incredibly rigorous and thorough adoption process?"

"Maybe," she harrumphed, folding her arms across her chest and her grumpy frown stayed where it was.

"In the meantime, I know how we can free up one kennel," he singsonged.

She turned her gumdrop eyes on him. "Yeah?"

He went over to Bryan's kennel and opened it. The hound immediately went to Rebelle's side and her hand automatically buried in his fur.

"Yeah. You could stop pretending he isn't yours," Will said, his eyebrow cocked in challenge.

Rebelle glanced down at the canine before turning back to Will, a gorgeous half smile quirking her lips. The sight of it was enough to knock the wind out of his lungs and Will's brain screamed *mine* with such force, it startled him.

"No, I can't."

"Yes, you can. I know you don't want to love things

because you're scared, but how would you feel if someone adopted him?" The fire in her eyes was all the answer he needed to know he was right. "I'll get him settled at home and change the kennel ready for the new arrival while you go and get them."

"Fine," Rebelle conceded.

"See, sex isn't affecting this, look at that teamwork!" He beamed at her and she rolled her eyes but he could see the smile that she was struggling to contain.

"I now own a dog thanks to you, stop smiling at me," she grumbled.

"Why are you resisting it? Didn't you hear that it's-"

"Award-winning? Yeah, I heard. You're such a goof," she snorted as he eased closer to her. She tried to leave but he pulled her back and dropped a kiss on her unsmiling lips that tasted like raspberries. She opened wide for him and he slid his tongue inside, seeking out hers and rolling them together, his stomach clenching when they touched. Heat and something *more* stirred in his chest at the way she melted against him, like she surrendered.

Maybe it was the fact that he knew everything now, that she didn't like people and didn't trust anyone and yet here she was every day taking a chance on him. He was chosen. Him above anyone. He'd never felt more worthy.

Will pulled away before things started getting X-rated in front of the dogs and contractors. She gave a final nibble to his bottom lip which had him nearly dropping to his knees. Her dark eyes, cloudy with lust, had male satisfaction roaring through his veins.

She cleared her throat. "Right, well that's settled then. I'll be back shortly."

His perma-smile remained while he situated Bryan at the home. The old boy immediately inspected all of

Parfait's kittens and curled up at her feet while she held him down with a paw and washed him. Confident they would become one big happy family, Will returned to the shelter and began readying the kennel for the new arrival when a familiar scent had him pausing.

He turned toward the door and saw his mother standing there, looking around her with an unpleasant twist to her lips.

"Darling!" she called when she spotted him.

He greeted her with an uneasy smile. "Mom? What are you doing here?"

"Well, you did sound so very attached to the place when we spoke last night so I thought I'd come down and see what all the fuss was about," she said, stepping forward on her sky high heels and clutching her white, hopefully faux, fur coat around her. The dogs looked at her like she was Cruella de Vil and Will nearly laughed, he'd have to tell Rebelle that when she was back later.

Diane peered into each kennel, pausing longer at Chihuahua brothers, Bruiser and Beast and cooed at them before she reached Will and hugged him. The simple touch took him from client to son and he felt her relax against him before she set him away and refortified herself. His disappointment at her professionalism surprised him. He usually didn't mind her 'momager' persona but too often lately he'd yearned for the relationship he had with young woman he remembered from his early days. His mom, sans manager.

She hooked her arm through his. "Aren't you going to give me a tour?"

He obliged, leading her around the shelter and introducing her to all the animals, Betty and Veronica took a particular shine to her. Oscar chose that moment to noisily investigate his undercarriage. Will showed her the new cattery under construction and took her outside to show her the land.

"Rebelle's got it all planned out. Once the cattery is completed, we'll move onto the next phase."

His mother's cool stare landed on him. "This woman, Mrs. Black-"

"Rebelle," he interrupted firmly, feeling his temper already stretching and yawning to life.

"I did some research into her. She's completely broke, Will." Her mouth flattened. "How much money has she asked you for?"

He laughed. He could see exactly where this was going and couldn't believe that he hadn't picked up on it sooner. "Not a cent, Mother, not a single fucking cent." It gave him great pleasure to say that.

His mother cocked her head, the only physical sign of confusion as her dermatologist was clearly incredible at their job. "Are you not bankrolling all of this?" she gestured around them.

He rocked forward on his heels. "I sure am."

Diane tutted. "Will, darling. She's taking you for a ride, I thought you were smarter than this. You're clearly enraptured by her and I'm not really sure why, shabby chic isn't really your style and-"

His good mood only stretched so far, even with his mother. "I think that's enough visiting for one day, don't you?" He turned and began walking back to the shelter and could hear the shuffle of her heels in the dirt as she followed him.

"I don't mean to hurt your feelings, darling, but she's just another gold digger."

He laughed again, this time picturing Rebelle's horrified expression each time he tried to offer her money. She was the furthest thing from a gold digger that he'd ever seen.

He whirled on her. "Your *research* can't tell you everything. Belle hasn't wanted a single thing from me except to leave her the hell alone and I wouldn't even do that! She has worked on this place entirely on her own and-"

"Are you in love with her?" Her shrewd gaze cut right through his argument, and suddenly he was a kid again, and she'd caught him red-handed stealing candy. His mouth floundered and in lieu of answering, he hurried back to the shelter. Because he couldn't say he was, but his heart also couldn't deny it.

"Will, you're being blinded by emotion, and I'm concerned. You've never behaved this way before in business. Maybe you should sign over some of your assets before you make any rash decisions?"

His anger crackled. "You think I'm not in my right mind? Because I took some time off and found a passion project? I did my research too. Do you think I've lost my touch? I knew all about her and I knew exactly what I was getting into with this charity. Name a more worthy cause than helping those who can't help themselves. Go ahead, I'll wait!" he challenged.

Her shoulders dropped. "But I don't understand *why*? You've buried yourself here, hiding from your life and responsibilities. You need to come back to reality darling, I don't say that to be cruel, but it's time. Too many people are counting on you. You owe them and it's time to come home."

The weight of everything he was avoiding, that he'd put a mental block up against to protect himself came crashing down, suffocating him. The knot in his chest pulsed sharply.

"What you've built, what *we've* built, comes with

responsibilities that can't be ignored. No matter how great this charity is, or how distracting the widow who runs it can be. I'll give you a week to finalize things here. I'll keep the dogs at bay. But there's only so much I can do."

He scoffed. "Really? The miraculous Diane Crawford-Wyatt-Miller-Harkins?"

"That's right!" she snapped, her eyes flashing angrily. He'd clearly hit a nerve. "We've worked too hard together to let it all go to shit now, it's our legacy!"

He shook his head sadly. "What happened to you? What happened to the vibrant young woman in the trailer park?"

"She grew up and it's time you did the same, you're nearly forty!" she shouted back but he saw the flicker of hurt in her blue eyes before she spun on her designer heel and left shouting "One week!" over her shoulder.

Frustration, anxiety and anger had him knocking the dog bowls to the ground. The clattering echo caused several dogs to start howling.

"Sorry," he muttered to them. He tilted his head back, trying to draw breath through his shrinking throat. He felt the mythical blade hanging above his head, aiming for his neck. Everything he'd been avoiding, the weight of responsibility creeping up on him.

He didn't want it, he wanted to hide.

He wanted Rebelle.

*

The way his mouth fit to her throat and sucked.

The way he grunted in bliss.

How his rough, strong hand made magic between her thighs.

Take A Chance

The feeling when he tunneled- "Uh, Rebelle?" Dr. Park clicked his fingers in front of her face.

She gave herself a shake, dislodging all her inappropriate thoughts. "Yeah! Sorry, Dr. Park."

He smiled. "Call me Jae. Is everything okay?" he asked, pushing his wireframed glasses back up his nose.

"Yep! What were you saying about the dog?"

"Unfortunately, she'd been in the process of being starved and we believe she's been used as bait for dog fighting. She was seized a few nights ago and we've kept her for observation and given her food and fluids. Other than being hungry and very wary, she seems okay. The owner is being prosecuted so we'll need to house her until they're either convicted or," his mouth flattened into an unhappy line, "or released."

Rebelle's stomach clenched at the thought of what the poor dog had gone through. "How long could that take?"

Jae shrugged. "Couple of weeks, maybe a couple of months. We'll keep in touch though as unfortunately she's also considered evidence."

"What? That's awful!" Rebelle exclaimed.

He began cleaning his glasses. "I know but that's the law, I'm afraid. You can't put her up for adoption, we just need to house her and then once this is all sorted, she can be rehomed, hopefully."

Rebelle swallowed. "Was it someone in our town?"

Jae shook his head. "No, next town over. They brought her here hoping the owner wouldn't know to come looking this far if she were released."

Rebelle's stomach dropped at the thought. She didn't want to bring any trouble to the shelter or herself. But she also couldn't turn her back on an animal in need. As long as she was updated on the owner's movements, she would be prepared. She could update Blake and keep him in the loop too if she needed him. She had to remind herself that she'd chosen this path, and this was what the job entailed sometimes. It wasn't always hand-feeding kittens and cuddling puppies, sometimes it was harsh and cruel but she could be the bright light at the end of the tunnel.

"You think you can handle it? You have the room?" Jae interrupted her thoughts.

"Sure. Did you know we're expanding? Things are taking off and we're adding a cattery at the moment. It's very exciting." Rebelle felt her cheeks flush. She wasn't used to telling people about the success of the shelter, until now there hadn't been.

Jae smiled. It wasn't as nice as Will's smile but nice enough. She smirked as she thought of Will reminding her once again that it was an award-winning smile.

"I'll have to come by and check it out sometime," Jae said, pulling her back into the conversation.

"Yeah, that'd be great."

"Then maybe after you give me a tour, we could grab some dinner?" He looked at her from under his lashes, seeming sheepish.

Her slight smile faltered at his offer. His smile stayed in place, friendly, his eyes wide open and expression soft. She didn't feel the rush of anxiety that would normally accompany this kind of request, and relief spread through her at the realization. She was growing and controlling her fears and recognizing what situations were worthy of her fear and how to handle regular interactions.

Will's handsome face flashed through her mind. She hadn't sorted through her feelings about last night and what they'd done or how she felt about that. Except that she knew her physical release had allowed an emotional release too. She'd woken less tense than usual, like a weight had been lifted from her shoulders, her body languid from her night with Will. With him, it felt like she'd lost her virginity all over again. Except she'd been safe, warm, cared for and in control. And she had enjoyed it. Was eager to keep exploring with him.

She hadn't meant to tell him about her past and she had even included details she'd sworn to never reveal. He knew all about her shame and degradation at the hands of someone else. Her brain reminded her of how she koala'd herself around him and described every degrading thing done to her. He knew it all and this morning she had looked for signs that he regretted what happened between them. But he still wanted her today. *He came to you this morning, kissed you, wanted you and wanted more...*her thoughts whispered. It was true, he'd been eager to go again, and she'd felt his impressive hardness against her belly.

"Rebelle, I think I lost you again?" Jae said, a wry smile on his lips.

"Oh sorry. Um, I'm flattered but I think I'm seeing someone. You already met him," she added just in case he thought she was making excuses.

His face twisted in confusion. "Will Crawford? The billionaire?"

Indignation sizzled in Rebelle. "He's not *just* a billionaire," she snapped, sick of hearing that word constantly associated with Will like it was the sum total of his parts when in truth he was so much more than that.

Jae held up his hands in surrender. "Sorry, I didn't mean it like that. I'm a big fan of the show, he's a great guy."

"He's nothing like he is on the show," she said, not backing down. Determined to stick by her man. *Whoa, hold on,* your *man? No, no, no.*

"He seems great. Is he sticking around Citrus Pines

then?"

A fair question which she didn't have the answer for. If you'd asked her a month ago, she couldn't wait to get rid of him. But now she wasn't so sure. She knew that his time here had an expiration date, because he couldn't stay here, he was needed elsewhere. Where the lights shone brighter than the stars and he wasn't saddled with some grumpy widow who ran a struggling shelter.

"Where's the dog?" she asked, needing to distract her mind from all the uncomfortable thoughts and questions racing through it.

Jae clapped his hands together. "I'll go get her crate. She won't come out of it just yet. She'll take a while to heal emotionally I think, but that's why I fought to be able to give her to you. You're great at this kind of care," he added, and Rebelle's previous annoyance faded slightly at his words. She was amazed someone had that kind of faith in her ability.

"You should bring your truck around back, it's probably easier," Jae said then disappeared.

He loaded the covered crate into the bed of her truck and came around to Rebelle's side. "She's all set, let's keep in touch on her development and the case."

Rebelle nodded. "Sounds good."

He swiped his thumb across his jaw. "I'm sorry about before, I feel like an ass. I didn't mean to offend you and…" he trailed off, twining his fingers together. "I value our professional relationship, so I don't want to ruin it."

She focused on unfurling her eyebrows to appear less imposing. "It's fine Jae, all forgotten."

He smiled again, his smile was nice yet she felt nothing. No chills or shivers or goosebumps or even annoyance like she did with Will.

"Great, well just call if you need me." He waved goodbye and she drove back to the shelter.

Her pulse kicked when she spotted the sleek white sportscar parked next to Will's, like matching his-and-hers midlife crisis cars. Rebelle assumed it belonged to Will's mother who seemed less than thrilled to meet her last night.

She parked up, trepidation filling her as she headed towards the shelter, needing Will's muscles to get the crate from her truck. She paused when she heard raised voices, the sound triggering flashbacks for her. She leaned against the wall and closed her eyes, drawing in breath through her nose and pushing it out through her mouth. When her emotions steadied, she opened her eyes to find Will's mom standing in front of her, watching her curiously. The blue of her eyes reminding Rebelle of Will.

"You seem like a good person, so I'll say this nicely. He doesn't belong here. You're keeping him here in a little bubble but it's time for him to come home. He has people counting on him." Her eyes flicked over the shelter, a slight curl to her lip before they settled on Rebelle again. "He was not made for mediocrity," she added, the fierce momma bear vibrating in her tone.

A few months ago, Rebelle would have balked at the confrontation, but she wasn't the same woman she was then and part of that was due to Will. "Well, neither was I. He's a big man, he'll come home to mommy when he's good and ready. Has it ever occurred to you that there's too much on his shoulders?"

Will's mom blinked in surprise.

"I take it you're leaving, which is a shame but please think of Take A Chance the next time you're looking for a cause to support, a pet to adopt or, hell, if you just have some time to kill. It was lovely to meet you," Rebelle said.

261

Then on shaky legs, she moved around the formidable woman and into the shelter.

She found Will with his arms braced on the table, his chest expanding deeply with labored breaths, his back muscles flexing beneath his shirt. She took him in, surprised to see him so...wrecked. She had only ever seen him smiling, not like this, and it unnerved her.

"Everything okay?"

He jolted at her voice, shoving a hand through his hair, pulling at the strands. "Yeah, how was the vet?"

She gave him a run down, skipping the part where she got asked out and accidentally told someone that she and Will were dating.

He followed her out to the truck and together they hauled the crate inside and settled it in the free kennel. She wanted to look at the dog but she didn't want to disturb her. She kept the blanket draped over the crate, just opened the door so if the dog wanted to, she could come out and have a sniff around while she got used to the new surroundings.

The tension never left Will's jaw. It remained when the contractor wanted to run through the work they'd done that day. It was still there when he spent time grooming the cats, a calming activity she knew he secretly loved but it didn't seem to work its magic and restore his good spirits.

It wasn't right. Rebelle was the moody melancholy one, not him. It upset their whole dynamic if he wasn't the bright ball of happy he usually was and she didn't like seeing him like this. She hosed down the dog bowls and toys, trying to think of ways to cheer him up when one particular one came front and center.

He needed shifting out of this funk and she just needed him.

She poked her head around the kitchen door. "Will, can you help me a second?"

His brow furrowed, a rare sight on its own. "Sure."

"In the home," she said and turned, heading out of the shelter. He trailed behind her, following her dutifully, just how she liked.

Rebelle went into the bedroom and he stopped in front of her, looking around him.

"What did you need help with?"

She examined her nails, trying to appear unaffected by the pounding of her heart. "I want you naked, now." She injected a bored tone to her voice, but her excitement still lurked beneath the surface. She had a newfound confidence being with him; one that was still shaky and could crumble at any moment.

"I see. Is this a treat for me, or you?" he smirked and relief coursed through her at seeing that damn smile.

"Depends on if you're a good boy and do as I say." She watched his nimble fingers immediately begin unbuttoning his shirt.

"Leave those on," she said when he went to slide his suspenders off. He stood before her in his dress pants and suspenders snaking over his bare inked chest and shoulders. She moved around him, her fingers trailing lightly over his skin, inspecting him. She observed his full back tattoo; the night sky, filled with constellations and her finger traced over Cassiopeia, the design so stunning and intricate.

She nibbled her way across his back before coming to stop in front of him. Their eyes clashed, his alight with lust, his lightly freckled cheeks rosy and his lip puffy from being chewed on.

He towered over her, a formidable man but she'd never felt safer. She'd tried to ignore his allure, his siren song but he'd invaded her senses and made it impossible. Now he needed to pay for that.

"Kneel."

The room echoed with the force of his knees hitting the floor, his breath evacuating his lungs in an excited huff. His eager expression and rapt attention fixed on her, ready for the next direction.

"Look at you, so handsome on your knees for me. Hanging on every word." She cupped his cheek and stroked her nails through the scruff on his jaw. He pressed his lips into her palm, maintaining eye contact and her pulse fluttered at the intensity. Her brain took a mental picture of this moment and locked it away to be pulled out on lonely nights.

Rebelle dropped to her knees in front of him and rose up, pulling her jumper off and removing her bra before slowly pulling down one of his suspenders, then the other. She wound her arms around his neck, pressing them flush together, heated skin to skin. She trailed her thumb over his bottom lip and leaned in but hovered just out of reach, watching his eyelashes flutter closed.

"You feel that?" she whispered.

His eyes remained shut. He nodded and she heard his thick swallow and shaky breath. She ran her nails back and forth over the back of his neck.

"That heat between us that feels like it's going to erupt and engulf us in flames? The urgency to press our lips together and give into the explosion?" She rubbed her lips against his soft wide mouth, not sealing them together, just teasing him.

"The way we're locked together, embracing, with just a puff of air separating our lips in something that can only be defined as an exquisite ache before we give in." Her stomach clenched sharply at the intensity of the moment, the need screaming in her veins. She held onto the amazing feeling, stretching it out and basking in it.

"I've never felt it before. I just wanted to tell you that and take a moment to appreciate it," she murmured. She released one hand from around his neck and brushed over his crotch, not surprised to feel how hot and hard he was. She squeezed and his mouth parted, a tangled moan slipping out and she dived on it, sealing their lips together.

Passion exploded between them as they ate at each other, tongues dancing to a wild beat, teeth banging but neither of them slowed the pace, they couldn't. When they pulled apart, breathless and wide eyed, she commanded him to strip and lay down on the bed.

Once he was splayed out to her satisfaction, she looked him over, unsure where to start. She gazed at his body, eyes homing in on his thick cock that was already damp at the tip and she ran her tongue across her teeth.

She climbed onto the bed and straddled his thighs, eyes locked on his crotch. Marcus had forced her to perform oral so many times that she thought she would never enjoy it. However looking at the man beneath her, she was intrigued and excited to drive him wild. His hands skimmed her thighs, gripping her tight and he rolled his hips.

She arched a brow at him. "I didn't give you permission to move."

"Sorry," he stuttered out, not appearing sorry at all. A sheen of sweat coated his chest and abs, she licked her lips and he groaned. "Please," he croaked.

How she loved it when he begged. "You want my mouth?"

He nodded eagerly and she smiled at his reaction, not trying to hold back. His eyes widened, locked on her smile. "Beautiful."

She rewarded his sweet words by licking up his shaft, pressing her tongue into the vein that ran up the thick column. His hands fisted the sheets at his sides as oaths fell from his lips like precious falling stars in the night sky.

Her mouth enclosed his length and she sucked him in deep, swirling her tongue before dragging her mouth back up to the head and focusing there. Her hand palmed his sac, rolling and squeezing while her mouth worked him. He rolled his hips, unable to stop himself but she didn't admonish him.

"Belle…" he warned.

She pulled her mouth off him with a pop and shook her head. "Not until I say you can." She thought that might be pushing him too far but judging by the expression of tortured wonder on his face she had pushed just far enough.

Rebelle descended again, sucking, licking, squeezing and she felt him tense up, ready to release and she stopped. He huffed in frustration but she could see the delight that her denial gave him.

The third time he tensed up, she brought her hand in to work him and she hummed deep in her throat watching as his orgasm hit and his face twisted with pleasure.

His muscles locked up tight and he burst on her tongue and she swallowed him down over and over, releasing him with another wet pop before placing kisses on his thighs and stomach.

He lay in a boneless heap, sweat plastering his skin and glistening enticingly and his expression was one of pure ecstasy and relaxation.

Mission accomplished.

Will reached for her but she shook her head. Although

she was aroused, she didn't want to take. He'd needed comfort for whatever was bothering him and that's all she wanted to give.

She pulled him to her, his face resting between her bare breasts. He placed reverent kisses to the skin between them while she stroked his hair. After a while, his steady breathing told her he was asleep and her own eyes closed and she slipped off with a smile on her face.

Chapter 19

"Where are you going?" Will grabbed her ankle when she tried to leave the bed, not ready to burst their bubble. His gaze roamed over her, sleepily, hungrily. She was dressed in just his white shirt which came down to mid-thigh, her hair would be a tangle all around her head and she knew she had creases in her cheeks from the pillow.

"You look mouthwatering. My little grump looks extra grumpy this morning. Come 'ere." He tugged her ankle and she fell back onto the bed. He wrapped his arms around her torso, pulling her back against his chest and instead of fighting it, she nestled in.

"You had to come back to bed eventually, I would have just waited you out," he teased.

She huffed. "Good strategy, in the meantime who looks after all the animals?"

Take A Chance

"Your practicality is not my friend," he groaned, relaxing his arms and giving her the opportunity to extricate herself. But she decided to indulge in his affection a little longer. She used to hate being touched but she hadn't realized how much she missed it in all her time alone and she loved being touched by Will.

When she didn't untangle herself, he tightened his hold again. "The cattery will be finished next week, you know what that is, don't you?"

"Nope?"

"It's Christmas," he whispered, and she stiffened in his arms. "You're not a Christmas person?"

"Not exactly, no."

She heard the smile in his voice. "Thank God, me neither."

She turned in his arms, putting them face to face and she lay on him, watching him curiously. His eyes were closed, his lashes so light they looked like rays of the sun streaking across the sky. "How come?"

His brow pinched and she rested her chin on her hand, waiting for him to speak. His tongue swiped across his lips. "It's a time for family and it's never really been like that for me."

She reached up, smoothing away the frown that had worked its way onto his beautiful face and he leaned into her touch. She said nothing, just kept stroking his forehead. She couldn't get enough of touching him, exploring him.

"I used to love Christmas when I was a kid. I knew it was about family and without a dad around that made it just me and Mom. She would steal the lights from the front lawns of the houses in rich neighborhoods, obviously not legal but she figured they wouldn't miss them. She always said, because they put them outside they must not want them so we were doing them a favor." He chuckled at the memory and she watched the way his cheeks reached up towards his eyes before dropping again. The lines deepening around his mouth. Again she didn't say anything, just continued stroking his forehead.

"It was just the two of us. She would do what she could, sometimes there was no dinner and sometimes dinner was just vegetables and no meat. There were never presents but I didn't need any, I just needed her."

He didn't continue but she could feel there was more. She got the impression he was sharing something that he hadn't told anyone before and knew it would take him a moment to find the words.

"Then when I was away at college, I was too busy working to make it back for Christmas. I was so focused on earning enough money to send her that I ended up never being around. And then when I was older, we were both building this empire and it never occurred to us to stop and celebrate. We were in different states, different countries sometimes and whenever I realized it was Christmas, it was usually too late."

Having met his mother, Rebelle found it hard to picture her as this carefree, young woman with a child. The woman who built an empire, that she could easily see, and it made her sad for the version of his mom that Will had lost. "What about now that she's married? You have step siblings?"

He snorted, opening one eye and pinning her with his green stare. "You met Kyle, right?"

She nodded and his eye closed, his hold tightened around her. "Kyle's sister isn't much better, damn socialites."

"Ava seemed nice," Rebelle said.

"Yeah, she is. I don't know how she ended up stuck

with Kyle though. Anyway, that's the story. Christmas is a time for family but we've not been one for a long time."

"I'm sorry, I know what it's like to be let down by family," Rebelle spoke softly.

He took hold of her hand and patted his chest. She rested her cheek against it, swirling her fingers over the roses he'd inked into the skin while he stroked her hair. "Tell me about it?"

Rebelle rarely shared any part of herself, but she trusted Will. They had formed a connection that was unexpected but was beginning to mean a lot to her. If she would open herself up to anyone it would be him.

"My mom died when we were kids. My dad didn't cope, he was already a gambler and once mom died, he turned into a drunken gambler."

"We?"

"Me and my sister."

He paused his movements, fingers entwined in her hair. "You have a sister?"

"Yeah, a twin."

He scoffed. "There's two of you? Damn. Wait, is she as surly as you?"

She made a move to get up and he laughed, holding her tighter so she couldn't get away. "I'm kidding, I'm just shocked you have a twin sister. Where is she?"

Rebelle settled against him again, secretly pleased she had longer with him and that wonderful drag of his fingers through her hair. "I have no idea. She left when we were sixteen. I liked to tell myself that she would come back for me, but she never did. Never wrote or visited, I haven't seen her since. Then Marcus came to town, he'd been blackmailing my father and I think that's how he convinced my dad to let us marry: Marcus would clear the debts, and his payment was me." Will's grip tightened in her hair at her words. "It's okay, relax. I'm fine now, everything is fine."

He tsked. "It should be me soothing you, not the other way around."

"I like soothing you. Soothing you soothes me."

He pressed a kiss to her head and rolled them over, kissing her cheeks, her lips, her neck before burying his face in her chest.

She closed her eyes, sinking her fingers into his flesh, reminding herself that he was real. He wouldn't be here much longer, and she was beginning to worry what she would do without him. The errant thought broke her out of the bubble they were in, and she tapped his bicep, wriggling free.

"Anyway, depressing conversation over. Animals need feeding and I need a shower."

As she walked away, her arm slid through his grip. "Do you want me to join you? Help you get those hard-to-reach places?"

She turned back to him and shook her head at his waggling eyebrows. "There's only room for one in that shower."

"Challenge accepted!" he shouted and vaulted out of the bed, chasing her into the shower.

She giggled as he pulled his shirt over her head and he sealed their mouths together. Licking into her, their tongues colliding as tingles danced along her skin. He backed her into the tiny stall, knocking his head on the top of the shower.

"Fuck," he hissed.

She smothered another laugh. "I told you."

"That proves nothing, I have faith in us," he said, turning on the shower, water spraying over them both.

"Ever the optimist," she sighed.

"Indeed." He moved closer, and she gasped as the cool tiles pressed against her back. His gaze fixated on her hard nipples and he slid his thumbs over them.

"So beautiful," he murmured, dipping his head and swiping his tongue over one, then the other. His strong arms circled her waist and pulled her into him. His hard cock pressed into her as his hands slid over her hips and palmed her ass, squeezing tightly as he pushed against her.

She reached between them, gripping him and his breath stuttered, just like she knew it would. Water trickled over his shoulders and ran in rivulets down his stomach which contracted with each labored breath as she worked him, her grip slick and fast.

"This was meant to be about you," he moaned as he thrust into her grip.

"Watching you unravel *is* about me," she said, biting his lip. "It's me doing this to you, it's me touching you, driving you wild."

He grunted and she slid to her knees. "Hands on the tiles," she commanded.

The slap of his flesh hitting the wet tiles echoed around the small, enclosed space.

"Do not move them, William, or I stop."

His head bobbed excitedly in agreement. She leaned forward and licked the tip of his cock and his head dipped back. She sucked him down, bringing her hand up to stroke his base as she focused her efforts on the tip. Harsh, unintelligible sounds spilled from his mouth as he slowly pumped his hips.

She pulled back and watched as his wide chest heaved, his arms tensed as they pushed against the tiles, doing as he was told.

"Do you like it when I tell you what to do?"

"Yes," he groaned.

"No one else has ever made you feel this good have they?"

"Christ, no."

"No one ever will." She said it as a statement, unsure where the need to express her desire was coming from.

"No," he replied, and she didn't realize how much she needed to hear that until he said the word. She went back for another taste, wrapping her lips around him again, her tongue flicking over the head as she squeezed the base and then she felt his hand in her hair. She pulled back immediately.

"William," she warned.

"Sorry, I just needed to touch you. Please, I'm so close," he panted.

"Do you want me to finish?"

"Yes!"

"Then you'll accept a punishment?"

"Yes fine, anything."

She smiled to herself, enjoying playing with his desire and expressing her own sexuality with him. She had never imagined she could be this assertive. She didn't know where the words came from or the confidence she had to express herself, only that he brought it out in her. He had created an environment of trust where she felt cared for, cherished and secure knowing he enjoyed and wanted her to exercise this level of control. That he got off on it.

"Good boy," she said and went back to driving him wild. His palm slapped against the tiles and she watched his whole body tense and water pummeled his skin as his shout echoed around them. She swallowed down his ecstasy as it flooded her mouth and his hips slowed their thrusting. She got to her feet and he gripped her tight, his body still going through little aftershocks, and pressed a

Take A Chance

kiss to her lips.

"Are you real?" he said against her mouth.

"I am. Are you?" she replied.

He nodded and his hand slipped over her thighs. It nearly broke her but she moved out of reach just before he touched exactly where she needed him. He looked at her quizzically.

"I told you there would be a punishment," she said.

His brows winged up. "Surely this is a punishment for you?"

"I guess we'll see. Now excuse me, I need to wash."

She moved under the water, the drops coasted down over her skin and she had the satisfaction of seeing that heat come back into his cool eyes as they tracked each droplet down her body. Then she grabbed the shower gel that smelled exactly like him and poured some into her hand. She proceeded to wash herself, slowly, paying extra care to her breasts and ass.

"Need some help?" he rasped.

She shook her head. "Nope, I got it." She knew the moment he spotted the wicked gleam in her eyes and he realized she knew how to torture him. She rinsed her hands before caressing her stomach and thighs, then dipped her fingers between her legs. Her head dropped back on a moan as she stroked over her clit.

"Rebelle," he growled.

She moaned and closed her eyes as she worked herself, dipping her hand to slide two fingers inside herself, pumping once, twice before circling back over her clit.

"Do you promise to behave and do as I say next time, William?"

"Yes. At least look at me when you come." A command and a plea rolled together and one she was only too happy to oblige.

He stepped closer, putting them chest to chest but he didn't stop her, or try to help. He just wanted to be near her and the idea spurred her on, pushing her arousal higher.

Her climax slammed into her and although she wanted to look away, the intensity in his stare held her firm. She saw everything in his eyes, his desire, his affection and something she didn't want to put a label on because it was too much, too scary to consider.

She sagged against him, surprised to find him halfway aroused again already. She was too boneless to move.

"Next time it's me who makes you moan like that," he grumbled.

"Only if you behave," she replied, and he made the noncommittal grunting sound he was so fond of. Then he proceeded to wash her hair, gently lathering and tilting her head back into the spray.

She turned off the water, contemplating the fact that they'd gone into the shower full of joy and silliness and she was leaving it feeling something much larger and intense.

Will went back into the bedroom and she took a moment to collect herself. She wrapped a towel around herself and wiped the condensation from the mirror. She came face to face with her reflection and was surprised to see the joy in her eyes. The plumpness of her cheeks now she was eating more, and dare she say, happy?

The fact that she knew it was *The Crawford Effect* bugged her. He wouldn't be around forever, he would leave too. She was getting used to him, relying on him and she didn't want to need him. She didn't need anyone.

Rebelle went back into the bedroom to find Will sitting on the bed with a towel wrapped around his waist and looking at his phone, his expression troubled.

Take A Chance

"Everything okay?"

His forehead smoothed. "Never better," he replied, tossing his phone aside and pulling her to him. His palms gripped the back of her thighs before trailing up and cupping her ass. He nipped at her neck before giving her butt a little squeeze which she felt right in her core. She was about to pull away, needing to set some boundaries between them but he must have read her mind.

"No time for any funny business, no matter how much you want it," he teased, winking at her. "We've got animals to feed."

*

"I know what we can do for Christmas!" Rebelle bounced in front of him, distracting him from thinking about yesterday morning when he had come to the realization that he wasn't ready to leave. He'd sat on her bed, listening to her putter around in the tiny bathroom, after the most erotic shower of his life, and knew he couldn't leave yet. He'd whipped out his phone and opened up his chat with his mom.

Will: Let's negotiate…
Momager: I'm listening.
Will: One more month.
Momager: Paha! You're joking? I told you, one week.
Will: Three weeks.
Momager: Back by Christmas and you do the GQ photoshoot…without complaining.
Will: New Year's Day, the GQ shoot with mild complaining and I'll throw in a sit down with that production company that keeps bugging us about the making the Will Crawford lifetime movie.
Momager: Deal.

He'd smirked to himself. Not his best negotiation but he'd got what he wanted which was more time. His win and her agreement had him softening towards his mother.

Will: Thank you.

Momager: Does this mean I don't see you for Christmas?

It was the first time she had mentioned it in years but maybe she was getting pressure from husband number four to have a family holiday.

Will: I don't think so. There's lots to do here if I need to be gone in two weeks.

Momager: I know you don't believe it but I only want what's best for you.

Will knew that she meant it, in her own way. She separated herself from him in order to drive their success but she didn't know how to come back to him.

Will: I know, love you Mom.

Momager: Love you too xx

Then Rebelle had appeared in front of him, still wet from their shower and all delicious looking in a towel and his thoughts had scattered.

"Earth to Will!" Present Rebelle clicked her fingers in front of his face, her sassy eyebrow raised.

He shot her a lascivious smile. "Sorry, I was just thinking about my punishment yesterday." He trailed his eyes over her body and had the satisfaction of watching her cheeks flush.

"William! Not in public," she hissed.

"Why not?"

She looked about them, checking no one was listening. "I don't want people to know."

He drew back. "Ouch?"

She rolled her eyes. "I don't want them thinking you're helping me out with the shelter because we're having sex."

"You guys are having sex?" Beau boomed, coming up behind Will and clapping him on the back in greeting. Rebelle squeaked in dismay and Will laughed at her awkwardness.

"I hate to break it to you, beautiful, but he already figured it out." Will nodded in Beau's direction.

"A beer please, Rebelle, then I'll keep your *secret*," Beau winked at her and she pulled a bottle from the fridge under the bar and flicked the top off.

"Did you have something you wanted to tell me?" Will asked, taking them back to their previous conversation.

"Just be at the shelter Christmas morning," Rebelle grumbled.

He planned on being there the night before and waking up with her. Not that he told her so, he could sense her pushing him away. He understood her reasons for doing so but it only made him want to cling on to her tighter. He winked at her and then headed off to a booth with Beau to catch up.

"I'm glad, man. I mean, I know you guys were messing around but I'm happy for you. You seem more at ease lately, barring the other night. Kinda seems like you've found your Taylor." Beau beamed at him across the booth and Will choked on his expensive scotch. "Come on, don't deny it. I've never seen you this gone over a woman before," Beau added while Will composed himself.

He glanced back at Rebelle, her short dark hair gleaming in the soft lights, looking silky smooth and practically begging for him to run his hand through it. She was huddled closely with Taylor, whispering fiercely and looking cute as hell in her red turtleneck sweater and blue jeans.

He couldn't deny it, there was something about her that was so different to other women he'd met and not just sexually. She didn't treat him like a billionaire, hell, he knew that she would prefer it if he didn't have money. She wasn't impressed by wealth, status or looks. It was actions and intentions with her, that was how she measured someone.

She soothed him, didn't have any expectations of him, didn't care about him being a celebrity. She treated him like an equal, a partner, her counterpart. She amazed and fascinated him, and he felt just like her roses, like she was the sun and his head turned in her direction whenever she appeared.

Two weeks.

He longed to keep peeling her layers back and seeing what more lay under the surface with her but he was running out of time.

He swallowed. "Is it that obvious?"

Beau snorted. "Yes. But there ain't nothing wrong with that. She's a good woman and you deserve that. And from what I know of her, she deserves you too. You're well matched, you just seem to fit."

Will didn't disagree.

"So, what are you gonna do?" Beau asked.

Will turned back to him, taking a sip of his scotch. "About?"

"You live in L.A. You have a life and a career over there. Are you just gonna give it all up?"

If only. Will recoiled. "I can't give it up."

Beau shrugged, peeling at the sticker on his beer bottle. "Why not?"

"Because people need me. The show needs me, the businesses need me and the charities."

Beau gestured to Rebelle with his bottle. "And what

about her? She needs you."

Will snorted. "If there's one thing I know about her, she doesn't need anyone."

"If you say so. But you're forgetting about someone else: me. I need you. Blake, Dean, Christy, Taylor, Justine. We all need you, it's been perfect having you here."

Anxiety rose in Will's chest and he struggled to breathe around it. Even though he knew that Beau and the others needed him in a different way, it was just more pressure piling on him.

"But what about you, what do you need?" Beau added quietly, like he could see how much this whole thing was stressing Will out.

Will looked around, imagining what it would be like to give it all up. The slice of happiness he'd carved out for himself after decades of feeling incomplete. Happiness he'd taken at the expense of everyone else. He could feel it all slipping through his fingers, feel *her* slipping through his fingers.

Two weeks...

"Hey fellas, sorry to interrupt but just wanted to say hi." The vet from the clinic appeared at the end of their booth. Beau extended his hand in introduction and the vet shook it, then Will's despite having already met him.

"I'm Jae, I know we've met but not properly."

"Nice to meet you, Jae. I'm Beau and I'm guessing you know this big lug?" Beau nodded at Will.

Jae nodded and proceeded to ask Will about the Pitbull that Rebelle had named Daisy. Will couldn't believe it when she offered up a name for the dog, knowing how she had resisted previously in her attempt to remain detached from the animals. Her tough shell was showing some cracks lately, and he hoped he'd had something to do with it.

"Yeah Daisy's getting there. She doesn't come out much, but you can tell she's getting more curious."

"That's great, I knew Rebelle would be perfect for helping her. Speaking of Rebelle, I just wanted to apologize for the other day. I didn't realize you two were a couple." Jae rubbed the back of his neck sheepishly.

Will's scotch paused halfway to his lips. "What?"

"With Rebelle. I asked her out, but she mentioned you were seeing each other."

Beau faced Will, a shit-eating grin spread across his mouth. "Oh she did, did she? Well, ain't that nice?"

Jae began to look nervous. "I didn't realize, I didn't mean any disrespect."

Possessiveness clenched Will's gut tight and a fierceness swooped over him. "We are. No apology necessary, excuse me gentlemen," he said, getting up from the booth.

He heard Beau sigh and say, "You'd better keep me company, Jae. This could be a while."

Will headed over to Rebelle, cocky swagger in every step. When she spotted him approaching, her eyes widened and she darted away from Taylor, flapping her hands at the redhead.

When she took in his expression her face morphed into a matching frown. "Everything okay?"

"I need to see you outside. Now."

He took her hand and pulled her out from behind the bar. There were catcalls, likely from Taylor, following them as they headed down the hallway and out the back door of the bar. He pulled her around the side of the building, the chill in the air not doing anything to cool the lust swimming in his veins like hot lava.

He caged her in against the wall. "The vet. Explain."

Defiance had her eyebrows setting firm. "What about

Jae?"

"He hit on you?"

"Yes. Is that a crime?"

"It should be." He softened his expression as he remembered the vital part of what Jae had said. "You told him we were seeing each other."

She faltered. "I-it slipped out, I didn't mean it that way."

"So he knows then?"

She threw up her arms, exasperated. "Knows what?"

"That you're mine." For a split-second lust was reflected back at him from her whiskey eyes, before it disappeared.

She folded her arms over her chest. "Excuse me?"

"You heard me. You can deny it all you want but you know it's true."

"Is this really about Jae?"

"Fuck the vet," he said, then buried his face in her neck, laving his tongue over her skin. "And fuck me," he purred, his lips to the shell of her ear.

She gripped his shoulders to remain upright. "You want me to fuck you, William?"

He shuddered when she used his full name. "You know I do." He gripped her chin, tilting her head back to look him in the eye as he slammed their lips together. Pleasure flooded him as she met him with her own fierceness, just as he expected. Just as he *needed*.

They nipped and sucked, teeth scraping flesh as they devoured each other. He kept leading the movements, making her adapt to him and he knew, hoped, it would rile her up.

Rebelle pulled back, glaring at him with wild eyes and swollen lips. "You're not in charge here."

He watched her, chest heaving with the effort to draw

breath after she robbed him of it, his pulse pounding erratically. He saw that gleam enter her eyes and knew he was going to be punished; he couldn't wait for his treat.

"Who's in charge?"

"You are," he replied.

"Who's in charge?" she repeated.

"Rebelle."

"Don't forget that." She pressed down on his shoulders and a smile split his lips as he realized what she wanted, what she was finally letting him do. He fell to his knees, stroking up her denim clad calves, to her thighs.

"I want your mouth on me," she demanded. His fingers trembled with anticipation as he worked her button and zipper, tugging the denim down to her ankles. He stared at her panties-covered center and buried his face between her thighs, spearing her with his tongue, using the fabric to abrade her. She gasped and he swallowed a moan at the sound.

"You're going to be so good at this, aren't you?" she stuttered out, her hand gripping his shoulder to steady herself, fingers curling into his skin. He nodded emphatically and tugged her underwear down, lifting one leg from her jeans and draping it over his shoulder. His hand skated over her soft skin, kneading the muscle in her calves, then her thighs before clasping her ass cheek and pulling her towards his mouth. Her hand in his hair, tugging firmly stopped him.

"What's wrong?"

"I've never done this before." There was a slight tremble in her voice that sucker punched him.

"Then I'll make it perfect, I promise," he vowed. Then leant forward and licked from her opening to her clit. She hissed and her grip tightened in his hair, tugging. The light pain driving his need higher, he loved seeing how she responded when they were together.

He feasted on her, licking and sucking at her clit, closing his lips around her and moaning, sending vibrations scattering over her sensitive nerves. She rolled her hips into his mouth, chasing each swipe of his tongue. She tasted sweet and a little spicy, just like her personality and he was addicted to her flavor.

He pushed two fingers into her and pumped as he sucked and a garbled noise left her throat. He flicked his tongue back and forth, torturing her swollen bud, before adding a third finger and curling them, teasing that rough spot inside her that had her eyes flying open, her mouth widening as she clamped down around his fingers and screamed.

He eased off, letting her ride out her climax and come down slowly. He got to his feet, his wet fingers tracing soft circles around her. "Thank you for my treat," he whispered against her mouth.

"You're welcome," she laughed, the sound husky.

He pressed a soft kiss to her mouth. "You're so beautiful when you laugh."

She sighed and sank into him for a brief moment before her hands were fumbling at his pants and she was gripping him, guiding him towards her. He barely had time to roll on the condom that he'd been storing for just such an occasion when she was hitching her legs around his waist and sinking down on him, so warm and wet and welcoming that he thought it would be all over far too soon.

She used the wall of the bar as leverage and true to her word; she fucked him. Pushing herself up and down, pumping her hips and bouncing on his dick. His head tilted back in bliss and he let her work him. His release started slow then barreled towards him and when he came, he could have sworn he saw shooting stars. His orgasm was teased from him, slow and intense and knee tremblingly good.

They didn't speak as Will helped her redress. Something big had just happened between them but neither of them addressed it, instead they walked back into the bar with small knowing smiles. Will disappeared into the bathroom to dispose of the condom then slid back into his booth with Beau.

He shot Rebelle a wink as she wiped down the bar demurely, like she hadn't just been outside riding him like a bull. Like she hadn't just rocked his entire world.

He downed his scotch, enjoying the burn in his throat and met Beau's smug grin.

Beau tipped his bottle to his lips. "You stake your claim?"

"Of course."

Beau chuckled, shaking his head.

"But only because she *let* me," Will clarified.

Beau whistled low. "Shit. It's like that, is it? No wonder you're glowing brighter than the north star."

"Actually, that's not the brightest star," Will contradicted.

"Glow-ing," Beau reiterated, smirking.

"Fuck you," Will replied, without any heat.

"No, seriously. It's super cute."

Will flipped him off and when the chuckles subsided, Beau fixed him with a serious look. "I'm happy for you."

Will clinked his empty glass against Beau's bottle. "Thanks, man."

Chapter 20

Rebelle fought with the final tangle of the lights, her pulse pounding as she heard Will stirring in the bedroom. Bryan and Parfait both angled their heads in critique of her efforts which she had to admit was not her finest work.

She heard a thud and the rattle of the door handle and decided she had done the best she could and quickly flicked the switch. The room lit up with three hundred multicolored lights, just in time for Will to emerge, looking rumpled, sleepy and fucking perfect.

He ran a hand over his jaw, and she stood there for a moment, dumbfounded by his beauty, waiting for him to notice what she'd done, her soaring pulse and breath bated.

He yawned. "Mornin'. Why didn't you wake me, I

slept-"

"Merry Christmas!" she rushed out, unable to hold back the glee any longer. He looked up and his eyes widened when he spotted her and the lights.

"Wha-" he began and trailed off as he came further into the room, looking around him at the lights. She noticed his sweatpants and matching sweatshirt and damn he looked good. She'd only ever seen him in his formal wear, or naked. He looked amazing in his formal wear but now he looked casual, relaxed and very, very huggable, not that she was the hugging type or anything.

Will tapped a couple of the lights before stopping in front of her.

"Thank you," he said, his voice was heavy with emotion. He cupped her jaw, brushing her hair back behind her ear and he kissed her lips, then each of her closed eyelids and nose before tugging her into his warm, crushing embrace. She used to fear his strength but now she reveled in it, feeling safe and secure and like there was nowhere she would rather be. She snuggled in, burying her nose in his sweatshirt and inhaling his mouthwatering scent.

"This is perfect. Thank you," he said again. She pulled him over to the couch and pushed him down, handing him a mug of warm cocoa with mini marshmallows that had melted into a congealed tasty rainbow on top. Parfait immediately leapt onto his lap and Rebelle curled herself into his side, despite the glare from Parfait. Bryan tried to join in, attempting to get onto the couch and clearly believing he was much smaller than he was. He settled for half-on, half-off with his head in Rebelle's lap.

They watched the lights twinkling, like a little family, Will playing with her hair, and she released a deep sigh of contentment, her eyes sliding closed.

I could stay here all day... That thought had her eyes springing open and she checked the time on her phone.

"You got somewhere else to be?" Will teased.

"There's something else I wanted to show you," she hedged, taking his empty mug from him and reaching across to wipe a bit of marshmallow from his top lip. His tongue poked out and licked her finger. "You've been spending too much time with Bryan," she scolded, wiping her finger as he laughed.

"I have something for you too." He moved a disgruntled Parfait and grabbed his car keys from the counter, disappearing outside. He came back moments later, bringing a slight winter chill along with a black box wrapped in a black satin bow.

"This is for you." He placed the box on her lap and sat beside her.

"You didn't need to get me anything," she grumbled, feeling awkward about accepting gifts.

He rolled his eyes. "Don't be a Scrooge."

She pursed her lips but gave in, untying the bow and pulling the lid off the box. She gasped spotting the beautiful black rose inside.

"Oh my God, where did you get this?" she breathed, gently removing it and staring at it with awe. She brought it to her nose and inhaled the sweet scent deeply. Pinching the petals between her thumb and forefinger she marveled at the crushed velvet feel of them. The color left her speechless: as dark as a starless sky and stunning with its delicately furled petals.

"It's dark, but soft and exquisite. Melancholy in its beauty. It's breathtaking. Just like you," he spoke softly.

Her heart twisted in her chest and tears sprang to her eyes at his words. This was how he saw her? No one had ever given her something so beautiful and thoughtful or used those words to describe her.

"I've never seen anything like it," she whispered, unable to take her eyes off it.

"This color isn't natural in the wild. You have to have them dyed to get this level of black. I wanted one just for you, something special. I see how much you love the white ones outside, but this felt like it was more you."

"You shouldn't have. But I can't deny how magnificent it is," she whispered, like any sound would disturb the flower in her hands. She stroked the petals lovingly, hardly able to tear her gaze away.

"I didn't realize you'd be quite so enamored, I'll get you hundreds of them."

She shook her head, the spell broken. "No way, I don't need a hundred. This one is perfect, more than perfect." She put the rose on the dressing table in her room and came back to the living room. "Thank you."

For the first time ever he looked sheepish, his cheeks flushing and he shoved his hands into the pockets of his sweats, looking at the ground. "It was nothing."

"No, it wasn't," she insisted, going up on tiptoes to kiss him. "Come on, we're not finished yet." She took his hand and led him out of the home and across to the shelter. He let her lead him, let her take charge and Bryan trotted dutifully behind them.

"What else have you got planned? You didn't need to get me anything else, what you did inside was amazing. Best Christmas ever," he enthused.

She swung the door to the shelter open. "Well, it's not just for you. It's for me too but most importantly, it's for all of them." She gestured towards the dogs.

"What do you mean?" he asked, but she went into the new office and reappeared, dragging two large boxes with her. They were overloaded with packages and some were in Christmas gift wrap.

"What is all this?" Will took the boxes from her and she allowed herself a moment to admire him picking up and putting down heavy objects again.

"So I was doing some social media research as to what other shelters do. Apparently you can set up wish lists connected to the website and share them. So I did. For cats and dogs, including toys, treats, food, blankets; and it turns out that people are very generous at Christmas."

Will stared at her, his mouth open in what she hoped was amazement.

"Isn't it cool?" she prompted when he said nothing.

"Cool? Fuck yeah, it's cool but you…I'm so proud of you. I can't believe I didn't think of it!" he exclaimed.

She arched a brow at him. "I'm surprised you didn't either Mr. Bigshot Billionaire Businessman. I'm a little disappointed in you. Here I was thinking you would bring all the expertise to this partnership, and I'm the one doing all the work." She left out the part where she was doing research in preparation for him leaving so she could manage on her own.

He threw back his head, his laugh booming around the shelter, startling the dogs. When his laughter subsided he just stared at her with a big grin and she started to feel itchy at the expression on his face. Like he knew she couldn't take much more, he tugged her into his arms and dropped a kiss on her lips.

"You're amazing," he whispered against her mouth and for a moment, a fraction of a second, she let herself believe him. "I mean it. You've battled and survived, grown and flourished and become this amazingly beautiful butterfly. The world needs more butterflies."

His thumbs stroked her cheeks and her throat worked but no sound came out. His words stunned her and she didn't know what to say. The whines and whistles of excitement from the canines peering over the tops of their kennels distracted her.

She swallowed, pulling herself away.

"Come on, let's not keep them waiting."

Will opened each kennel, letting the dogs all come out and play together and there was furious sniffing of each other's butts and wagging of tails in joy. They left Daisy in her pen as she was still very shy. Rebelle handed out toys, feeling like Santa Claus as each one was snatched away by an excited pooch. She took out her phone, beginning to film it all.

"What are you doing?" Will asked as he was engulfed by dogs wanting attention.

"We've got to show the people what their donations meant to the animals, the joy they brought these little guys," she replied.

"I'm torn between wanting to keep this moment private for us and you putting all the joy on social media," he grumbled.

"I won't put it *all* on social media. I'll hold back some bits just for us," she promised and that seemed to placate him.

The toys were handed out, gift wrap was shredded and cardboard boxes chewed with furious excitement. The shelter was filled with wagging tails and the sound of squeaking toys.

Bruiser and Beast fought over a bone, each of them with their jaw clamped around one end playing tug of war until Will introduced a second bone and they calmed, sitting their little butts side by side as they chewed.

Sasha enjoyed a meat-filled Jumbone, nibbling in bliss with her eyes closed. Doug The Pug was tearing into the gift wrap and thrashing his head happily.

Take A Chance

In all the frantic excitement Rebelle thought she spotted Daisy poke her head out of the crate so she took a break from the carnage to step into her kennel and have some downtime with her. When Daisy spotted Rebelle had treats, her little gray tail started thumping gently and she looked at Rebelle with wide, hopeful eyes.

Rebelle fed her one treat at a time, speaking to her in soothing tones and stroking her softly while she ate. After a while she realized Will was leaning on the plexiglass front watching them and Daisy wasn't at all worried by his presence.

Rebelle shook her head at him. "She's so gentle, I don't know how anyone could have done such horrible things to her."

"It's okay, Belle. She's safe now, she has you and hopefully soon she'll have a wonderful new family to give her the life she deserves." He watched for a few more minutes before he went back to the chaos the dogs were causing although the noise was dwindling like they were worn out. Rebelle spent some more time with Daisy before she left her in peace, not wanting to over-stimulate her.

"The dogs are all either sleeping off their treats or exhausted from playing with new toys," Will said with a smile once she joined him again and together they shut them all back in their kennels.

"Cats next," Rebelle said, and Will practically ran into the new cattery. She laughed at the eager cat dad ready to play with them.

Parfait's kittens played with the gift wrap, ignoring the catnip mice and scented fish that wiggled enticingly which the other cats gravitated towards. Betty and Veronica got high from their mice, which were dribbled on so much that the blue color of them had turned to a greeny gray.

Will trailed string along the ground for the kittens and they all pounced on it before climbing his leg and squeaking for attention. Rebelle dished out the gourmet mousses and wet food and before long the cats were all collapsed in fat happy heaps on their blankets, washing luxuriously after their feasts.

"This is the most fun I've ever had at Christmas," Will said, putting away some kittens who had fallen asleep on him. "Definitely a new tradition."

Rebelle tried not to think about the fact that traditions were repeated and surely Will wasn't sticking around or moving to Citrus Pines. She looked at her phone again, conscious of the time.

"Okay, seriously do you need to be somewhere?" he asked.

"Yes," she replied.

She watched as disappointment settled over his features. "Oh, sure. I didn't mean to keep you."

She tried not to smile. "We've *both* got somewhere we need to be. Come on."

*

Rebelle insisted on driving them, Will offered to let her drive his Bugatti but she declined. She liked her beat up old Ford truck. She'd had confirmation from the *Rebelle's Angels* chat that everything was set up and ready to go.

"So, you gonna tell me what we're doing?" Will slid his gaze to her but she couldn't look at him. Not when he was dressed in jeans and the Christmas sweater she'd bought him that featured a reindeer straddling a candy cane and read Pole Dancer. She found him incredibly attractive today in his relaxed state and if he dared whip out the award-winning smile, she was liable to pull over and have him in some very compromising positions. She almost laughed at her thoughts. A few months ago, if someone had told her this would be what was floating through her mind, she would have accused them of having too many of Taylor's cocktails.

"You'll see in a minute," she all but growled. She was stressed that things wouldn't go according to plan, or she had gone too far or too emotional with this.

He frowned and fidgeted next to her, not happy with not knowing what was going on, but she was in charge now and she bit back a smile at his need to know. "Shame they didn't teach you to have some patience at that fancy-ass business school," she drawled.

"I'm just keen to get home and crawl back into bed and give you my *other* Christmas present."

Heat spiraled through her at the promise in his tone. His hand reached across and settled on her thigh, squeezing gently. She swallowed but refused to look at him, determined to get them to their destination with no detours for hanky-panky.

His palm slid higher and squeezed again and her breath hitched. His smug chuckle filled the cabin of the truck, and her brows dipped.

"There's my favorite scowl," he purred, which only caused the scowl to deepen. He inched his hand higher, dipping between her legs and the turn off for The Rusty Bucket Inn thankfully came into view.

"We're here!" she cried, her voice strangled. Although she was relieved, she was slightly disappointed. She was uncomfortable accepting gifts but something told her she would have welcomed the one he wanted to give her.

He glanced through the windshield. "The Bucket?"

She didn't answer, just parked up in the lot next to

Dean's truck.

"Rebelle?"

"Let's go," she said, getting out of the truck and he followed her.

"I don't think they're going to be open today, Belle," he said, shaking his head.

"They are for a private function," she teased, smiling up at him.

He cupped her chin and brushed his thumb across her lip. "I love it when you smile, it makes me lose my breath," he murmured. She struggled to swallow, looking into his eyes, so warm and inviting.

She took his hand. "Come on." She pushed open the door and immediately started to salivate over the mouthwatering aromas that filled the room. The bar glittered with more twinkly lights, as per Rebelle's instructions, reflecting off the tinsel that decorated the space. A rather haphazardly decorated Christmas tree sparkled in the corner and mistletoe dangled throughout the room. A couple of the tables had been pushed together to make one long banquet table. And what a banquet it would be, the table was piled high with delicious-looking food and Rebelle's stomach started growling dramatically.

"Finally!" Beau cheered when he spotted her and Will.

"What are you guys doing here?" Will asked, his smile wide at seeing all his friends gathered together.

"We wanted to give you a special Christmas or some crap like that." Blake waved his hand dismissively, but Rebelle saw the amused sparkle in his gray eyes.

"It was Rebelle's idea," Christy added from her position on Dean's lap. Rebelle's cheeks heated with awareness as seven pairs of eyes landed on her.

"It's our family Christmas," Taylor said, hugging Will's

Take A Chance

side and crushing Rebelle against her too.

Will looked around. "Guys, this is..." he trailed off.

"We're awesome, we know," Dean joked, and Christy playfully slapped his arm.

"We wanted to do this. We're all so close and it just made sense to do it together," Justine added, stroking her now very pronounced belly.

Rebelle watched Will as his eyes swept around the room before landing on hers. An emotion she couldn't place flicked across his face briefly before he pulled her to him and kissed her deeply, pouring everything into the kiss. There were cheers and catcalls before Blake spoke up. "Alright you two, this is a family event."

"Ooh, Daddy Blake stepping in to reprimand."

"Only one woman in this room calls me Daddy," Blake grunted, and Dean spat his drink out.

All eyes swerved from Rebelle to Justine who just shrugged with a small smirk on her face.

"Gross...did you bring the dessert?" Taylor asked.

Rebelle cringed before handing the box over. "I'm not very good at this whole baking thing."

Taylor patted her hand. "I'm sure they'll be fine."

"You baked?" Will whispered in her ear.

"We all had to bring something and I picked dessert. I Googled how to make cookies."

His nose wrinkled. "That explains the smell this morning."

She frowned at him but before she could retort, Christy was bouncing in front of her. "You need to put this on." The blonde held up a pale pink sweater that read *Jingle Bells* and had little gold bells stitched onto the shoulders. Rebelle took it from her, her fingers sinking into the soft material.

"When you told us that you'd gotten Will a Christmas

sweater, which is perfection I might add, we all decided to wear them, and we picked this out for you."

Rebelle looked around and spotted everyone wearing Christmas sweaters. Taylor's cream sweater bragged about being *On The Naughty List*. Christy's black sweater said *Gold, Frankincense and Merlot* while Justine's green sweater had a red bow stitched around her bump and read *Best Present Ever*. The guys had also stepped up with Dean's navy sweater saying he would *Sleigh-All-Day* and he clicked his fingers sassily. Beau's red sweater boasted that he was *Sexy and I Snow It* and Blake's plain black sweater just said *This Is My Christmas Sweater* in basic font, which made Rebelle laugh.

She met Christy's eyes and held the sweater tight to her chest. "Thank you," she whispered, her eyes misty for the second time that day. Why were the holidays so emotional?

She ducked into Taylors office to change and the whole time she held back happy tears listening to all the playful bickering going on in the main bar. She was here with her friends, who had now become her family. Six months ago, she would never have envisaged this moment. Hell, three months ago, when she bumped into Will for the first time, right here at the bar, she never would have thought she'd be here.

When she left the office everyone was sat around the table, the guys talking about basketball and motorbikes. Will caught her eye and winked, patting the seat next to him. She listened to them go on and loved that they just had regular conversation. No one was asking Will what it was like in Hollywood or what celebrities were secretly assholes. No one was hitting him up for money or asking for selfies and autographs. Will was relaxed, the tension from his shoulders gone and she was pleased.

"You luuuurve him," Taylor teased next to her.

Rebelle's head whipped around and her eyes narrowed. "I *so* do not!" she hissed.

"Do too!"

"Leave her alone, you would have skinned us alive if we'd said that to you about Beau a few months ago," Justine said.

"I know, but I needed a push to admit it, which is what I'm trying to do for Rebs."

Rebelle held her breath when Will's arm rested on the back of her chair and he began absently stroking the back of her neck, twirling the ends of her hair. When she realized he wasn't paying attention to them she turned back to Taylor. "Nothing needs pushing and he's leaving soon anyway."

"He'd better not be, he belongs in this town," Justine griped.

"Justine's right. Also that would make Beau sad and that's not okay with me." Taylor leaned back in her seat, trying to see past Rebelle and get Will's attention.

"Don't!" Rebelle whisper-yelled. "Please don't say anything."

Taylor must have seen the desperation on her face as she sat back in her seat. She pouted though. "Fine. But for what it's worth, I think he feels the same way about you."

The subject was dropped and Dean distracted Rebelle by asking about the shelter while they all chowed down. Eventually it was time for dessert and anxiety gurgled in her stomach, threatening to expel all the amazing food she'd just eaten. She served the cookies to everyone along with a scoop of ice cream and watched as they all dug in.

There was silence as everyone tried the cookies.

"Erm, Rebelle?"

"Yeah, Beau?"

"What did you make these from?"

Her brow furrowed. "Just a recipe from the internet. Why?"

Beau held a cookie up in the air then brought it down on the edge of the table with a hard *whack* that echoed around the bar. He raised his hand and the cookie was still completely intact. Rebelle's hands flew to her face in mortification. There was a hard silence before everyone burst out laughing.

"Oh my God!" she wailed, horrified.

Will pulled her into a hug. "Let's cross cookie making off your list of talents," he joked. Everyone laughed again and as she looked around their faces, she found the corners of her mouth lifting up and she burst out laughing too.

"I'm so sorry!" she wheezed between breaths.

"It's fine darlin'. We still got ice cream," Dean piped up.

"Mmm, it's delicious!" Blake winked at her, always having her back. "Did you make it?"

"No."

"Oh…" There was another pause before the laughter resumed.

When they finished their ice cream, a very untraditional Christmas dessert but it was all they had, Christy raised her glass in a toast.

"Merry Christmas and Feliz Navidad all! It's been amazing and can't wait to do it again next year and every year after that!" There was emphatic agreement and she continued, "To new traditions!" Everyone repeated the sentiment and clinked their glasses, and when she and Will clinked theirs, he squeezed her thigh meaningfully. "To new traditions," he said softly, his eyes burning into hers.

She didn't know how to respond. She didn't know how he could say that knowing he would likely be leaving soon and going back to his normal life. Would he come back next year? Would he come back *ever*?

She couldn't bring herself to agree, just smiled at him. He turned back to the guys and her thoughts whirred away until she heard a gasp and Justine bolted up from her chair.

"Did you spill your drink?" Rebelle asked, taking in the wet patch on her orange skirt.

Justine raised wide eyes and looked at Blake. "No, I didn't."

There was a pause, then Blake leapt to his feet. "Oh, shit!" He gripped Justine's hand. "Are you okay? You feeling okay? Are you in any pain?"

Justine released a shaky laugh. "I'm fine but ask me again in a few hours."

"Oh my God!" Christy and Taylor shouted in unison.

"Your water broke?" Dean asked.

"I think it did, yeah. Taylor, sorry about the chair."

Taylor waved her hand. "Don't worry about that."

Blake took her hand and steered her away from the table. "Sorry to cut this short everyone but we need to go." He looked about him, patting his body.

"I've got the keys, but we need to go home and get the hospital bag," Justine said, clinging to his arm.

"I've had one packed and ready in the car for months, we're good to go," he replied.

Justine paused her waddling and promptly burst into tears. "That. That right there is why I love you," she wailed.

"Do you want any of us to come with you?" Beau asked.

"No, we're goo- ah!" Justine yelped.

"Okay, we gotta go," Blake said, leading her to the door. Justine blew kisses over her shoulder as she went. "I'll get Blake to keep you all updated," she called and then they were gone.

"A Christmas baby, cute! I hope they give him or her a Christmas related name," Christy gushed.

Dean snorted. "You remember the bet, right? It's Blake's pick so it's definitely going to be motorbike based."

They stayed for a couple more drinks then set about cleaning up and rearranging the tables before all going their separate ways.

Later that night, Rebelle lay naked on top of Will, her head resting on his damp chest as his fingers twirled down her spine, both of them catching their breaths as they came down from world-shattering orgasms.

"Thank you for my favorite Christmas ever," he rasped against her hair, his fingers tracing patterns over her back. The thought drifted through her mind again that she could stay like this forever and fear gripped her, cutting off her oxygen. The fear doubled when she realized that the pattern this adorable man was tracing around her scars were little love hearts.

A lump rose in her throat, but she had to address the future before they both continued on pretending. "You're going to leave soon. Aren't you?"

His fingers paused their dalliance and she heard the thud of his heart pounding through the wall of his chest.

"Yes."

She closed her eyes. She knew he would. He had another life to get back to. "Soon?"

A pause. "Yes."

Now she knew. Now she could prepare. She'd never

Take A Chance

grown to rely on a man, and she wouldn't start now. She would miss him but she'd get over it. She was resilient. She'd just dropped her guard too much for a time, but she would refortify.

She always did.

Chapter 21

"Don't be nervous, everything will be fine," Will soothed, stroking his hands down Rebelle's arms and trying not to get aroused just from looking at her, but dang, it was hard. Pun intended. He couldn't get enough of her, had been trying to sate his lust for her. They both had, because they knew time was running out. There was one week to go until Will had agreed to return home and unfortunately, he was a man of his word and always upheld his agreements.

He had tried blocking it from his mind; that was the only way to get through the days. Instead, he focused on the amazing Christmas Rebelle and his friends had given him. They'd had confirmation from Blake that baby girl Harley had arrived yesterday morning after an intense twenty-six-hour labor for Justine. The shelter was opening today for adoptions. Life was great, if he just

Take A Chance

ignored what would happen in a weeks' time.

Both he and Rebelle were nervous but they knew it was time to start letting some of the animals go, no matter how much Rebelle fought against it. Parfait's kittens were now old enough to be separated from their mother and while Will had worried about how Parfait would handle it, Rebelle assured him that the little calico would be ecstatic to get rid of her brood who never gave her a moment's peace. And as usual, Rebelle was right. It was Will that had a harder time with the separation. He wanted to keep all the little rascals and he felt like a dad sending his kids out into the world for the first time. He wanted to bundle them all back into the trailer and keep them there forever.

The thought of leaving Parfait, Oscar, Betty, Veronica and Bryan, had his stomach clenching with nausea, let alone how his body protested at the idea of leaving his Belle.

"I know, I'm just...what if no one comes? But also, what if people come and take my fur babies away?" Rebelle peered up at him with her wide doe eyes full of worry and he wanted to kiss all her concerns away. Yesterday they had put fliers out all over town and Palm Valley to announce the opening as well as posting on their website and social media which now had 150k followers. Their socials had blown up after the Christmas post Rebelle had uploaded with the animals opening their presents. The comments came flooding in wanting to know about adoptions and supporting local charity so Will had a suspicion that they would do just fine today. Rebelle had managed everything online and it had amazed him how quickly she had learned and become something of an expert.

"Belle, it's time to let them go," he replied, and his

heart leapt into his throat when he saw her eyes pool with tears.

"I don't know what's wrong with me," she wailed and he chuckled, pulling her against him.

He stroked her hair soothingly. "It's all your dreams and hard work coming to a head. You've been planning for this moment and focusing all your time and passion on it for so long. I'm not surprised you're emotional." *Hell, I'm emotional.* "It just shows how much you care and that's what makes you so damn special here. And the best advocate for these animals."

Rebelle pulled back to look up at him and he swiped his thumbs over the curve of her cheeks, wiping away her tears. "You think I am?"

"Of course. I wouldn't have gotten involved otherwise. It was *you* I believed in."

Something passed behind her whiskey eyes and she stepped back, a cool mask slipping into place, like it had a few times in the last couple of days. Since Christmas day.

Will had noticed her distancing herself from him, like she was getting ready for him to leave. It reminded him of what she was like when he first came here, and he didn't like it. She had been so closed off, so scared of people and he was so proud of her, amazed at how she'd grown in the last few months.

He never wanted her to go back to the way she was before, but he sure as shit couldn't blame her for putting that space between them. It was needed.

He brushed it off, trying not to let it get to him. They had more important things to focus on today. He pasted a smile on his face and clapped his hands together. "Come on, let's do this!"

It was like the animals all knew something was going on and were on their best behavior.

Take A Chance

After an hour of pacing and Will trying to distract Rebelle, Ben and Kayleigh arrived. Will didn't know them very well but knew they worked at the bar with Rebelle. He'd seen Ben perform his Elvis tribute act and the dude was impressive.

They greeted the couple and exchanged pleasantries before Ben got right down to it. "Have you got any rabbits? I'm looking for a friend for Geralt."

"Geralt?" Rebelle's nose wrinkled adorably. "That's an interesting name for a bunny."

"Like *The Witcher*," Will told her but she just shook her head.

"Tell me he has long, white fur?"

Ben grinned. "Why else would he be called Geralt?"

Will laughed.

"And he's grouchy too, which is why we need to get him a friend," Kayleigh added.

"Nothing wrong with being grouchy," Will heard Rebelle mutter under her breath. He fought a smile before turning back to Ben. "A Jaskier?"

Ben nodded. "Exactly."

"I have no idea what's happening, but we don't have any rabbits at the moment. If you're not in a hurry then we can let you know when some come in?" Rebelle said.

"No hurry, thanks that would be great. Come on Kay, I can see kittens!" Ben said gleefully and the young couple disappeared to explore.

Rebelle turned back to Will. "What's a Jaskier?"

"Someone sweet but annoying," Will joked.

"Oh. So, a Will then?"

He barked out a laugh. "You made a funny," he quipped and enjoyed watching her stern features fight a smile.

They turned away as a large burly man came in, his

eyes darting around and taking everything in. Will recognized him as the mechanic at Dean's garage. He couldn't remember his name, just that his chat was minimal and he knew his way around a car.

"Bear? What are you doing here?" Rebelle spoke softly to the giant.

The giant, Bear, rubbed the back of his neck, looking towards the door like he wanted to run through it. His big hand moved to tug the end of his beard.

"Uh, I was thinkin' about getting a cat for my mom? Maybe some c-company for when I'm out workin'?" He spoke slowly, carefully, with his southern drawl shortening words like he was trying to save time.

"That's great. How is your mama?" Rebelle asked.

Will was taken aback by her interest in the husky man and how her voice gentled when she spoke to him. Jealousy tried to nip at him but he pushed it away, he had no right. Usually Rebelle avoided strangers but was quite confident around their friends now, though he wasn't aware that she knew anyone else.

Bear's hand found its way to the back of his neck again and he cleared his throat. "Uh, not too sure. W-waiting for some more test results."

There was a pause and the guy looked so weary that Will's heart ached for him. He couldn't be any older than Rebelle judging by the lack of wrinkles on his forehead and around his eyes. Yet there was an air of exhaustion that seemed to age him. When Bear didn't offer more, Rebelle nodded. "Fingers crossed for good results. In the meantime, shall we find someone who can give her a little joy?"

"Sounds good."

"The cattery is just there, pop in and have a look and I'll be by in a second to see if anyone takes your fancy.

Take A Chance

We'll find your mama her purrfect match!"

Bear's lip twitched under his thick mustache. "It's real good to see you looking so ha-happy, Rebelle," he said before nodding at Will and heading towards the cattery.

"How do you know him?" Will asked as Rebelle watched Bear leave.

Rebelle got this far off look in her eye. "He was in the year below us at school. I didn't really know him but one time when I was a bit younger, in the early days Marcus was shouting at me in the street for some stupid reason, and Bear came and pushed himself between us. He got in Marcus's face, I never heard what he said but Marcus went super pale and it shut him right up. Bear told me if I ever needed help to just let him know and he would help, no matter what it was. I wish I had said something or reached out, but I didn't." She drew in a shaky breath, folding her arms over her chest. "I heard through the grapevine that his mom was sick, in and out of hospital and he's been caring for her. He's a good man."

Will found himself owing Bear a debt of gratitude for standing up for Rebelle when he realized something wasn't right. Although Dean was generous with his staff, Will knew how bad hospital bills could get and made a mental note to see what he could do to help Bear and his mom.

Another couple came in looking for a dog and Will introduced them to Alfie, the border collie mix and let him into the yard so they could play and see if they were a good fit.

Taylor and Beau also showed up to support, which Will was grateful for and he and Rebelle proudly gave them the tour.

Bear ended up adopting Betty and Veronica. As taken as he was with a couple of Parfait's kittens, he knew they would be too much work for his mom. He needed older cats who were already self-sufficient. A bittersweet pang hit Will at the thought of his girls getting adopted. Although it was amazing, he would miss them.

High on the success of the day, Rebelle and Will buzzed about the shelter, talking to various people and working on the spiel they'd come up with. Will handed out 'Purrfect Match' forms and Rebelle answered questions.

Towards the end of the afternoon, Will noticed a man trying to peer into Daisy's kennel. They had left her crate covered with a blanket to give her some space from all the visitors and they made it clear that she wasn't available for adoption.

"Can I help you find your purrfect match today?" Will asked in his best salesman voice.

The guy turned to him and smiled, a gold tooth sparkling in the lights. He looked to be older, his skin wrinkled and craggy with gray showing in his beard.

"I was wondering if you'd had any Pitties come in? Wife's a big fan of the breed and she's just desperate for one now we've retired," he said.

"No," Rebelle replied firmly, appearing next to them and Will frowned at her. The guy didn't react to Rebelle's shortness, just tucked his hands in his jeans pocket and rocked on his heels.

"No problem, missy. Is there a wait list we can put our details down on?"

Rebelle shook her head. "N-"

"Sure thing," Will interrupted. "Come right this way." He took the gentleman over to the little waiting area they'd created with a coffee machine and comfy chairs and tables for adoptees to fill out the necessary paperwork. They planned to expand it to sell toys, beds

Take A Chance

and litter trays so people could get everything they needed to bring their new bundle of fur home, he just needed to find the right supplier.

Will talked to the man and took his details down. He had another look around before waving goodbye and leaving the shelter. Will spotted Rebelle scowling at him and not in the sexy way she usually did. *You are so gone if you think her scowl is sexy…*

"What's going on?" he asked.

"I don't trust that man," she answered.

"Gerry? Why not?"

"He was too interested in Daisy."

Will shrugged. "He's looking for a Pitbull?"

"And he just happened to come here on the first day and find the Pitbull that's not available for adoption because we're waiting for the outcome of a cruelty case? I don't trust him. I'm getting a vibe and I don't like it, Will. We need to move her."

Will scoffed. "You're being paranoid."

Rebelle rounded on him, her eyes flashing angrily. "Excuse me?"

He immediately regretted his words. "I just mean, I think you're being overprotective and seeing trouble where there isn't any."

She ignored him. "I need to call Jae."

Will's pride rankled at the mention of the sexy vet who had already shown interest in his woman. "Jae?"

"And Blake."

"You can't, he's just become a dad."

"Then, I'll call someone else," she snapped, pulling out her phone.

"Rebelle, hey," he gripped her arms, steadying her. "Slow down. Look, if you want to move her then we'll do it but after everyone has left. Only another hour."

She peered up at him, her expression carefully blank. "You don't believe me, do you?"

He cocked his head to the side, sighing. "I didn't say that."

She pulled herself free of his grip and fixed him with a look that made his balls shrivel up inside his body.

"Excuse me, I'd like to have a look at the kittens if possible?" A woman interrupted their stare off. Rebelle pasted a smile on her face and went to help her. They were busy for the next hour so didn't get a chance to talk again. Then the shelter was closed, and Rebelle fed the dogs while Will tackled his beloved felines.

He found her in the kitchen, furiously scrubbing at the food bowls. "Great first day! Alfie's adopted. Bear is taking Betty and Veronica, we've got some names down on our mailing list and that woman is going to take two of Parfait's kittens. How do you feel?" he asked, coming up behind her and kissing the back of her neck.

He felt her shoulders tense and hated it. "It's great," she said, sounding unenthusiastic.

"Are you still worried about Daisy?"

"Of course."

He clapped his hands together. "Come on, let's move her. Where do you want her?"

Rebelle dried her hands on a dish towel, brushing a damp lock of hair off her forehead. "Put her in the home."

He faltered. "Is that a good idea?"

Rebelle matched his stare. "I'll protect her no matter what."

"That's what worries me, Belle. Nothing is going to happen to her, besides I'll be here."

"You have drinks with the guys."

He groaned. He'd forgotten about that. "Okay but

after that, I won't be long."

She turned away from him, wiping down the surface. "Actually, maybe you should stay at the cabin tonight."

Her words landed with a blow. "What?"

"I think we need a break and it'll be good for us to be apart, with you leaving soon and all. It'll give us a chance to get back to reality." She wouldn't look at him and he could feel panic rising up as the truth he'd been hiding from leapt out from behind the wall he'd put in front of it.

He was losing her. She was sliding through his fingers and yet, he had to let her.

"If that's what you want…"

"I think it's what's best," she said, her tone flat. He helped her tidy, then moved Daisy so she was in the home.

"I guess I'll see you tomorrow then?"

Rebelle nodded, folding her arms over her chest and he hated the awkwardness between them. He wanted her back already, knew he was losing her and he hadn't even left yet. Fuck, leaving town was going to be harder than he thought. He turned and stalked out of the home before he grabbed her and begged her to go back to what they'd been just that morning.

*

Rebelle glanced through the telescope, looking at the stars and trying not to think about the hurt look on Will's face when she asked him to stay away tonight. It had hurt her too. She hadn't wanted to do it but she was stung by his dismissal of her concerns.

She had grown to read people's behavior and she recognized it when it was shitty and suspicious. She had expected Will to believe her and have her back, not dismiss her suspicions. She'd thought they were a team, but it just showed her that you could only rely on yourself.

Maybe it was better this way. Rebelle didn't like how attached to him she was getting. She was beginning to rely on him, to expect him to always be there and that wasn't what she wanted. Now she feared the idea of him leaving her all alone with the shelter and business and she didn't like how much that bothered her. She was used to being on her own. She had *wanted* to manage the shelter on her own. He was a distraction that she couldn't afford.

They were kidding themselves anyway. They'd always had an expiration date. What she hated was that she already missed him. Missed sprawling over his naked body, their damp skin connected, covering him with her own like she was owning him. Protecting him even. She missed hearing his booming laugh that used to terrify her and set her nerves on edge. Now it set them on fire. Missed him enough to be out in the chilly fall air looking up at the stars because now they somehow made her feel close to him.

She sighed and got up, heading inside for her phone. She grabbed it, scrolling through WhatsApp and smiling at the pictures Justine sent of Harley, the newest Rebelle's Angel. Harley was gorgeous, the spitting image of her mother and Blake would make the best girl dad.

Rebelle hovered over her chat with Will, wanting to talk to him.

"Jesus, you saw him three hours ago," she scolded herself, dropping her phone. "You don't need to speak to him. You. Don't. Need. Him."

This is why she needed to separate herself from him, before she grew any more attached.

Take A Chance

A low rumble filled the home and Rebelle frowned before she realized it was coming from Daisy's crate. Rebelle peered into the crate and saw Daisy huddled in the corner, tense, her eyes wide and growling.

"It's okay, Daze. It's just me," she cooed, trying to soothe her but the rumbling continued and grew louder. Bryan sat up from his place on the couch and began whining. Rebelle thought she heard a noise outside and a chill trickled down her spine.

They were warning her.

So many thoughts raced through Rebelle's mind and fear tried to choke her but she focused on her breathing, just like Justine taught her. She grabbed for her phone and dialed Jae.

"Rebelle?"

"Jae, I think someone's here. They've come for her, get the police here now, please," she hissed.

"What? Are you okay? Oh my God, do you want me to come?" he panicked.

"No, you're too far away. I'll call someone else just get the police here. I've got Daisy with me." She huddled down by a window, trying to see out into the pitch black and so thankful that she had left the lights off in the home to stargaze.

"Jesus, Rebelle. Stay on the line."

"No, call the cops and I'll call you back."

"Reb-" She cut him off. Her hands trembled with fear as she got up the call log and ducked down from the window in case the phone was illuminating her.

Daisy continued to growl and Bryan had positioned himself in front of her crate, protecting her. Rebelle scooted over to them for comfort while she called Blake. There was no answer, so she left a garbled voicemail. She called Will, praying he would answer, that he wouldn't be mad and ignore her.

He answered on the first ring. "I'm sorry, beautiful, I didn't mean-"

"Will! Someone's here. I think they've come for her, is Blake with you?"

"Shit, no he's not. Okay, I'm coming, stay on the line." She could hear the panic in his voice. Heard him telling the guys, minus Blake, and running through the bar with Taylor shouting after him. Then she heard his car start up, jumping at the blast of heavy metal music before it was silent.

"Belle, you with me?"

"Yeah, I'm here. Hurry please," she whispered. The dogs in the shelter all began barking their warning and her heart stuttered in terror.

"There's definitely someone here, Will. The dogs are all barking, I need to do something."

"No, I'm coming, Belle, I'm nearly there."

She heard the distant sound of glass smashing then the barking grew in volume. "Shit, they've broken in. The animals!" she gasped, her heart just about beating out of her chest in fear for them.

"Belle, don't do anything stupid. Stay put. I'm nearly there," he growled like he knew exactly what was running through her mind.

"I can't leave them, Will," she whispered.

"Dammit Rebelle, please. I'm begging you, stay there!" Will was shouting now and she could hear his tires screeching. She couldn't worry about him, she needed to focus on her fur babies. She hung up and glanced down at the phone and saw a message.

Jae: Police ETA 5 minutes.

She heard a dog's whimper through the night and Daisy growled again and barked. Rebelle's stomach turned at the thought of something happening to the animals and she couldn't wait any longer. She was terrified of what might be out there but needed to protect them.

    She opened the door to the home and went out into the night.

Chapter 22

"Fuck, come on!" Will roared as Rebelle ended the call. He smacked the steering wheel and put his foot down, the pedal flat to the floor. He was minutes away, a million thoughts racing through his mind.

Time stretched on and he pulled onto the lane to the shelter, his tires spitting out gravel, churning to get to her quicker. His headlights lit up the building and he spotted Rebelle at the door wearing just her pajamas. He slammed on the brakes and was out of the car and running to her moments later.

A man appeared and blew past Rebelle as he ran out of the shelter and headed towards the trailer.

"No!" Rebelle cried.

Will ran after him, determined not to let him get anywhere near Daisy. His pace was fast thanks to all his training, and he was gaining on him. A second later, Will tackled him to the ground and wrestled the guy onto his front and the moon came out from behind the clouds.

"Let me go!" the man snarled.

"Not a fucking chance, Gerry!" Will spat, seeing it was the guy from the shelter earlier. Rebelle had been right, as usual and he felt like an even bigger ass than he did earlier.

"Will?" Rebelle called; her voice filled with worry.

"Stay back!" He didn't want her anywhere near Gerry.

"I've got the police and Blake," she called.

"Will?" Blake shouted and then a flashlight was blinding him. He held up one hand to signal Blake when Gerry tried to make an escape. But Will was at least twenty years younger and stronger so Gerry didn't go anywhere.

Blake appeared with two officers behind him, and they took Gerry. Will turned, ready to hold Rebelle tight and never let go, when her body plowed into him as she threw herself into his arms. He enveloped her shaking form, stroking her back, soothing her as she gripped him tight.

"It's okay, you're safe. Everyone is safe and nothing is going to happen to you," he soothed.

When they finally let each other go, Blake was there, making notes and questioning Rebelle, then Will. Then Will set about boarding up the smashed window of the shelter with some leftover wood panels from the cattery while Rebelle checked on each of the animals.

Knowing her past he didn't like showing anger around her but his temper was frayed and at boiling point.

"You okay?" Blake appeared at his side as Will pounded in the final nail to the door.

Will put his hands on his hips and blew out a shaky breath. "I don't know, man. She scared the shit out of me, running around out there."

"Trust me, I know." Blake snorted. "Justine did something similar to me once. I get it. But she's fine, you're fine and the animals are fine. We got the guy thanks to you and from talking to the officers on the case this should actually help secure a conviction."

"That's something then, I guess." Will looked about helplessly, not knowing what else to do.

Blake regarded him. "She's a strong woman. Loving her sure as shit won't be easy but it'll be the best thing you do. From one man with a strong, stubborn *infuriating* woman, to another."

Will shook his head. "I don't lo-"

"Yes, you do. It's written all over your face, hotshot. It's why right now you could tear the world apart and also fall to your knees and cry like a damn baby. It's a big, beautiful emotion."

Will turned away, feeling some of that emotion overcoming him. He put the tools back in the box and took them into the shelter with Blake following him.

"You don't get it, it's not meant to be. I'm leaving in a few days."

"I get it, I do. I was a stubborn ass about it too."

Will scoffed. "I'm not the stubborn one for once."

Blake chuckled. "Well, halle-fucking-lujah! You've met your match."

Will shot him a withering look and the sheriff stifled a yawn. "What are you even doing here? You have a newborn baby. Go home to your fiancée and child."

Blake's thin mouth stretched in a wide smile. "Damn, that sounds good."

"Thanks for coming out, man. I know how much you look after her and I appreciate it."

Blake clapped him on the back. "No worries, all part of the job." But they both knew he went above and beyond.

Will and Rebelle closed the shelter and he walked her back to the home where she hurried over to give Daisy rubs and pats, cooing at what a good guard dog she'd been.

She glanced over her shoulder at Will. "I'm not going to apologize."

He snorted. "I'm not surprised."

She faced him, her skin pale from the shock of the evening, her rosebud mouth drawn thin. "I was concerned for my animals, and I made a choice to fight for them. A choice I would make over again."

She had a fire inside her and he loved when those flames erupted, bright and hot. He was constantly amazed at the level of care she had, about anything, after all that she'd been through. She had a big courageous heart that she hid in her chest but he saw it.

"You scared me. I was concerned for you." He knelt down beside her. "You scared me," he repeated softly. Her face lost its fierceness and gentled. He loved her fiery side but he also loved her gentle side, her softness. Because she was so guarded it was rare to see which made it all the more special.

He *needed* her softness. Will pulled her into a hug, resting his head over her heart and her fingers delved into his hair. His soul let out a sigh at the contact, the closeness.

They didn't argue. She took him to bed where they both tried to sleep but couldn't. She surprised him by reaching for him, pressing wet kisses to his chest that had him twisting his hands in her hair and holding her to him. He rolled over on top of her and meshed their mouths together, pouring every ounce of fear and frustration until their tongues were tangling and they were fighting for breath.

"One more time, please?" he whispered against her mouth. Usually she would have taken control by now but tonight she was leaving it up to him, like she knew he needed it.

He figured he was reading too much into it, but he had to believe that she submitted to him. She was trusting him and conceding to him, giving him what he needed once again, it had to mean something. *He* had to mean something to her.

He settled between her legs which wrapped around his hips, locking behind his back. He kissed his way down her chest, his hand sliding under her and cupping her ass, tilting her up into him. He detoured to swirl a tongue around one hard nipple, then the other. Her moans of pleasure fizzling like lightening in his veins, sparking to life through his entire body. What he'd had with her was what he'd been missing his whole life. Connection.

Profound hunger gripped him and it was an urgency she matched, reaching between them and wrapping her fingers around his cock, pumping him and twisting her hands in punishing strokes that had his toes curling and curses spilling from his lips.

"Please, William. Now." Her plea in that stern voice, coupled with the way she sighed his name had him gripping himself and pushing into her.

She was warm, wet and welcoming and he grunted as he slid through her. His thrusts soon turned languid and slow, taking his time. If it was their last time, he wanted it to last forever.

He committed every breath, every utterance to memory. Every scratch down his back she created as she fought against the intensity that she tried to hide from. He wouldn't let her. He made her relax into it, accept the slow thrusts and affectionate words and meaningful touches and he swallowed her strangled moan as her body finally gave in to him. He followed right behind her, his climax rippling through him in a jaw clenching, bone snapping breathless burst.

They hadn't fucked, they'd made love and looking in her eyes, she knew it too.

And as she lay, draped across him as was now customary, snoring softly, he whispered those three words into the night.

*

Rebelle woke the next morning, the heat of Will at her back, his heavy arm draped over her, holding her to him in a crushing grip. Like he was scared to let her go. Instead of making her anxious or claustrophobic, she relished his embrace.

Will's face nestled into the curve of her neck, his warm steady breaths coasting over her skin, causing small shivers to wrack her body and push herself back against him.

The idea that they weren't meant to be doing this anymore briefly flitted through her mind until she shoved the depressing thought away. She gave herself another moment to enjoy the sleepy bliss before she reluctantly extricated herself from his octopus arms.

Rebelle petted Bryan on the head and went to the bathroom to wash up. When she came out, Will sat on the bed, facing her, wearing just his boxers and her stare raked over him, taking in this giant of a man in her tiny trailer. It was almost laughable how at home and right he looked here. She memorized the thick, muscled, tattoo-covered body, her eyes catching on the odd designs, but they were all familiar now. She knew his body almost as well as her own.

In lieu of having an awkward conversation where they just reiterated that last night was the last time, she clapped her hands together. "You wanna take the cats or dogs today?"

His cool stare pierced her, assessing before a look of resignation crossed his face. He offered her a small smile. "What do you think?"

They dressed in silence and went their separate ways at the shelter. She thought at one point she could hear him talking to the cats but when she went into the cattery, he was silent.

Just as she was opening the doors to the public for the second time, Jae, Blake and another man that Blake introduced them to as, Neil, Daisy's caseworker arrived. Apparently after the police had threatened Gerry with a lengthy jail sentence, he'd sung like a canary. They had enough evidence that they believed Daisy was home free but just needed the court to make it official.

Rebelle was relieved to know this was nearly over and Daisy could find a new family who would give her the home she deserved. As they were leaving, Jae mentioned he had some kittens that had been picked up from a farm. They were feral and hated human contact and Rebelle caught the glee in Will's eyes, knowing he couldn't wait to get his hands on them and gain their trust.

"I think the mother got spooked and left them but we're keeping an eye out for her. They just need some fluids. I can bring them by tomorrow?" Jae said.

Rebelle nodded. "Sounds good."

The day went quick. More people turned up to view the animals and more *Purrfect Match* forms were completed. Rebelle was on a high throughout the day and each time she spotted Will he seemed the same, big smile on his face, friendly with those who came to the shelter. But she could see his sparkling eyes were dimmed, his smile held a bit of strain and though he tried to hide it, she could tell.

At the end of the day, he helped her finish up then left and she didn't hear from him all evening. She tried to distract herself by playing with Daisy and socializing her with Bryan who was desperate to play with her.

She tried to stargaze but just found herself thinking about Will and wishing he was there. Which was precisely why it was a good plan to stay apart. She was already so dependent on him, and she had promised herself she would never depend on a man again.

The next day, Will turned up and greeted her before heading straight into the cattery. She didn't get a chance to do as much admin now they were open to the public. It was a huge step for the shelter but she wasn't sure how she would juggle dealing with the public, spending time with the animals and tackling the business side of things too.

She cornered Will later in the day to discuss. "Do you think we should hire someone?"

He cocked his head to the side, a lock of auburn hair falling over his forehead and she ached to brush it back. "Why?"

"Because it's busy and you'll be gone soon. I won't be able to do all this on my own."

His smile stayed in place, but she saw a muscle tick in his jaw.

When he didn't say more, she added, "Do we need to hire or find volunteers?"

"Probably one of each so we know for sure that you have someone helping every day. I'll get it sorted, you don't need to worry about a thing. Whatever you need, I'll make it happen." He smiled again but it wasn't anywhere near its full wattage.

She shrugged. "I can do it. I just, I don't know, wanted to confirm that was the right thing to do? Hire versus volunteers."

"Whatever you think, that's the right thing to do. I'll handle it."

She liked that she was able to have input still. He'd been true to his word, and she still maintained control and he'd switched the dog food supplier back as requested.

Will's phone rang and he pulled it out, a slight frown appeared as he looked at the screen and it took everything in her not to reach up and smooth away the crease. She had struggled without him last night and although he wasn't being distant, rude, or mad, he was being different. He wasn't himself and she didn't know why.

By New Year's Eve she realized why he was so down. There was a bone-deep sadness in him that he was trying hard to hide and it was tearing her up inside. She didn't know how to make it better so she decided to confront him.

Rebelle found him in the cattery with the feral kittens who hadn't stayed feral for very long once Will had gotten his hands on them. He definitely had a talent for taming wild things, her throat closed when she realized that included her. She had amazing self-preservation skills and she had managed to avoid thinking about him leaving. She could tell from his deepening sadness that the day to say goodbye was fast approaching.

"Isn't life better when we're not all grumpy and hissy anytime someone touches you? This way you get treats and cuddles but don't tell Mommy Rebelle just how many treats you're getting or she'll think I'm spoiling you." Her heart lurched as she overheard him. She didn't want children but the idea of fur babies and lots of them with this man suddenly sounded like her idea of heaven. She pushed away the vision of them adopting all the strays and needing a second home just for animals.

"Will?"

He turned to her, one kitten perched on his shoulder, patting at his ear lobe, two climbing up his pants legs and one clinging to the back of his shirt. She burst out laughing at the sight of this formidable Viper covered in howling kittens. His phone rang and he extricated the tiny felines before pulling out his phone and silencing it.

"Who are you ignoring?"

"Everyone," he muttered and turned away, putting the kittens back in their bed and closing the pod door. Tension radiated from him, and she hated seeing him so tense, it wasn't good for him. They had switched roles, he was the surly one and she was the one who would do anything to make him smile.

"Will," she pulled his arm, turning him to face her. She reached up to cup his cheek, standing on her tiptoes. His eyes met hers and she saw the sadness churning away in the ocean depths.

"What's going on? Talk to me."

"What's the point?" he shrugged.

"Because you'll get it off your chest and go back to normal."

"No, I won't. Because going back to normal is the fucking problem," he said, pulling away from her and shoving a hand through his hair in frustration.

She shrugged. "So then don't go back to normal. Stay."

He scoffed and spun away, bracing his hands on the

table against the wall that they used for prepping food and giving the cats medication. "I can't stay. I have to get back, there's too much riding on me."

"Like what?"

"Businesses, all these small businesses that aren't getting the support and attention I promised them. Charities, fundraisers I haven't attended. The show, my colleagues, my mom," he ticked off each one on his fingers. "They all need me, need my money!"

"But what do *you* need?"

He paused, stumped by her question. His lips rolling inwards, and he made a dismissive noise in his throat.

"Come on Mr. Billionaire. What do you need?"

"It doesn't matter."

"Then what do you *want*?"

"It doesn't matter," he gritted out.

She watched the wretched expression on his face and took pity on him. "It's okay to not want that life in L.A. anymore. If you want to stay, then stay. Choose yourself. You need to pick you because no one else can make that decision for you."

He looked about him, his hands flailing with all the words he didn't say.

"Haven't you *earned* it by now? Haven't you helped so many people that you can rest easy now?"

He shook his head. "There's so much more that I could do."

"Why is it up to you?" she burst out.

"Because that's what happens when you have lots of money, you're successful and you have fame. Everyone wants a piece, a small chunk of it. Of you. And you can't escape. You have a responsibility to help those who don't have those things. I won't turn my back on them like others would. Like my father did."

"Is that why you helped me?"

He took a step towards her, his face softening. "No. I *wanted* to help you, I believed in *you*. Not the other way around."

She knew he was telling the truth. His phone rang again, and he growled a curse and silenced it.

"Someone clearly wants to get hold of you. It might be important."

"It's not."

She scowled. "So that's it then? You're just gonna go home to L.A. and hide how miserable you are and make everyone else happy instead of yourself because you don't have the courage to go after what you want?"

He just looked at her with puppy dog eyes full of despair that broke her heart. She'd had to make the choice once, different context of course. Her or Marcus, and she'd chosen her. She knew it was hard. She was disappointed in Will for not seeing what he was doing to himself and angry at him for everything he did to help her and others, yet he wouldn't help himself.

"You're not the man I thought you were," she said and spun on her heel, leaving the shelter and stomping back to the trailer.

Chapter 23

You're not the man I thought you were...her words battered around his brain, pinballing from one side of his skull to the other. They haunted him all night, kept him awake, hovered over him while he packed up the little cabin for a second time.

He had hardly slept, the whole situation too frustrating. He'd disappointed Rebelle, and now the seconds were ticking away until he left for good. He hadn't wanted to spend his last night, New Year's Eve, alone. He wanted to spend it with her. He'd heard an old saying once that the way you spent New Year's Eve was the way you would spend the rest of the year, and he had wanted it to be with her. Wanted to ignore the world, his life just a little longer but it just wasn't possible. Duty called.

There was a knock on the cabin door and that cruel

mistress, hope, sprang to life. In two strides he was across the room and swinging the door open wide.

"Happy New Year!" Beau called.

"Screw You For Leaving!" Taylor said at the same time and gave him a big hug. He smiled and hugged her back.

"I can't believe only three months ago we were saying goodbye and now we're doing it all over again. I'll ask you one more time, stay?" Beau practically begged him with his dark eyes.

Will pulled him into a bone crushing hug. "If I could, I would. In a heartbeat."

Taylor put her arms around them both grumbling, "I don't see why you can't."

Will chuckled, swallowing the lump in his throat. He didn't deserve them. He pulled back, blinking to clear his watery eyes. "Invite me back for the wedding?" he asked, handing her back the keys to the cabin.

Taylor playfully punched his shoulder, wiping her eyes. "You know it."

"But I haven't even proposed yet!" Beau said, indignantly.

Taylor smirked. "Oh sweetheart, we both know you will. You need to lock this down." She gestured to herself, and Beau just shook his head. Will loved their back and forth, and once again he was profoundly grateful that his friend had met his match. Will nearly reached out, wanting to pull Rebelle into his embrace forgetting she wasn't there. He felt her beside him even when she wasn't.

Like he knew exactly what Will was thinking, Beau said, "You gonna go see her on your way out of town?"

Will scrubbed a hand over his stubbly jaw. "I think she's too mad at me right now."

"If you leave without saying goodbye, you'll make her madder. And that will make me, Christy and Justine mad and trust me, you don't want that," Taylor warned, arching a brow.

"I don't think it'll go well," Will hedged.

"Better than not at all."

"Yeah, yeah. I hear you. Haven't you got a bar to run? And a gym?" Will grumbled.

"Not on New Year's Day, but we'll let you go. If you come back again, make sure it's for good. You hear?"

Will made a noncommittal noise and hugged them again.

With one last look around and a heavy heart, Will grabbed his bag and left. He dropped it in the trunk of his car which was much emptier now that his telescope wasn't taking up space. He figured he would leave it at Rebelle's seeing how much she now enjoyed looking at stars.

He drove out of the parking lot, pausing in the entrance. Left was out of town towards the airfield where his private jet was waiting for him. Right was through the town and out towards the shelter. He turned left and drove about halfway down the road before shouting, "*Fuck!*" and turning around. Rebelle might be mad at him but he couldn't leave without seeing her one last time.

His phone rang, interrupting Disturbed's *Down With The Sickness*, a personal favorite of his. He saw the name flash up that he'd been ignoring and once again canceled Adrienne's call. A moment later his mom called him and he canceled that too.

"You think she'd at least wait until the end of the day to chase me home," he grumbled to himself. She rang again and once again he canceled the call. Then Adrienne called again and when he pulled onto the dirt road leading up to the shelter a sinking feeling settled in his gut. Why were they both ringing him? Adrienne had been chasing him for days, maybe there was an emergency. He was about to call her back when he spotted all the cars and TV vans.

"Fuck!" he shouted as he took in the number of reporters flooding the ground, crawling around the shelter. His temper flared, his blood boiling with rage and he had no trouble summoning his TV villain.

He drove right up to the home, barely avoiding running down the paparazzi, and got out. Lights flashed in his eyes, microphones and cameras were shoved in his face as questions were fired at him.

"Are you having a breakdown?"
"How's your mental health, Viper?"
"What's the widow like in bed?"
"How do you feel shacked up with a murderer?"

His steps towards the home halted and the burning lava flowing in his veins erupted. He spun, getting in the face of the last guy, his voice low. "Call her that again, I fucking dare you."

He saw the reporter swallow, and he took several steps back but Will moved with him.

"William?" The soft, scared tone of her voice, combined with her saying his full name dampened his temper. He turned and saw her peeking out through a crack in the door, her beautiful whiskey eyes wide with terror and he needed to get to her. He shoved through the swarming crowd and then was inside the home, hauling her trembling body into his arms.

"It's okay, I'm here. I've got you," he murmured, stroking a hand over her silky hair. Trying to soothe her and himself.

"The things they called me..." her voice was muffled

against his chest, but he could hear her chattering teeth.

"They don't know what the hell they're talking about. It's not about you, it's me. It's my fault they're here. I thought I'd bought myself more time, but I was wrong."

She pulled back to look at him and the tears gathering in her eyes shredded his calm. He cupped her cheeks, thumbs swiping away the droplets that spilled over her lower lids.

"They called me a murderer but I didn't do it, Will, I swear. Is that why you wanted to leave?"

"No, God, don't think that. Of course, I know you didn't do it. This is all just about selling news and me being out of L.A., plus the sheriff's death has given them something to sink their fangs into. I can fix it." He let her go to pull his phone out and dialed Adrienne, suddenly realizing exactly why she wanted to speak to him.

"I had a feeling I'd finally hear from you," she said when she answered.

"Call off the hounds, Adri. I mean it, you crossed the line coming for her."

"I know you've been feeding me bogus stories. You went back on our agreement, and so did I."

"You've got five minutes to get them all out of here or I'll start doing it myself."

She tsked. "That's not how this works and you know it."

He sighed, exhaustion sweeping in. There was a time when he lived for the thrill of the negotiation but that wasn't him anymore. "What do you want?"

"I'm glad you asked. An exclusive. No-holds-barred, no topic off limits, including your childhood and the trailer park."

"Fuck you, Adri! Of all people you should get it!"

"I did, until you reneged on our deal."

Rebelle squeezed his bicep to calm him down and he glanced at her, staring up at him, concern pinching her forehead. He met her stare, amazed that she wasn't scared of his anger, only concerned for him.

She shook her head. "No, don't give them that." She must have heard what Adri said and still fought to help him keep his privacy.

The problem was he loved her, and there was only one thing he wanted to keep private. He would do anything to protect her.

"If I give you this, you'll leave her alone. Call off your hounds and leave her alone, forever. You hear me, Adri?"

"They'll be gone in minutes," she replied, gleefully.

"There's one topic of limits."

"What's that?"

He turned his back on Rebelle and lowered his voice. "Her." There was a heavy silence. "You owe me."

"Deal," Adri spat through gritted teeth knowing it was better to get something than nothing. And what she would get would be enough to set her up for life. He hung up on her and turned to Rebelle.

"Why did you do that?" she demanded.

"I did it for you."

"I didn't need you to. Don't give them the private pieces of yourself for their trashy stories!"

"Aw, you worried about me, beautiful?" he teased, trying to lighten the tense mood.

She shook her head. "You do so much for others, give so much of yourself away."

"You wanna be my protector?" He tugged her towards him and risked it, kissing her lightly, adoring the way she melted into his hard body. Just then, he wanted her to protect him forever. Wanted them to protect each other.

"Marry me?" he whispered, smiling against her plump

lips.

She reeled back, her brows creasing. "Excuse me?"

"Marry me?"

She shook her head. "No."

"No?"

"How could you ask me that? I would never marry again. Would never tie myself to a man."

"No, that's not why I asked. Don't you see though, he didn't love you but I-"

"But you found something to fix, to distract yourself from going back to a life that's making you miserable. You have a savior complex, Will. You're trying to save me, the animals. Only I don't need saving. I don't need fixing and I don't need you, Will," she added softly, trying to convince them both.

His throat dried. "I know you don't need me. But don't you…don't you want me?"

There was a pause. A long silence stretched between them. Will was never afraid of silences, he'd used them as a tool in negotiations, happy to sit in the uncomfortableness of it until the other person cracked. But this was the most agonizing silence he'd ever endured.

Rebelle squeezed her eyes shut before meeting his stare. "Thank you for all your help, I couldn't have done this without you."

His heart shattered, small shards poking at him. He didn't say anything, just bent down until their foreheads pressed together. Of course she didn't want to marry him. He'd been stupid to think otherwise. They knew this was just a casual thing until he left; he knew this wouldn't go further, what had he been thinking? Both of them closed their eyes, him trying to figure out how he was going to walk away from her and this place and not break.

When they pulled apart, Will cleared his throat. "I'd better go. Obviously, I'll be in touch about the shelter, and you have my number if there are any emergencies or something you're not sure on."

She stepped back, pushing her hands into the pockets of her black jeans, biting her bottom lip. "I'm sorry."

He waved a hand. "Psh, don't worry. I'll deal with the press." He turned, unable to look at her any longer. He moved to the door and paused when she called his name.

"William?"

God, he'd never get over the way she said his name. He turned. "Yeah?"

She smiled, full and wide and his eyes gobbled up the sight of it. "I mean it. Thank you. For…" she tailed off, looking about her. "…everything."

He couldn't speak so just sent her a smile in return.

He tugged open the door and ran out, shouting, swearing and raging. Swinging for paparazzi without trying to hit them, giving them the show they wanted. His performance worked, they followed him, their focus on Rebelle completely forgotten. He knocked over equipment, barged cars, every inch the nasty Viper they all wanted him to be. By the time he reached his car they had abandoned her completely.

He paused, desperate for one last look before he got in his car and drove away. She was in the doorway, her long gray cardigan pulled tight around her as she hugged herself, a small smile on her face as she watched his ridiculous behavior. God she was amazing when she smiled. He shot her a wink before getting in his car, blasting Disturbed again and speeding off, spitting up gravel as he went.

He watched in his rearview as the reporters all scrabbled to their cars to chase after him. He watched her get smaller and smaller, his chest aching, caving in on itself until he couldn't see her anymore.

He drove to the airfield and boarded his private plane, yelling at the pilot to go. He was strapping in as the cars all pulled up and he gave them all the finger as the plane taxied away.

He spent the journey in contemplative, heartbroken silence. When he landed, he didn't want to go to his home. For the first time since he was a child, he wanted his mom. So he had his driver take him straight to his mother's new mansion.

Diane was standing in the doorway like she'd been expecting him, which he guessed she had or maybe she just knew he needed her. She opened her arms and even though he was nearly twice her size, he let her arms engulf him. The sorrow he'd been fighting back finally overtook him.

She patted his back, soothing him. "I know what'll help. Let's get you back to work."

Chapter 24

Rebelle: Thanks for sending the new photographer around. She took some great shots, can't wait to share them on socials and in the next newsletter.

She waited for those ticks to turn blue and drew a deep breath when they did. She saw Will typing. He kept pausing and typing and her anticipation at his response turned to frustration the longer it took for his reply to come through.

Will: You're welcome.

"That's it?" Rebelle yelled, startling Bryan from his snooze on her bed. She huffed and threw the phone down, watching it bounce on the mattress and fall to the floor. She lay back, draping an arm over her eyes in despair.

She couldn't reach him. Whenever she messaged him, she got one word replies or sometimes even just an emoji which she found infuriating. She sent him updates about the not-so-feral kittens, he hearted the message. She told him about a meteor shower that was happening, he gave it a thumbs up. He refused to engage with her, and it bothered her more than she'd ever imagined it would.

She hated how much she missed him. She longed to see that stupid award-winning smile. She even stooped as low as Googling images of him just so she could see it. But it lost some of its gloss compared to in person, the effect just wasn't the same. She missed hearing his booming voice and laughter that used to scare her. She missed his energy, the vibrance and sunshine that emanated from him and lifted her up in turn.

She missed his kisses, him pulling her against his hard body. The way his deft fingers and tongue would weave a spell of magic on her that she had thought long gone. Missed the way that he would worship her, giving her the confidence and space to take control like she needed. The way he loved how she commanded him. She would see it behind his eyes, in his expression how he loved it, reveled in giving himself over to her.

She watched clips on YouTube, desperate to have his deep voice around her. Playing clips of the show and old interviews. She had to fight back the tide of jealousy threatening to consume her every time she stumbled on old footage of him with other, stunning women. At least she hoped it was old footage.

Rebelle wanted him to come back. Wanted to beg him to come back and be by her side, running the shelter together because that's what would be good for the business. She could see it now, now that she'd had the space, time had revealed how she *could* continue on her own, not letting anyone help her, but it would be a lonely road, one she never wanted to travel again. *Been there, done that and I don't want the fucking t-shirt, thanks.* Or she could accept help and the shelter could flourish, exactly as it had done.

Rebelle heard her phone beep and she scrabbled to the edge of the bed, stretching to pick it up and Bryan huffed at her jostling him. Excitement pounded through her but deflated a little when she saw it wasn't Will.

Christy: We all set for in an hour?

Tonight was the beginning of another new tradition: the monthly sleepover that the women had been doing for years and Rebelle finally had an invite. The only rules? Turn up in your pajamas and for the love of all that is holy, bring snacks. A fairly open brief in terms of what to bring and although Justine would be coming, she wasn't staying and hadn't had time to bake her signature brownies.

Rebelle stepped in and offered to make them but remembering the not-so-successful attempt at cookies a few weeks earlier, she'd reached out to Beau and asked him to give her a baking lesson seeing as how he loved it so much. At first, she'd been a little skittish in his company but he was gentle with her, gave her space and something about his energy reminded her so much of Will that she just missed the stupid billionaire even more.

But having never spent a night away from the shelter before, she grew anxious.

"Come on, buddy," Rebelle gestured to Bryan and let him out for the last time until she came back first thing in the morning. She stood on the deck of the trailer, watching as Bryan pottered around in the dark, trying to find the best place to pee.

She pulled her new flannel pajamas around her against the chill and tilted her head back, looking at the stars. The sky blazed full of them, flickering brightly and the vastness of them brought her peace. How could she have never paid much attention to them before? She was fascinated with them.

She caught one, winking brighter than the rest and her eyes flicked towards the telescope Will had left behind. She shivered at the memory of him behind her, his heat at her back, his body against hers as he guided where she should look. Her eyes fluttered closed imagining his warm breath on her neck as he inched closer. The way he compared her to a beautiful star. Her throat tightened and she went to the telescope, peering through, desperate to feel a connection with him.

She found the constellation and discovered the winking star was indeed Rho Cassiopeia. She stared at it, feeling so in tuned to it that she could reach out and grab it. Her body hummed like she could sense Will was near. So convinced of it, she spun around, expecting him to be leaning against his midlife crisis car, that dazzling grin spread across his face but all she saw was darkness.

Disappointment choked her and tears filled her eyes at the way she *needed* him before she stopped and pulled herself together. She turned away, ignoring the telescope now, and called out to Bryan. He trotted back into the home, collapsing next to Parfait who Rebelle hadn't had the heart to put in the shelter for adoption. Call her selfish but she just couldn't give the calico up, it felt like losing a pivotal connection to Will.

He had messaged her, asking if Parfait had been adopted and Rebelle confirmed that the cat had been, she just neglected to mention it was by her. Rebelle popped into the cattery quickly to feed the newest batch of kittens who squawked for their food.

She studied the completed cattery that was a combination of her and Will's designs. There was a window so the cats could watch the birds from their pods. A huge part of the wall had rows of rope, like a giant scratch post for the cats so that when they got out of their pods, they could have a really good stretch and scratch. There were numerous cardboard boxes because according to Will, "Where they fits, they sits". And tall cat towers dotted here and there for them to look down on everyone.

In short, it was perfection.

But it was as if the echo of Will ricocheted off the walls, she couldn't escape the stamp he'd put on the place and dammit he was all around her. She tried to find a part of her life that he hadn't touched, hadn't marked with his presence but she couldn't.

She escaped the cattery and went back to the home, grabbed her phone, keys and the cooling brownies. She kissed Bryan goodbye who was in a state of bliss as Parfait held him down with her paw and proceeded to give him a thorough wash.

Rebelle got into her truck and drove over to Christy and Dean's house. Apparently, the guys were also getting together tonight and although she knew it was unlikely, she couldn't help but wonder if Will was there. Was he planning another visit anytime soon?

Christy flung the door open and gestured to herself. "We're matching!" She was wearing the same flannel pajamas as Rebelle but where Rebelle's were red, Christy's were blue. The blond enveloped her in a huge hug that included squishing.

"I'm so glad you came!"

"I may not be much fun tonight."

Christy tilted her head. "Nonsense, you're always fun." Rebelle was hustled inside and the brownies were snatched away and swiftly replaced by a cocktail.

"You like raspberry, right?" Taylor asked. Rebelle nodded, eyeing the red liquid in the champagne glass and wondering how Taylor knew that. "Good, it's a raspberry Bellini. Just raspberry syrup and Prosecco. See what you think?"

Rebelle took a tentative sip then the sweet fizz exploded on her tongue and she drank the whole glass down.

Christy cheered.

"I think she likes it!" Taylor sang.

"I think she *needs* it," Justine said, appearing with a baby carrier.

"What's going on?" Christy asked.

Rebelle shrugged. "Oh, I'm fine."

"No more Bellinis until you tell us," Taylor threatened.

Rebelle snorted. "When did you get so responsible?" There was a pause and Rebelle clapped a hand over her mouth, wishing she could snatch the words back.

Justine snorted and Christy guffawed.

"Dang, she's got me there," Taylor grinned. Relief calmed Rebelle's nerves and she realized she was safe with these ladies. She didn't need to try and be someone else. If anything, they liked her the way she was, all sharp edges, and enough sarcasm to rival their own.

They moved into the living room and settled on blankets in front of a roaring fire. The brownies were handed out, along with bowls of chips and dip.

"Talk to us, then I'll pour." Taylor held the Prosecco bottle aloft over the champagne flute and arched an auburn brow at her. Rebelle looked around them, still struggling to open up but their faces each projected real concern.

"First rule of sleepover club is that we get drunk. The second rule of sleepover club, much like Fight Club, is the same as the first. But the *third* rule of sleepover club is that we talk about our worries," Christy said, and Rebelle wondered what a fight club was although it sounded pretty self-explanatory.

She nibbled her lip and took a page out of Will's book: negotiating. "Another raspberry Bellini then I'll share."

Taylor looked at the others. "Damn, she drives a hard bargain. Fine, you win."

Rebelle swallowed down another drink and let out a small hiccup as the bubbles flared up her throat.

"That's my girl," Taylor said, proudly.

"Now spill!" Christy added.

"There's nothing to spill really, except that Will left."

The women looked at each other.

"Did you want him to leave?" Justine asked.

"No."

"Did you ask him to stay?"

"Kinda?"

"Kinda?" Taylor and Christy repeated.

"You don't get it, he does so much for everyone else and never thinks about what he wants. He takes on so much and feels so much obligation to everything and everyone that I didn't want to be yet another thing he felt responsible for. He's so focused on making everyone else happy that he forgets to make himself happy. He needed to choose himself and I can't make him do that." Rebelle hiccupped again.

Christy eyed her. "Ah, I see."

"She's in love with him," Taylor nodded.

Rebelle scoffed. "I'm not."

"You so are," Justine teased, rocking Harley who had stirred.

"You just want him to be happy!" Christy cooed. "That means you love him."

"It's cool, he loves you too," Taylor shrugged casually.

"What!" Rebelle spluttered. "How do you know that?" A weird sensation prodded at her gut.

"It's obvious. Also, Beau told me."

"Well how did Beau know?"

"I'm assuming guy chat?"

Did he? He had done so much for her, never faltering at anything she said or did to rebuff him. She didn't know what she'd done to deserve his attention, loyalty and unwavering kindness. Maybe his proposal had been real, not savior-complex based?

"If he did, why didn't he tell me that when he proposed?"

"He proposed!" they all shrieked.

"He didn't discuss any feelings. I thought he was just doing it to make himself feel better, like he was looking after me and I don't need that so I said no."

The women looked at each other. "I don't think that's why he did it," Taylor said.

"I think maybe he wasn't sure how you felt?" Justine spoke softly.

She swallowed the lump in her throat. "I don't deserve him." She looked around the other women, unable to take the concerned looks. "Bellini me!"

"Did you ever consider that after *everything* you've been through, the sheer hell your life has been, that you deserve a kind, gorgeous, billionaire, goofball sex-god?" Justine mused.

"God?" Taylor's nose wrinkled.

"I'm speculating."

"Nah, she's right," Rebelle said, the Bellinis loosening her tongue and she slapped a hand over her mouth again. The shrieks of joy stirred baby Harley. They all quieted and waited until Harley was settled again before speaking.

Take A Chance

"Worth it," Justine snickered.

"For what it's worth, I think you're finally getting what you deserve, and so is he," Taylor said.

Christy hugged her. "Don't be afraid of it like I was," she whispered, for Rebelle's ears only. The advice that came from them, the way they cared about what happened to her and worked to help her achieve happiness had gratitude bubbling up inside her.

"Uh oh; Bellini her, Taylor. I can see tears coming and if they do then we'll all go!" Christy snapped her fingers at Taylor who worked hard to pour the drink.

"Someone change the subject!" Rebelle wailed.

Justine talked about mom life and they listened to how amazing Blake was as a father, not that they ever doubted he would be.

"We have news," Justine teased them.

"You're not pregnant again already, are you?" Christy's face paled.

Justine tutted. "No. We're getting married!"

Taylor frowned. "We know that. You got engaged nearly a year ago."

"No, like married in a month. We just want to get it done so we're going to have a small ceremony."

"But you always wanted a big wedding?"

"I know, and now I want to be with Blake more." Justine rolled her eyes at the chorus of *awws*, but her grin was huge. "We just want to get married here, like you did Christy, and have a small reception at The Bucket. And I want you all to be my bridesmaids?"

The shouts of *Yes!* once again stirred Harley and as the cheers faded in Rebelle's ears, she stared at Justine. The woman who had helped her so much, who she had grown close to, now wanted Rebelle to be part of her wedding. Tears filled her eyes again as she looked around at these women.

"I have friends," she said quietly but the noise soon subsided at her words.

"Of course you do," Justine said.

"Now, let's get drunk. We have lots to celebrate!" Christy said. They talked and laughed until alcohol came out of Christy's nose and Justine stood up laughing.

"I think it's time to go," she said dryly and waved off the boos. "Rebelle, walk me out?" She said goodbye to the others and Rebelle followed her, watching as she secured Harley in her car seat.

"I know we've worked on some of your issues but I want to be clear. You are worthy of love, whether it's us, Will or someone else. You're a strong, wonderfully independent woman with a kind heart and you deserve the world. We can continue our sessions if you like?"

Rebelle nodded. "That would be great. Thank you for everything you've done for me. I don't think I'd be here without you." Her throat closed over the words.

"Yes, you would. Now, come here." Justine pulled her into a hard hug which Rebelle just accepted. She was getting better with affection and remembered when Will first hugged her. Would he be proud of how good she was getting at them?

Justine turned back before getting in the car. "Can I ask you something?"

"Sure."

"Why did you really say no to Will's proposal?"

Rebelle shrugged. "I thought he was trying to save me and I didn't need him to. I didn't want to be tied to a man again, I don't want to need someone."

Justine cocked her head, studying Rebelle. "Everyone needs someone. You need them to push you, to complete you and to elevate you to be the best person that you can be, and you do it for them in return. You've had one, horrific, example of a toxic relationship. True relationships are about partnerships and isn't that what you've built with Will?"

Rebelle thought over how she'd grown in the last few months and saw that yes, she'd done it herself, but Will had given her the tools she needed. They had become partners who each had different strengths but worked best together. She had drawn strength from him to grow and develop. And he'd done the same. He'd let loose in a way she knew he couldn't in his normal life.

She shook her head. "I just don't know if I can open myself up to being weak again when I've worked so hard to be strong."

"Honey, that's not weakness. It takes strength and courage to let someone into your life and heart and to trust them, and you have strength in abundance."

"I do?"

"Yes, *mamacita,* you do! You have it *because* of your past experiences."

"I feel so confused. And a little Bellini-drunk."

Justine laughed and took Rebelle's hands in hers. "Okay, close your eyes."

Rebelle narrowed her stare at Justine before huffing and closing her eyes.

"Imagine you're at the shelter. You're doing your thing and then, the most amazing thing happens. What is it?"

Rebelle felt a smile lift her lips. "Daisy gets adopted by a wonderful family."

"Okay, so who do you tell?"

"Will."

"How do you get in contact with him?"

"Well I don't need to, he's right there with me."

"Exactly, Rebelle."

Rebelle's smile slipped into a scowl once she realized what Justine had done. She opened her eyes and found her friend smiling at her.

"I don't think you're confused at all. I think you need to get out of your own way." Justine blew her a kiss before getting into her car and driving off, leaving Rebelle dumfounded.

She returned to the house, thoughts of Will plaguing her.

"How did you know you were in love?" she asked the others.

Christy's brow pinched in thought. "Dean made me feel like I could fly. Like anything was possible. I was truly happy and whole."

"What she said. Like I could do anything with him by my side," Taylor added.

Rebelle had similar feeling towards Will, except Justine was right, theirs felt more about partnership. About what they could achieve together.

"How does Will make you feel?" Taylor asked gently.

Rebelle paused, thinking it over. "Safe. He's got this big, big heart. And I don't doubt that he's hiding a part of himself from me, like Marcus did, because he's the same around everyone. When he's on his own in the cattery, he talks to cats, he thinks I don't hear him but I eavesdrop and he's authentic. He's the same person whether it's a room full of rich investors, the cats, his fans or me. He's open and vulnerable and doesn't hold anything back. He makes me feel like I deserve to be loved."

"Tell him," Christy urged.

Rebelle shook her head. "It's not just me. He needs to choose this too. He hasn't come back, hasn't chosen what he wants for himself. He's barely spoken to me so I guess I'm not what he wants after all."

"He'll figure it out, I have faith," Taylor said, handing her another Bellini and they put on a horror film and ate brownies.

"Did you make these from scratch?" Christy asked, bits of brownie stuck in her teeth.

"Yes, why?" She omitted Beau helping her.

"No reason. They're delicious," Taylor snickered, and Rebelle shook her head before pelting the banshees with remaining brownie pieces until they were laughing and she looked forward to a long future of sleepovers with these women.

Chapter 25

"I dominate. That's why you come to me. Why you need me. I'm the only one who can explode your business. My contacts, my name, my experience. It's why you're here. If you weren't serious about this you wouldn't be here. This is my territory and if I accept then I'm letting you play in it. Now, have you got a better counter-offer than the bullshit you just put forward?" Will snarled.

"Cut!" the director shouted.

Immediately Will shook off his 'viper stance' and rolled his shoulders, willing the ick factor to slide off him.

"Perfect! That was fucking perfect, Crawford!" A random executive producer gushed at him but he didn't want to hear it. He detested himself and everything he'd just said.

There was a time when he would have relished giving a

monologue like that. But times had changed, *he'd* changed. He wasn't the same man he'd been ten years ago when he would say shit like that. Hell, he was a different man even to just three, four months ago.

His time in Citrus Pines had changed him. He'd seen what really making a difference looked like. And it wasn't some harsh words, big ballsy attitude and making those who need your help practically grovel for it. It was care, kindness and hard work. Not flashy sets and celebrity friends.

His work no longer satisfied him, it wasn't meaningful. He'd made himself, and others, rich but now the thrill of the deal had never felt less appealing. He needed more. He needed worthwhile. He needed to get out of here.

He stalked over to the director, Carlos. "How long have we got left?"

"Just a couple more hours to do some more pitches and some blocking," Carlos replied. Will wanted to have a tantrum and it must have showed. "What's up with you? You had your little time away, we put everything on hold so you could *live your best life*, now it's hard work time," Carlos mocked him.

Will took a step forward but a hand on his shoulder stopped him. He turned and saw Ezra Jackson, one of the newer Vipers.

"Not worth it," Ezra's deep voice warned. Will eyed Carlos again before deciding Ezra was right and turned to stalk back to his dressing room. It wasn't hard to miss, it was the biggest one in the fucking place. Too big. He preferred smaller spaces now, like a cabin or a trailer home.

It was a moment before he realized he wasn't alone. He spotted Ezra leaning against the doorframe, arms folded over his chest. He had only spoken to Ezra a few times before putting him forward as a new Viper on the show. Ezra was a tech mogul who made his fortune selling apps before becoming one of the pioneers in software development. His company soon joined the Fortune 500 list and he became the ninth Black executive to be on that list.

Will liked him, not only for his business acumen but because, like Will, he'd had a tough start in life and had worked his way up through sheer grit and determination. Ezra called people on their shit but wasn't easily riled. His calm persona was the perfect opposite of Will's explosive, aggressive one and they worked well together on set, becoming rival Vipers. But it was all an act.

"Talk to me," Ezra said.

"Nothing to say," Will replied, dropping down on the couch.

Ezra pursed his lips and pulled at the cufflinks on his shirt. "Wanna try that again?"

"Fuck!" Will shouted, to try and shift some of his frustration. He ran a hand through his hair. "I just…" he couldn't get the words out.

"What happened in Citrus Pines?" Ezra asked, shocking Will. "Oh, come on. You didn't expect me not to figure out where you'd gone?"

Will didn't say anything, surprised that Ezra had known the whole time where he was and he was touched that Ezra had never leaked the information.

"Was it a woman?"

"Yeah."

Ezra bared his teeth in a terrifying grin. "Of course it was. And now you're questioning everything you thought you knew and the weight on your chest is slowly crushing you and you want to punch every fucker who tries to talk to you?"

Will stared at him, amazed. "How are you in my head?"

Ezra chuckled, a low rumble that sounded like the beginnings of an earthquake. "I've been there, my friend." He pushed off the wall and took a seat beside Will.

Will scrubbed a hand over his face. He'd had his break and yet being here, he felt more exhausted than ever. "Honestly, I've been questioning things for a while."

"Tell me about it?"

He told Ezra how he'd been feeling before going to Citrus Pines. How he'd been conflicted about business and didn't have the same passion and hunger for the deal. That he was bone *tired*. Then he told Ezra about finding the shelter, building it up, and about Rebelle.

"Man, I've never seen your eyes light up like they did just then."

Will sat with the words for a moment, playing with his watch. "Have you ever wished..." he trailed off.

"Wished I was still in my studio apartment that I shared with two other people, tinkering with an old computer where no one knew my name and I was just having fun?" Ezra said.

Will nodded.

"Sure. But I'm only just starting out. I've got years to go until I think it'll get too much. And if those thoughts ever overshadowed how often I was grateful for you finding me and where I am, then I'd make a change." Ezra stood up, signaling the end of their chat. "What I will say is; you've been in the game for nearly twenty years. You've done your time, you've made your mark and helped other young people get a footing on the ladder. If you decided to stop, people would shit themselves."

Will snorted. "Helpful."

"They'd shit themselves and then be onto the next thing. People are resilient, we both know this, they'd get over it and have moved on before you know it. It's not quite the tragedy you think it would be." Ezra held out his hand and tugged Will to his feet.

"Man, you don't pull your punches."

"I know, it's one of the reasons I caught your eye, remember? It's harsh but true."

Will tucked his hands in the pockets of his slacks. "But what about all I can do with my money, isn't it selfish to stop helping?"

Ezra laughed and Will honestly felt the ground shake. "Fuck no! You've done your time, bro. Besides, you need to retire, old man. Let some of us younger boys step up."

"You're only ten years younger than me," Will scoffed.

Ezra quirked his pierced brow. "Exactly. I'll even help you find a retirement home."

Will flipped him off and Ezra slung an arm around his shoulders. "Come on, man. Let's go make some more young entrepreneurs cry and then we can go for a drink. I need my old Will back, I don't like you like this."

By some miracle Will made it through the rest of the shoot and went for a drink with Ezra. When the women started crowding him and Will realized he wasn't needed there anymore, he said goodbye to Ezra and went to his mother's place.

Will let himself in, grabbed a beer and dropped onto her uncomfortable, fancy-ass sofa. His phone beeped and he pulled it out.

Rebelle: Thanks for sending the new photographer around. She took some great shots, can't wait to share them on socials and in the next newsletter.

Will's heart pounded, excitement flooded him at her message, followed by the sudden pain. He missed her.

Take A Chance

Every heartbeat was a thudding ache in his chest that stole his breath.

He began replying.

I miss you.

I love you.

How are the kittens?

I miss your frown.

How is Parfait?

Do you miss me?

Tell me what to do.

Instead he kept his distance, just like he had been for the last month. Trying not to think about her. Trying to forget her. Trying to forget how she followed him into his dreams and taunted him. How he should have just told her he loved her. Loved her sharpness, so at odds with her caring nature. Her bravery, her selflessness, her loyalty, passion and dedication.

But he didn't.

Will: You're welcome.

He hated himself. How could he have thought he could be on the board for the shelter and not let his feelings get in the way? He'd never been so wrong. Did she even miss him? Did he haunt her every waking thought like she did for him?

Will lost himself in some shitty movie until a few hours later when his phone beeped again. He saw Taylor had sent him a picture. He tapped it open and Rebelle's face filled the screen. Her dark eyes alive with happiness, her cheeks flushed and the widest smile he'd ever seen. The text read *living her best life* and she was doing it, without him.

Rebelle was right, she didn't need him. Didn't miss him. Didn't love him after all like he'd hoped she was starting to.

He got another message through and reluctantly swiped Rebelle's face away.

Blake: Getting married in a month. Be there or be a dick.

Will snorted. He got excited, planning his trip out in his mind. Then the thought of going back to Citrus Pines sat heavy with him. He wanted to go with every fiber of his being. But having to leave that place *again* and the reminder of her not loving him split his heart in two.

No, he would stay here and pout. Like a fucking grown up.

*

"Will, I'm tired of you slobbing around my house. It's been nearly a month and frankly, I've had enough."

Will lifted his head from the TV where he was watching another crappy Christmas movie on the random Christmas365 movie channel he'd found. He was obsessed with them now. Each one made him think of Rebelle's face as she stood in the trailer with all the lights, the scent of burnt cookies in the air and the apprehension on her face. He blinked in frustration, willing the image away.

"I did what you wanted. I finished filming this series. I did the GQ shoot and I hardly complained. My place is so empty and I like being here."

Diane huffed. "Well, at least shower. We've got a benefit to attend and you need to be ready in an hour."

"I'm not going," he grumbled like a petulant child.

"It's a benefit for a charity you're on the board for, you have to. Also, I put you forward as an auction item. People can bid to win you for the day, it'll be fabulous!" She clapped her hands excitedly.

"Then they're gonna be disappointed."

"The Jenkins' daughter will be there. Maybe if she won you, you might get out of this funk and-"

"Jesus Christ, I'm heartbroken, Mother!" he shouted. "I'm not getting over this, don't you understand? It's not what you do when you love someone, and they don't love you back! You don't just go to a party or get a new suit or an extra round of fucking Botox. You sit and be miserable and do nothing except think about that person until you're broken all over again from torturing yourself. Until your soul *hurts* and your body is weak and you can't even *think* about your next breath. So no, Mom. I don't want to go to an event. I don't want to shower and get dressed up, and I sure as shit don't want to meet another woman."

There was silence as his words hung in the air around them. "Now can you please leave so I can cry and then hit something and then watch a sappy movie? Thank you."

She didn't say anything, just stared at him with an unreadable expression on her face and he turned back to *A Castle For Christmas*. After a moment the clack of her heels against the marble floor signaled that she was gone.

Will didn't cry. He didn't have the energy for that. His phone beeped with a new message and he lazily glanced at the screen.

Dean: No word on if you're coming to the wedding?

Beau: I know you're busy but Blake would love you to be there.

Blake: If you don't come, I'll hunt you down and fucking kill you.

Blake: So, I'll see you next week.

Blake: Dick.

Will wanted the ground to swallow him whole. He

couldn't do this right now. More people wanting things he couldn't give because he only wanted one person to need him, and she didn't. He didn't think he could be in the same town as her and not beg her to love him. His phone beeped again and he growled, silencing it but not before he saw the message.

Beau: You came here for salvation once before, maybe you'll find it again.

Chapter 26

Rebelle ran around the shelter, trying to get through all the people waiting to ask questions. Her volunteer, Stacey, had to go home early with the 'flu and Rebelle thought she could cope on her own but she was wrong. Once again she realized that relying one hundred percent on herself just wasn't possible. She needed help and there wasn't anything wrong with that.

She had learned now that it was okay to ask for help, that asking for help made people stronger. If only she'd realized that much sooner, maybe life wouldn't have been so hard, maybe she would have achieved her progress with the shelter a bit quicker. *If you had, you might never have met Will...* The thought stopped her in her tracks. Maybe she was on the path she should have been all along.

Ben and Kayleigh turned up, ready to look at the new bunny that had come in. A cute little black lion-haired female. Ben took one look at her and declared her perfect for Geralt and filled out the Purrfect Match form.

That made three adoptions just today and Rebelle's heart filled with pride. Her fingers reached for her phone to message Will and tell him the good news. She opened their chat but stopped. She scrolled through the messages she'd sent and the one word replies she'd received and her joy was doused.

She had thought that he cared about her, that he would always put the shelter first and any personal stuff that happened between them second. But the way he was behaving suggested he couldn't put the shelter first, and it hurt her. She wanted to share the highs with him, and the lows. She wanted him to be here by her side, but he'd chosen a different path.

"And constantly wishing him here doesn't make it happen," she mumbled to herself. She put her phone away and continued running around like a mad woman until the crowd thinned and she'd gotten on top of things.

When it was quiet, she heard the roar of an engine, the blast of loud music and hope lit her insides on fire. She rushed to the entrance of the shelter, eager to see if it was him, if he'd come home to her.

Disappointment crushed her when she saw it wasn't him. Although she was confused, was that really his *mother*?

She watched Diane step out of the white Bugatti in her big, hopefully faux, fur coat, her glasses perched on her head, the smooth forehead not belying a single emotion. She tottered over to Rebelle and looked about her, dismissively.

"Diane, what a pleasant surprise." Rebelle would be polite to Will's mother if it killed her.

Diane just looked down at her and then gestured

inside. "I'd like a tour, please."

Rebelle blinked in surprise, shocked that the word please had come from her mouth. She bit her cheek at being ordered around but complied. She showed Diane the cattery that reminded her so much of Will she could hardly bear to be in it sometimes. Past the dogs to the office that had been built. She took her outside in the cool winter air and outlined her plans for expansion.

"I want to see the dogs again," Diane declared.

Rebelle hesitated, she didn't understand why Diane was here and why she wanted to see everything. At the same time she just wanted to get rid of her. Maybe if she just did what the woman wanted then she would leave? Rebelle was dying to ask about Will. She had seen his GQ shoot, well, had specifically searched for it. And then drooled over the pages, him shirtless, his arms behind his head, his thick biceps flexed and the tattoos covering him that she ached to trace. She couldn't get it out of her head, wanted the man himself right here.

She took her back to the dogs and Diane lingered over the two Chihuahua brothers, Bruiser and Beast. For the first time since she arrived, Rebelle noticed her expression soften.

"They came to us after being rescued, someone had left them in the woods, and they managed to survive until they were found."

"Oh!" the cry slipped from Diane taking Rebelle by surprise.

"They're fine now, we found them and they're looking for their *fur*ever home," Rebelle said, emphasizing the 'fur' and Diane snorted.

"That's good, I like that pun."

Rebelle hid her smile behind her hand and for some reason felt extremely proud of herself for cracking

Diane's harsh façade.

"I'll take them. I can pick them up in a week. It would be sooner but my husband is whisking me away for a few days. I saw them when I last visited and couldn't stop thinking about them," Diane revealed, barely taking her eyes off them.

"Would you like me to get them out, you can play with them for a little while we do the paperwork?"

"No," Diane said firmly. "I'll want to take them now if I do."

Rebelle understood. Diane didn't want to get attached to them until she could take them home. Rebelle had a similar feeling, had worked hard to not get attached to the animals but now she couldn't help it, she was weak.

She gestured for Diane to take a seat in the office and they filled out the paperwork together. Then once it was done, Diane said a quick goodbye to the pups and Rebelle walked her to the sportscar that reminded her so much of Will.

The whole encounter with Diane, although great because Rebelle had adopted out more animals, felt a bit strange. "Diane, why did you really come here?"

Diane turned to her and arched a formidable brow. "For the dogs."

"Okay, why else did you come here?"

Diane pulled on her expensive looking leather driving gloves. "I was interested."

"In the shelter? I won't sell it, no matter how much you offer for it," Rebelle replied fiercely, and amusement lit Diane's blue eyes.

"No darling. I was interested in you."

"Me?"

"Yes, I wanted to see if you're as miserable as he is."

Rebelle choked on the air leaving her lungs. Eternally

optimistic Will was…miserable? Visibly, not trying to hide it, miserable? She needed more information, was greedy for it.

"And?" she asked, her voice strangled.

"You're hiding it better than him but I'd say you're about as bad as each other. In his entire life, I've never seen him the way he is now." Diane flicked some invisible lint from her coat, feigning boredom but now she had revealed a weakness. She cared for her son, deeply, to be here checking up on Rebelle.

"I like you, Rebelle. You're a good woman and I did my research on you. I have a feeling I know the things you've overcome, and I will forever admire your courage and tenacity. We're a lot alike and for that, I'm excited to get to know you. He's chosen his match well." Diane hit her with a hard stare. "But if you hurt my son, I will destroy everything you love." Then she put her glasses back on and turned, getting into her car.

Rebelle stood there, no words coming to her, the whole conversation had left her in shock, and her brain couldn't compute the information or form words.

"Thank you for letting me adopt those two beauties in there, even though I know I've been difficult. I look forward to having them in my life, and you." Diane waved and then she drove off, leaving a gobsmacked Rebelle tripping over her thoughts.

Will was miserable, without her? If he was so miserable, why hadn't he chosen her? Why hadn't he come *home*? It didn't make sense.

The dogs started howling, it was past their dinnertime and she jumped to work, realizing that meant she needed to be at Christy's in one hour.

It was the night before the wedding and Justine wanted to spend it with all her bridesmaids. Rebelle hadn't heard from the others if Will was coming or not, although she had assumed he would be, knowing he and Blake were friends.

She finished her jobs at the shelter and packed up the things she needed for the night then hopped into her truck to head to Christy's, as the men were holed up at Justine and Blake's.

Christy let her in then went off to get drinks and Rebelle used the opportunity to speak to Justine. "Do you know if Will is coming?"

Justine shook her head. "I don't know. He hasn't said and I think Blake is hoping he'll just turn up, but he might be busy or he might not want to come back."

"You think he wouldn't want to come back?"

"I think maybe he's hurt and a little lost right now."

"God, Justine what did I do? I messed everything up. I should have begged him to stay. I *wanted* him to stay. Why didn't he pick me?" Rebelle fought back the tears and Justine's arms came around her.

"Men are dumb, it's as simple as that," she sighed and Rebelle burst out laughing.

"His mom came to the shelter today. She wanted to see if I was as miserable as him."

"No way? Scary Diane?"

Rebelle shrugged. "She's not so scary."

"So he's miserable, huh?"

"Sounds like it."

"Have you reached out to him?"

"I wanted to, so bad. But it's got to be his decision, he's got to choose happiness for himself."

"Then let's hope he makes it, and quick." Justine hugged her again.

Then there was a swell of noise as Taylor entered the house like a little tornado shouting, "Let's get this bish married!"

*

Will flicked off the shelter's Instagram page. He couldn't look at another post of happy animals being rehomed and know that he wasn't there. That he had chosen strangers and money over what fed his soul. He didn't care if he let them down anymore. Like Ezra said, they would get over it.

He had made a huge mistake and he needed to fix it now, whatever it cost. He needed to get back to Citrus Pines, back to the shelter, back to *her*. Just the thought had the weight lifting from his chest for the first time in weeks.

Watching Rebelle lead the life she wanted and achieving her dreams gave him the same urge. It showed him that no matter what, he could do it. After everything she had been through, she'd had the courage to go after what she wanted, to succeed, to take risks and trust him. She inspired him. Rebelle had said he needed to choose himself, but choosing Rebelle and the shelter was choosing himself. He was picking the thing that made him happy, that he could see a future in, that he *loved*. She had helped him find his courage.

Will called his mother but she didn't pick up. He tried her again and again and was ready to tear the world apart when she finally came home.

"Where have you been? You've been ignoring my calls, you're my manager and I need to talk to you!" Will's voice was raised and he flinched, knowing his mom would destroy him for raising his tone with her. She sauntered into the house, like she hadn't a care in the world.

"I just got back from my trip and you haven't asked me how it's gone?"

He sighed. "How was your trip?"

"Lovely, thank you."

Frustration had him clenching his jaw. "That's it? Okay well I need to talk to you."

She shrugged, pulling off her gloves and examining her nails. "Aren't you going to ask me where I went?"

He closed his eyes, counting back from ten slowly. "Where did you go?"

"Citrus Pines."

His heart stopped cold in his chest. "What did you go there for?"

"I wanted to adopt a dog. And I wanted to see why you've been so sad."

"And?"

She sat down on the couch and patted the space beside her. "Will, I know I haven't been the best mother to you. In fact, at times I've been a better manager than mother. We've built an empire together and I wanted to protect that. But not as much as I will *always* want to protect you."

Her expression softened and for a brief moment he thought he saw her, truly saw the mother from his childhood.

"I pushed you too hard at times and I know it. I wouldn't say I regret it because look at what we've done. I'm eternally proud of you. But when I look at you now and see how unhappy you are, it makes me feel like the biggest failure in the world. None of the money, the fame or the business mean anything if you're unhappy. And you're unhappy because it's not what you want anymore, and I wouldn't listen."

Hope lit his chest for the first time in weeks. "Tell me

Take A Chance

we can fix this?"

She smiled at him. "We can fix this. *I* can fix this. After all, I am Diane Crawford-Wyatt-Miller-Harkins."

"Thank the Lord, because I'm done. I can't do this anymore, I won't do this anymore. I want to work at the shelter, I want to open more. I want a more fulfilling life. I want her."

His mother's smile widened. "I fully support that. I spoke to her earlier and I give my seal of approval."

"You do? How is she? Is she okay?"

"She's fine, on the surface. But she needs you."

He snorted. "Belle doesn't need anyone."

Diane tilted her head. "I can't believe I already know her better than you. She *does* need you." She pulled him into a hug and he relaxed into it, really hugging her.

"Now what do we do?"

"You let me do what I do best as your manager."

"Okay but after this, you're fired." He held his breath, waiting for her to argue but she didn't.

"Sounds good to me. That way I can focus on just being your mom."

A lump rose in his throat at her words, he wanted that so much. For them to go back to the way things were.

She let go of him and stepped back. "Now, you'd better hurry if you want a chance to make things right with her before the wedding. The private jet is waiting, go pack your bag."

He kissed her cheek. "I love you."

"Love you, too."

Will was impatient to get to Rebelle but that grew tenfold when the plane was delayed. He spoke to the pilot who assured him they were working as quickly as possible to solve the issue. Will stressed the urgency of the journey and they agreed to source another plane. One thing he would miss from his old life was the speed with which he could get shit done, just from his name alone. That would probably change once he left the limelight, but he would deal with it. As long as he had Rebelle and the shelter, he could deal with anything.

When he finally landed on the airfield outside Citrus Pines it was much later than he'd anticipated. He decided to head straight to Blake's to spend the night with the groom and best men. He would catch Rebelle after the wedding tomorrow. Even though the thought of waiting killed him, he didn't want to interrupt Justine's evening and pull attention away from their special day.

Will rang the doorbell of the modest farmhouse and waited for Blake to answer. The sheriff appeared, his scowl etched on his face and it didn't shift when he spotted Will. He stood in the doorway and folded his arms across his wide chest.

Will knew he'd been a dick in ignoring Blake, his own issues getting in the way and he owed the man an apology. But he settled for humor first. "I see fatherhood hasn't mellowed you."

The sheriff's lips pursed. "You suck at apologies."

"I know. I was a dick and I know it. I was too wrapped up in my own thing and I'm sorry. But I'm here, if you have room for one more best man?"

The scowl remained in place for long enough to make Will worried before it slipped. "Get in here, dickhead."

Will grinned and they hugged, slapping each other's backs so hard they winded each other. He followed Blake into the house.

"Look who finally pulled his head out of his ass," Blake said, entering the living room which was decorated bright orange. Will came in behind him, a sheepish smile on his face.

"Well it's about damn time," Beau grinned and got up to greet him.

"I'll second that. What the hell took you so long?" Dean asked.

"It's a long story, gimme a beer and I'll tell you."

Chapter 27

"You ready?" Rebelle asked Justine, pulling her veil down over the back of her head, careful not to muss her bun and smoothing it. Taylor finished buttoning the back of Justine's dress. It had taken a long time, the buttons were tiny and ran down the entire back. Christy was buckling up the thin straps on her orange heeled sandals.

"Very. So freaking ready," Justine replied.

Rebelle laughed. "Then what are we waiting for? Let's go!"

Justine smiled at her. "It's so good to see you smiling and laughing."

"Well, a lot of it is down to you so you can thank yourself." They hugged quickly before Taylor chivvied them along.

The guests had all arrived and Justine's family could be heard from inside the house. The ceremony was taking

Take A Chance

place in Christy and Dean's backyard which was sprawling with citrus fruit trees and wildflowers dotted the grass. It looked like a meadow and even though Justine would have preferred a more traditional church wedding, she just wanted to be married already.

"This is it. See you at the end of the aisle, sweetheart," Taylor said, giving Justine a kiss on the cheek and then heading outside.

"Love you," Christy said, squeezing Justine's hand and then followed Taylor out.

Rebelle turned to Justine, handing her the bouquet of white, peach and deep orange flowers. "Just checking you don't want to run?"

Justine laughed. "Are you kidding me? You see that man down there? He's my guy, forever."

Rebelle could have melted at the cuteness. "I figured, but just wanted to check. He's a wonderful man, you know he's special to me too."

Justine smiled. "I know. I'm glad you have a strong bond."

Tears welled in Rebelle's eyes. "Oh God, why am I emotional?" she cried.

"Stop it, you'll set me off!"

"Okay, I'm going. Bye." Rebelle took off after the others. Pausing just before she left the house and started the journey down the aisle. She smoothed her hand down the plain peach satin gown that Justine had them all in, for some reason the woman was obsessed with orange.

Rebelle shook her head, her curled hair tickled her jaw with her movements. She took a deep breath and stepped through the gossamer curtain that led to the backyard and when she looked up, she nearly stumbled. Will was down the end of the aisle, smiling at her with that stupid grin of his that she missed so much she nearly sobbed with relief at the sight of it. She could barely focus on moving forward and somehow managed to keep going.

She made her way, without stumbling and took her place next to Christy and Taylor. Taylor nudged her and waggled her eyebrows in Will's direction and Rebelle rolled her eyes, her cheeks flaming. She avoided Will's stare, it would be the only way she would get through the ceremony without throwing herself at him.

Justine came down the aisle to murmurs of excitement. Blake clutched his chest when he saw her, and Rebelle nearly burst into tears again. The ceremony was thankfully short and they were whisked away to do photos with Harley who was being looked after by Justine's beaming mom. Then it was up to them to get everyone to The Rusty Bucket Inn after for the reception. With Justine having such a big family and lots of folks from the town, there was a lot to do and she barely caught a glimpse of Will.

Once they were settled at the bar and the happy couple had arrived, there were speeches and food and finally everyone was free to do what they wanted.

She spotted Will. It was hard to miss him being so darned tall and broad, and he stood out with all his tattoos and fierce expression. They locked eyes and her breath fled her lungs. She had forgotten what it was like when his beautiful eyes captured hers, ensnaring her.

She started towards him, but a couple intercepted him, and she lost him to the crowd. Taylor and Christy snagged her away to dance and she didn't see him again. She looked for him but couldn't see him anywhere.

She went up to Beau. "Has Will left?"

Beau frowned, his mouth pulled tight. "Yeah, he mentioned something about needing to get back, sorry Rebelle."

Take A Chance

She swallowed her disappointment. She had needed to talk to him and thought he wanted to speak to her but maybe not, maybe she'd read this all wrong and he didn't feel the same after all. Maybe Diane was wrong.

Rebelle should have realized by now that life didn't always work out but the disappointment ate at her and she wanted to leave. She found Blake, pulling him away from a conversation with Justine's father.

"I'm gonna head back to the shelter and check on the animals but I just wanted to say congratulations once again," she said.

Blake surprised her by pulling her into a hug. "I'm so glad you're here, that you came. That everything's worked out."

She didn't want to disappoint him so just agreed and hugged him back. She was getting good at hugs now, especially around this affectionate bunch. She grabbed Justine who was dancing with one of her brothers and hugged her goodbye too and then she was leaving.

She trudged back to the shelter, watching the stars and trying not to let the sadness consume her and dampen the wonderful day that she'd had, watching two people unite with love. Instead she thought about the time that Will walked her home, when she felt the first stirrings of *something* between them.

Finally the shelter came back into view and the moonlight lit the way for her. When she got closer to the home, she spotted someone on her porch looking through the telescope and her heart leapt in her chest. A small whimper escaped her at seeing him.

He hadn't left, he'd come home.

She hurried up the porch and stopped in front of him panting.

He casually pulled back from the telescope and hit her

with his cool stare. "You know I was wrong to compare you to Rho Cassiopeia. Watching you tonight, you shine far brighter."

She ran her gaze over him, snagging on the fact that he was wearing the constellation suspenders that she'd bought him. "Every night I check the stars, making sure they're still there and didn't implode and disappear. Like you."

He flinched at her words and although she was eager for reconciliation, she was hurt too, and she vowed a long time ago to stop smothering who she was for fear of someone's reaction.

He stood up. "I'm sorry about that. I didn't mean to disappear but it was too hard to talk to you, to see you, when I was so overwhelmingly in love with you."

She gasped softly and took a step towards him.

"I know you don't want to get married but when I asked you to marry me, I didn't articulate myself very well. I wanted to marry you because I love you. Not because I was asking for power over you or to look after you but because I was asking for partnership, love, affection, passion. I'm finally choosing what I want, what I should have chosen a long time ago. I want to build a life together, just the two of us, because I've never found someone I wanted to do that with before."

She shook her head. "Will-"

He stepped towards her, crowding her with his big body and scent that had her wanting to curl up against him and purr like a damn kitten. "Don't you see that it's you who has power over me? That it has been since the moment I met you? Hell, how many times did you ignore me? Try and send me away? I am *weak* for you, always have been. Always will be. I have no plans to change that for the rest of my life." He took her hands in his, the

Take A Chance

rough callouses scraping her skin so wonderfully. "You're it, Rebelle, I knew the second I saw you. You're the love of my life and I'm not just saying that. I've lived nearly half of it so I should know by now. If I could prise my soul from my body and hand it to you to keep forever, I would. Just to show you how much you mean to me. How much I need you. How much I want you." He pressed their foreheads together, their breath mingling. "Tell me I'm not out here alone in this?"

She pulled away, shivering from the cool air. "I told you I didn't need you. Yet you forced your way into my life, no matter my efforts to discourage you. I tried so hard to get it through to you that I didn't want you here." He hung his head, nodding in agreement.

"But you didn't listen. And every day I'm so thankful that you didn't." His head snapped back up and a slow grin unfurled across his lips.

"You were so damned annoying I wanted to kill you, then kiss you, then kill you then kiss you again. I was wrong, I do need you, in all the ways you can need a person. I need you to smile that gorgeous award-winning smile at me, I need you to be proud of me when something goes right. I need you to talk to me, to share your thoughts with me and your life with me."

He released her hands and cupped her jaw as she continued.

"You bulldozed me, tore down my defenses, which were so high I thought they would never come down. But you did it. I don't even know how but you did. With your smiles, your stars, your care for the animals and me. You made me believe in the good of others, in kindness again and love. Dammit, you made me love you!" she shouted like she was mad, and he burst out laughing.

"It's not funny, William," she murmured darkly, and

his eyes flashed at her, a moan slipping from his lips and his arms came around her.

"Say that again," he whispered to her, under the stars.

"William."

He backed her against the door and cupped her jaw, tilting it up so her eyes locked with his. Then he smiled as he licked the seam of her lips and her knees turned weak.

"Let me in, Belle."

She slanted her lips across his, taking control of the kiss and prised his mouth apart, swirling their tongues together, pouring out all her love for him. They kissed until they were out of breath and she pulled away, fumbling with her key to unlock the door to the home.

She finally managed it as he trailed kisses down her neck, focusing on the sensitive spot behind her ear that had her eyes rolling back in her head. She finally got the door open and rushed inside tugging him with her. There was a loud sound, like a rumble of thunder, followed by a sharp bark and then a crash.

"Oh my God!" she shouted and ran to flick the light on then turned, doubling over with laughter when she saw Bryan had tackled Will and was smothering him with licks. Will tried to fight him off but he had clearly missed the big oaf.

"Bryan, stand down," she choked out through her laughter. When Will was free she helped him up and he repaid her by lifting her over his shoulder and heading into the bedroom where he dropped her gently onto the bed.

A loud wail had them tearing apart and then Parfait was leaping at Will, trying to climb into his arms.

Will turned to Rebelle with wide eyes. "Oh my God, *you* adopted her?"

She shrugged. "I kept her for you, I was hoping you

would come back, and I couldn't let her go. Bryan was meant for me, and Parfait was clearly meant for you."

He squeezed the frantically purring Parfait again before he apologized to the cat for making their reunion so short and dropped her outside the bedroom door, closing it and stalking back to Rebelle.

They peeled their clothes off between hurried kisses until they were naked. She didn't try to take control, just gave in to what they both needed which was to be together.

And when he rocked slowly into her, their hands entwined. "Let me have it, beautiful," he whispered. His reverent kisses became her undoing and she whimpered into his mouth as her body took over. Her climax shattered her, leaving her breathless and his desperate groan followed and she held him as he shuddered.

Then she lay across him, as was now customary, tracing little patterns over his chest as he did the same on her back. Previously he'd drawn hearts but there were different shapes that she couldn't discern.

"What are you drawing?" she mumbled, so close to blissful sleep.

"Our future. Happiness, love, amazing sex, and lots and lots of fur babies," he replied, sleepily.

She chuckled. "That sounds perfect to me…"

Chapter 28

10 months later...

"What is stuck in your fur, madam?" Will grunted, combing out the tail of the Maine Coon which had been dropped off at the shelter yesterday. Her elderly owner was struggling with the maintenance required on a cat like this and didn't want to do it anymore. At first Will was frustrated but Rebelle soothed his annoyance, reminding him this was why the shelter existed. To help those when they were in need.

He managed to extract a lump of something he didn't want to look at too closely. "Not very regal, is it?"

"Will!" Rebelle appeared in the cattery, panting. He shut the Maine Coon back in her pod and faced the love of his life.

"What's up, beautiful?"

She flapped her hands. "It's happening!"

His eyes widened. "It is?"

"Yes, get your sexy ass back to the home now!" she yelled and was gone in a flurry and he chuckled to himself at her exuberance.

He tidied up the brushes and combs and closed up the shelter. He sauntered back towards the trailer, stopping briefly at the small paddock they'd added to the back of the shelter on the way to say goodnight to Rufus, a horse and Walter a donkey that were sharing it.

His phone rang and he pulled it out. Leaning against the fence of the paddock, he answered.

"Yes, Mother?"

"Did you see?" Her excited voice came down the line.

He laughed. "I did see, I'm super happy for him."

"Ezra's second award in ten months, astounding!"

When Will fired his mother it left her with a lot of time on her hands so naturally she went after the next big thing, Ezra. She had become his manager and together they had worked on developing his brand. Ezra had stepped up and taken over as lead Viper on the show which had earned him a ton of recognition.

"Yes, it is. I congratulated him already."

"Good. Also the contractor is coming next week to start installing the hydrotherapy room."

Not only had she become Ezra's manager, but she had also taken over management of some aspects of the shelter while he and Rebelle focused more on growing the charity and running the place. Rebelle had wanted to include a hydrotherapy room to help cats and dogs with arthritis or injuries to regain mobility.

"Fantastic, Rebelle will be so pleased."

"I know, I already told her. She screeched, Will, screeched with excitement."

He shook his head, laughing again. "I can't believe you two talk more than you and I do. I'm your son," he grumbled but secretly he loved it. Since he and his mother parted business ways, they'd spent more time together as a family and Diane and Rebelle had developed an incredible bond.

"And she's my daughter. So, I'll be down on Boxing Day, I'll leave Richard behind this time."

He frowned, worried about her. "Trouble in paradise?"

She made a dismissive noise. "He would rather spend it with his children. Which is fine and his right but I just…" she paused. "I just can't stand Kyle. I feel bad for Ava though, she's so sweet, why is she tying herself to him?"

Will sighed. "I don't know. But the twins are cute, she sent pictures. I've told her if she ever wants to escape, she can come here."

"That's good of you. I hope she does, does it make me a bad stepmom that I want her to leave him?"

"No, that makes three of us," Will chuckled.

"Speaking of, where is she?"

Will looked back towards the trailer. "She's in the home, I need to go, it's showtime."

His mother squealed. "Ooh please send me pictures. I can't believe I'm going to be a grandmother again!"

"Will do, see you in a few days, Mom. Love you," he said.

"Love you, too."

He put his phone back in his pocket and looked up at the stars, at the vastness of the night sky that he found so oddly comforting and wondered how he'd gotten so damn lucky. Since he and Rebelle said *I love you,* he and his mother had worked at unpicking his contracts, selling off

Take A Chance

some of the businesses he was involved with and he'd found replacements for the charity boards he was on so no one suffered. It had taken a few months but together they had worked at securing him the life he wanted.

Now he looked after the shelter with Rebelle which kept him busy. They were expanding out to another city and the work that had come with it had been daunting, but he had found that new challenge to sink his teeth into.

Life with Rebelle was more than he could have ever wished for. She challenged him, soothed him, dominated him and best of all, she needed him.

The door to the home swung open and there she was.

"Hurry up, you're going to miss it!" she snapped, his favorite frown on her face.

He almost laughed but instead just smiled at her and watched the frown instantly dissolve.

"Damn that stupid award-winning smile," she muttered, shaking her head, and went back inside.

He made a quick stop by his car and grabbed the box that contained a single black rose, her Christmas present. Well, one of them anyway. He was beginning to worry the other wouldn't appear in time.

When he was inside the house, he stowed the box behind the couch in the living room. "You didn't see anything," he said to a snuggling Bryan and Parfait who were relegated to the living room for this evening.

He took a seat on the bedroom floor beside Rebelle, stroking a hand down her back. "How's she doing?"

"Okay so far. You nearly missed it though," she grumbled, folding her arms across her chest.

"It's only just started, we'll be here for hours yet," he laughed, pulling her into his arms and kissing the top of her head.

There was a mewl from the pregnant tabby, Princess, laying in the cardboard box, squirming on her blanket as her belly clenched with a contraction. Last time Will had watched a cat give birth, he'd been petrified and wishing Rebelle were here with him. Now, she was here and he knew what to expect and couldn't wait for Rebelle to experience this.

"Do you think they'll be here by midnight?" Rebelle whispered.

He nodded. "I think so. Christmas kittens, what more could anyone ask for?" He grinned down at Rebelle before dropping a kiss on the tip of her nose. She ran her fingers through the stubble on his jaw and pressed their lips together. He nibbled at the seam of her lips until they parted letting him inside and she pulled back abruptly.

"Your mom!"

He arched a brow. "That's who you're thinking about right now?"

Her frown slid into place. "No, we need to tell her what's happening."

"Already done it."

Her frown disappeared and she snuggled up against him and they quietly sat, soothing Princess when she began panting.

"Oh look, there's one!" Rebelle gasped. Princess immediately began washing the first kitten, a squirming little black and white bundle. Over the course of six hours, she had four more kittens. When it was over, Rebelle was cooing gently at Princess about what a good mom she had been. Princess kept blinking at Rebelle, padding her paws.

Will watched Rebelle fuss over them and eventually, Bryan and Parfait were allowed to visit the new kittens and were introduced.

"What are you smiling about?" Rebelle asked as she looked at him over their brood of animals, her dark eyes twinkling at him.

He just shook his head. "Everything."

*

"Merry Christmas!" Christy exclaimed, raising her glass. They all clinked glasses and dug into the amazing food everyone had brought. The Rusty Bucket Inn filled with the sounds of excited chatter as everyone caught each other up on what they'd been up to recently. Rebelle watched as Harley babbled away on Blake's lap, reaching up to tug at his beard. Will tucked his hand under the table to feed Bryan some scraps when no one was looking. And Taylor and Beau were whispering furiously between themselves.

"Can I have everyone's attention?" Beau called and the noise died down.

Will turned to Rebelle, winking and shot her that award-winning smile which had been her downfall. She frowned at him, wondering what he was so happy about.

"Next year we're going to have to set another place at this table," Taylor said, squeezing Beau's hand.

"We've started the adoption process!" Beau exclaimed.

"Oh my God!" Justine cried.

"I'm going to be an uncle?" Dean asked, his voice slightly wobbly. The noise level erupted again as everyone descended on the couple to congratulate them and find out more info. Then it was time for dessert and Rebelle nervously brought out the cookies and ice cream.

"Don't panic, they're store bought," she said, shooting the entire table a withering look when they all breathed a sigh of relief. She fought back her smile at the reaction, secretly loving the way they teased her.

Once the food was all gone, everyone loosening belts and groaning at the fullness, Blake turned to her. "So where to next?"

Rebelle shot Will a frown as he draped an arm around her shoulders. "He won't tell me. He's keeping it a secret."

"I've got to have some control here, now you're such a hotshot businesswoman." He dropped a kiss on the tip of her nose.

"Wait, so you don't know where the next shelter location is?" Christy asked, sliding onto Dean's lap.

Rebelle shook her head. "I'll get it out of him eventually."

"Don't you leave in two days?"

"We sure do," Will replied, his smile bright.

"I guess you'd better hurry up and start torturing him for information then," Justine joked.

Later on, once they'd tidied up all the food and returned the tables back to their normal place, they hugged each other goodbye.

"Hey, you guys, mistletoe. You need to kiss," Christy said, pointing at Beau and Rebelle who were hugging goodbye. A low rumble emanated from Taylor.

Rebelle looked up at Beau awkwardly and he smirked down at her, a twinkle in his dark eyes.

"I've just realized something. Rebelle's the only woman here I haven't kissed."

Will tugged Rebelle away from him. "Yeah, and it's gonna stay that way."

Beau laughed and instead grabbed Will who, in his retrieval of Rebelle, had stepped under the mistletoe. Beau dipped him backwards, no mean feat given how huge Will was, but Beau could handle it. He planted a big, sloppy kiss right on Will's lips.

"Yes, finally, that's what I'm talking about!" Taylor hooted.

At that moment the door to the bar opened and a woman entered.

"I'm sorry, sweetheart, but we're closed for a private function," Taylor said but the woman peered around her and Rebelle nearly fainted when she saw her own reflection staring back at her.

"Rebelle?"

"Holy shit, there's two of them," Dean hissed loudly.

"I forgot she had a twin!" Justine said.

Rebelle, stunned, could only stare at her sister. Her mouth opened but she had no words.

"I, uh, was told you might be here today," her twin said, an impish smile on her face.

Rebelle reached for Will who was by her side in an instant, holding her up, supporting her. He walked her forwards, so she was just inches away. Her eyes ran over her twin.

Her hair was a different color, likely dyed the honey blonde that hung around her in soft waves. Her eyes were lighter than Rebelle's, her jaw not quite as sharp but there was no denying that it was her.

"Rose?" she choked out.

"Hi," Rose said simply.

"How…what…you came back?" Rebelle stuttered.

Rose flicked her gaze to Will. "Someone found me and reached out."

Rebelle spun around to Will who had a sheepish expression on his face. "You?"

"Merry Christmas," he sang weakly. He smoothed his hands over her shoulders. "I knew you wanted to know what happened to Rose, that you missed her, and I wanted you to be happy and whole."

Tears filled Rebelle's eyes at what her wonderful man had done for her, the lengths he must have gone to in order to track Rose down.

Rebelle was suddenly aware of their audience and looked at each person in turn.

Justine swiveled on her feet. "Yeah, we've gotta get Harley home anyway."

"Got to get back for the Christmas edition of Bake Off."

They all darted around each other awkwardly before leaving and Taylor pressed a key into Rebelle's hand. "Stay as long as you need to, just lock up when you're done."

Will turned her to face him and she looked up into his eyes, concern filling the ocean depths.

"Do you want me to stay? Do you want to do this alone?"

She nodded. "I think it's best if I do."

He kissed her. "Just call me if you need me. You can do this, beautiful, I love you. Come on Bryan." Will patted his leg to get the dog's attention but her ever faithful canine wouldn't be moved.

She glanced down at him where he settled himself on her feet, his weight already taking away all sensation in her toes. "Go with your dad," she told him and he grumbled but reluctantly slunk off with Will.

Then she was alone with Rose.

Rose tangled her hands together awkwardly. "So, how've you been?"

Rebelle pictured this moment a thousand times. She had pictured a tearful reunion, a happy reunion, and an angry, bitter reunion. She wanted to be mad at Rose for leaving but she couldn't find the energy. Rose was alive and here and honestly, Rebelle understood why she'd left, over the years she wished she had done the same.

Rose shot her a pained look. "Say something, please?"

Rebelle whooshed out the breath she'd been holding. "I need a drink."

Rose nodded. "I could use a drink, too."

Rebelle ducked behind the bar and grabbed a bottle of scotch, two glasses and poured a shot into both, pushing one across the bar to Rose. She downed hers before Rose even had a chance to lift the glass to her lips. Then Rebelle poured another one, the burn knocking her out of her haze.

She eyed her sister, wanting to throw her arms around her and beg her to never leave again.

"Are you back for good?" she asked, trying to keep the hope from her voice.

Rose nodded. "I guess so, no plans to go anywhere else. I'm here to make amends. I want to hear about your life."

Relief flooded Rebelle but she didn't know what to say to that except, "You left."

"I did." Rose's lip wobbled and it took everything in Rebelle not to wrap her in a hug. Which under different circumstances would have made Rebelle laugh thinking back to how she used to hate touching others. "And I have regretted it for years. I didn't know how to come back after running away and leaving you. Then I heard you got married and probably wouldn't have wanted to see me anyway and I got scared that you moved on and didn't need me in your life."

"Are you kidding? You're my baby sister, I will always need you. I *have* needed you," Rebelle said, softly. Thinking again how ironic it was that she used to believe she didn't need anyone.

"I'd like to earn a place back in your life, if you'll let me?" Rose asked, biting her lip, her voice trembling slightly.

Rebelle came around the bar and stood in front of Rose, her eyes rushing over her sister's face and taking in every nuance like she didn't have exactly the same features. She pulled her into a hug and squeezed tightly. Rose grunted but wrapped her arms around Rebelle and squeezed back just as fiercely.

Rebelle wasn't sure which of them started crying first only that when they pulled away, they both had tear tracks down their cheeks. She cleared her throat and grabbed the bottle of scotch, pouring them another three fingers each and gestured to a booth.

"I think it's time we had a proper catch up, sister to sister."

*

When Rebelle finally got back to the trailer, after situating Rose in one of the cabins at The Rusty Bucket Inn, she found Will on the deck, looking at the stars.

She stumbled over to him, the scotch sloshing in her belly.

He spotted her, his lips lifting in that iconic smile. "I'm gonna play it cool and pretend I haven't been out here riddled with anxiety for you."

She snorted. "You're too cute."

His eyebrows winged up. "You're drunk."

"You're fully clothed."

His laugh boomed out, louder in the still night. He gifted her with a lazy smile. "Come 'ere." He opened his arms and she fell into them, nestling herself against him. He kissed her temple and she closed her eyes, breathing in his salt and sandalwood scent.

"How did it go?"

"Fine, she's fine. I think she needs mending. She wants forgiveness."

"Can you give her that?" he said, his lips moving against her skin.

"Of course, I'd give her anything she wanted. But I think she needs it from herself."

"So, what are we gonna do now?"

"She wants a couple of days to settle back into the town so we're gonna stick to our plan and go open that new shelter, wherever it is. Then when we get back, she and I'll be ready to start trying to build our relationship, I guess."

Will squeezed her tightly. "Sounds good to me."

"Thank you for bringing her back to me," she whispered.

"I'd do anything for you."

She leaned back and looked up at him. "Then can we go to bed now? I want to unwrap my Christmas present."

He groaned and pressed his lips to hers, chasing away the chill from the winter air. He lifted her into his arms and carried her inside. Although they had expanded the shelter, they were both happy to continue living in the small home. It had everything they needed: room for fur babies and room for each other.

Will took her into the bedroom and fell back onto the bed, Rebelle bouncing on top of him. She dragged off his sweatshirt and his hands worked to pull her sweater over her head but she stilled them.

"I want to negotiate," she said, sliding her tongue across his lower lip.

He groaned. "I knew I'd regret teaching you how to do it. What do you want?"

"You. Forever."

He stilled, staring up at her with a tender look on his face. "You already have me."

"I know but, like, in a legal sense."

He reared back slightly. "Are you asking me to marry you right now?"

"Yes."

"Holy shit."

"I know. It's a lot, especially after I rejected your proposal."

He shot her a sarcastic smile. "Thanks for the reminder."

"I'm being serious though. Marry me?"

His eyes sparkled with amusement. "If I say yes, I have some conditions."

She rolled her eyes. "I should've known you would try and negotiate."

He brushed her hair back from her face and cupped her jaw. "Never try and negotiate with a negotiator, beautiful."

"This is super romantic by the way," she sighed, nipping his bare chest.

He held up his hands. "Hey, it's your proposal."

She walked her fingers across his pec, tugging at the ring through his nipple. "What are your conditions?"

His mouth parted and she heard his breath tangle in his throat when she tugged again, before he found his words. "You, me, going around the country, opening shelters and rescuing animals, for the rest of our lives."

She pretended to think about it. "I think I can live with that."

He rolled his eyes. "Then, yes."

"Yes?"

"Yes, woman!"

Rebelle whooped and he laughed, rolling them over and pinning her beneath him. He teased her lips, trailed his tongue down her neck, kissing across her bare collarbone.

"Wait, I need to tell Diane!" Rebelle shouted, shoving Will off her and searching for her phone.

"Now?" he huffed in frustration.

She turned towards him. "Yes now. You know how close we are."

He frowned at her and she reached forward, smoothing the crease away. "Frowning doesn't suit you, William."

A noise rumbled from his throat at her use of his full name. She found her phone and decided to take pity on Will and instead of calling Diane, she shot her a message. She turned back to Will to find him kneeling on the bed. Her gaze roved over him, snagging on the *Belle* he'd had tattooed on his chest, nestled amongst the roses, right over his heart. A shiver moved through her at the thought of having this man forever.

"Look at you on your knees for me, like such a good boy," she purred.

She saw the change in him. His hands gripped the sheets next to him and his lip curled slightly as arousal settled over his face. Heat simmered in his eyes and one hand released the sheets to grip himself through his boxers.

She tutted. "Uh-uh. That's mine."

He grunted but released himself and she stroked over his thighs, loving the strength there. She pushed him back on the bed and arranged his arms and legs so he was spread wide for her, reminding her of the Vitruvian Man image.

Rebelle worked her mouth over his skin, teasing him,

pushing his self-control to the limit with each ghosting of her lips. She explored his body, she could never get enough of him.

His breath snagged in his throat when she slicked her tongue over his thick length before moving up his body and laying on him, rubbing her wet sex over him. Her breathy moans in his ear tipped him over the edge and he took over.

"Enough teasing," he growled and flipped her onto her back, entering her with a hard thrust. He licked into her mouth, feeding her reverent kisses that took her to a fever pitch and just when she was ready to fall into oblivion, he slowed the pace. The bump of his hips easing to an agonizing slowness. He rocked into her slowly and she clawed at his back, desperate for him to *move*. He drove her wild and she caught the gleam in his eyes as he stared down at her that told her he was doing it on purpose. He wanted her to completely unravel.

"I love you," he whispered, and she cursed. He wasn't playing fair, she was only human, she couldn't help the way her body reacted.

"Damn you," she hissed. His dark chuckle unfurled like velvet across her skin when she frowned at him. Then her body seized around him and stars exploded behind her eyes.

"You should've known better than to try and best me. I always get what I want and I always want you," he murmured, placing kisses over her damp skin before his hips started swinging again and he grunted with his own release.

Rebelle lay across his body, covering him with hers, needing his touch, his soft snores soothing her. She was exhausted but her brain was too wired, thinking about what's next with the shelter and with Rose. Her thoughts

Take A Chance

battered around in her brain so she tried her old technique to relax.

Count out what's good...

She took a deep breath, ready to start but her mind settled on one word. She smiled slowly and she whispered;

"Everything."

The End.

Keep your eyes peeled for Rose's story coming soon...

If you LOVED this story then please, please for the love of Henry Cavill leave a review, thank you x

Acknowledgements

Thank you so much to you, the reader, for taking a chance on Rebelle & Will's story, I really hoped you enjoy it and please consider leaving a review on Goodreads, Amazon and any socials you have. Reviews really help indie authors, and we need all the help we can get from awesome readers like you.

This was a really hard book to write, for so many reasons but some people that helped make it a little easier are my alphas: Mimi Flood, Anna P and Anna Lindgren. These are some amazing friends and authors, and I'm so lucky to have them in my corner. Make sure you check out their books!

Thank you to my betas, Michelle and Annie. You both provided me with feedback that shaped the story and just made it all a lot better! I truly appreciate your input and support xx

About the Author

Lila is a thirtysomething writer living in Derbyshire, England with her *cough* parents *cough*. She loves romance, sharks, cats and has an ~~un~~healthy obsession with Henry Cavill.

Take A Chance is the fifth novel in the Citrus Pines series, head to Amazon to check out the series if you haven't already! Lila is a huge fan of the romance reading and writing community so why not say hello, she can be found on Instagram, Facebook, Pinterest, Tiktok, Goodreads and contacted via her shiny new website www.liladawesauthor.com.

Also By Lila Dawes

Citrus Pines Series In Order

It's Only Love: Dean & Christy

Color of Love: Justine & Blake

Sweet Surrender: Taylor & Beau

Love Me Good: Kayleigh & Ben

Take A Chance: Rebelle & Will

Printed in Dunstable, United Kingdom